BETSY ROSS:
ACCIDENTAL SPY

MARILYN CLAY

BETSY ROSS: ACCIDENTAL SPY
First Mayfair Mystery Print Edition released December 2012
Copyright © 2012 Marilyn Jean Clay

Expanded Second Print Edition January 2014
Copyright © 2014 Marilyn Jean Clay

Printed in the United States of America

ISBN-10: 1494789973
ISBN-13: 978-1494789978

PROLOGUE

October 1773 - Philadelphia, Pennsylvania

"What must thee be thinking, Elizabeth? Thee knows to marry outside thy Quaker faith is forbidden!"

"But, Mother, I love him so!"

"What doth thee know of love? Thee is surely mistaking the kindness of John Ross for love."

Elizabeth Griscom, called Betsy by her family since she was a little girl, was Samuel and Rebecca Griscom's eighth child. Although ten of the seventeen babes born to Betsy's mother had perished as infants, three of Betsy's younger siblings, Hannah, Rachel, and George still lived at home. Two of the older girls, Deborah and Susannah, were already married and had children of their own. Sarah, to whom Betsy was particularly close, had recently married and left home.

"I daresay Sarah's marriage hath put this rebellious notion into thy head."

Betsy's lips tightened as she carefully pulled a long handled griddle of piping hot corn cakes from the brick oven in the kitchen of the Griscom's fine three-storey home in Philadelphia. "I confess I have spoken with Sarah regarding my feelings for John. And she agrees that what I feel for him does indeed run deeper than mere friendship."

Mistress Griscom stirred the bubbling contents of an iron pot suspended over the flames. "The penalty for marrying this man is far too great, Elizabeth. Thee would be read out of The Society of Friends and never be allowed to attend another Quaker Meeting for the whole of thy life." Betsy's mother brought the wooden spoon in her hand to her lips in order to sample the savory stew she was preparing for her family's dinner that night. "Clearly, thee hath not weighted the consequences of marrying outside thy faith."

Betsy exhaled an exasperated breath. "I have thought of nothing else for months, Mother."

"Ah. So, thee hath *not* been thinking about thy feelings for John Ross?" Turning from the hearth, Mistress Griscom leveled a stern look at her recalcitrant daughter. "Thee are a good Quaker girl, Betsy."

"Yes, mother," Betsy huffed. "I am a good Quaker girl. I have always been a good Quaker girl. I have never given thee a moments concern."

"Then why would thee start now?"

The older woman skirted past her tight-lipped daughter. "Put the corn cakes on the table. Then summon thy father and George whilst I portion out the stew. I trust Rachel hath placed napkins all around."

"Where is Hannah this evening?" Betsy asked.

"Your sister is staying the night with Sarah."

Alone in her bedchamber that evening, Betsy lay in the darkness unable to sleep. All that she had earlier declared to her mother was not, in fact, the whole truth—that for months she had thought of nothing else but how dear the cost to wed John Ross would be. The truth was, for a good many months, she had thought of nothing save how very, *very* much she wished to become John's wife and to bear his children.

Betsy Griscom had known John Ross since she was a girl of twelve, the year she left Friends School and began her apprenticeship at William Webster's Upholstery Shop. John Ross, son of a clergyman who was *not* a

Quaker, and a few years older than Betsy, was already apprenticed to Mr. Webster. From the start, the two young people had gravitated toward one another. John had been kind and helpful to the shy Quaker girl whose remarkable talent with a needle and thread had astonished everyone.

John Ross had never once taunted Betsy for thinking she could compete in what was generally considered a man's trade. But then it had never occurred to Betsy that any occupation would be closed to her. Quakers believed that men and women were equal in all ways; that no person, regardless of gender or rank, was superior to another. It was *that* particular belief that had brought Quakers to the New World in the first place. Quaker men did not remove their hats or bow down to anyone, not even a king; an act in England that was perceived by royalty as treasonous.

Yet it was another Quaker belief that had lately begun to gnaw at Betsy, namely, that for Quakers there was no actual marriage ceremony, or prescribed wedding vows. Quakers did not observe rituals of any sort. When a couple wished to marry, all that was required of them was to profess their love for one another before witnesses, and thereafter, in the eyes of God and the world, they were husband and wife. If that were the case, Betsy reasoned now, then she and John Ross were *already* married. Had they not more than once professed their love for one another . . . *before* witnesses? Their employer William Webster knew of their abiding love for one another. Their friends knew how deeply they cared. At picnics and other social gatherings, which she and John Ross had attended together, they were often teased about being sweet on each another.

Betsy sighed. For her parents to refuse to give them leave to marry was simply not fair. It was true that John would never pass the rigid tests and disciplines required by The Society of Friends. Those Quaker men charged with the task of investigating the prospective bridegroom would most certainly declare John Ross unfit, given the fact that both his father and grandfather had been ministers of another faith.

But they loved one another. So, why, Betsy wondered now, did her mother *also* not recognize that, in accordance with their strict Quaker beliefs and in the eyes of God, she was not *already* wed to John Ross?

Webster's Upholstery Shop, October 1773

"There is a public dance tonight at the Aubrey House Inn, Betsy," John Ross whispered as the pair of them worked side-by-side stretching a square of burgundy damask over the seat of a heavy mahogany chair.

Betsy kept her eyes on her work. "I had meant to learn ten new French words tonight, John."

"You are far too studious, Betsy."

"Perhaps, I am; but as you well know Mr. Webster is scarcely able to converse with the immigrants. One of us should be able to speak French. I already know a good many German words," she added. Already the largest city in the colonies, Philadelphia expanded weekly as boatloads of new settlers arrived from France, Germany and many other European countries.

John, a handsome young man with dark brown hair and brown eyes, grinned. "I meant to teach you ten new dance steps tonight."

Betsy blushed prettily. "I am uncertain if I could sneak out again tonight, John. The last time we attended a dance together I was staying the night with my sister Sarah." In a softer tone, she added, "Mother is pressing me to cease seeing you altogether."

John's head jerked up. "You've reached yer majority, Betsy. You are yer own woman now." His eyes began to twinkle. "Oh, botheration. I know very well ye'll not heed a single thing yer mother says."

Betsy's lips twitched. John Ross knew her *very* well.

"What are the pair o' you a-whisperin' about now?" William Webster strode into the cluttered workroom of his busy upholstery shop. The white-haired man, who always looked as if he slept in his clothes, stood with arms akimbo as he observed his young apprentices. "I for one will be relieved when you two tie the knot, although I'll not want to lose you, Betsy, when ye become . . . that is, the day ye announce ye're . . ." the elderly man grew flustered at the direction of his own thoughts. Clearing his throat, he said gruffly, "I'll need ye to deliver those chairs tonight, John. Plenty more work to be done a'fore this day ends." Turning, he disappeared into another chamber.

John glanced over his shoulder as if to confirm that their employer had indeed exited the workroom. "There's yer excuse to be getting home late tonight, love. We've three more chairs that must be upholstered before morning."

"Oh, John, you know I dislike telling falsehoods."

"But, I'll wager ye like dancin' with me a good deal more than ye dislike fibbin' to yer mum."

Betsy grinned. "You know me too well, John Ross."

His grin turned wicked. "Not well enough."

"Jo-h-n!" Betsy scolded, her blue eyes widening. After a pause, she said, "Very well, I shall send a note 'round. But, for a certainty, I must be home by ten of the clock."

"Which will give me a good two hours to enjoy holdin' ye in my arms."

Betsy's lashes fluttered against her flushed cheeks. Two delightful hours spent in John Ross's arms was well worth the discomfort of deceiving her mother.

* * * * *

That night a huge harvest moon hung low in the sky. The golden orb cast long shadows across the tree-shrouded lane as hand-in-hand Betsy Griscom and John Ross hastened toward their destination, a good half hour's walk beyond Philadelphia on King's Highway. On the way they passed several taverns, each ablaze with light as both travelers and local patrons alike flocked to the establishments to enjoy the delicious food and free-flowing ale.

In 1773 Pennsylvania inns were generally two-storied affairs, most built of stone with a porch across the front and two doors, one giving on to the taproom, the other leading to the living quarters of the proprietor's family. Sleeping chambers for travelers were located on the second floor. Although most roads in all thirteen colonies were still rough and unpaved, traveling in "stages" where one covered a certain distance of one's journey, then changed horses for the next stage, was becoming commonplace. These days, one often saw "stage-coaches" tooling up and down King's Highway, which was the quickest and straightest route from Philadelphia to New York. Twice that night Betsy and John had to hug the outside of the dusty road in order to allow a stagecoach pulled by six large horses to rumble past.

"Perhaps we will take a stage-coach journey one day," John said.

"Where shall we go?"

"Anywhere you like. Perhaps New York City or Brook Land Heights. Perhaps we'll journey up to Canada. Now that the Indian wars are over, a trip up north should be safe enough. Would you like that?"

"I would like going anywhere with you, John."

Upon reaching the busy Aubrey House Inn, but before advancing up the narrow stairs to the second floor where a spacious room, typically used for political meetings, wedding feasts, and tonight, a public dance, was located, Betsy and John paused in the common room where John purchased them each mugs of small ale and half servings of shepherd's pie. The sounds of music and laughter drifting down from overhead caused them both to eat quickly.

Once above stairs, John wasted no time pulling Betsy onto the dance floor where amidst the chatter and gay laughter, dozens of couples were performing a lively *contredanse*. Those who were not dancing stood on the sidelines clapping their hands together. Because Betsy was not yet a proficient dancer, she had to concentrate to keep up with John, who was both nimble on his feet as well as musical. He often made up words to the music and, to Betsy's delight, sang his impromptu ditties to her.

"My sweet Betsy is the prettiest girl here; her eyes are blue and her lips are rosy; had I a fistful of daisies, I'd give her a posy!"

Betsy laughed gaily. To be with John, away from the shop always lightened her heart. With John she felt happier than she'd ever felt in her life. She trusted him completely and knew that he would never do anything to hurt her, nor would he allow any harm to come to her.

After dancing non-stop for close on an hour, Betsy begged exhaustion and gratefully allowed John to lead her to a row of ladder-backed chairs positioned beneath the opened windows where wafts of cool air drifted in from outdoors.

"How about another mug of ale, love? I daresay I could do with a dram."

Betsy nodded assent and watched as her handsome escort disappeared into the crowd of young people milling about on the edge of the dance floor. Other girls were also seated beneath the windows awaiting their beaus to bring them refreshments. Nearby, the deep-timbered voices of a knot of young men drew Betsy's attention. Fanning her flushed cheeks with a hand, she began to listen when phrases like "the demmed tea tax" and "hung in effigy" reached her ears.

Her brow furrowed when she heard one fellow declare, "These days Lobsterbacks 'er swarmin' all over Boston!"

"Why, only last week, a hundred or more British soldiers marched bold as you please off a ship anchored in Boston harbor," said another.

It quite surprised Betsy when John, carrying pewter mugs of ale in each hand, paused to speak to them.

"What were you and those young fellows talking about?" she asked when John returned and handed her a mug.

"The rebellion in New England," he said before tipping up his mug.

Betsy's gaze grew troubled. "I shouldn't want something like that dreadful Boston Massacre to happen here."

"Don't fret, love." John grinned. "I'll protect you."

Betsy's pretty face relaxed into a smile. "I know you will, John."

On their way home that night, John slowed his pace more than once to draw Betsy close for a kiss. As his kisses deepened, both his, and her, breath grew short.

"John." She turned her head away. "We mustn't."

"I'm on fire for you, Betsy," he gasped, burying his nose in her thick chestnut curls. "Sometimes at the shop, it's all I can do to keep from kissing you then and there; Mr. Webster be dammed."

"I feel the same about you, John." Although it wasn't what she *really* wanted to do, she pulled from John's embrace and urged him back onto the road toward town.

"Perhaps it would make the waiting easier if we—" He turned to gaze into her deeply troubled eyes. "What *are* we waiting for, Betsy? I see no reason why we shouldn't get married right now!"

"*Now,* John?" It was on the tip of her tongue to tell him that according to her Quaker beliefs they were *already* married.

"I doubt we'll ever gain your parent's blessing. We've wasted too much precious time as it is. We should do as your parents did and elope."

"If we did throw caution to the wind and married now, where would we live? I shouldn't want us to begin our married life living with your sister and her husband, and I couldn't ask Sarah . . ."

"I've some money tucked away. There's a little house for rent on Mulberry Street, not far from Webster's shop." His tone grew excited. "I've been thinking, Betsy. Once we marry and have our own place, there's no reason why we shouldn't open up our own upholstery shop. With my skill and your talent, why, we'd be successful in no time. What say ye?" He brought her fingers to his lips and kissed them.

"Perhaps we should wait a bit, John . . . I-I mean, it would take a great deal of money to start our own business. We'd need so much, needlework supplies and trim and a vast quantity of fabric and . . ."

"I'll wager yer Uncle Abel would extend us credit. He and his partner Mr. Drinker import fabric from all over the world. One shipment and we'd be in business."

Betsy chewed on her lower lip. She'd often thought the two of them might one day own their own upholstery business, but . . . *now?* So soon after they married? "I-I don't know, John."

"Promise me you'll think on it. And ye'll also think about us eloping. I don't know what your Quaker Bible says about marriage, but mine says it's better to marry than to burn and . . . I'm burning up for you, Betsy. I don't know how much longer I can wait."

Late October 1773 - Webster's Upholstery Shop

"There'll be trouble if yer Uncle Abel's ship docks in Philadelphia, Betsy. I believe it's my duty to warn him."

"I don't understand, John. How can you know such things?"

The hour was late and Mr. Webster was above stairs taking supper with his wife, leaving his apprentices in the workroom to complete the tasks they'd been assigned for the day; Betsy stitching gold braid onto a pair of velvet draperies, John tacking canvas backing onto a sofa he meant to upholster the following day. Because they were alone in the rear of the shop, the two felt free to converse in normal tones.

"Don't ask me how I know, love."

"You've never before kept secrets from me, John."

He pulled a printed handbill from the pocket of his breeches and handed it to her. "Here. You can see for yourself."

Betsy's curious gaze scanned the page. "It says Captain Ayers will be tarred and feathered if he lands the *Polly* in Philadelphia." Her face a question, she looked up. "What does it mean, John? Why would he . . .?"

"The *Polly* is carrying *tea*, Betsy. *British* tea. And it's consigned to James and Drinker, Importers. If I warned your uncle, perhaps he could get word to Captain Ayers to dock the ship downriver instead of sailing up the Delaware to Philadelphia."

"But, cannot Uncle Abel also read this?"

"The handbills are not to be widely distributed. A protest is planned."

"A protest?" Betsy murmured. "John, you are frightening me."

He continued to work. "I know how you feel about war and fighting, Betsy, but colonists will not allow England to impose injustices on them forever. You are aware of the rebellion in New England. Whether Philadelphia Quakers like it or not, war will soon reach our doorsteps."

Betsy did not reply. It was true; Quakers did not believe in raising arms, and certainly not in war or fighting. Still, Betsy knew of the heated debates going on now between the colonies and the king, about the hated Stamp Act in which Parliament had imposed a tax on every sheet of paper the colonists used for wills, deeds, books and newspapers, even for playing cards. The crown had also heavily taxed other commodities the colonists imported such as molasses, glass, lead, paint, and of course, tea. To be honest, she did not believe it was right, or fair, for the king to impose severe penalties on the colonists simply for wanting to live as freely as English citizens did in England.

"Betsy," John's voice cut into her reverie. "There are hundreds of British soldiers already garrisoned in Boston; even the governor of Massachusetts is loyal to the king. They say British soldiers are freely entering colonist's homes up north and seizing whatever they want. Where will the tyranny end, Betsy?"

"Oh, John, I cannot bear to think on it!" Betsy dropped her needle and covered her face with her hands.

John flew to her side. On his knees before her, he cupped her tear-stained face in his hands. "I'll never let anything happen to you, Betsy. I promise I will always be here to take care of you."

Betsy flung her arms around his neck. "But how can you stop the British from coming *here,* John?"

"Since Quakers refuse to fight," he spoke into her hair, "your family and others like them will be safe from the British. It is only we rebel Patriots who will be hanged for treason."

"But *you* are a Patriot." She drew away, her blue eyes moist with tears.

He nodded. "And I hope my wife, my *future* wife, will understand that I must fight for the freedom of every single colonist in the country, whether they be Patriot or Quaker."

Betsy sniffed back her tears. "I do understand, John. Truly, I do. And I do not wish to spend another day, or night, apart from you. I love you with all my heart, and more than anything, I want to become your wife and . . . and to help you fight your battles. I *will* marry you, John Ross," she said decisively. "I will marry you *now.*"

November 4, 1773, Philadelphia

Crossing the broad Delaware River could be hazardous at any time of year but it was especially hazardous in winter. Tidal currents were strong, at times running over two knots. Even a moderate wind could whip up nasty waves which when they crashed down onto a small skiff could easily sink it, or at the very least, send up an icy spray that quickly drenched the vessel's occupants.

"I had hoped we might leave work in time to catch Cooper's last ferry this evening," John told his pretty little wife-to-be, the pair huddled together on a backless bench of the small fishing boat John had hired to row them across the mile-wide river on that chilly November night.

"No matter, John, I can already see land." Betsy's long gaze scanned the horizon. "We'll make it across in no time." She tugged her worn cloak tighter about her shoulders as a brisk wind churned up the dark water.

John snuggled closer to her. "So long as we don't get drenched and the marriage license in my pocket ruined."

"Perhaps I should hold on to it."

"I'm the man." John grinned. "I'll keep our marriage license safe, just as I'll keep *you* safe." His arm tightened about her shoulders as the small boat dipped perilously close to the choppy black water.

Upon reaching shore, John and the other man dragged the small boat onto dry land. Once John paid the fisherman, he and Betsy trudged up the slippery slope to Hugg's Tavern located near the waterfront of the neighboring colony of New Jersey. John's friend, William Hugg, Jr., proprietor of the tidy tavern, had Justice of the Peace James Bowman waiting inside to marry the couple. Once there, John handed over the required ten shillings for Bowman's services then, he and Hugg, as his witness, signed the surety bond declaring to the officials of the province of New Jersey that the proposed marriage was lawful, free of impediment and that both parties were of a legal age to marry.

While the men took care of business, Betsy glanced around the dimly lit tavern. Next to the bar stood a tall case clock that had only one hand. Betsy surmised the hour to be seven, but how many minutes past that it was impossible to tell. Suddenly, a serving wench burst into the common room from the kitchen, her hips swaying as she sashayed across the room balancing two platters of steaming hot food and freshly baked bread. The aroma of the bread tempted Betsy, who'd eaten next to nothing all day. The girl's full breasts bounced as she advanced toward a table where two scrubby fishermen sat. Noticing the men's leering grins, Betsy expected the girl would no doubt receive extra pennies for her trouble tonight.

Standing before the hearth, her gloved hands clasped behind her back, Betsy inched closer to the crackling flames in an effort to warm her backside. A wave of sadness washed over her when she realized she was about to be married in a common tavern wearing no new finery and without her mother or sisters present, and carrying no flowers. But, that didn't matter. She was a grown woman and she loved John Ross, and more than anything, she wanted to become his wife, to make a home for him and to bear his children. It was silly to put off their nuptials simply because her parents disapproved the match.

On the other hand, John's sister Joanna was sympathetic to their plight.

As a wedding gift, she had given John enough money for the newly wed couple to spend their wedding night at the splendid new Wayfarer Inn located a few miles inland. Betsy had brought along her nightshift and hairbrush and before leaving work today, had sent a note to her mother telling her she would not be returning home tonight . . . and not to worry. Her parents would know soon enough that she and John Ross had married. Betsy had confided their plans to her older sister Sarah, who would relay the news to their parents on the morrow.

CHAPTER 1

THREE YEARS LATER

Philadelphia - January 1776

"There is nothing more necessary than good intelligence to frustrate a designing enemy, and nothing that requires greater pains to obtain." . . . *George Washington.*

"Must you go out today, John?" Betsy Ross peered through the window of the small upholstery shop the young couple had established soon after they married. Snow mixed with ice blew in swirling funnels down the street. "The snow has turned to sleet. The streets are deserted."

"I gave my word, love." John shrugged into his great coat and dug into the pockets for the red woolen gloves Betsy had knitted him for Christmas. "If I don't take my turn guarding the warehouse today, some other fellow will be obliged to go in my place."

"But there'll not be man nor beast abroad this afternoon." Betsy turned from the window. "Do stay home with me, John. We can sit by the fire where it's warm."

"I'll be home before ye know it, love."

Betsy watched as John wound a woolen muffler around his neck and pulled his cap down over his ears. "I wonder why gentlemen do not wear pattens on their boots when they venture out into the snow. Although I suppose a gentleman would look silly wearing pattens on his shoes."

His lips twitching, John dropped a kiss on his little wife's flushed cheek. "My feet will be fine, love." His dark eyes twinkled merrily as he pulled open the door of the shop. "And ye can warm up the rest of me tonight."

"Do be careful, John. I shouldn't want you to slip and fall to your death."

Muffled sounds of his merry laughter drifted back to Betsy as he stepped from the snow-covered stoop onto the slippery walkway. She hurried to the window to rub a clean spot on the frosty windowpane in order to wave goodbye to her intrepid young husband as he passed beneath the window. At least he was only setting out to *guard* the warehouse filled with muskets and gunpowder; he wasn't marching off to join the rebels in their fight for independence. Betsy didn't know how she'd cope if, or *when,* that day came.

She hadn't drawn a peaceful breath since the war began last year in New England, with bloody battles at both Lexington and Concord. When news reached them of yet another battle fought near Boston, at a place called Breed's Hill, and it was said the rebel troops lost simply because they ran out of gunpowder, local militias up and down the seaboard hastened to stockpile weaponry. Betsy's husband John, a member of the local Citizen Guards in Philadelphia, had set out today to protect the Pennsylvania Militia's valuable stash. Unfortunately for all Patriots, the newly formed Continental Congress had no money with which to provide General Washington's hastily formed army with muskets or ammunition, or with tents, blankets, or even food. Betsy prayed daily that this wretched war with England would draw to a swift close, and that the fighting would never reach as far south as Philadelphia.

After watching John's ghostly form disappear from sight, Betsy turned from the window. Although she couldn't help worrying about him setting out in such foul weather, she knew he'd given his word to take a turn at guard duty today, and John Ross never went back on his word. It was one of the many things she loved about the responsible young man she'd married.

Thus far, her life with John Ross had been all she could have hoped for. Despite the challenges they faced making a go of their upholstery business, they rarely disagreed. Real monetary success had not yet arrived, of course, since by the time they opened their shop doors, England had already cut off all trade with the colonies, meaning fabric and supplies were virtually impossible to come by. Still, when a customer brought in draperies or bed hangings to be mended, they praised the Lord and enjoyed completing the work together. Not for one minute did Betsy regret her decision to go against her Quaker faith, or defy her parents, in order to marry John Ross.

But she did regret *not* insisting he stay home with her this bitterly cold day! With no carts or horses able to navigate the icy streets, who would possibly attempt to steal heavy crates of muskets and gunpowder?

Betsy managed to stay busy all afternoon tidying up the kitchen, mending a pair of John's breeches and trying to keep the fire in the parlor going despite gusts of cold air seeping into the house. By evening, with the sleet and snow still falling, her worry escalated. John should have been home above an hour ago. If the weather weren't so wretched, she'd walk down the hill to Dock Street to see what was keeping him. John was always punctual. He knew she worried. Growing hungry, Betsy nibbled on a wedge of bread, leaving plenty for John who would come home famished. He'd taken no food with him today.

Suddenly, a rap at the door caused Betsy to spring from her chair in the back parlor and run through the darkened house to the shop door. Who could be calling? John had his own key and would let himself in. Jerking open the door, she was surprised to find fellow Guardsman Thomas Hull on the doorstep. She was about to invite the young man in out of the cold when the grim look on his face caused her breath to catch in her throat.

"What is it, Tom?"

For answer, he cast a troubled gaze over one shoulder. Wrapping her arms about herself, Betsy stepped onto the icy stoop to anxiously look past Tom. When she caught sight of two men struggling to carry another man prone between them, her heart plummeted to her feet. The trail of bright red blood dripping onto the stark white snow was clearly visible.

"John!"

"The warehouse exploded," Tom said simply. "I heard the blast as I approached to take my turn at guard duty. Suddenly, the whole damn building burst into flames."

"No-o!" Terror gripped Betsy as she clutched the doorjamb. *"No!"*

* * * * *

Although Betsy kept a constant vigil at her husband's bedside, dressing his many wounds, spooning warm broth into his mouth and doing all she could to lessen his pain, in a few short days her beloved John, his limp head cradled in her arms, drew his final breath.

Two cold winter days later, Betsy, still numb with grief, followed behind the men who hefted John's casket aloft and carried it to the graveyard adjacent to Christ Church on nearby Second Street. Standing next to John's sister Joanna, Betsy's eyes filled with tears as the church bells tolled a dull thud in her ears. Huddled together, they watched the men pitch clods of hard black earth onto the plain pine box containing John's broken body.

"How will I manage without him?" Betsy murmured through her tears.

"You will put your faith in God and know that He is watching over you. And John will also be watching."

Alone now and a widow at four and twenty, Betsy Ross slowly returned to her home on Mulberry Street; her world and the life she had believed would go on forever, now taken from her forever.

CHAPTER 2

Throughout the blur of days that followed, ladies from Christ Church rapped at Betsy's door bringing food and well wishes. Husbands were dispatched to the woodpile behind the Ross home to carry in logs for the fire, and to pump fresh water from the public well on the corner. Betsy scarcely knew when her visitors arrived, or when they departed.

One day as she lay in bed, an insistent rap at the door roused her from a fitful slumber. When it appeared the caller would simply not leave, Betsy dragged herself to her feet and pulled a wrapper on over her nightshift. Not caring who'd come to call or what they wanted, she numbly crept down the stairs to peek from the front window. A small smile lifted the corners of her pale lips when she saw it was Sarah, the only member of her family brave enough to risk censure from the Quaker elders by coming to see her. Her older sister had stopped in regularly when Betsy was nursing John's wounds.

"I've brought food," Sarah said as she entered the darkened house when Betsy finally pulled open the door. Though the sisters resembled one another, Sarah's light brown hair and blue eyes seemed insipid next to Betsy's vibrant coloring. Sarah, wearing a tattered gray cloak over her traditional Hodden gray gown, walked briskly through the shop to the parlor. "I'll wager you've not been eating properly, if at all." The sound of Sarah's voice diminished as she hurried through the tall, narrow house.

Like most dwellings on Mulberry Street, the ground floor of Betsy's home contained only two rooms; the one facing the street served as the shop while the rear chamber with an adjacent pantry was the family's private parlor. John had painted the walls of both rooms a cheery lemon yellow and in the early days of their marriage, Betsy kept the planked wooden floors shiny with beeswax. At one end of the parlor stood a fireplace framed with pretty blue and white Dutch tiles. A small drop-leaf table and chairs sat pushed against the sidewall; a cupboard holding pewter plates and Betsy's precious china teacups rested against the back wall. On those rare occasions when Betsy and John had had a guest for dinner, the parlor also served as the dining chamber.

Slumping onto the sofa before the hearth, Betsy didn't notice that the fire consisted merely of a few charred logs resting upon a bed of white ash. She also did not notice Sarah setting out two bowls on the table or pulling open the lower drawer of the cupboard to retrieve a pair of spoons.

"Have you tea made?" Sarah asked without looking up. "If not, I shall make some."

Dragging her wrapper closer about her body, Betsy muttered, "I have no tea. Nor any bread, or meat, for all that."

Sarah's brows snapped together. "You cannot continue on in this fashion, Betsy. I have decided it best that you come and live with me. I shall brook no objection." She paused as if expecting to hear one. "So . . . there's an end to it. After we eat, we shall gather up a few of your things and . . ."

"John would not want me to abandon the shop." Betsy pushed aside the tangled chestnut curl that dangled over her brow.

"John also would not want you to perish from neglect." Sarah gazed down upon her sister, her legs tucked beneath her body in an attempt to stay warm. "I daresay you have not brushed your hair in a sen'night."

"I have no reason to brush my hair."

Sarah bustled from the room. Betsy heard her footfalls ascending the steep stairs to her bedchamber in search of her hairbrush, she assumed.

"There," Sarah said minutes later, after she'd tugged the stiff bristles through her sister's thick tresses. "At least you look a far sight better. Now, let's get some food into your stomach."

Betsy couldn't recall when she'd last eaten. Or what she'd eaten. But, she admitted, the Brunswick stew and cornbread Sarah had brought tasted good.

"It feels quite cold in here," Sarah exclaimed moments after both girls had finished their meal and moved to the sofa. She directed a gaze toward the smoldering embers. "You need fresh logs for the fire, Betsy, and water with which to wash. You need help. If you refuse to live with me; then I shall come and stay with you a spell." She held up a hand. "Just until you get back on your feet."

"But what of William?"

"My husband has gone. After reading, nay *devouring,* the pamphlet everyone is reading now called *Common Sense* in which the author declares that: *'the time for deliberation is over and action must now be taken,'* William answered a call for volunteers from a man named Henry Knox at an obscure fort somewhere up north called Ti . . . con-der . . . osa, or . . . oga; I am not certain which. At any rate, the rebels are attempting to cart the heavy artillery they confiscated from the British all the way from this fort-place down to Boston." Sarah's voice faltered. "It seems an impossible task to me and I cannot fathom William's reason for wanting to assist. William is a Quaker. He will not fight."

Sarah's distress seemed to jerk Betsy from her own. She reached for her sister's hand. "If William refuses to fight, he should remain safe, Sarah." Her tone was gentle.

"I pray that will be the case." Sarah sniffed. "Do forgive me, Betsy, I do not mean to diminish your loss."

Betsy gazed into the sputtering flames. "Truth be told, I've come to realize that if John hadn't died when he did that . . . he, too, would have marched off to join the fighting." A rush of tears clouded her vision. "John believed so very strongly in the Patriot Cause."

"As do we all," Sarah murmured. "I expect that's why William wants to assist." After a pause, she said, "Even our parents are suffering from this wretched war. Father says the king is making it far too difficult for any of us to scratch out a living. I suppose the time has indeed come for us to declare our independence." She turned a questioning gaze on Betsy. "But who shall we be if we are not English subjects? Who shall be our king?

We've no royalty in the colonies."

Betsy shifted on the sofa. "I suppose they'll dig up some distant kin of a royal duke or earl and declare him king. Or . . ." she absently twisted a strand of chestnut hair, ". . . perhaps we shall become a different sort of nation, sovereign unto ourselves. At least . . . that is what . . ." her voice fell to barely above a whisper, "John used to say."

"Well, that seems a rather odd notion to me. How shall we get on without a king?"

Despite the pain still searing her heart, Betsy's back straightened. "Perhaps His Excellency General Washington will become king and his wife Martha our queen. We already address her as Lady Washington." Hearing echoes of John's voice in her head fervently speaking of freedom and independence, her chin trembled. "John said that to declare our independence from the crown is a far sight better than to remain slaves to the King of England." Repeating his words caused fresh anguish to grip her insides. "John says," she faltered. "John *said* we could all be hung for treason if we refuse to obey Parliament's laws, which . . . he says . . . *said,* are designed to keep us enslaved."

Sarah gazed at her younger sister. "You seem to have quite a good grasp on the matter, Betsy."

"John had a good grasp." Tears pooled in Betsy's already red-rimmed eyes. "Oh, Sarah, how shall I go on without him?"

Sarah drew her sister's trembling body close. "Dear Betsy, I know how deeply you cared for John, but it has been weeks now since he perished. You really must give a thought to yourself and to your own future. Surely you do not mean to carry on your upholstery business without John. You are a woman; you cannot manage a business alone. And with goods so very scarce now . . . why, the shelves of the apothecary shop and the mercantile are very nearly empty. Only Loyalist merchants continue to prosper. God only knows from where they procure goods."

Betsy sniffed back her tears. "John said Loyalists survive because they believe the crown has every right to levy taxes upon us. And since they openly pledge their allegiance to the king, they manage still to receive goods, although . . . not even John knew from where."

"If our little army is not successful against the British soon, I fear we shall all be hanged as traitors to the crown. Is that how it is to end for us, I mean, for those of us who are *not* Loyalists?"

Betsy bit her lower lip before replying. Repeating John's sentiments felt like ripping her heart from her chest, but somehow it . . . also made it seem as if he were . . . still here. "John said that since the king has never visited us, he has no idea how modern we've become, or that we're quite capable of managing our own affairs." Speaking his words aloud seemed to lift some of the cobwebs from her mind. "I, too, believe we can manage very well on our own."

Sarah gazed raptly at her younger sister. "But would you *fight* for what you believe?"

Suddenly the words she'd just spoken, that she believed colonists could manage very well on their own, sent a fresh surge of strength through Betsy, as if John truly *were* right here, telling her she *was* strong, that she *could* go on, without him.

Betsy slowly rose to her feet and reached for the poker. Prodding the remnants of the charred logs, she managed to coax one small flame to life. She watched the tiny orange finger of fire grow stronger and brighter, then, she leaned the poker back up against the bricks and returned to the sofa. "I believe I would fight, Sarah. In his own way, John was already fighting this war. He believed it was his duty to guard that warehouse full of muskets and ammunition so if the British marched this far south, our militiamen would have sufficient weapons on hand with which to fight. My John gave his life for the Patriot Cause, the same as if he were killed in a bloody battle in New England." Fresh tears pooled in Betsy's eyes. "Oh, Sarah, John is *dead* . . . what am I to do? Where am I to turn?"

Again, Sarah enfolded her sister's trembling body in her arms. "I am alone now, too, Betsy, and I am also frightened. Please let me stay with you a spell; at least until William returns home."

Betsy dried her tears. John's sister Joanna was right. She had no choice but to trust that God *and* John were watching over her. As long as she remained in this house, John would be right here with her; and now God had sent Sarah to help steady her. She gave her sister a shaky smile. "Very well, Sarah. We shall help one another cope."

In February, newspapers reported that skirmishes between the rebels and the British had been fought in several colonies fronting the Atlantic. Because Philadelphians hadn't realized the rebellion had reached the southern colonies, they were surprised to learn that a battle at a place called Moore's Creek Bridge had been fought in faraway North Carolina. They were also shocked to learn that Royal Governor Dunmore of Virginia had actually ordered colonists to set fire to the village of Norfolk when his demand for recruits and provisions for the *British* army went ignored by the Patriots! Clear to Betsy and Sarah now was that the entire country was at war and the fighting would not cease until the Continental Army declared victory.

Every day, Betsy thanked God that Sarah was there to keep her company. And with each passing day, she felt her grief lessen and her thoughts return to the future. One bright sunny day she put a sign in the window stating that beyond upholstering chairs and sofas, and fashioning draperies and bed hangings, she also made ladies clothing. She fervently hoped the sign would bring in some much-needed new business. With John gone and the war escalating her ready cash was fast dwindling to nothing. Right after John was injured the landlord had graciously ceased to badger her about the back rent she owed, but she was now four months behind. She fully expected the man to come knocking on her door any day now.

Helping the girls with the heavy chores was the young man Sarah's husband had hired to lend a hand whilst he was away, a sixteen-year-old youth named Toby Grimes. Toby's father was one of those zealous men who'd marched off to fight at the onset of the war, leaving behind a wife and four children. A responsible young man, it was clearly evident Toby was doing his best to care for his abandoned family. Every morning, he carted in fresh logs for Betsy's kitchen fire, pumped water from the well, and performed other tasks deemed too arduous for the ladies.

Twice each week on Market Day, Betsy and Sarah walked down Mulberry Street to the open-air stalls where they purchased fresh milk, meat, and produce from farmers who brought their goods into town to sell. One crisp morning in mid-March, excitement fairly crackled throughout the marketplace as everyone talked about how General Washington's Patriot army had stormed Boston and successfully liberated the city!

"My," Betsy declared, her blue eyes glittering, "the sight of those redcoats scattering must have been marvelous to behold!"

All around them cries of *"The war is over!"* and *"Lobster-backs go home!"* rang out.

"Surely this means William will be coming home soon!" Sarah exclaimed. She and Betsy, both carrying parcels tucked beneath their arms, hurried back up Mulberry Street. "I expect I should get the house ready for him. Do not fret, Betsy, I shall continue to send Toby around to help you and I will also pay his wages. You will allow me to do that for you, will you not?"

Betsy nodded absently. "Yes; thank you, Sarah." Listening to talk of war just now had brought back images of that terrible night in January when the men brought John home. Those dark days after the explosion, she had been so busy tending his wounds she hadn't thought to question him about the actual events of that night. What exactly *had* happened at the warehouse? Had someone overtaken John and set fire to the dozens of cases of gunpowder stored there? Why hadn't the authorities come to question him the next day? And, why had nothing been said about the explosion since?

"I do not believe you've heard a single word I've said, Betsy. Is something troubling you?"

"I've been thinking about the events of that night."

"What night?"

"The night of the explosion."

"Oh," Sarah said. "I thought you had put all that behind you and were moving forward with your life. With the war over now, everything should return again to normal. I understand you are determined to carry on with your upholstery business, Betsy, you have always been quite headstrong."

"Indeed, I am headstrong. And I am determined to keep our shop doors open. But I also cannot help wondering about the events of that dreadful night. All I know is that Tom Hull said the warehouse suddenly burst into flames. Just now at the market, I overheard men talking about how British soldiers in the Massachusetts colony had learned where the rebels had stored their muskets and gunpowder and had broken in and stolen everything. Could not the same thing have happened here? Did British soldiers attempt to steal the weapons in the warehouse that night and John tried to stop them? John once said the British were offering gold to Loyalists in Massachusetts who sabotaged the Patriot Cause. The more I think on it, Sarah, the more I'm convinced that a Philadelphia Loyalist was responsible for the explosion; perhaps even *rewarded,* for setting that fire. Otherwise, why would the warehouse suddenly explode? What *caused* the explosion?"

"Guns and ammunition were stored there," Sarah said as if that were sufficient reason to explain an explosion.

"Gunpowder doesn't just ignite on its own, not during a snowstorm inside a leaky old warehouse. What caused the building to suddenly burst into flames?"

Sarah's lips thinned. "You have been feeling so well lately, Betsy; please, can you not just let it be?" When her sister said nothing, she added, "Continuing to dwell on the accident will not bring John back. You are needlessly oversetting yourself."

Betsy was still deep in thought. "Perhaps I could inquire of the night watchman on duty that night. Perhaps he saw something, or even knows precisely what happened."

"I cannot think that a good idea, Betsy. You simply must put that nasty business behind you. With the war over now, ladies will want to decorate their homes again. They'll want new bed hangings, and bolsters, and draperies . . ."

"But do you not think it odd that the authorities never launched an investigation? No one ever came to ask John what happened that night."

"I expect an explosion at a munitions warehouse tells the entire story; an official inquiry was not deemed necessary."

"But I need to know what happened," Betsy insisted. "Surely a record exists somewhere telling which night watchman was on duty the night of the explosion."

Later that day Betsy decided to consult with the girl's Uncle Abel. As the respected proprietor of *James and Drinker Importers*, an inquiry from Abel James would be taken seriously. When she and John married, Uncle Abel had helped them acquire the fabric and supplies they needed in order to launch their upholstery business. If Uncle Abel informed Betsy that nothing was amiss that night, she would believe him. Uncle Abel didn't lie.

A few days later, a message from Abel James arrived at Betsy's shop. Sarah was above stairs gathering her things in preparation to return to her home that afternoon. Betsy hurriedly unfolded the note and after reading it, ran up the stairs and burst in upon her sister.

"Listen to this, Sarah. Uncle Abel says that the constable did, indeed, recall who had been on duty at the wharf that night because the following morning the man's *frozen body was found floating in the Delaware River just below the Dock Street warehouse!*" Betsy's tone reverberated with agitation. "It was assumed the Watch had slipped on the ice and fallen into the river and was unable to climb out."

Sarah did not look up from her task of folding up garments and neatly fitting them into an opened valise on the floor. "That sounds reasonable to me, Betsy. The cobbles were icy that night; if you recall, it was not only snowing, it was sleeting."

"I clearly recall that wretched night, Sarah. But this says nothing about *why* the warehouse suddenly burst into flames! What if the night watchman did *not* simply slip and fall into the river, what if he was *pushed?*"

"Oh, Betsy." Shaking her head, Sarah looked up. "Surely you do not believe the night watchman was murdered."

"I do, indeed. I believe that both John *and* the night watchman were murdered. I believe someone deliberately set fire to the warehouse and in the doing, was seen by the Watch, and to protect himself from being apprehended, the perpetrator silenced the man. Permanently. Or perhaps, *before* he set the fire, he took the precaution of killing the night watchman and *then* he . . ."

"Oh, Betsy. Why can you not just let it be? If the authorities do not believe anything was amiss then why must you dredge it all up again?"

"Because I am convinced that my John was murdered! I cannot let it go, Sarah." Betsy began to pace back and forth between the makeshift bed upon which Sarah had slept and the curtained window in the spare room. "A crime was committed, Sarah; and I *will* not let it go unpunished! I will not!"

CHAPTER 3

Beyond asking the questions she'd already asked, Betsy had no clue how to conduct an investigation. Where did one begin? Should she attempt to look for a suspect? How did one go about doing that? Of only one thing was she *fairly* certain. The motive was sabotage . . . unless; the explosion truly was an accident. But not for a minute did she believe that. Unfortunately, with Sarah now gone, she could not devote all day every day to her investigation since she also had to earn a living. Not only did she owe four months back rent on the shop but in the short time she and John were married, they'd racked up a mountain of debt with merchants all over town, including the apothecary who'd been kind enough to send over whatever medicines or ointments Betsy requested after John was injured. Somehow she had to climb her way out of debt *and* conduct an investigation. How to accomplish both gnawed at her both day and night.

Thankfully, in the next few weeks, a slow but steady stream of work began to trickle in. But it took nearly every cent Betsy earned to purchase logs for the kitchen fire and food for the table. Whatever was left over she set aside to go toward paying off the back rent she owed. She was exceedingly grateful that Sarah continued to send Toby Grimes around. Being a petite person, Betsy found simply carrying logs into the house an arduous task. Without Toby's help, she didn't know how she'd cart them down the steep steps to the underground kitchen.

In late April, in an effort to learn more about what was politically afoot in Philadelphia, perhaps even who was responsible for the warehouse explosion, Betsy decided to join a group called Fighting Quakers, composed mainly of people like herself, who for one reason or another had been read out of Meeting. Most members still clung to the traditional Quaker belief against fighting or bearing arms, but these particular men had declared that if necessary they would indeed sling a musket over a shoulder in order to fight for their rights as independent Americans. John had attended several meetings, but Betsy, fearing women would not be welcome, hadn't gone with him. When John came home from the last meeting he attended saying that several young ladies with whom Betsy was acquainted had been there, she had planned to attend the next meeting with him. That time never came. Now, Betsy decided to join the rebel group; although she'd keep her decision to herself. Sarah would only scoff at her stubborn refusal to abandon her quest for the truth.

Unfortunately at the first Fighting Quaker meeting Betsy attended, she learned only that, contrary to what many Philadelphians believed after the liberation of Boston, the war was far from over. Instead, the British evacuating that city merely left General Washington . . . who'd been awarded a gold medal for accomplishing the feat without sacrificing a single rebel in the process . . . now wondering when and where the British would strike next?

Even today, fighting was taking place in far away Canada, a matter of particular concern to Sarah, whose mental state was fast spiraling towards depression over the fact that William had not yet returned home. To Betsy's chagrin, throughout that first month as a Fighting Quaker member, she did not hear anyone mention sabotage of any sort. That she was making no headway whatever with her investigation only made her more determined than ever to uncover the truth.

Aware in May when the second Continental Congress convened in Philadelphia and statesmen from nearly all thirteen colonies descended upon the city, Betsy was pleasantly surprised one spring afternoon when a delegation of high-ranking Congressmen, amongst them General George Washington himself, with whom Betsy was acquainted from Christ Church where she and John had worshipped and she continued to, and John's uncle, Colonel George Ross, called at her shop. Delighted to receive such esteemed callers, Betsy brewed a pot of tea, using the last of the leaves Sarah had brought, and served it to the gentlemen. Because Toby was there, she asked him to carry the heavy tray up the stairs to the parlor. Before the men left that afternoon, she was thrilled when they asked her to sew a large banner representing the unification of the thirteen colonies. Overjoyed by the commission, Betsy offered up a prayer of thanksgiving to God for bringing her such an important and lucrative piece of work.

A few days later, Betsy folded up the enormous silk banner she'd

created, consisting of red and white stripes with thirteen five-pointed stars,
one for each of the thirteen colonies arranged in a circle on a blue canton,
and carried the package to the State House on Chestnut Street to present to
the delegation. The gentlemen were so pleased with her work that they
ordered a dozen more flags just like it. Betsy was thrilled beyond measure.
Although the men did front her a sum of money to purchase bunting for the
new banners, she had yet to be paid for the task, therefore, she had no
choice but to live on expectations of the vast sum of money she would
eventually receive.

In order to complete the time-consuming project, she sat up long into
many nights industriously stitching on the banners by candlelight. The
sooner she finished the job, the sooner she could satisfy the landlord's
persistent demands for the back rent she owed. Lately, she'd begun to feel
guilty that Sarah continued to pay young Toby's wages. Especially since
he seemed to spend the better part of every day at Betsy's shop rather than
helping Sarah.

One morning, Betsy's Uncle Abel stopped in to see her.

"I'm on my way back from City Tavern and thought I'd check on
you," the elderly Quaker said by way of explaining his unexpected call.

Betsy knew her uncle went every morning to City Tavern, a meeting
place for businessmen in Philadelphia who wished to learn which ships had
sailed into the harbor during the night and which were expected to arrive
that day. Betsy invited her uncle into her parlor where she was hard at
work on the Continental banners.

"Please, sit down." A hand indicated a chair opposite the sofa where
her work was spread out around her. "I'm sorry I haven't anything to offer
you, Uncle Abel, no coffee, or tea."

"No matter." The white-haired gentleman smiled. "I have it on good

authority that anyone caught drinking English tea in New York is arrested on the spot. Loyalist citizens gleefully turn over their Patriot neighbors who still have tea on hand, to the authorities."

Betsy sighed. "What a dreadful pass our world has come to."

"Tell me how you're getting on, my girl, now that you're alone."

"I am bearing up." Betsy smiled somewhat tightly. "With the Lord's help."

"You seem to have garnered a nice bit of business."

"I do have quite a large commission before me now." Betsy told her uncle about the new flags she was making for General Washington and held one up to show him.

"Very nice, my dear. And do you have sufficient supplies on hand to complete the project?"

"I have plenty of bunting for this task. However, were a customer to want new draperies, or a sofa or chair upholstered, I've nothing suitable on hand, no damask, or silk, or linen."

"Perhaps I can help."

Though she'd welcome her uncle's assistance, Betsy shook her head. "Thank you for your kind offer, Uncle Abel, but I've no money to pay for whatever fabric you could supply."

"I extended you and John credit when you first opened your shop doors. You are every bit as talented and resourceful as he was. I am quite confident in your ability to carry on, my dear."

"Thank you, Uncle Abel. Your confidence in me means a great deal."

"As it happens, I am expecting a large shipment of piece goods: Chinese silk, bombazine, harrenteen, cheney, damask, velvet, even brass tacks and chair nails. If you'd like me to set some parcels aside for you, I will be glad to extend you credit. What say you?"

"Oh, Uncle Abel," Betsy breathed, "I don't know what to say. Thank you, indeed. Once I've been paid for this project, I hope to settle the remainder of my debts and have enough left over to see me through several more months. I should be able to begin repaying you straightaway for whatever goods you provide."

"So it is settled, then. In the meantime . . ." The distinguished Quaker rose and reaching into the pocket of his frock coat, withdrew a pouch jingling with coins. "Perhaps this will help see you through." He dropped the pouch onto a nearby table. "Consider it a gift from an uncle to his favorite niece." An indulgent grin spread over his still strong features.

Relief washed over Betsy's face as she set aside her work. "Thank you ever so, Uncle Abel." She followed the older man into the corridor that separated the parlor from the shop.

"I'll send a note 'round later this week telling you when my ship is expected to dock, or you can stop by City Tavern, if you like."

"You are too kind, Uncle Abel."

"To help you is always a pleasure, my dear."

Betsy knew she was not the only shopkeeper in Philadelphia scrambling for business. Merchants all over the city were having a difficult time obtaining goods to stock their shelves. Since mandates from the crown had halted all imports from England, ships carrying goods were now diverted to the West Indies before being allowed to dock. Only after the value of the shipment was tabulated and a judgment made on how to disperse the goods was a ship allowed to put into harbor. Betsy had no idea from where, or how, her uncle was procuring supplies but so long as the Implementation Officials who patrolled the wharfs and inspected the cargoes of every ship that arrived in Philadelphia found nothing amiss; that was good enough for her. As a highly respected Quaker businessman, and therefore perceived to be a Loyalist, Betsy knew her uncle's fealty to the crown went unquestioned.

A few mornings later, although it was not yet seven of the clock, Betsy was up, dressed and anxious to get to market. After making her purchases, she planned to head over to City Tavern to consult with her uncle. Snatching up her basket, she flung open the door of her shop, and as usual, left it unlocked behind her before she hurried down the sloping thoroughfare toward the waterfront. Although the sun had not yet burned off the fog that crept inland every night off the Delaware River, the city was already bustling with activity. Other women, also hurrying to market, joined her on the brick flagway, most calling out friendly greetings, although most went unheard above the noise of carts and wagons clattering by on the cobbled street.

Nearing the open-air market on High Street, farmer's wagons, some still loaded with produce . . . potatoes, carrots, onions, cabbages, and corn . . . lined both sides of the busy thoroughfare. Attempting to maneuver her way across the thronged street, Betsy nearly collided with a lanky youth whose head was ducked against the brisk wind sweeping up from the river.

"Beg pardon, Miz Ross." The young man politely touched the brim of his cap. "Didn't 'spect to see you out and about so early, ma'am."

"Good morning, Toby." Betsy paused for a fleeting second. "The door is unlocked. Bring in logs for the fire, please, and put the kettle on. I'm off to market. If anyone stops in, tell them I shall return straightaway."

"Yes, 'um. I'll also tidy up the workroom and sweep off the stoop for ye, ma'am."

"There's a good lad," Betsy called over her shoulder as she hurried away.

Upon entering the marketplace, Betsy made her way around the colorful stalls manned by apple-cheeked farmers, butchers wiping bloody hands on their aprons, and sleepy-eyed city merchants hoping to earn a few extra shillings before returning to their shops for the day. Choosing carefully, Betsy managed to fit all her purchases into her basket, then quickly made her way back up Second Street to City Tavern to ask Uncle Abel if the ship he'd been expecting had sailed into the harbor. She hoped that in addition to a dozen or more bolts of fine fabric, her parcels would also contain tape and braid, canvas webbing, tacks and upholstery pins, and, of course, spools and spools of multi-colored thread. She recalled how excited she and John had been when their first shipment of supplies had arrived back when they first opened their shop doors. It had been months since she'd felt anything akin to excitement, but small tremors of it surged through her now.

She found City Tavern also crowded and noisy that morning. After locating her uncle and exchanging greetings with him, the older man told his niece that, indeed, the ship they'd been awaiting had been spotted on the horizon and should dock in a few hours.

"I expect to be at quayside the bulk of the day so it will likely be tomorrow before I can dispatch a driver to deliver your goods."

"Oh." Betsy's face fell.

Abel James smiled. "You may send Toby around this evening to fetch my cart and the pair of you can load up your supplies tonight, if you like."

"Oh." Betsy brightened. "Thank you, Uncle Abel." She turned to go, then turned back. "How will I know . . .?"

"I'll send 'round the official receipt which you'll need to present to the excise officer when you arrive at the quay. It contains all the necessary information to collect your parcels."

Betsy's smiled broadened. "I cannot thank you enough, Uncle Abel."

"My pleasure to help you, girl." The Quaker merchant escorted the pretty little widow through the crowded tavern to the door. Apparently it had not escaped his notice that her appearance in the predominately male-dominated arena was garnering undue attention. "I promised John before he died that I'd look out for you, Betsy."

Seated beside Toby on the bench of her uncle's cart that night as they approached the wharf, a delicate chair whose seat cushion Betsy had mended that afternoon stood upright in the bed of the wagon. Betsy's long gaze took in above half a dozen stately schooners, their square-rigged sails straining against the breeze as the huge ships swayed in the choppy water. Even this late in the day, the wooden piers jutting out over the river still buzzed with activity. Men shouted orders amid horse-drawn conveyances rumbling over the cobbled street, it littered with crates, chests and kegs that had been unloaded but as yet unclaimed. Once again excitement arose within Betsy as she climbed down from the cart to search out the excise officer to whom she must first present her receipt before being allowed to claim her parcels.

"Deliver the chair to Mrs. Martinson, Toby, then come straight back here," she instructed. "By then I shall know which packages are ours and we can load them up."

"Yes, ma'am," Toby replied cheerfully. A cluck of his tongue and a quick shake of the reins set the brown mare in front of him in motion.

A half hour later, her mission complete, Betsy stood alone amongst the clutter on the wharf, her stamped receipt in hand as she scanned the cobbled street for Toby and the cart. The brisk wind off the Delaware River caused her long gray skirt to flap about her legs. *What was keeping the boy?* Not a patient person by nature, Betsy soon began to feel more than a tad bit irritable over being left stranded on the crowded quay. Toby had had sufficient time now to drive back and forth to Mrs. Martinson's home at least thrice. At length, Betsy began to pick her way along the cluttered dock in the direction she expected Toby to be coming. On the opposite side of the wharf, warehouses eventually gave way to noisy pubs and taverns, which, Betsy noted were already full of bawdy sailors and . . . women of a dubious sort. More than once, she was obliged to step aside as a drunken sailor, reeking of sweat and sour ale, stumbled onto the flagway.

"Hey, mateys! Look what I foun'!" A bleary-eyed limey leered at Betsy. "Wha's yer name, swee-heart?"

Refusing to answer the uncivilized query, Betsy thrust up her chin and skirted past the inebriated seaman. Her agitation mounted as she crossed one narrow alleyway after another all the while spotting nary a sight of Toby or the cart. Upon reaching the very street upon which Mrs. Martinson lived, she turned and marched up to the door of the fine home and inquired if Toby had yet delivered the chair she'd sent over.

"Indeed, he has, Mrs. Ross," the maid replied. "Your boy was here above half an hour ago."

Quite beside herself now, Betsy retraced her steps back to the pier. *Where was Toby?* In the weeks he'd been coming around, he'd never once given her a moment's concern. He'd dispatched every duty she'd given him with a sense of urgency and responsibility. *Where could the boy have got off to now?* Toby was not the sort to dawdle; nor would he pop into a pub for a quick nip.

Although she didn't expect to see him inside an alehouse, she did pause to peer through the mullioned windows of several crowded taverns. She did not spot Toby, but in the common room of one of the more respectable establishments, she did catch sight of her Uncle Abel enjoying a leisurely supper at a table surrounded by a half dozen of his acquaintances.

Betsy hurried away before her uncle spotted her looking in. Darkness was full upon the city now and the night air felt quite chilly. She pulled her shawl more tightly about her shoulders even as more sailors poured from the wharf onto the flagway. She shouldn't be on the dock at this hour. Even during the day, quayside was not a desirable area for a woman; after dark, it was downright foolhardy for a lady to be here.

Hurrying up the cobbled lane, Betsy attempted to keep to the walkway but found doing so nigh on impossible as the passageway was narrow and in some places, non-existent. When yet another knot of sailors, deep in their cups, approached her, she ducked into a dimly lit alleyway to avoid colliding with the seamen who were having a difficult time holding one another up. Betsy's blue eyes rolled skyward as she waited for the rowdy riff-raff to pass by.

Suddenly above the din and confusion on the waterfront, other sounds claimed her attention. Casting a curious gaze over one shoulder, Betsy spotted two shadowy figures scuffling further up the alleyway. By the dim lamplight filtering through a half-opened door, she was able to ascertain that one of the men was considerably larger than the other, although the slight one was holding his own in a valiant attempt to ward off his attacker's blows. Grunts and curses punctuated their struggle. A rush of sympathy for the smaller fellow overtook Betsy and without thinking, she cried, *"Let him go!"*

Her cry caused the larger man to glance up. Unable to see his face, she was stunned when suddenly, he flattened the boy against the wall and with a single lunge, thrust what appeared to be a knife into the smaller fellow's midsection. Without a sound, the slight man crumpled to the ground as his burly attacker fled.

Stunned, Betsy leapt into action. *"Stop!"* she cried, dashing into the alleyway. Nearing the figure crumpled on the ground, she sank to her knees. The boy's head hung limply to one side. Recognizing him at once, Betsy gasped, *"Toby!"*

Her stomach lurched when her gaze dropped to his shirtfront already stained by a great quantity of crimson blood. More pooled beneath him as it freely poured from a gash in his neck.

"Toby! Who did this?"

At the sound of her voice, the boy's eyelids fluttered and his chalk-white lips attempted to move, but Betsy could see that his strength was fast ebbing away.

"I'll fetch help!"

Springing to her feet, she ran all the way back to the alehouse where only minutes earlier she'd spotted her uncle through the tavern window. Every step she took, she prayed he'd still be there. He was, and, the very second Betsy told him that Toby lay wounded in an alleyway; he and two of his companions lurched to their feet.

Clutching Betsy's arm, Abel James steered her toward the door. "Robert, see my niece home. Harry, fetch the Watch, and bring my wagon around. Don't fret about your goods, Betsy; I'll have someone deliver them to you. I'll take Toby home and have my wife patch him up."

Betsy and the men fairly ran down the street. Tears trickled down Betsy's cheeks as she hurried to keep up with her uncle's long strides. "You'll tell me how Toby fares, will you not?"

After Betsy thanked the gentleman her uncle had dispatched to see her home, she hurried inside and shakily locked the door of her shop, then realized she'd been so overset when she'd rushed into the tavern to fetch Uncle Abel she had neglected to give him the receipt with which to claim her goods. Nor had she told him she had actually witnessed the crime.

CHAPTER 4

Betsy lay awake long into the night. The sight she'd witnessed in the alleyway, Toby's limp body, the river of blood gushing from his neck, was simply too gruesome to thrust aside. It also brought back vivid memories of that awful night when the men brought John home. Grief threatened again to overtake her. Only this time, it was coupled with guilt.

If she hadn't insisted that she and Toby go to the pier *tonight* when Uncle Abel said he'd deliver her supplies tomorrow, this would never have happened. A sob caught in her throat. She had just wanted to feel the same elation that she and John had felt exclaiming over all the lovely fabric and tassels and braid they'd received in their first shipment of goods. Back then, they'd both been full of ideas for pretty new bed hangings and attractive window coverings. She had so looked forward to feeling that way again. Instead, her selfish impatience had caused . . . oh, if only she hadn't insisted they go to the dock *tonight.* Just then, Betsy clearly heard a voice inside her head telling her she was not the one at fault, that if the man who stabbed Toby hadn't chanced upon him tonight at the quay, he might have sought him out at her shop, or perhaps at Sarah's home, thereby placing her sister, and perhaps herself, in grave danger.

Betsy sat straight up in bed.

Could it be true?

She covered her face with her hands. *Dear God, please, please do not let Toby die!*

The following morning, Betsy's thoughts were still churning. Her uncle had not yet sent word of Toby's condition, although, like John, she feared the boy couldn't possibly survive such massive wounds. She was so overwrought she could scarcely swallow a bite of the lumpy oatmeal she'd mindlessly prepared to break her fast. Later that morning, she took up her sewing. Left to do on the new flags for General Washington was to cut out and attach all the five-pointed stars.

Mid-morning a rap at the door caused Betsy's head to jerk up. Her heart in her throat, she hurried through the house to find a portly man on the doorstep. An insignia on the pocket of his frockcoat identified him as a city official.

"A fine mornin' to ye, ma'am. I'm Constable O'Malley."

The grim look on the man's face sent a shudder through Betsy.

The constable stepped inside accompanied by a gust of cool air pungent with the scent of impending rain. Politely removing his cap, he said, "Abel James asked that I relay to ye the sad news of Toby Grimes' passin', ma'am."

"Oh-h." Betsy's eyes squeezed shut. A second later, after regaining herself, she said, "I-I neglected to tell my uncle last night that I was . . . standing at the far end of the alleyway the instant Toby was stabbed."

The constable blinked. "Are ye saying ye witnessed the crime, ma'am? That ye can identify who kilt the boy?"

"No." Betsy shook her head. "I caught only a glimpse of the man's face a split second before he . . . plunged his knife into . . . " Her breath caught in her throat. "I-It was far too dark to clearly see the man's face, sir. I saw only that he was of a greater height and girth than Toby. He was quite . . . burly-looking."

"Ah. No doubt a presser." The constable fingered his cap. "They's two ships anchored in the harbor what's short-handed. Watch said pressmen has been rounding up hands. No doubt young Toby refused to go and the presser jes' kilt him." He jammed his cap back on his head and turned to go. "No use investigatin' the matter further, ma'am."

"Wait!" Betsy cried. "A murder was committed, sir! It is your *duty* to investigate the crime."

The constable shrugged. "Wouldn't rightly know where to begin, ma'am. Would be nigh on impossible to determine who was on the wharf last night. Like I said, the perpetrator was most likely a presser. Lessen you, or the boy's mother, can think of a reason why somebody'd want Toby Grimes dead; ain't no reason not to conclude it weren't no random killin'. Dockside stabbin's 'er quite common, ye know."

"But you must make some sort of effort to find the killer!"

"Ma'am, they's a stabbin' most ever' day down at t'quay. What with sailors from ports 'round the world, and now soldiers an' unsavory sorts hangin' around, there's no way I could run the guilty party to ground. Like as not, the fellow what done Toby in is twenty leagues out to sea by now."

"Well, perhaps someone other than myself observed the pair enter the alleyway, or . . . or perhaps heard them arguing beforehand. To ascertain why they were quarreling might lead you straight to the guilty party."

"Even if'n the two of 'em was seen, like I said, the killer is likely long gone by now. Sailors what gits their-selves stabbed generally jes' ties a rag 'round the wound and gits right back on the boat. If'n they dies out to sea .

. ." he turned palms up, "well, you know what they does with the body then." He turned to leave. "Good day to ye, ma'am."

Betsy watched in disbelief as the constable advanced to the flagway.

Once there, however, he paused. "Do ye s'pose Toby was involved in some sort of shady dealin's, ma'am?"

"Toby was a fine young man; reliable and responsible. I once entrusted him with five shillings, and upon his return to the shop, he handed over every cent due me along with the goods I'd sent him to purchase."

"Well, then, there's yer motive, ma'am."

"What are you saying?"

"Robbery. Not a penny found in the boy's pockets. In all likelihood, the fellow what kilt him stole his money. Robbery was the motive, pure and simple." He touched his cap and strode away.

Betsy could hardly believe her ears. How could the authorities dismiss Toby's death in such an offhanded fashion? It was bad enough that dozens of young men were being shot dead on battlefields up north. It was unthinkable that fine young men, like John and Toby, could be slain right here at home and no one bothered to seek out the killers.

At length Betsy's outrage turned to frustration, and then to gloom when she realized that at least part of what the constable had said was true. It would be impossible to determine who had been on the quay last night. She herself had walked past dozens of drunken sailors who by today would not recall anything they'd seen or heard last night. Also true was that by morning, half the ships that had docked yesterday had already put out to sea, quite likely taking Toby's killer right along with them. Still . . . something should be done. But . . . *what?*

Returning to the parlor, Betsy continued to mull the matter over as she returned to work on General Washington's flags. Eventually the sound of raindrops pelting the windowpanes penetrated her consciousness. If her uncle hadn't yet sorted out which parcels on the wharf were hers and claimed them, the downpour would very likely ruin her fine new fabric and costly supplies. But she could do nothing to remedy that either. Exhaling a frustrated sigh, she turned again to her sewing. And an hour or so later, was relieved when the hard rain let up. Soon after that, an employee of her uncle's delivered a dozen boxes and crates to her doorstep. If Toby had been there, Betsy would have set him to unpacking the boxes and hefting the heavy rolls of fabric off the floor and carrying them across the room to lean against the rear wall of the shop. Instead, still wracked with grief over poor Toby's death, Betsy tackled the cumbersome task herself.

Some time later, her work was interrupted when a shabbily dressed woman balancing a drowsing babe on her hip entered the shop. The woman's free hand clutched that of a whimpering three or four-year-old girl. From Betsy's position on the floor where she was removing supplies from a wooden crate, she noted the muddied hem of the woman's brown fustian skirt. Although the rain had ceased, it was evident the woman had slogged through ankle-deep water on her way here. Also evident was that she was not the sort of patron who generally frequented Betsy's shop. Rising, Betsy thrust aside thoughts of Toby as she dusted her hands on her apron.

"Good afternoon, madam. What might I do for you today?"

The woman's eyes narrowed. "You Betsy Ross?"

"Indeed, I am, madam. And you are . . .?"

The woman thrust her sleeping babe toward Betsy. Caught off-guard, Betsy wordlessly took the infant as the woman bent to pick up the little girl who was now loudly bawling.

"I'm Toby's mum. I come to ask ye what happened to m' boy.

Constable said you was with him last night on the dock." The woman bounced the squirming toddler in her arms.

Fresh mist pooled in Betsy's eyes. "I'm so sorry, Mrs. Grimes. I told Constable O'Malley all that I know." She shifted the rather heavy babe in her arms from one hip to the other. "Could I offer you and your little girl a . . . cup of water?"

"Water ain't gonna' bring back my boy!" the woman snapped. "Toby was a big he'p to me. How am I gonna' manage without him?"

The woman's outburst caused the little girl's cries to intensify. Her balled-up fists pushed against her mama's shoulder.

"I got all I cin handle jes' lookin' after these two and there's another one at home. What am I gonna' do now, Miz Ross? I ain't got no money to feed my youngin's or pay the rent!"

Betsy winced as fresh guilt swept over her. "P-perhaps you could send word to your husband, ma'am. Given the circumstances, I expect his commanding officer would excuse him."

"Ain't nobody cares 'bout no one but they-selves no more." Setting the little girl down, Mrs. Grimes reached into her apron pocket. "I come to give ye this." She held out an object. "Found it in Toby's pocket. Ain't mine. Figured it belonged to you, or yer sister. I don't rightly know where she lives."

Because Betsy's hands were full, she did not take the object, nor did she see what it was. Something small. In a fumble of confusion, the woman dropped the object onto a nearby table before snatching her babe from Betsy's arms. Her long gaze took in the array of colorful items scattered about the floor.

"Looks like you got the blunt to buy ye'self plenty o' fancy geegaws."

"Perhaps I could give you something for the children to eat," Betsy suggested weakly. "I-I have fresh bread."

The woman's eyes narrowed. "A reward fer returnin' yer property to ye would be nice."

"Of course." Betsy hurried to the parlor and returned carrying the last few coins Uncle Abel had given her. She dropped them into the woman's outstretched hand. "Perhaps this will see you through the next several weeks, Mrs. Grimes."

The woman brought one coin to her mouth and bit down on it, then deposited them into her pocket. "Thank ye kindly, Miz Ross." She scooped up the little girl's hand and turned to go. At the door, she paused. "Don't s'pose ye know the name of Toby's *other* employer, do ye?"

"His . . . other employer?" Betsy stammered. "I-I was unaware Toby had another employer, other than my sister, Mrs. Donaldson."

"Paid far better than you, an' that's a fact."

"I wish I could help, Mrs. Grimes."

"Humph."

Betsy turned back to her work. *Who, other than Sarah, had Toby been working for?* And when did he *do* the extra work? He was here at sun-up every morning and again before sundown every night and lately, a good many hours in between. The rest of the day, she assumed he was with Sarah. Toby had never mentioned *another* employer.

Perhaps she should alert Constable O'Malley to this new turn.

She resumed unwrapping supplies and storing them in the proper cupboards. An hour or more passed before it occurred to her to see what possession of hers Toby's mother had returned.

CHAPTER 5

A key.

To *what?* It didn't match the key to the lock on the shop door, and there was no lock on the rear door. To secure it, one merely settled a wooden bar into an iron bracket designed to prevent someone from pushing open the door from the outside. Furthermore, Betsy kept nothing . . . no chests, cabinets or cupboards . . . secured under lock and key.

Perhaps it belonged to Sarah. Deciding at once to find out, she dropped the key into her apron pocket, snatched up her shawl and this time, locked the shop door behind her before she set out to walk the short distance to Sarah's house. She had seen her sister only a few times since the day she returned to her own home. Hurrying up the street, Betsy wondered if William had written to say when he would, or would not, be returning to Philadelphia now that the war had started up again.

The glum expression on Sarah's face told Betsy she hadn't heard from her husband. In addition, she appeared as disturbed as Betsy over Toby's death. Sarah declared the key wasn't hers and had no idea who, other than the pair of them, the boy might have been working for.

"I do hope you will leave the solving of *this* crime to the authorities, Betsy."

"The authorities' attitude regarding crime in this city is a travesty!" Betsy exclaimed.

"I expect they are doing the best they can, Sister."

Betsy saw no need to discuss the matter further. She did accept Sarah's invitation to take supper with her, and later that night, before climbing into bed, turned again to studying the key. Because it did not belong to either her or Sarah meant it must belong to Toby's *other* employer. She turned the object over in her hand. Or, perhaps it didn't. Perhaps Toby had simply found it and carried it in his pocket as a token of good luck. Her little brother George used to carry a pebble in his pocket. John always carried a thimble in his breeches pocket, which was silly since he never used one. Betsy carried needle and thread in her reticule, and since John died, she'd taken to carrying *his* thimble. Somehow it felt as if she always had a part of him with her.

Before drifting off to sleep, it occurred to Betsy that perhaps the key itself was the key to Toby's murder. Perhaps Toby had been killed *because* he had the key and if *she* hadn't called out to the man with the knife, he might have rifled through Toby's pockets after he killed him in search of it. That *she* was in the alleyway prevented the murderer from doing so, which meant that because the man with the knife hadn't found the key, he, or perhaps a conspirator, would still be looking for it. Icy fingers of fear washed over Betsy. If someone were to appear at her door inquiring about a lost key, it would either mean the person was Toby's killer, or was somehow connected to the crime. Surely, at *that* point, Constable O'Malley would agree to investigate the murder. In the meantime, she'd be extra vigilant to lock her front door when she left the shop and to secure the windows and doors every night before she climbed the stairs to her bedchamber.

A few mornings later, Betsy was struggling to cart heavy logs, one by one, down the steep steps to the underground kitchen. After stacking the dry wood on the stone floor, she reached into the bucket where Toby stored twigs and sticks for kindling when her fingers touched . . . something odd.

Drawing forth the object, a small wooden box; the lid fastened with a lock, her pulse began to pound.

Clutching the little box, Betsy raced up the steep stairs to the ground floor, then up the second flight to her bedchamber and the cupboard where she'd put the key. Fumbling with it, she managed to insert the key into the lock, which was a wee bit rusty, then carefully turned back the lid.

Her brow puckered when all she found inside were three scraps of paper, one with a crude diagram drawn upon it, another containing an odd assortment of words that looked like no words Betsy had ever seen before. The third page . . . appeared to have nothing at all written upon it. She turned it over and over, even carried it to the window and held it up to the light, and after turning it this way and that, had to conclude . . . it was completely blank.

Shaking her head, Betsy returned the pages to the little box, locked it and stowed it and the key beneath a pile of neatly folded linens in the cupboard, then she returned below stairs to build up the fire and prepare something to eat. Nibbling on bread and jam, thoughts of Toby and the mysterious pages inside the wooden box swirled through her mind. No doubt, if John were here, he'd quickly sort out the puzzle and also know where to begin to track down Toby's killer. As usual, frustration set in when Betsy realized she was making no progress whatever in solving the mystery surrounding John's death, and now she had no clue where to begin looking for Toby's killer.

That night Betsy attended another Fighting Quaker meeting. Two of her young lady friends . . . Minette Dubeau, a pretty French girl whose parents had recently immigrated to Philadelphia, and Emma Peters, a new friend she'd met since joining the group . . . arrived just after dusk to walk with her the quarter mile to where the meetings were held. When Betsy told them of Toby Grimes's death, both girls expressed heartfelt sympathy.

"Perhaps zee will find another helper soon," Minette said, her words colored by a thick French accent, which to Betsy sounded charming. All three young ladies were identically dressed in long gray frocks adorned with plain white collars and snug white caps on their heads. Short blond curls bobbed beneath Minette's cap.

"Do the authorities have any notion who might have killed Toby?" Emma asked, gazing around Minette to address Betsy. Emma was the tallest of the three, her plain features and straight brown hair a contrast to both Minette's fair coloring, and Betsy's vibrant prettiness.

Betsy told her friends what the constable had said, concluding with his reasons for making no attempt whatsoever to solve the crime.

"None at all?" Emma exclaimed.

"No." Betsy sadly shook her head.

"Eet would indeed be difficult to question all zee reef-raff on the wharf," Minette said.

Nodding, both Betsy and Emma had to agree.

Betsy chose not to mention the key Toby's mother had brought her, or the little wooden box she'd found in the kindling bucket, instead she steered the conversation to another topic. Attempting to sound cheerful, she said, "All I have left to do on my project for General Washington is stitch on the stars."

"If you like, I could come tomorrow afternoon and help you stitch on stars."

"That would be lovely," Betsy replied.

"If zee wishes, I veel also come."

Betsy smiled. "Thank you. You are both very kind."

An announcement their leader read aloud that night regarding the public reading of an important document the Continental Congress had been hard at work upon brightened the spirits of every Fighting Quaker. It was said the document would soon be read aloud from the steps of the State House with a parade to follow. More sobering news delivered at the meeting focused on the British warships that had lately begun to arrive in New York harbor. Despite the lowering effect of that revelation, by the end of the meeting, everyone was again optimistically declaring that the colonists had little to fret about as no doubt, General Washington would chase the British out of New York the same as he had done in Boston.

After the meeting adjourned, Minette wished to introduce her friends to her older brother, François, whom she said had only just arrived in Philadelphia from France.

"I am pleased to make your acquaintance, Mrs. Ross; Miss Peters," the tall Frenchman declared after his sister presented her girlfriends to him.

"Thank you, sir." Monsieur Dubeau's *lack* of an accent surprised Betsy, who found herself smiling up at the handsome gentleman. Since John's death she hadn't felt the least desire to meet another man, but the Frenchman's refined good looks, his thick dark hair and alert black eyes, quite appealed to her. She surmised him to be a few years older than she, perhaps six, or seven and twenty.

"Please, address me as François." The Frenchman's intent gaze remained fixed upon Betsy's smiling face.

"Very well." Betsy's long lashes fluttered against her flushed cheeks. "François." Even speaking the man's name felt . . . exhilarating.

After exchanging additional pleasantries, the gentleman bid the ladies a good evening. Walking home, the girls chatted and laughed amongst themselves.

"I zink my brother find you . . . how you say? Pret-ty."

Both Betsy and Emma laughed gaily.

Emma said, "I zink Betsy find your *brother* . . . pretty."

All three girls giggled. Betsy didn't protest, although in the back of her mind, she couldn't help wondering why the gallant Frenchman hadn't offered to escort the ladies home? Aloud, she remarked on the fact that François seemed not to have the least trace of a French accent.

"My brother, he grow up in England . . . in home of our *cousine*. François learn very well heez . . . *Anglais*."

"I see." Betsy nodded. Of a sudden, an odd prick of guilt assailed her. Thinking about another man somehow made her feel as if she were . . . betraying John.

"What does your brother plan to do now that he's joined your parents here in the colonies?" Emma asked.

Minette shrugged. "He mean to become . . . how you say? Man of state. States-man. In England, François study just-ezz. He very much like all things to be . . . fair. François very *un*happy when our *cousine* killed in war."

"Which war?" Betsy queried.

"Theez war," Minette replied, her tone saying the answer to that question should be obvious. "Our *cousine*, he killed in Boss-teen."

"O-oh, Boston," Betsy murmured. "I am so sorry." Her brow puckered. If Patriots had killed their cousin, why were François and his sister now siding *with* the rebels? If he were angry that Patriots had killed his cousin, why was his allegiance not *with* the English rather than *against* them? Perhaps, Minette had got things backward. The little French girl often mixed things up. Perhaps Betsy would have the opportunity one day to learn the truth from François. Although exciting, that thought also caused another prick of guilt to stab her.

Upon reaching her doorstep, Betsy bade her friends a good night and unlocking the door to her shop, entered the house alone. Crossing the front room in the darkness, she tripped over something, which . . . surprised her as there shouldn't be anything lying in her path over which to trip. A few steps further, she stumbled again. Feeling her way to the table upon which rested a candlestick, she fumbled for a Lucifer to light the taper. Holding the flickering candle aloft, she turned around and . . . gasped.

Every item in the room was in complete disarray! All her new supplies, tape, braid, boxes of tacks and pins, her carefully organized spools of thread, were all scattered helter-skelter upon the floor. Her eyes wide, she stepped around overturned chairs and tables as she made her way to the parlor. Once there she also could not believe the clutter. Cupboard drawers had been yanked open; the contents scattered. Cushions from the sofa and both chairs had been tossed to the floor. Upon catching sight of two of her lovely china teacups shattered to pieces, tears sprang to her eyes.

Her heart pounding, she ran to the staircase and scampered to the second floor of the house. Relief washed over her when she saw that nothing there was disturbed. Suddenly an insistent pounding at the front door claimed her attention. Hurrying back downstairs, she picked her way through the house to the door.

"Miz Ross?" came a male voice. "It's the Watch. Are you all right, ma'am?"

Betsy flung open the door. The alarmed expression on her face was sufficient answer to the night watchman's question.

"I spotted a man runnin' from yer side yard a few minutes ago. I give chase, but he disappeared down Bread Street a'fore I could catch 'im. Thought I should check on ye. Perhaps I should take a look around inside."

"Please, do, sir; come in," Betsy breathlessly replied.

The night watchman entered the house and Betsy, holding the candle aloft, led him through the disorderly shop and into her untidy parlor. Checking the rear door and both windows, the watchman came upon the shattered window in the small pantry adjacent to the parlor through which he declared the intruder had entered the house.

"Ye'll want to git this windowpane replaced on the morrow, ma'am." He bent to pick up shards of glass and bits of wood that had separated the thin panes. "If you've a piece of chip board, ma'am, I'll patch this up for ye tonight."

Betsy fetched one of the empty crates her new supplies had arrived in and gratefully allowed the night watchman to cover the gaping hole. She thanked him profusely and was also grateful that, as he made his way through her shop, he paused to set upright several items of furniture, including her heavy worktable and a bulky cupboard.

Again, Betsy spent a restless night. She had no doubt what the prowler had come in search of . . . the wooden box and the key that fit it. Had she not returned home when she did, the housebreaker would have likely found his way above stairs and torn up her bedchamber. She'd checked the kitchen before she climbed the stairs to bed and was vastly relieved the interloper had not had time in which to also tear apart that room.

Lying abed, she thought back to the night Toby had been killed and the explanation given her by the voice in her head. If Toby had been involved in something sinister that resulted in his death, her impatience to retrieve her supplies that night had truly *not* been the cause of his death. On the other hand, she had no doubt now that the burglar would return sooner or later to resume his search for the wooden box. What the pages within the box might signify, she had no clue. She wracked her brain trying to imagine what the diagram drawn upon one of the pages in the box meant, and what message did the unintelligible words on the other page convey? Not a scrap of it made sense and furthermore, to hand over the box to the constable at this juncture would prove useless for how would the intruder know the box was no longer in her possession.

CHAPTER 6

The following morning, Betsy was up early, bustling about to put things to rights before Minette and Emma arrived to help sew on stars. Because the shop very often looked untidy, Betsy's friends would think nothing of the inch-tape draped over a chair, the ledger books stacked upon her desk, and two or three pasteboard boxes littering the floor. Earlier that morning, Betsy had summoned the glass-smith to replace the broken windowpane. The man was just finishing up his work when the girls arrived, so Betsy suggested the three of them sit in her sunny sitting room above stairs, the room where Sarah had stayed. Choosing to mention nothing of the previous night's disturbance to her friends, the girls spent a pleasant and productive afternoon. Nearly all the stars were now sewn onto the red, white and blue banners.

Later that evening, as Betsy was tidying up after supper, another rap sounded at the door. Her heart in her throat, she tried to remain calm as she made her way through the house. *Might it be someone asking about the key?* Opening the door a crack, Betsy was both relieved and surprised to find a former friend standing on the stoop.

"Why, Joseph Ashburn. I've not seen you since . . . well; I cannot recall when we last saw one another. What brings you back home to Philadelphia?"

Of middling height, Joseph Ashburn was a rosy-cheeked, rugged sort of fellow with wind-tossed blond hair. He wore blue breeches tied below the knees and his white linen shirt was open at the neck. "It's a pleasure to see you again, Betsy." Ashburn's smile was warm. "May I come in?"

"Indeed." She swung wide the door. Joseph Ashburn had been quite an ardent suitor of hers before she settled her affections on John Ross. As the workroom was in shadows, Betsy said, "I'll fetch a candle," and hurried to light the one she always kept on the small table in the shop. "Shall we sit in the parlor and talk?"

The broad-shouldered young man followed behind her as she, holding the candle aloft, led the way to the rear of the narrow building.

Betsy set the candlestick down and indicated a chair for Joseph. "I would offer you a cup of tea, but . . . I've none to offer. I might have enough lemon-water to fill a mug." She smiled. "Had I rum and sugar, I could whip you up a nice grog."

Joseph grinned. "I require nothing, Betsy. Do tell me how you've fared these past months."

She evaded the question. "You are looking well, Joseph, your sea travels appear to agree with you."

Hazel eyes twinkled from his sun-bronzed face. "I confess I do feel more at home on water than I do on land."

When they were young, all their friends had been amazed by Joseph Ashburn's prowess at the helm of his catboat as well as his athleticism as a swimmer. On several occasions, Joseph had swum across the mile-wide Delaware River, then turned around and swam right back.

"I confess I've thought of you often in recent months," Betsy said. "Now that the British are intent upon capturing our ships, I have prayed that you were . . . safe," she added softly.

"I am quite safe. Although, I admit my seafaring life has now become tenuous, at best. We privateers were exceedingly grateful when Congress granted us leave to confiscate the cargoes of any British ship we could capture and board."

"Oh, my." Betsy grimaced. "That sounds quite dangerous, indeed."

"It can be. Especially for a small schooner such as mine. But fortunately the *Swallow* is fast."

"What brings you to shore in the middle of summer?"

"I mean to fit out my rig with weapons."

"Weapons? Dear me, you must be in a great deal of danger."

"To be armed will at least give me a fighting chance. I plan to install a couple of four-pounders on my deck and procure muskets for my entire crew."

Betsy detected a hint of pride in his tone. "Sounds as if you enjoy the danger."

Joseph chuckled. "Danger does keep things interesting. I also plan to install a couple of *quakers* on my deck."

When Betsy appeared puzzled, Joseph laughed. "A *quaker* is merely a large log shaped like a cannon and painted black. From a distance, it looks like a real cannon. We privateers take great delight in making fools of the British. I can purchase a good-looking *quaker* for about twelve pounds whereas real guns will set me back twenty-five hundred."

"My, such a vast sum." Half that would pay off *all* her debts.

"I'll earn it back in no time. My travels are far more profitable now than when I first took to the sea for my aunt."

Betsy was acquainted with Joseph's aunt, the widow Ashburn, who kept a lovely home on Front Street. It was common knowledge that Mrs. Ashburn had purchased the schooner Joseph sailed, which he formerly used only for trade with the West Indies, bringing home rich cargoes of molasses, rum, tobacco, and in the old days, tea. As a boy, Joseph lived with his aunt. Betsy knew she missed her favorite nephew whenever he sailed away.

"I've not seen your aunt in a long while."

A small silence ensued, during which Betsy tried to decide whether or not to tell Joseph about this week's disturbing events.

"Is something troubling you, Betsy? You seem distracted."

She looked down. "Something . . . has happened, Joseph; and I confess it has me quite perplexed."

He leaned forward. "Perhaps I can help."

With no further prompting, Betsy told him about witnessing Toby's death, how the constable refused to investigate the murder, how she'd found the little box and last night, about arriving home and finding her shop ransacked.

Joseph moved to take a seat beside her on the sofa. "When you said you *witnessed* the murder, do you mean you got a *good* look at the man who stabbed Toby?"

"It was quite dark in the alleyway. I daresay if I saw the man again, I'd not recognize him. It's far more likely that he would recognize me. I was standing in the light. He and Toby were in the shadows."

"You arriving home last night obviously interrupted the murderer's attempt to burgle your shop," Joseph pointed out.

Betsy winced. "You believe the man who ransacked my home is also the . . . murderer?"

"Who else could it be?"

"I-I don't know. When the constable said the murderer had put out to sea, I thought . . . oh, I am so confused, Joseph. Should I tell Constable O'Malley about the box and the papers?"

"How about if I take a look at them?"

Betsy sprang to her feet to retrieve the wooden container and waited beside Joseph on the sofa while he carefully studied the pages.

"I believe these are military messages, or at least, the garbled one is a message; words appear to be written in some sort of code," he said. "The diagram could be a map, perhaps telling Toby where to meet his contact."

"Are you saying you believe Toby is, I mean, *was* a . . . spy?"

"Appears that way to me. Which doesn't explain why he was killed, but it could certainly be why your shop was torn up. Someone, if not the murderer, then perhaps an associate, wants this message, and the map, before it falls into the wrong hands."

Betsy inhaled an uneven breath. "Oh, Joseph, what shall I do? I should have simply left the box lying out in plain sight so the thief could have found it and been gone. Now, I am left to wonder *when* he will return to resume his search."

"You could consult with Dr. Franklin."

"Dr. Franklin? What would he . . .?"

"Some say Benjamin Franklin is a spymaster."

"But are you certain?"

"It behooves me to know such things, Betsy. I'd bet my life Dr. Franklin will know what this means."

"I would never have suspected Toby, *or* Dr. Franklin, was involved with . . . oh, dear, me."

Joseph set the box aside and turned back to Betsy. "Franklin will have a theory. In the meantime, promise me you'll keep your doors and windows locked."

"I shall indeed."

Joseph's warm gaze held hers. "I have missed you, Betsy."

Her lashes fluttered. "I have missed you, as well, Joseph."

"I was saddened to learn of John's death."

Her chin trembled. "Losing John was . . . *is* the most difficult thing I have ever borne."

He reached to brush away the errant tear that slid down her cheek. "Has your family come around? I thought given John's death, your parents might . . ."

"No." She shook her head. "I've not seen my parents. Once shunned, always shunned. Of course, I would gladly welcome them back into my life, and into my heart. I sorely miss my sisters, Rachel and Hannah. And George. He would be quite the young man now. Sarah is the only one who comes around. When John died, she wished me to give up the shop and come live with her. Her husband had just marched off to war." She looked up. "Were you aware Sarah married William Donaldson?" She didn't wait for a response. "Our little shop meant such a great deal to John. I knew he would want me to carry on. He upholstered the pretty chair in the window. I can't bear to remove it."

Joseph patted her hand. "I admire your courage, Betsy."

At length, they began to talk of shared memories from their past.

Sometime later, Betsy said, "So, you believe I should consult with Dr. Franklin about my . . . troublesome matter."

Joseph stood. "I do, indeed. If the garbled message was meant for the Patriots, then it might very well have ended up in Franklin's hands anyhow. If not, then, it would be best to have it out of yours." He glanced about. "Before I take my leave, might I bring in wood for your morning fire, or a bucket of fresh water from the well?" His gaze was expectant.

Betsy thanked him for the kind offer and after Joseph had completed both tasks, she escorted him to the door. "It was lovely to see you again."

"Might I call again, Betsy? I'll be in the city a good while longer."

She smiled. "I would like that."

Grinning, the handsome seaman turned to go. "Bolt the door behind me, lass."

"I will. Good night, Joseph."

On the following Sabbath, Betsy walked around the corner to worship at Christ Church on Second Street. A cool breeze wafting inland off the river kept the summer heat from becoming oppressive. Following services, she stood on the grassy lawn before the red brick building hoping to catch sight of Dr. Benjamin Franklin who also worshipped there, as did a good many of the statesmen who had gathered in Philadelphia at the Congress to join in unifying the colonies. Betsy had met the brilliant Dr. Franklin back when she and John married and began attending services here. Since John's death, the elderly statesman had often greeted her.

Thinking back now, she realized it had taken a while to become accustomed to worshipping in a manner that was such a vast departure from a Society of Friends Meeting. At a Quaker gathering, silence reigned until someone felt led by the spirit of God to speak; here, the music and singing were loud and spirited. The Christ Church minister, wearing a flowing scarlet robe, stood high in a pulpit and delivered an interesting and *different* sermon to his parishioners every single Sunday morning, a feat that in itself amazed Betsy.

She also enjoyed observing the other women's clothing. Although she still clung to Quaker garb, she found the colorful silks and satins the ladies wore to services here astonishingly beautiful. The fashionable gowns featured gold or silver braid on the stomachers, plus colorful ribbons or lace at the neck and sleeves. Wealthier women wore panniers to widen their skirts. Betsy thought wearing a host of petticoats beneath one's skirt must make sitting a trying ordeal. She wore only a single petticoat and her long gray skirt was not puffed out at the sides, or decorated with ribbons or rosettes.

Gentlemen's clothing also seemed fanciful to her; although since the war began, their blue, green, or burgundy satin breeches and frock coats had been replaced by more somber colors, browns and grays, but most still featured lace cascading down the shirtfronts and at the coat cuffs. Men either wore their hair powdered or donned a white wig, most with a queue at the nape of their necks. Women also wore wigs, and those that didn't, powdered their hair. Perhaps one day, when she had enough money to do with as she wished, she would make herself a stylish new gown of blue silk, with kid slippers, and gloves to match. And a bonnet adorned with lace and flowers.

Watching the churchgoers climb into their smart two-wheeled chaises or shiny black closed carriages, she at last caught sight of Dr. Franklin conversing with a knot of impeccably dressed gentlemen. When he bid the gentlemen farewell, Betsy hurried onto the flagway in time to meet the elderly statesman as he walked by.

"Good day, Mrs. Ross." His shoulder-length brown hair streaked with gray, the older gentleman studied Betsy through the small spectacles perched on the end of his nose.

"I wonder if I might walk with you a bit, sir?"

"Indeed." Franklin's black walking stick, fashioned from crab tree wood and tipped with gold, made a tapping sound upon the red bricks as he walked.

Heading toward the gentleman's home located near his print shop on High Street, Betsy said softly, "There is a matter I wish to discuss privately with you, sir."

"Ah. Then I shall persuade my housekeeper to brew us up a nice kettle of tea. What say you to that, Mrs. Ross?"

Betsy's eyes widened. "You have tea, sir? Forgive me. I confess it has been quite some time since I enjoyed a cup of tea."

Franklin's eyes twinkled merrily. "I generally only indulge if I deem the occasion . . . special."

Upon realizing the gentleman had paid her a compliment, Betsy blushed. "Thank you, sir. Tea would be lovely."

In his parlor, Betsy noted that all the sofas and chairs in the room were home to stacks and stacks of papers and books. She wondered if he had read them all. In no time, a matronly housekeeper appeared bearing an ornately carved silver tea service, complete with a plate of warm scones and pot of apricot jam. After doing the honors, the woman left the room, closing the double doors behind her.

"Now, what is it you wish to discuss, Mrs. Ross?"

Betsy wasted no time telling Dr. Franklin everything that had happened the past week.

Franklin listened intently. "I do recall hearing about the demise of a young man on the wharf. Quite unfortunate, that." He set aside his teacup and saucer. "But I must concur with the constable, Mrs. Ross. It would be nigh on impossible to ascertain who the killer might be."

"I quite understand, sir, although I think it dreadful that Toby's killer will never be brought to justice. Still, I wonder if you would mind looking at the papers I found inside the little box." She pulled the folded pages from her reticule.

Adjusting his spectacles, Franklin squinted at the small print. The third page, the one that appeared blank, he held up to the light. "Quite possibly the message was set down in invisible ink," he said. "My guess is young Toby was acting as a courier for a spy."

Betsy's head shook with dismay. "Joseph was of the same mind."

"Joseph?"

"I consulted with my friend Captain Joseph Ashburn. It was he who suggested I confer with you."

"Ah, yes. Fine young man, Ashburn. In the past months, he and his crew have confiscated two shiploads of much-needed guns and ammunition for our troops. Amongst other things." He grinned. "This tea very likely came from the cargo of a British ship that Ashburn plundered."

"Are couriers compensated to convey messages?" Betsy asked. "Toby's mother said his *other* employer paid quite handsomely."

Franklin nodded. "On the whole, spies are very well compensated. I understand the British are offering gold to Loyalists who pass along information they overhear regarding the rebels, as well as anyone who sabotages the Patriot Cause."

Betsy's eyes widened. "And I believe, sir, that either a British spy, or a Loyalist, was responsible for causing the explosion at the munitions warehouse that killed my husband John. If you recall, sir, my late husband was guarding the warehouse on Dock Street during that awful blizzard this past January."

"I, too, thought that fire seemed suspicious." Franklin nodded. "I am deeply sorry for your loss, madam."

"To my knowledge the authorities never conducted an investigation."

"A great many injustices are taking place in our world today, Mrs. Ross. Not everything that happens as a result of war can be remedied."

Betsy's chin began to quiver. "Regardless, sir, I am determined to see both John's killer, and now the man who murdered Toby Grimes, brought to justice."

Franklin's head shook. "I cannot think that a wise course, Mrs. Ross. Philadelphia is the largest city in the New World and therefore, teeming with unprincipled characters. I would not wish harm to come to a pretty young lady like yourself, Mrs. Ross."

"But I cannot sit idly by and watch those dear to me being brutally cut down by unprincipled madmen. A killer is at large, sir. Something must be done."

"Your zeal for justice is admirable, my dear. But investigating explosions and murders is best left to the authorities."

"Who have done nothing!"

Despite her outburst, Franklin remained calm. After a pause, he said, "I understand you are sewing fine new banners for our Continental army."

Betsy nodded.

"Then you are doing your part to aid the Patriots in their fight for independence."

"I am capable of doing far more than sewing flags, sir."

"I am certain you are. You are a capable young woman, and a very pretty one," he said again. "I expect you will soon find another young man to marry and will provide him a lovely home and fine, healthy children."

"Perhaps I should go now, sir." Betsy set her teacup and saucer on the table at her elbow. Dr. Franklin was treating her as if she were little more than a foolish woman.

Franklin stood. "To offend you was not my intent, Mrs. Ross."

"I am not offended, sir. I merely wished to consult with you regarding this . . . trouble that, whether or not I wish it, I have become embroiled in."

"With your permission, I shall pass these pages along to someone who might be able to unscramble the code. Until then, there's no way of knowing which side Toby was working for."

Betsy pulled on her gloves. "I can scarcely believe Toby would aid the enemy."

Franklin thoughtfully tapped one page with his spectacles. "Interesting. These pages contain no stamp, meaning no tax was paid upon them and consequently no imprint affixed. Which is a clear indication to me that whoever penned these messages was not one of our own."

"I had not noticed that," Betsy murmured. "I own, sir, that I am rather frightened that the man who broke into my home might be Toby's killer, and that he will not give up until he finds what he came in search of."

"He may or may not return. It is possible that this particular information is now outdated and consequently of no use to anyone. It is also possible that Toby was working both sides, which might explain why he was killed. Perhaps one, or the other, of the agents he reported to learned of his duplicity and rather than turn him over to a superior officer, simply silenced him on the spot."

"Oh, how dreadful! Poor, Toby."

Franklin escorted Betsy to the door. "I will forward the blank page to someone who possesses a solution that will bring the message to light. Then we'll know for certain upon which side of the fence young Toby sat."

Betsy thanked Dr. Franklin both for his wise counsel and the lovely cup of tea.

"You are welcome to call again, Mrs. Ross. I confess I am not often visited by delightful young ladies."

Betsy smiled up into his kind face and after murmuring additional pleasant words, took her leave.

Walking back home that afternoon, Betsy's thoughts were a-jumble. Despite Dr. Franklin's condescending attitude, his observations had been enlightening plus his theories regarding the possible reason for Toby's death did, indeed, have merit. If Toby had been working for both sides, he certainly would have been paid handsomely. With his father away fighting, clearly Toby believed it was his duty to care for his family and was doing so the best way he could. That he lost his life in the process was tragic beyond measure.

Distracted by the anxious thoughts swirling through her mind, Betsy was unaware that a lone figure followed a few paces behind her, the burly man's hands stuffed into his pockets, a cap pulled low over his brow.

CHAPTER 7

Betsy was tidying up her kitchen that evening when a noise startled her. Every muscle in her body tensed as she paused to listen. Hearing nothing further, she decided that perhaps she had absentmindedly left the front door unlocked when she came in. Perhaps a gust of wind had blown the door against the wall, or toppled one of the bolts of fabric propped against the far wall. Still, before venturing upstairs to investigate, she glanced about for something with which to defend herself in case wind was not the culprit. Reaching for an iron pot, she decided it was far too heavy to hold above her head as she stole up the narrow steps, so instead she snatched up a long-handled knife.

Stealing across the flagstones toward the stairwell that led up to the ground floor, she heard another noise. Fear gripped her insides as she slowly climbed upward. Without a light to guide her, each step she took thrust her deeper into darkness. By the time she gained the landing, she'd heard no further sounds. Moving noiselessly into the corridor, the tight knot in her stomach lessened a mite. At that instant a sudden blow from behind knocked the knife from her hand. It clattered to the floor and before she could scream, a muscled arm coiled around her shoulders and dragged her backward. Feeling a sharp object touch her throat, a cry of alarm escaped her.

The man had a knife!

"Scream and ye'll die," the intruder growled.

Her heart beating like a drum, Betsy involuntarily clutched at the muscled arm gripping her throat.

"Where's the box, lady?"

As the man's arm tightened around her neck, the point of his knife actually pricked her throat.

Betsy's heart lurched at the sting. Feeling a trickle of blood ooze from the cut, she said, "I-It's in the cupboard. Above stairs."

"Then, we'll jes' walk that way and ye'll get it for me."

Her captor propelled her towards the steep stairs that led upward. At the bottom of the stairwell, he gave her a rough shove. "Turn around and ye won't live to see another day. I'm countin' to three. If ye ain't tossed the box down to me by then, I'm comin' up after it."

Betsy scampered up the stairs. In her bedchamber, she snatched up the box and hurried to toss it down the darkened stairwell. When she heard the lightweight container hit the floor, she feared it would break apart. Terror gripped her as she wondered what the man would do when he found the box empty. Hardly daring to breathe, it surprised Betsy to hear the man's footfalls running back through the shop. Apparently she had left the door unlocked when she came in earlier this afternoon, which saved him the trouble of breaking yet another window in order to enter her house.

For several tense seconds, Betsy stood stark still, until the silence was shattered by another male voice.

"Betsy? Betsy, are you all right?"

"Joseph!"

Running down the stairs and into the darkened front room, she cried, *"Did you see him? The man? He was here!"*

Joseph attempted to gather her into his arms. "Are you all right?"

Squirming from his embrace, Betsy ran to the shop door. "He was *here,* Joseph! Just now!"

The instant that what she was saying registered, Joseph flew past her and out onto the street. Betsy stood on the stoop and watched as he ran to the corner of Second, then turned around and run back up as far as Third.

His chest rose and fell as he returned to the shop. "I'm sorry, Betsy. I saw nothing. The Watch has not yet trimmed the lamps. It's too dark to clearly see anything." He ushered her back inside and threw the bolt. "When I arrived and saw your door standing wide open, I grew alarmed."

Still dazed by the terrifying incident, Betsy murmured, "Evidently I'm not yet in the habit of locking the door behind me when I come in. I'm more accustomed to leaving my shop door unlatched."

"Even on the Sabbath?"

"Especially on the Sabbath. Ladies from the church, or Sarah, often drop in to see me on Sunday." Lighting a candle, she led the way into the corridor.

Candlelight illuminated the smattering of debris on the floor. "What's this?" Joseph knelt to gather up bits of wood scattered about. "Looks to be what's left of Toby's box."

"The man held a knife to my throat and demanded I get it."

"He held a knife to your throat?" Spotting the trickle of blood on her neck, Joseph exclaimed, "Betsy, you're hurt."

A shaky hand reached upward. "The knife pricked me."

"Did you get a look at the man?"

"No. He said if I turned around, he'd kill me. Oh, Joseph, I was terrified what he would do once he found the box empty. I left the pages with Dr. Franklin this afternoon. However . . . just now, when the man didn't find anything inside the box . . . he said nothing."

Joseph studied the shattered pieces. "Perhaps the container wasn't entirely empty. The scoundrel may have found what he came in search of after all. Look at this."

Betsy gazed at the shards of wood. "I don't understand."

"Appears the little box had a false bottom."

Betsy's mouth dropped open. "Something else was hidden inside. And, *that's* what he wanted all along."

"Evidently."

"And we shall never know what it was."

"Hang what it was!" Joseph steered her into the parlor and tossed the remnants of the container onto the hearth. "Your troubles are over, lass. May I sit down?"

Relief softened Betsy's features. "Please do."

Taking a seat beside her, Joseph said, "Let me have a look at that cut."

"It does sting," Betsy admitted.

Joseph dabbed at the still moist blood with his handkerchief.

"I'm certain it's not serious," Betsy murmured.

"Nonetheless . . . perhaps I should search further."

"No." She touched his arm. "Please, don't leave me, Joseph."

Frowning, he sat back down. "I worry about you, Betsy."

"You just said my troubles are over."

"Are you certain you didn't recognize the man?"

"I heard a noise and when I came up from the kitchen, he grabbed me from behind. I could tell he was a large man. His chest felt hard and . . . muscled."

"What did he say?"

"That he wanted the box and for me to get it and . . . if I didn't, he would kill me."

Joseph pulled her to him and held her close, a comforting hand patting her shoulder. "Clearly you need someone to look after you."

Betsy drew away. "He won't bother me again, Joseph. Now that he has what he wants, he has no further cause to harm me. I am no longer frightened."

Joseph inhaled an uneven breath. "Perhaps you are right." He reached into a pocket and withdrew a soft pouch. "At any rate, I've brought something that might cheer you."

"What is it?"

"The finest Black Chinese tea in the world," Joseph announced. "Seditious contraband."

"Oh!" Betsy giggled. "How deliciously wicked!"

"Now you can offer me a cup of tea when I come to call."

Betsy was already on her feet. "I shall brew a pot straightaway." She smiled up at Joseph as they both hurried down the steep steps to the kitchen. "You are being very solicitous of me, sir."

"It's clear you need someone to look after you," he said again.

Betsy flushed. Of late that did appear to be the case. How fortunate that Joseph turned up tonight when he did. He was a kind caring man and it would be easy to allow him back into her life. But, the ache in her heart over losing John was not yet completely healed. And even if it were, she wasn't entirely certain she was ready to commit to another man, or if that man would be Joseph Ashburn.

CHAPTER 8

July 1776, Philadelphia

The following week, Colonel George Ross called at Betsy's shop to retrieve the flags she'd completed and to compensate her for making them. Betsy was vastly relieved when he paid her in coin as opposed to the freshly minted Bills of Credit Congress had authorized in an effort to defray military expenses. All thirteen colonies were now issuing paper money, called Continentals, which, despite their official status, everyone suspected weren't worth the ink it took to print them.

Colonel Ross seemed pleased with Betsy's work and promised to refer her services to the commanders of local regiments in the hope they'd commission her to fashion colors for them. "You may very well become Philadelphia's premier flag-maker."

Uplifted by her former uncle-in-law's promise of referrals, Betsy turned to the mending on her worktable and prayed that additional work would soon follow. Although pleased to once again have cash in hand, she soon realized that after paying the back rent she owed and discharging a few other debts, she'd have little to nothing left in her pocket. Uncle Abel would have to wait a bit longer to receive what she owed him.

One sunny day in early July, Sarah stopped in to visit. "I pray this dreadful war will end soon," she fretted.

The day being especially warm, both girls untied the long sleeves in their gowns and pulled chairs nearer the opened window in Betsy's parlor while they sipped mugs of cold tea.

"So, Joseph brought tea?" Sarah marveled. "I recall he was quite keen on you before you wed John."

Betsy nodded, a bit absently as thoughts of Captain Ashburn were not uppermost in her mind. The previous evening, she'd attended another Fighting Quaker meeting and tomorrow afternoon, she and Minette and her brother François, and Emma planned to attend the public reading of the document the Congress had recently ratified called the Declaration of Independence. Betsy was especially looking forward to seeing M'sieur Dubeau again.

"I've received two letters from William," Sarah announced. Setting aside her mug, she reached for her reticule. "One, written quite some time ago, concerns his mission with Henry Knox, which is now complete. The second one," she sighed, "contains quite lowering news." Unfolding the crumpled pages, she declared, "William has decided to stay on."

"He has agreed to fight?" Betsy exclaimed. "But he is a Quaker."

Sarah's head shook. "I never expected he would fight."

"Evidently he believes as strongly as John did in independence." A moment later, Betsy asked anxiously, "How are you getting on without Toby's help?"

"Our parents have been sending George 'round. I do wish they'd let him look in on you. Our little brother is quite grown up now." She paused. "I would expect *you'd* miss Toby far more than I. He seemed to spend a good deal more time helping you than he did me. I am especially grateful Joseph is coming to see you. He will be a great help."

Betsy said nothing. She hadn't told Sarah about finding Toby's locked box, or the intruder. Believing that nasty business was now behind her, she saw no need to speak of it again. She also hadn't told Sarah about joining the Fighting Quakers, or meeting Minette's brother, François. No doubt Sarah would also disapprove of her interest in a foreigner.

"Shall I read bits of William's letter to you?"

"Indeed." Betsy sipped the cool tea. "Wherever William is, I pray he is safe."

Sarah scanned the page skipping past the intimate passages meant only for her. "He says that our army appears quite rag-tag, that none of the men have proper uniforms, most wear the clothing they joined up in, homespun shirts and britches of every color; cowhide shoes or moccasins, tattered caps or broad-brimmed hats. He says they have very little to eat." Her chin trembled. "It breaks my heart to know my dear husband wants for food.

"He says the bread they're given is hard enough to break a rat's teeth; and that if they have meat, they stick the flesh on a stick and cook it over an open flame. He says it gets black on the outside and stays raw on the inside but the men are so hungry they eat it anyway. He says they prepare something called fire-cakes, from flour and water. I assume it to be some sort of bread. He says it also blackens on the outside but stays raw on the inside."

"Sounds as if fire-cakes never get hard enough to break a rat's teeth," Betsy murmured.

Sarah smiled sadly. "He says that now the days and nights are warmer, the men forgo sleeping in their tents and simply stretch out on the ground, but that it's difficult to stay asleep due to the flies and mosquitoes and the call of the whippoorwills."

"To be serenaded by whippoorwills sounds peaceful," Betsy said. "Does he say anything of . . . actual fighting with the British?"

"He says the British prefer to attack on the Sabbath, since they believe God is on their side then. He says during a recent skirmish the enemy drove them into a creek and showered them all with grapeshot." The letter fell to her lap as Sarah covered her face with both hands. "Oh, Betsy, I cannot say how it saddens me to think of William fighting."

Betsy reached to squeeze her sister's hand. "God will keep William safe, Sarah." Never had she thought her own countrymen would fight against their English brothers. To hear actual accounts of battle from someone she knew made the war seem all too real.

Two years ago when the first proud Philadelphia sons had marched off to war, it had all seemed quite festive then with the thunder of horses' hooves on the cobbles and the shuffle of men's feet as they marched to the beat of the fife and drum. She recalled when the parade passed by her shop, pretty girls rushed up to give the soldiers a peck on the cheek and that the boys had blushed and grinned. She supposed the whole thrilling sight would be repeated again tomorrow afternoon following the public reading of the new proclamation.

"War is indeed wretched," Betsy said aloud as her sister tucked away her precious letter.

"Will you pray with me, Betsy?"

"Indeed." Kneeling on the floor before the sofa, both girls folded their hands. Later, after extracting a promise from Sarah to call again soon, Betsy bade her beloved sister farewell.

"We hold these truths to be self-evident . . . that all men are created equal . . . that they are endowed by their Creator with certain unalienable rights; that among these are life, liberty, and the pursuit of happiness."

Applause, cheers and shrill whistles arose from the crowd gathered on the grassy slope of the new State House building on Chestnut Street that sunny July afternoon. Congressman John Nixon's deep baritone carried to the far reaches of the crowd as he read aloud the document that nearly every delegate from all thirteen colonies had signed.

"Isn't it thrilling?" cried Emma Peters standing between Betsy and Minette and her brother François that hot afternoon.

"Indeed." Betsy applauded along with everyone else during the pauses that followed each and every phrase of the beautifully written manifesto.

Church bells had begun to peal early that morning and continued to ring throughout the sultry afternoon. At the conclusion of Mr. Nixon's speech, a parade composed of dozens of foot soldiers and more on horseback, one man from each regiment carrying a flag depicting the company's theme such as a coiled snake, a bear, crossed muskets, or some such fanciful symbol, marched past the State House. A thrill raced through Betsy when she caught sight of General Washington, resplendent in his buff and blue uniform, astride his huge white stallion, the Continental army following behind him. Upon reaching the State House, General Washington paused to wave and nod at the cheering crowd. Betsy squealed with delight when she spotted the very flag she'd sewn with her own hands fluttering in the breeze beside the great leader.

"Look! Our flag!" Emma cried, pointing to the red, white and blue banner. "The one we sewed stars onto!"

Thunderous cheers and applause drowned out Betsy's reply. Accompanying the tramp of the infantrymen's feet and the rumble of artillery wheels, the lilting sounds of the fife and drum filled every heart with pride, renewing their determination to win this bitter battle for freedom.

Later that afternoon, the stirring words of the Declaration of Independence still ringing in their ears and the spectacle of the parade still dancing before their eyes, Betsy and her friends walked from the State House up Sixth Street to North East Square. The pretty tree-lined park soon filled up with scores of other Patriots crying *"Freedom or die!"* and *"Lobster-backs, go home!"* Betsy, Minette and Emma and their gentlemen friends, Jack Thompson and Caleb Lawton, all settled down to enjoy a picnic luncheon and watch the parade pass by all over again.

Betsy's shining gaze met that of the handsome Frenchman, François Dubeau. "How fortunate that you arrived in Philadelphia in time to experience this glorious occasion along with the rest of us, sir."

He nodded. "Our fighting men are . . . very brave."

"Will you be marching off to join the rebels?" Betsy asked, excitement evident in her tone.

François did not respond at once. At length, he said, "I am needed at home. My parent's grasp of the language is . . . sorely lacking."

Betsy smiled. "I have noticed Minette often mixes up her words."

"I was fortunate to learn the language whilst living in England. I mean now to teach my family what I have learned."

His remark corroborated what Minette had said; that her brother had studied in England. Still, Betsy thought the handsome gentleman did not seem quite as elated as the rest of them. But, perhaps being a foreigner, he had not yet fully grasped the plight of his newly adopted country. She continued to try and draw out the Frenchman but apart from teaching his parents the language he gave only cursory answers to her questions without elaborating upon anything.

Later that evening as she thought back on the day, she realized that while François was a pleasant and agreeable young man, he often seemed guarded, even evasive, going out of his way to never divulge anything of a personal nature about himself. Moreover, throughout that long afternoon, he'd never asked a single question of her. Apart from knowing she was a seamstress, he knew nothing about her. Eventually she concluded that perhaps it was his aloofness that made him seem so intriguing. That and his dark good looks. Joseph, on the other hand, kept no secrets. He was always open and forthcoming; but perhaps that was because they'd known one another since childhood.

Of a sudden, another prick of guilt stabbed Betsy. It had been six long months since John died and although she would never cease loving him, she was slowly coming to realize that life was for the living. Already she'd begun to long for the husband and family John's death had denied her. Was it too soon to be thinking of another man, or was she merely a young lady with ordinary wants and desires?

CHAPTER 9

At the next Fighting Quaker meeting, everyone's spirits were still high as a result of the Independence Day celebration. Leaders said the landmark document had been read aloud in towns and villages throughout the colonies. Following the reading in New York City, a cheering mob had overturned a gilded lead statue of King George seated atop a horse. The mob severed the king's head, mounted it on a spike and displayed it outside a tavern. When told that the statue would be melted down and recast for bullets, cheers erupted amongst the Fighting Quaker members.

Other news filtering down from the north was not quite so uplifting. Vast numbers of British troops were now quartered in the homes of New York City residents. The number of British ships pouring into New York harbor exceeded over one hundred, amongst them the 50-gun *Centurion,* the 40-gun *Phoenix,* the 64-gun *Asia* and the 30-gun *Greyhound,* which had conveyed British General Howe to the city. It was said that the combined number of cannons on those five warships alone exceeded all the rebel guns awaiting the enemy on shore.

Hearing such specific disclosures, Betsy wondered how her little Quaker group in far-away Philadelphia could be privy to such detailed information regarding the enemy?

On their way home that evening, she decided to ask François as they walked a few feet behind Minette and Emma and their gentlemen admirers, the foursome up ahead gaily discussing more frivolous topics.

"There are a number of ways in which we might glean information about the British military," François responded. Betsy couldn't help noticing that his tone sounded more animated than she'd ever before heard from him. "I, for one, regularly correspond with several British officers now occupying New York City."

Caught off-guard by the admission, Betsy gasped. "Are your British soldier friends aware that you have joined the *Patriot* Cause?"

François shrugged. "Apparently to question my fealty has not occurred to them. I daresay I am not the only citizen in Philadelphia who communicates with the enemy."

Betsy could hardly believe her ears. *What else might her foreign friend know about the enemy?* In an attempt to learn more, she boldly said, "I suppose information about the British could also be uncovered by . . . spies." Noting the hint of a smile lift the corners of François's lips, her pulse quickened. *Was she finally about to learn something useful?*

"That you express an interest in such matters rather surprises me," François remarked.

Betsy worked to remain calm. "I have recently learned a bit about . . . covert activity," she replied softly.

Her companion's black eyes cut 'round.

At that instant, Jack Thompson also turned to address them. "There is a public dance tomorrow night at Old Square Tavern, what say we all attend together?"

"Sounds like a capital plan to me," Caleb Lawton chimed in. He smiled down at Minette. "What say you? Will you show us how the French dance?"

In minutes it was decided that the three couples would attend the public dance the following evening at Old Square Tavern. Despite the recent decree that entertainments, plays, concerts, and the like, were banned due to the war, a good many young people had been pleased to discover that not all amusements had been set aside. Everyone knew that Philadelphia's elite, the bulk of them Loyalists, including those British officers who were quartered in the city, continued to amuse themselves in blatant disregard of the ordinance.

Following Jack's interruption, Betsy's private conversation with François and the miniscule inroad she'd made with him, ground to an abrupt halt. She vowed to broach the sensitive topic with him again, perhaps as they walked home from the dance tomorrow evening.

The next day a courier rapped at Betsy's door delivering a message from Dr. Franklin. Tearing into the missive, Betsy noted it bore the requisite tax stamp in the upper corner. The one-word message *'British'* set her heart racing. *So, Toby had been working for the enemy. Is that why he was killed?*

The disheartening news drove the excitement Betsy had been feeling over the proposed outing that evening from mind leaving in its place a gnawing sense of foreboding.

Walking back to the parlor where she'd been sewing, Betsy stuffed the note from Dr. Franklin into her pocket and reluctantly turned her attention to mending the rebel officer's uniform a woman had brought in that morning. The simple task would not net much but she could certainly put the few pence she'd earn to good use.

As her needle expertly whipped in and out of the rough cloth, thoughts of François Dubeau filled her mind. Why had he joined the Patriot Cause when it was rebels who had killed his British cousin? Could François be secretly aligned with the British in the hope of avenging his cousin's death? If so, how could she ferret out the truth regarding his allegiance? She knew it was a stretch but she couldn't help wondering if perhaps François had had a hand in Toby's slaying? That is, if the boy's death was indeed related to spying. She regretted not discovering the secret compartment in the little box before the intruder carried it off for it might have provided a clue to the answers she sought.

As ever when she thought in this vein, frustration soon set in. If only she could gain so much as a toehold into Philadelphia's spy underworld she might begin to put the pieces together. Thus far, she hadn't heard so much as a whisper regarding the munitions warehouse explosion. Had the night watchman, whose frozen body was found floating in the river the following morning also met with foul play? Had he observed a stranger lurking about the warehouse that wintry afternoon and unfortunately paid for the knowledge with his life?

If she hadn't been so consumed with grief those early weeks following John's death, she could have at least questioned the proprietors of those taverns located near Dock Street; for despite the foul weather, undoubtedly a few had remained open that day. Perhaps the proprietor or a serving wench had seen, or heard, something out of the ordinary. Unfortunately it was too late now to expect anyone to dredge up a memory of what they might have observed that icy day last January. But, that did not mean the killer could not still be brought to justice. With characteristic determination, Betsy renewed her vow not to give up until she uncovered the whole truth . . . no matter how long it took.

That night Old Square Tavern was ablaze with light and brimming with noise and laughter. Although many of Philadelphia's fresh-faced young men had marched off to war a week ago with General Washington, many more still remained behind. Being out amongst gay young people lifted Betsy's spirits, but the music and dancing also brought back painful memories of the lighthearted fun she and John used to enjoy before they married.

Tonight Betsy, Minette and Emma were dressed in their customary

Quaker garb, Hodden gray gowns with white collars and snug white caps on their heads. Jack and Caleb looked clean and fresh in white linen shirts and dark knee breeches with white hose and plain black leather shoes. François's appearance, however, was another matter altogether. Double rows of ruffles marched down the front of his white linen shirt and lace fluttered from the cuffs of his green satin coat. Green satin knee beeches and shoes with silver buckles completed the Frenchman's fashionable attire. Betsy felt like a small gray dove standing beside a proud peacock.

Although she thoroughly enjoyed the dancing, tonight was the first time she'd ever danced with anyone besides John. Because François was a good deal taller than John, twirling in his arms somehow felt . . . not right. That François remained especially attentive to her throughout the evening, however, did please her. He was a fine looking man and of all the eligible young ladies in Philadelphia he seemed to have singled *her* out. Despite the many flirtatious smiles aimed his way, never once did he leave her side to dance with another young lady.

During the interlude in which the three couples stood on the sidelines sipping small ale, François did excuse himself. Thinking he was headed for the necessary, Betsy thought nothing of it. However, when it seemed he'd been gone overlong and she did not see him on the dance floor, she grew a trifle concerned. She finally spotted him standing near the entrance conversing with a knot of other young men, all unknown to her. When François at last returned to her side and without a word, ushered her onto the dance floor, Betsy longed to ask the identity of the men and what they'd been discussing. But, she refrained. Perhaps she could draw François out on the way home.

When the case clock at the top of the room struck eleven, Betsy was about to declare that she'd like to leave when she caught sight of another young man standing on the fringe of the crowd, this one intently watching her. A bright smile lit up her face. *Joseph!*

She gazed up at François. "Will you excuse me, please?"

He inclined his dark head. "*Mais certainement.*"

His sudden use of French struck her as odd; still she hurried away. Upon reaching the seaman's side, she exclaimed, "You are on shore this evening!"

Joseph regarded her coolly. "And you are on the dance floor."

"Do dance with me, Joseph, please."

"And what would your finely-turned out escort say?"

"François is the brother of my friend Minette Dubeau. Come, I will introduce you . . ."

"Another time. I was just leaving. Good night, Betsy."

Stung by his curtness, Betsy watched the proud seaman head for the door. His blond good looks also garnered a deal of attention from the pretty girls he passed by. "Good night, Joseph," she murmured.

As the three couples walked back through Philadelphia's lamp-lit streets, François wasted no time questioning Betsy about the young man she had abandoned him for.

Betsy gazed up at her handsome escort. In the lamplight, the shadows dancing across the planes and angles of his face made him seem all the more attractive. "Mr. Ashburn is a childhood friend of mine."

"Who appears to care a great deal for you."

Betsy blinked. "I-I . . . am not privy to Mr. Ashburn's private feelings."

"He stood watching you from the shadows for a lengthy spell and with quite a disagreeable look upon his face. You invited him to join us, *oui?* And he refused?"

Betsy looked down. "He . . . needed to return to his ship."

"Ah. Your Mr. Ashburn is a seaman."

"He is a privateer, the captain of his own ship, the *Swallow.*"

"I see."

When François said no more on the subject, neither did Betsy. To her chagrin, François said little else on any subject at all. Her remaining attempts to draw him out proved useless. Despite her enjoyment of the dance, in the end she was forced to conclude that the outing had been somewhat of a disappointment.

The following evening, Betsy was surprised when once again François Dubeau appeared at her door. She had hoped Joseph would call tonight. That she actually felt stung by his aloofness the previous evening told her she cared a good deal more for him than she realized.

"Good evening, *mam'selle*. Might I come in?" The Frenchman's confident tone said he fully expected to be welcomed into her home.

A nervous smile flickered across Betsy's face. It would never do for Joseph to find her with François again tonight. "The evening is quite pleasant, sir, perhaps we might take a stroll." She noted he was once again impeccably turned out, this time in blue damask breeches and a matching vest over a white muslin blouse.

"As you wish."

Withdrawing a key from the pocket of her apron, Betsy locked the door behind her before joining François on the walkway. Not wishing to come face-to-face with Joseph if he might, indeed, be on his way to see her, she suggested they walk *up* Mulberry Street instead of downhill towards the river.

"The sunset is beautiful." Betsy's long gaze took in the vivid streaks of amber and rose peeking through the treetops. When her companion made no reply and in fact said nothing for above half a block, Betsy grew a bit impatient. If he did not wish to be with her, why had he called? What did the Frenchman want from her? And, when did he mean to apprise her of his wishes?

The two walked in silence for another long block before he finally said, "Minette tells me you sewed banners for the rebel General Washington."

"Indeed. It was quite a large commission, which, I . . . welcomed."

"So, now the project is complete, how fares your upholstery business?"

Asking a personal question of her now, was he? "I have taken in a bit of mending."

A few more paces elapsed before he said, "I assume you mend uniforms for . . . military officers."

Betsy nodded, although did not elaborate. She could also be evasive.

"Have you mended uniforms for . . . British officers?"

"No!" Her head jerked up. "And I daresay I never shall!"

François cast a somewhat bemused look at her. "Not even if it would further the Patriot Cause?"

Her eyes narrowed. "How could mending a uniform for a British officer further the Patriot Cause?"

Walking with his hands clasped behind his back, François's demeanor remained maddeningly calm. "Let us say a British officer, or perhaps, several, came into your shop and whilst you were reattaching a button or turning up a hem, the men began to speak on matters that might be of interest to a . . . Patriot general."

Betsy's heart began to pound. *Was he at last broaching the very topic she so longed to know more of?*

They had turned down Fifth Street and were now approaching Chestnut where the State House stood, the very spot where they'd watched the Independence Day parade. The grounds surrounding the brick building looked especially inviting tonight with patches of colorful flowers surrounding the base of every tall tree. Other citizens were strolling about the lawn. To Betsy, their presence felt . . . reassuring.

"Shall we sit on the steps?" François suggested.

Betsy nodded.

Once they were seated upon the cool marble steps, François began to speak. "I have no doubt that you are a fine *grisette, mademoiselle.* Despite your talent as a seamstress, however, I suspect your business has . . . faltered."

"The business of every merchant in the city has faltered," Betsy returned tartly.

"Perhaps . . . I could provide a solution to your problem."

Betsy swallowed hard. *What was this oh-so attractive man about to suggest now? And why was it that instead of enjoying his company as she'd fully expected she would when she first met him, the infuriating man seemed only to irk her? A part of her wished to trust the foreign gentleman; yet the voice in her head clearly advised caution.* "I am listening," she said.

"During wartime," his tone dropped to scarcely above a whisper, "there are . . . shall we say, less conventional ways in which one might turn a profit."

Goose flesh popped out on Betsy's arms.

"I, for one, recently joined a Patriot group called the Secret Committee of Correspondence."

Swallowing hard, Betsy worked to remain calm.

"Committee of Correspondence members are similar to the Sons of Liberty groups in the north," François told her. "Members pass along information that has been handed to them by more . . . well-placed constituents, men who freely move amongst the various enemy camps and have intercepted missives from say, British generals, confidential dispatches that regularly pass between officers, or intelligence directed to their superiors in England." He paused as if to gauge her reaction thus far. When Betsy provided none, he went on. "Rebel leaders such as the great General Washington are coming to realize that the activities of the Secret Committees of Correspondence provide an excellent way to learn what the enemy is up to. Being hungry for intelligence, Continental officers are willing to pay handsomely for it."

Betsy was now on pins and needles. *Was he telling her straight out that he did, indeed, spy on the British?* "Is not passing along these packets of information considered . . . spying?"

He shrugged. "Not at all. A member's involvement is no different than if I handed you . . ." . . . he withdrew a folded up piece of paper from his pocket . . . "this." When she did not take the offering, he returned it to his pocket. "For the most part, committee members merely hand off packets to one another. We form a sort of chain, if you will, from one colony to another. The information reaches its destination far quicker than one might think, actually. Member's identities are unknown; no words between contacts need be spoken." Leaning back, he casually propped his elbows on the stair behind him. "One member in Virginia simply digs a hole in a graveyard, buries his packet and walks away. He never knows who retrieves it, and doesn't care."

"But, how are Committee members compensated? You said they are . .

. paid handsomely." Betsy kept her tone low despite the excitement building within her. Although no other citizens were near them on the marble stairwell, it would never do for such a conversation to be overheard.

"A senior officer in each committee handles that function, but it, too, is dispatched in a clandestine fashion. A person watching the exchange would not know what he had just witnessed. And," his next remark sweetened the deal, at least for Betsy, "we are paid in coin, not that worthless Continental paper money, or those foolish Codfish bills being circulated in Massachusetts."

Betsy grinned. Codfish bills were supposedly worth a full shilling, which was considerably more than Continental bills, generally worth only a sixth of a pound or less and considered quite easy to counterfeit. Because the so-called Codfish bills contained an engraving of a codfish across the top, artfully done by the renowned Patriot Paul Revere, they were thought to be more difficult to copy.

"To be paid in coin would indeed be a bonus," she murmured, her interest indeed aroused. To earn a bit of money in such a simple fashion would be quite grand. "How does one become a member of this . . . Correspondence Committee?"

"The proper title is Secret Committee of Correspondence. So, my proposal interests you, *oui?*"

Despite her intrigue, Betsy hedged. "Before I . . . commit, I have a few questions to put to you, sir."

He inclined his head a notch. "It would surprise me if you did not, *ma petite*. You are an intelligent woman."

Betsy's lips pursed. Even his veiled attempt to praise her into doing his bidding had the effect of irking her. For an intelligent man, he was quite transparent. "You once mentioned, sir, that your English cousin was killed by rebels. I cannot help but wonder why you have now aligned with the Patriot Cause? It would seem more likely that you would . . ."

A sharp tone cut her off. "That a rebel bullet felled my cousin makes him an unfortunate casualty of war. I have aligned with the Patriot Cause, *madame,* because I am a staunch believer in justice."

His sudden anger seemed somehow . . . *too* sudden. "I see."

"On the surface my reasoning might seem incongruous, but by justice, I mean I do not believe England has the right to subjugate the colonists, or control their lives. I am now a *colonist, madame,* the same as you are."

"If you feel that strongly, sir, why have you not marched off to join the rebel army?" she pushed.

"I have explained to you that I am needed at home. As a Quaker, I do not believe in bearing arms. I can do more for the Patriot Cause by *not* fighting."

Betsy noted his long gaze fixed somewhere on the perimeter of the State House grounds. She gazed that direction but spotted nothing out of the ordinary. The sky had gown darker and the grounds were now quite thin of company, but noting the Watch come round a corner and begin to trim the lamps, diminished some of her unease. The Watch would soon begin to call out the hour, declaring to citizens within earshot that all was well. She fervently hoped that to be the case.

When François spoke again, he seemed also to have reined in his ire and his tone was now again almost pleasant. "I arrived in Philadelphia with a number of letters of introduction in my pocket, Mrs. Ross; letters designed to introduce me to prominent American families. Unfortunately, I have learned that the majority of those families are Loyalists. How best to turn those introductions to my advantage has puzzled me . . . until now."

Betsy gazed up with interest. *What was he saying now?*

"I recently received an invitation to a *soiree* at the home of a gentleman named Edward Shippen."

"Judge Shippen?"

He shrugged. "I know not the gentleman's rank. I originally meant for Minette to accompany me. Instead . . ." He turned to her. "I am asking you."

Betsy blinked. *He wished her to accompany him to a party?* The bit of pleasure that swept over her dissolved the split second his look turned disdainful.

"Do you possess a finer costume, *ma chérie?*"

Betsy's lips firmed. She was a Quaker. He should know she owned nothing fashionable. *He* may have abandoned Quaker attire, but she still clung to it.

When she did not reply, he said. "When I earlier spoke of British officers frequenting your shop, *madame*, I was suggesting a method whereby you might gain bits of useful information which you could pass along for profit to a Secret Committee of Correspondence member. A tailor in New York City recently learned of a plot to murder General Washington, a plot the tailor overheard being discussed between a pair of British officers in his shop as he fitted one of them for a jacket. When I heard of it, I thought of you."

So, the elegant Frenchman had singled her out not because he felt drawn to her but because she *could further* his *cause.* "I am unacquainted with any British officers, sir, and I refuse to tailor a British officer's uniform. Furthermore, if I were to accept your offer to spy on the British, how would you suggest I entice British officers into my shop?"

"That, *ma fleur,* is what I am attempting to explain." His tone again sounded a trifle impatient. "To gain the enemy's trust, *mademoiselle,* it is necessary for one to consort with the enemy."

"How am I to do that? I am a Patriot."

She noted the muscles of his jaws grinding together. "Attending the Shippen *soiree* with me will allow you to cultivate the friendship of Loyalist women, Mrs. Ross. Your new friends will then recommend your services as a *grisette . . . pardon,* 'seamstress' to those British officers quartered in their homes."

"I have no desire to cultivate the friendship of Loyalist women," Betsy declared before realizing that her quick response meant she was foolishly tossing aside an excellent opportunity, the only one she had received thus far, to further *her* cause. Nonetheless, her growing irritation with the Frenchman made her continue on in the same vein. "I do not wish to lie about my true feelings, sir, or speak disparagingly of . . ."

"It is not uncommon these days for citizens to slip-slide from Rebel to Tory. The Shippens entertain British generals one week and Patriot generals the next. By inviting you to accompany me to the Shippen *soiree,* I am providing you with a superb opportunity to lure the enemy into your confidence. If you are a competent enough seamstress to fashion a suitable garment by Thursday evening next, I will gladly escort you to the *soiree.* To do so will place us both in a prime position to embark upon our shared subterfuge."

Shared subterfuge? Although this was precisely the opportunity Betsy had dreamed of, she realized that to link herself with the duplicitous Frenchman actually set her teeth on edge. Still, if she were to learn anything at all about covert activity in Philadelphia, she had no choice now but to agree to his plan. "To fashion a gown in a sen'night, sir, will not pose a problem," she replied coolly.

"Perhaps my sister can help."

Betsy took umbrage. "I am quite capable of fashioning a gown for myself, sir!"

"For our plan to bear fruit, *ma petite,* your gown must be fashionable." Another scornful look raked over her dowdy costume.

Betsy managed to hold her tongue.

"Minette only just arrived from Paris," he reminded her. "Amongst her possessions are a number of dolls. One is wearing a gown I am told was fashioned for our beautiful Queen, Marie Antoinette."

Betsy knew he was speaking of French Fashion dolls, which, might, indeed, prove useful in designing a truly fashionable frock. She swallowed her pride. "Minette's help with the cut of my gown will be most welcome, sir. Thank you."

"I shall ask her to call upon you and to bring the dolls. You are agreeing to my plan, *oui?*"

As François had obviously intended all along for their association to be nothing more than a business arrangement, Betsy felt foolish for having ever thought otherwise. Still her stubborn streak did not wish him to think she was agreeing to his proposal so easily. "I must be assured, sir, that once my new friends, the Loyalists and their friends, the . . . British officers, come to my shop, that all I am required to do is . . . listen."

"And set down whatever you overhear and to pass along your report."

"Pass along my report to whom?"

"I will be your contact, *madame.* For the nonce, you must concentrate upon gaining the enemy's trust. So . . ." he pressed, "you agree to accept my offer, *oui?* "

Lifting her chin, Betsy stood. "I would like to return to my home now, please."

"*Certainement.*" He also stood.

At Betsy's doorstep, François leaned to whisper into her ear. "I must have your word, *ma petite*, that nothing we have spoken of tonight will be bandied about. Most especially not to your friend, the South Sea trader."

Betsy bristled. The moniker 'South Sea trader' referred to *pirates*. "Captain Ashburn is a *privateer, sir,*" she declared hotly. "He and his crew operate entirely within the law and he possesses the Letter of Marque to prove it."

It was too dark for Betsy to see the smirk of amusement on François' lips. "Forgive me, *ma petite fleur.* I meant no disrespect to your friend."

The Frenchman's flowery phrases were also beginning to annoy her. Did he think if he called her his *little flower* enough times, she would turn into a simpering milk-and-water miss who would agree to anything he wished? Betsy unlocked her shop door. Decidedly irritated with the Frenchman now, another part of her admitted that she had always wished to attend a *soiree* at one of the lovely mansions on Society Hill. And to do so wearing a beautiful new gown . . . how could she possibly refuse?

But . . . did she dare? Would her presence amongst Loyalists forever brand *her* a traitor? Indeed, not. François had said General Washington supped with Judge Shippen and General Washington was not a traitor.

Turning to François, she said, "I have decided to attend the dinner party with you, but I must give your other proposal a bit more thought."

"Very well. *A bientôt.*" With a polite nod of his head, he turned and strolled away.

Walking through her darkened house, thoughts of spying and subterfuge swirled through Betsy's mind, as well as the perplexing problem that has plagued women throughout the ages . . . what on earth would she wear to a fashionable dinner party?

CHAPTER 10

The following day Minette appeared at Betsy's door bringing two beautiful French Fashion dolls. "François say you agree to attend *soiree* with heem, *oui?*"

"I did, indeed." Betsy invited her friend into her parlor.

She had never before seen a French Fashion doll. Atop their painted porcelain faces, both dolls wore tall powdered wigs featuring feathers and ribbons; one had a strand of pearls woven through the stiff white hair. Minette said the wide Polonaise gowns were generally worn only at court, or fancy-dress balls, but the square cut of the neckline, the stiff stomachers, and elbow-length sleeves on the doll's dresses were now all the rage in Paris. Betsy could hardly wait to begin cutting the fabric and stitching together a lovely new gown for herself.

At length Minette rose to go. "I leave with you my fashion *bébés.*"

Betsy thanked her and at once began to sketch a design, and then to sort through her bolts of costly new fabric. Knowing it would not be proper to wear bright colors so soon after her husband's passing; she chose a soft gray silk that had arrived with her shipment.

"You will look lovely, Betsy," Sarah exclaimed the following afternoon when Betsy told her sister why she was making the dress. "I shudder to think what our mother would say if she knew what you are planning."

"Well, it is not as if I could be read out of Meeting again," Betsy replied. She'd been pleased when her sister hadn't chastised her for attending the dance the other evening with Emma and Minette, and her brother François. Now, Sarah also hadn't scolded her for accepting the Frenchman's invitation to attend a fashionable dinner party. Above stairs in her sunny sitting room, the girls began to carefully cut into the fine fabric.

"Rachel would be quite envious if she knew of your plans. Our younger sister is so like you, Betsy, and I do not mean only in countenance. She is every bit as headstrong as you are when she sets her mind to something. To be sure, Rachel daily tries our mother's patience."

"I would dearly love to see her and Hannah, and George. I thank the good Lord every day that you are brave enough to come around, Sarah."

"I will never abandon thee, Sister." Sarah studied the lovely Fashion Dolls. "We would have adored sewing frocks for dolls such as these when we were children."

Betsy smiled, recalling fond memories of their childhood and the many hours she and her sisters had spent together sewing. Hearing Sarah's occasional affectionate use of "thee" and "thy" also warmed her heart.

"I daresay you will receive commissions to make many more such beautiful gowns after the women see you at the party."

If everything went as François expected, Betsy thought, she might very well earn enough from the new business she garnered to repay Uncle Abel for all her new fabric and supplies. She would also accept François's *other* offer, of course. To earn money simply by listening and setting down on paper whatever she might overhear would indeed further the Patriot Cause, although she would *never* tell Sarah of her involvement in that venture.

"Shall we embellish the stomacher with bows from the same gray silk or do you prefer a contrasting color?" Sarah asked, sorting through the many fabric swatches.

"I think the selfsame color will look more elegant. I plan to trim the square neck and sleeves with silver braid and also a lace frill."

"With bows at the sleeves?"

Betsy considered. "Perhaps small ones. I shouldn't want to gaudy it up with too many furbelows."

"You are such a pretty girl, Betsy, I am persuaded it will not be too very long before thee receives another offer of marriage."

Betsy laughed. "So long as it does not come from a Loyalist."

"Have you told Joseph you will be attending a society dinner party?"

"I have not seen Joseph since that night at Old Square Tavern."

"Clearly he was jealous of François." Sarah held up the bow she'd just tied. "What do you think? Bigger, or smaller?"

"It is perfect as it is. Thank you for helping me, Sarah."

"Perhaps I might meet your Frenchman one day."

"I will need thee to dress my hair on Thursday evening next."

François Dubeau arrived to collect Betsy in a smart two-wheeled chaise pulled by a single black horse. After charmingly expressing his pleasure over meeting Betsy's sister Sarah, he surprised Betsy by remarking on how lovely she looked tonight in her new silk gown. As expected, he was elegantly attired in a three-piece suit of burgundy silk, the breeches tied below the knees with ribbons, the coat adorned with a velvet collar and cuffs. Froths of white lace dripped from his wrists and cascaded down his white linen shirtfront. White silk stockings and gleaming black pumps completed the Frenchman's stylish costume.

Sarah had piled Betsy's chestnut hair up on her head leaving three glossy ringlets to dangle over one shoulder. Betsy nestled a delicate pink silk rose amongst her shiny curls. This being the first occasion she'd ever worn anything other than a plain gray frock and white apron, she felt breathless with excitement. She succeeded in remaining calm as François handed her into the chaise. Smiling, she waved goodbye to Sarah who stood on the walkway.

Drawing up to the Shippen's elegant home, Betsy recalled that she and John had often exclaimed over the grand house as they strolled down South Fourth Street. Formal gardens and fruit orchards surrounded all the mansions here, but the Shippen home was by far the largest; maintained, she and John had assumed, by slaves. The majority of Philadelphia's wealthier citizens owned slaves. Before the war, it had not been uncommon for a black boy or girl to accompany the well-to-do patrons into John and Betsy's small upholstery shop.

"I expect the bulk of the conversation tonight will center around the British ships sailing into New York harbor," François told Betsy as the tidy chaise fell in behind a string of other coaches making slow progress toward the Shippen home. "No doubt, there will be a good bit of cheering over the fact that the British now occupy the city."

"Must we also cheer?" Betsy asked, beginning to feel a trifle uneasy about what lay ahead.

"If you feel you cannot join in, *mam'selle,* simply remain silent. Your task is to impress, not to debate political matters, which . . ." he flicked an imaginary speck of lint from his coat sleeve, "I am persuaded is far and away beyond the capability of women anyhow."

Betsy blanched but ignored the rude remark. François would never be an especial friend of hers, so his opinion of her capability to discuss anything mattered not a whit to her.

"Depending on the size of our host's guest list," he continued as if instructing a child how to go on in polite society, "you and I may, or may not, be seated near one another at table. Consequently whomever you are seated beside, instead of attempting to converse with the gentleman you must . . ."

"Despite your low opinion of me, sir," Betsy exploded. "I am persuaded I shall not embarrass you with a display of ill manners."

François's lips pursed. "I see no need for prickliness, *madame.*"

"You seem to think me completely lacking in propriety."

With a sniff, he abandoned their quarrel. "Our host and hostess will no doubt introduce the pair of us around."

"So long as you and I are not viewed as being *linked* together."

François's lips twitched as he turned a bemused gaze upon her. "Quite clearly I have misjudged you, *ma chérie.* When it suits you, you can be quite saucy." A dark brow quirked. "As it happens, I find saucy women rather . . . attractive."

"What a pity," Betsy said. "For I find rude gentlemen quite *un*-attractive."

Edward Shippen and his wife, Margaret, were high-standing Philadelphia citizens whose wealth had accrued over the years from their extensive real estate holdings. As the dinner guests entered their lovely manor home, a liveried butler ushered each one into a beautifully appointed withdrawing room.

"Welcome to our home, Mrs. Ross," Mrs. Shippen greeted Betsy. "I am delighted that M'sieur Dubeau invited you to accompany him tonight."

"Thank you, Mrs. Shippen; I am delighted to be here. I believe I once met your lovely daughter Peggy." Betsy knew the Shippen's had been blessed with four daughters and a son.

"We meant to bring Peggy *out* this year, but . . ." the older woman sighed, "the war; you know."

Betsy smiled prettily. "The conflict has dramatically changed all our lives." She directed a speaking look at her escort, as if to say, there, you see, I can be quite civil. He appeared not to notice.

For the next quarter hour Betsy nodded and smiled when introduced to other guests, and derived great pleasure from simply viewing her surroundings. Being an upholsterer, the silk-covered walls, the richly draped sofas and chairs and the other ladies' gowns greatly interested her. Attired in her own stylish creation, she did not feel the least bit out of place. It did surprise her to note that several of the other ladies gowns were not quite as fashionable as she'd expected, however, some being made in a style popular some fifteen years ago called the *sack*, featuring a fitted bodice in front and two wide pleats hanging straight to the floor in back. Only a few ladies' skirts were held away from their bodies by panniers and none were too terribly wide. However, nearly every gown featured the popular square-cut *décolletage*, as did Betsy's. A few elderly women modestly wore crossed handkerchiefs tucked into their low-cut bodices.

Betsy became so caught up studying her surroundings, she was scarcely aware of François, who, she eventually realized was still hovering near her elbow. Relieved that he was saying nothing, Betsy continued to amuse herself perusing the colorful gowns and costly jewels glittering at the ladies throats. Noting that a good many of the gentlemen's silk waistcoats seemed stretched quite tightly over their well-fed bellies brought a smile to her lips.

"What do you find so amusing, *madame?*"

François's caustic tone drew Betsy from her reverie. "I am merely enjoying the sights," she replied quietly.

"So long as you do not enjoy yourself to the detriment of our . . . *cause*." François's cool tone was low.

His remark reminded Betsy that despite their pleasant manners, everyone here was, in fact, the *enemy* and she was not here to enjoy herself, but to cultivate false friendships.

Eventually the Shippens led their guests into the dining chamber, which Betsy noted was every bit as elegantly furnished as the drawing room. Scarlet silk covered these walls and on the floor, her slippers sank into a thick Turkish carpet. A pair of crystal chandeliers, ablaze with dozens of candles, hung low over the polished mahogany table where gleaming silver serving dishes and silver goblets made it seem to sparkle. Against the wall, exquisite, etched-glass panels fronted the sideboard. The costly elegance displayed here nearly took Betsy's breath away.

Upon realizing that each guest's name had been lettered upon a small ivory card fronting the place settings, she found herself seated between a Mr. Whitmore and a Mr. Boggs, both of whom she was unacquainted with but did recognize their names from the *Pennsylvania Packet*, as both were wealthy and influential Philadelphians.

After liveried servants solemnly poured rich red wine into every guest's long-stemmed crystal glass, Judge Shippen raised a toast to the success of the British troops in New York. Although Betsy cringed at the sentiment and the cheers of approval that followed, she managed to swallow a few perfunctory sips of wine and was relieved when no other gentleman rose to offer a similar toast. Dinner conversation soon became lively amongst the men and, as François predicted, focused mainly upon the British occupying the New York colony.

"Loyalists are a decided majority in New York City," a gentleman sitting near Betsy declared. "Upwards of three-fourths of the land there is owned by Loyalists."

"I understand the royal governor of New York, William Tryon, has set up headquarters aboard one of the king's own ships," declared another gentleman, "and is secretly directing all Loyalist operations from the harbor."

"Is that a fact?"

"Make no mistake, the conflict in New York will not last long."

"Staten Island is another Loyalist stronghold."

"The Virginia farmer's rag-tag army don't stand a chance in New York and that's a fact," predicted another gentleman.

Upon hearing General Washington being referred to, with derision, as the Virginia farmer, Betsy squirmed, but said nothing and instead turned her attention to the sumptuous meal upon the delicate china plate before her. Never in her life had she tasted such delicious pheasant pie. The asparagus compote was topped by a thick cream sauce, and the green peas, creamed carrots and new potatoes were seasoned to perfection. Silver platters littering the table contained an assortment of puddings and breads all garnished with nuts, raisins, and thick treacle. Being accustomed to far simpler fare, Betsy thoroughly enjoyed the meal. Having never been served dinner by a liveried footman, it amused her when the alert gentleman seemed to know the instant she drained the last swallow of wine from her long-stemmed goblet and silently appeared out of nowhere to refill it. Twice his presence had so startled her she'd nearly dropped the sterling silver fork in her hand.

When the dinner discussion turned to the Oath of Allegiance to the Freedom Cause that Judge Shippen declared he was currently being pressured to sign, Betsy's ears again perked up. Aware of the official decree, she knew that if a man refused to set down his name, he could be arrested, have his property seized, or be banished altogether from the city. But, where could a man safely go, she wondered (but did not inquire aloud) if every colony and village within it enforced the same law?

She overheard a gentleman across the table remark that only last month Dr. Franklin's son William, Royal Governor of New Jersey, had been arrested for refusing to sign the oath. How, she wondered, did Dr. Franklin feel about his son taking sides against him?

"Governor Franklin declared that he had an everlasting duty to his king," said Mr. Boggs. "He was still staunchly maintaining his position even as he was being hauled away to Connecticut, where unfortunately he is now imprisoned."

Betsy became aware of women at the table murmuring with dismay regarding the topic under discussion. Mrs. Shippen remarked that she had lately been urging her husband to sign the oath.

"After all we must think of the children. How would they get on if their father were banished to Connecticut?"

When Mr. Whitmore, to Betsy's left, said he favored reform over rebellion and compromise over confrontation, Betsy could no longer keep silent. "I quite agree with you, sir."

Whitmore rewarded her with a nod of approval; whilst Mr. Boggs to her right, said, "You appear to be a discerning woman, Mrs. Ross."

"Thank you, sir," Betsy replied, although following the minimal exchange, she noted the critical look François, seated across from her, aimed her way. Defiantly lifting her chin, she turned away.

Later, in the drawing room, after the gentlemen had rejoined the ladies, Betsy was appalled to overhear a remark François made to a pair of women who had him cornered before the mantle-piece. Apparently the women had been discussing the agreeableness of having children in one's life and asked François his opinion.

"*Madame,* I like children only when they are properly prepared and served with a savory sauce." With a nod, he abruptly excused himself and left the women staring after him, their mouths agape.

Her blue eyes rolling skyward, Betsy hurried toward the affronted ladies. "Please accept my apologies on behalf of M'sieur Dubeau. I am certain he did not mean what he said. He has an . . . unnatural sense of humor."

"Unnatural, indeed!" snapped one lady.

"The French do seem to think themselves superior to the rest of us. Make no mistake, you would do well to rid yourself of such a disagreeable young man," admonished another woman.

"That is a lovely gown you are wearing, Mrs. Ross," said a pretty young lady who had stolen up to the group and was now hovering near Betsy's elbow. "Did M'sieur Dubeau procure it for you from Paris?"

Betsy turned toward the young lady, whose gown she had earlier noted was quite soiled about the hem. "No, he did not. I made my gown myself."

Hearing Betsy's reply, all eyes widened.

"But that cannot be," cried one. "I am certain I saw that exact same design in the pages of *La Belle Assemblee.*"

"I assure you I made my gown myself, madam. I am a seamstress. I have an upholstery shop on Mulberry Street."

"Yes, well, I cannot believe you made *that* gown."

"Nor do I believe it," said the one who'd declared the French believed themselves superior to others. "Apparently her sense of humor is as unnatural as M'sieur Dubeau's." Lifting her chin, she swept away.

Before Betsy had a chance to reply, another said, "My dear, did I hear you correctly? You made your gown yourself? It is quite lovely!"

"Thank you." Betsy directed a smile her way. "I am a seamstress, madam."

"Perhaps she means she made the gown *over*," said the first woman, who had rejoined the group. "I cannot believe it possible for a colonial seamstress to fashion such an exquisite creation. Do come along, Regina." Taking the arm of her friend, she dragged the more submissive woman away.

"I am so sorry," said the young lady who had first remarked upon Betsy's gown. "I did not mean to cause a stir. I think your gown is quite beautiful and I do believe you made it yourself." One hand fingered her soiled frock. "Had I sufficient funds, I would commission you to make such a gown for me."

"And I would be happy to do so, my dear. Do tell me your name."

"I am Miss Anne Olsen," said the slight girl who looked to be no more than seven and ten years. She had light brown hair and an unassuming demeanor. "I live with my aunt and uncle, Mr. and Mrs. Dearborn."

"It is a pleasure to meet you, Miss Olsen."

"Perhaps we shall meet again one day, Mrs. Ross."

"I look forward to it."

Later that evening, seated beside François in the little chaise as it bounced over the cobbles toward Betsy's home, she feared all her efforts aimed at impressing the Loyalist women had come to naught. If they refused to believe she had made her gown, not a single one would commission her to make gowns, or upholster a chair, for them.

"Well, it appears your little frock impressed no one," François remarked dryly.

"Unfortunately the same cannot be said for you," Betsy countered.

"You've no need to blame me for your failure to impress, *madame.*" That said, he closed his eyes, laid his head against the squabs, and did not rouse himself even to help her alight from the carriage, opting instead to let the coachman perform the honors.

Betsy unlocked her front door and entered the darkened house. Despite her failure to impress, she had quite enjoyed the outing. However, one evening spent in the Frenchman's disagreeable company had turned what little remained of her regard for him into distinct dislike.

CHAPTER 11

"You must admit that for us to settle out differences with England, *without* bloodshed, would be a good deal healthier for all concerned," Betsy declared to Joseph the following evening as they sat together on the sofa in her parlor.

She had been pleasantly surprised to find the sun-bronzed seaman standing on her doorstep that night. Carrying a bulky package tucked beneath his arm, she invited him in and assured him that after last night's dinner party, she had no intention of ever seeing the Frenchman again. She was vastly relieved now that she and Joseph seemed to once again be on a friendly footing.

However, his tone still sounded a trifle miffed when he replied, "It sounds as if after spending one evening in the company of Loyalists, you have now joined ranks with them."

"On the contrary. What I am saying is that I now better understand their viewpoint and I believe it unfortunate that our differences are so great that we think we must kill one another in order to settle them."

"I wonder if we are not being naïve in our fervor to engage the greatest force in the world in battle. If we all turn up dead after the smoke clears, whether or not we've gained our independence from the king will become a moot point."

"Exactly. Mr. Whitmore said he favored compromise over conflict and I quite agreed with him. However," Betsy worried her lower lip, "the king did refuse to read the Olive Branch Petition we submitted last autumn. If we cannot gain the king's ear, that does rather dash any hopes we might have for compromise."

"In the interim," Joseph added, "you must agree this war is a damn thrilling drama!"

A sudden image of John's bleeding and broken body dimmed the sparkle in Betsy's eyes. "I fear the cost for this particular drama is far too dear," she murmured.

"Forgive me." Joseph reached to squeeze her hand. "That was thoughtless of me." Some moments later, he leaned to retrieve the package he'd brought with him. "I came by last evening and . . . again tonight . . . to ask if you might mend something for me . . . that is, before you get too busy making fancy gowns for your new Loyalist lady friends."

"Of course, I will be glad to help you, Joseph. What do you need?"

Tearing apart the wrapper, he withdrew a somewhat tattered Union Jack and two British officer's uniforms.

Betsy flinched. "And you have now joined ranks with the British army?"

Joseph grinned as he stood and shrugged into a scarlet coat. Holding up an arm, the sleeve hung a good five inches beyond his wrist. "Just preparing to plunder the high seas and hoping to avoid getting killed in the process. A British ship that spots a Union Jack waving in the breeze and a couple of British officers strolling the deck will think twice before firing on us. I wondered if you could mend the flag for me and shorten the sleeves of these coats?"

"That coat does appear to have been made for quite a tall man, or perhaps an ape."

They both laughed.

"My first mate is near my size; neither of us being too very tall, so the sleeves of both coats can be the same length. Lack of stature on board ship can be an advantage, you know; easier to squeeze through hatchways and whatnot."

Betsy rose to get the inch tape and after jotting down the necessary measurements for the alteration, folded up the redcoats and flag, and set the bundle aside.

"Several uniforms I absconded with perfectly fit others of my crew plus I've managed to acquire all the necessary accouterments," Joseph added, "helmets, boots, swords, scabbards and a half dozen British muskets."

"When do you plan to leave Philadelphia?" Betsy asked as they both sat down again.

"As soon as everything is ready, guns, cannons, *quakers* . . . and the flag and red coats."

"I see." Now that she'd reconciled with Joseph, she didn't particularly wish to see him leave the city so quickly. The more she learned about François, the more she disliked the man but quite the opposite was true with Joseph. Not wishing to withhold anything from him, she began, "I have not yet divulged . . . everything about M'sieur Dubeau."

"Ah. So, the Frenchman wants more than merely to help you increase your business, eh?"

Betsy nodded.

"I thought as much." A booted foot commenced to tap upon the floor.

"Joseph, I was being truthful when I said François does not fancy me, nor I him. Not in *that* way."

"Then what exactly does the demmed Frenchie want?" Joseph's nostrils flared.

Betsy quickly told him about the Secret Committee of Correspondence and François's proposal that she help him gather information and hand off reports to other members, and about the monetary reward she'd receive for doing so. "I have a good many outstanding debts, Joseph; my rent has increased, and since the war began, the cost of food and firewood has doubled; plus I still owe Uncle Abel a great deal. I find I am constantly in dire straights."

"So the Frog means to compensate you in exchange for spying for him."

Misgiving flickered across Betsy's face. "I do not look at it that way, Joseph. I have no intention of actually . . . becoming a spy. But in order to learn who killed John, and perhaps even Toby, I must . . . put myself forward. If François is willing to give me a few shillings in exchange for whatever information I might glean, then . . ." She shrugged. "At any rate, it will probably come to nothing. Only one of the ladies at the dinner party believed I'd actually made my gown, so it's not likely I shall gain a single bit of new business from the venture. Or learn anything useful," she added wistfully.

"Well, you've not asked for my advice, but it appears to me that you could easily get in over your head. Spying is dangerous business, lass. As evidenced by what befell poor Toby. I shouldn't want anything to happen to you. You've only just met the Frenchie. Are you certain you can trust him?"

"At this juncture, I am uncertain who I can trust."

"You can trust me!"

"Of course, I trust you, Joseph. No doubt, it will all come to nothing," she said again. "If I gain no new customers from my sojourn into society, whether or not I trust François will also not matter. Quite possibly, I shall never see him again."

"You just declared you intended *never* to see him again."

"I shall be obliged to see him again if I am to hand off a report to him. What I meant to say was . . ."

"I know what you meant." Joseph rose to take his leave. "For what it's worth, I have heard a bit about the Secret Committees of Correspondence. There are members in every colony up and down the seaboard." He reached for her hand. "Come, walk with me to the street. And promise me you will be careful in your dealings with the Loyalists, *and* the Frenchie."

Betsy smiled and when Joseph offered before he left to bring in logs for the kitchen fire and water from the well, she gratefully accepted his kind offer. "I am glad you came to see me again, Joseph."

When he said good night at the door, Betsy could tell from the look in his hazel eyes that her gallant seaman wished to draw her into his arms and hold her close, but . . . she held back, still uncertain she was ready for any sort of intimacy with another man.

Betsy spent the following afternoon altering the sleeves of Joseph's redcoats. In preparation to mend the flag, she searched for a bit of bunting left from the banners she'd made for General Washington. Suddenly, becoming aware of feminine voices, she glanced up as two ladies stepped into the foyer of her shop. Betsy recognized one of them from Judge Shippen's dinner party.

"How nice to see you again, Miss Olsen; do come in."

The younger woman greeted Betsy and presented her aunt, Mrs. Dearborn, a portly woman of some forty years, who, judging from her fine clothes, Betsy surmised to be quite well-put. However, Betsy thought the green linen frock she wore was more suited for a girl of Miss Olsen's years, and that Mrs. Dearborn should be wearing the somber gown her niece had on. She politely invited the women into her parlor where both scarlet coats lay draped over the backs of chairs, the Union flag spread out on the dining table.

"Oh, I see you also sew for gentlemen," remarked Mrs. Dearborn.

"I am merely altering the coats," Betsy murmured, hoping the woman did not inquire the names of the British officers to whom the coats belonged.

"I will tell my husband about your services," Mrs. Dearborn said.

A smile flickered across Betsy's face. Perhaps there was hope for new business after all.

When all three ladies were seated, Mrs. Dearborn addressed Betsy. "Mr. Dearborn and I were unable to attend the Shippen's dinner party the other evening but when Anne told me you were wearing one of the most beautiful gowns there, I decided we should come and see you. My niece has been invited to a ball in New York City in honor of General Howe and she is in dire need of a new frock."

Miss Olsen smiled shyly while Betsy's heart pounded over the prospect of garnering such a lucrative commission.

"Anne attempted to describe your gown to me, Mrs. Ross. If it's no trouble, I would very much like to see it."

"Of course." Betsy sprang to her feet and led the way upstairs to the sitting room where her gray silk gown was displayed on a wooden tailor's form. Both women exclaimed over the fine fabric and the design, however upon spotting the French Fashion dolls, Mrs. Dearborn positively flew into raptures.

"Oh, my dear!" She held up one of the dolls. "If you could make a gown half as stunning as this, I am persuaded Anne's young man will propose the instant he sees her!" She turned a smile upon her niece. "We must tempt him beyond all endurance the night of the ball, my dear. I have decided your gown must be flaming scarlet, to match his coat."

Miss Olsen turned to Betsy. "Might you have scarlet silk on hand, Mrs. Ross?"

"Indeed, I do." Betsy led them back downstairs to her shop where several dozen ells of fabric in a variety of colors leant against the wall.

After the women had chosen the fabric, Betsy sketched a design for the dress, incorporating ideas from both the Fashion Dolls and those suggested by Mrs. Dearborn. The ladies then decided on trim and lace for the gown, and Betsy took Miss Olsen's measurements. After agreeing upon a date for the first fitting, both women expressed delight over discovering Betsy right here in Philadelphia and wearing pleased smiles, took their leave.

Exhaling with relief, Betsy headed back to the parlor and flung herself onto the settee. *Dear God in Heaven, François's plan was working exactly as he predicted!* Although, she expected the two scarlet coats draped over the chairs in the parlor had gone a long way toward forwarding the notion that she was a *bona fide* Loyalist. She could hardly wait to tell Joseph of her good fortune.

CHAPTER 12

Sarah came to see Betsy one afternoon, declaring she'd received a letter from her husband telling her that he was quartered in New York City with Henry Knox's regiment. The sight of the British officer's red coats in Betsy's parlor gave Sarah pause but after Betsy explained how they came to be there, Sarah expressed her delight that Captain Ashburn had called again.

Sewing on the scarlet ball gown, Betsy told her sister about her new commission and mentioned that Miss Olsen would be arriving within the hour for her first fitting. When Sarah offered to help, Betsy assured her that all that remained was to baste together the side seams of the bodice, so Sarah began to read aloud parts of her husband's letter.

"William says the troops are in a quandary wondering from which direction the British will strike and that British warships continue to come. *'I counted eight ships one day, ten the next and twenty-five only yesterday. Commander Knox saw a swarm of them this morning and said as best he could make out, there are now upwards of one hundred British warships in New York harbor. We are so close to them that at times we can hear the soldiers on board talking. One evening last week, after the Watch had called out the hour and declared all was well, we heard a British soldier on board ship reply that by this time tomorrow evening that would not be the case. I don't believe a single one of us slept a wink that night. Commander Knox says that for a certainty the British fleet has absolute control of the waterways.'"*

"Oh, dear," Betsy murmured. "That sounds quite distressing."

"William says that General Lee maintains that whoever commands the sea, commands the town. William says the troops are busy digging trenches and building mud embankments to protect themselves from an enemy attack, which they daily expect. *'Both Staten Island and Long Island are Loyalist strongholds. In addition to scores of British soldiers in the city, armed Loyalists hide in the swamps of Long Island and attack us without provocation. With so many Loyalists abroad, the potential for conspiracy and sabotage is all too real; so no one is to be trusted.'* "

Betsy's brow furrowed. Apparently spies lurked everywhere. She hadn't said a word to Sarah about François's plan that *she* spy on the Loyalist ladies who came to her shop and she had no intention of doing so.

"William says frightened rebels are deserting in droves, most stealing away during the night, taking their muskets and as much gunpowder as they can carry. One man lugged home a cannon ball which he meant to give to his mother to grind mustard seed."

"Why, I cannot imagine!" Betsy looked askance.

"He says many of the deserting soldiers simply change sides, that the rebels are so hungry, they willingly trade information for food. *'We survive on half a cup of rice a day and a thimbleful of vinegar.'* Oh, Betsy, I weep every time I read those words. If only I could get food to my poor, dear husband."

"I, as well, feel heartsick for our fighting men."

Sniffing back tears, Sarah resumed reading. *"'Scores have perished from dysentery. I read in the New York Post that General John Tomson, who was sent north to set things straight in Canada, has succumbed to smallpox.'"* Sarah paused. "I truly fear for my husband's life now, and not just from the fighting. If only he would come home."

"William would never desert his regiment." Betsy continued to sew, her needle flying in and out of the scarlet silk with speed and accuracy. "He is too fine a man to act in so cowardly a fashion."

"I suppose it is encouraging that despite a lack of food, he continues to thrive." Sarah's gaze scanned down the page. "He says that even after the rebel troops had positioned one hundred cannon about the city, they had to station patrols to guard them as the Loyalists, who've been promised cash rewards for doing so, sneak up at night and either sabotage the guns by packing mud into the mouths, or they steal them."

Betsy looked up. John, indeed, had the right of it when he declared how important it was to guard both day and night the muskets and ammunition stored in the Dock Street warehouse.

"William says that when Commander Knox realized there was an acute shortage of artillerymen, he elevated William to command those that remained. So," Sarah sighed, "at least, my husband is no longer digging trenches . . . with no food in his belly." The pages of the letter fell to her lap. "I will be so glad when this dreadful war is over."

"We all pray for an end to it."

"Are you certain I can do nothing to help you, Betsy?"

"Umm . . ." That her Loyalist client would soon be arriving suddenly dawned upon Betsy. "I daresay it would be a good idea to put away your letter, Sarah, and please say nothing of it when the ladies arrive. After all, they are Loyalists."

Sarah sat up straighter. "Oh, I hadn't realized. Your Miss Olsen is the enemy."

* * * * *

"Why, it's lovely, Mrs. Ross! You look beautiful, Anne!"

"I do look beautiful." Miss Olsen preened before the looking glass.

From the corner of her eye, Betsy caught sight of Sarah standing in the doorway, her pale lips a thin line of disapproval as she looked on.

"Scarlet quite becomes you, my dear. I'll wager your captain will propose the minute he sees you in that gown!" Mrs. Dearborn reached to tug at the neckline. "Can we not make it a tad bit lower?"

Betsy withdrew a pin from the pincushion strapped to her wrist. Tiny scissors hung from a chatelaine on the bodice of her frock. "Indeed, we can, but . . . are you certain?"

"You are certain you want your captain to take notice of you, are you not, Anne?"

"Well, I-I suppose just a tad bit lower wouldn't hurt, would it?"

"Absolutely not!" her aunt exclaimed.

After Betsy had turned down the neckline and pinned it, Mrs. Dearborn, talking non-stop all the while, helped her niece carefully remove the unfinished garment. Handing it to Betsy, she assisted her niece into her own clothing. "When you are presentable, dear, I am sure Mrs. Ross will offer us a nice cup of tea and you can read your letter. You do have English tea; do you not, Mrs. Ross? But, of course, you do." She directed a conspiratorial look at Betsy. "Only our Patriot counterparts are obliged to brew their tea from bitter-tasting raspberry leaves."

Betsy darted a rueful look at her sister. "Sarah, dear, would you put on the kettle, please?"

A quarter hour later, all four women were seated below stairs in Betsy's parlor, each sipping precious black tea from Betsy's precious china teacups.

"Now, then," Mrs. Dearborn said after taking only a small sip of her tea, then setting the cup aside. "You must read your letter, Anne. To be sure Mrs. Ross and her sister are as hungry as your uncle and I were for news from our brave young men."

Betsy noted Sarah's hard gaze trained upon the older woman.

Miss Olsen pulled several folded up sheets of paper from her reticule. "'*My very dear Anne.*' Oh." Her lashes fluttering, she looked down. "I-I suppose I needn't read *all* of it."

"Skip to the part about the war, dear. Unless a woman has a son, or husband, at the front, which I assume neither Mrs. Ross, nor her sister do, we've no other way to receive first-hand news from our soldiers." She cast a gaze at the sister's simple gray gowns. "I daresay you Quakers have the right of it. To refuse to fight is the only sensible choice. If you cannot discern which parts to read, dear, I shall have no trouble. There are no sweet words meant for me." Laughing, she fairly snatched the letter from the hands of her timid niece.

" '*We enjoy very comfortable accommodations here in New York City and are surrounded by generous folk who supply us with plenty to eat and lavishly entertain us.*' " Mrs. Dearborn glanced up. "I understand concerts and plays have not been left off in New York City, more's the pity for us." She turned back to the letter. " '*We are actually experiencing greater luxury here than we have since the onset of the hostilities with fresh meat aplenty, milk, eggs, butter, the plumpest vegetables and the sweetest pastries.*' "

Betsy's heart plummeted. Casting an anxious look at her sister, she noted moisture already flooding Sarah's pale blue eyes.

"'*News of the Patriot's Declaration of Independence greatly amused us and served only to underscore the impertinence of these poor misguided people. Their leader, the rebel farmer, is too languid by half and takes action only when he deems it necessary to defend himself which clearly tells us he is far too cowardly to launch a frontal attack; therefore we are persuaded that to squash the Yankee psalm-singers will be little more than child's play.'* " Mrs. Dearborn laughed. "Your captain is such a clever fellow, Anne." She resumed reading. " '*Hardly a day passes without a score of Patriot deserters turning up to entertain us with their tales of woe. The boys attempt to gain our trust with snippets of information but there is no believing the deluded wretches. We reward them with a bit of food, and then either shoot them or . . .'* "

Betsy heard Sarah's squeak of alarm and squirmed when her sister suddenly fled the room.

" '*. . . transport them to a prison hulk where in less than a fortnight they die of disease or starvation. It is said that our troops outnumber the combined population of the two largest cities on the continent, New York and Philadelphia. The rebel army don't have a clue that above seventeen thousand German soldiers are now on their way to these shores, which means that we will surely have done with this bothersome rebellion before winter sets in. I think of you every day, my dearest darlin. . .'* " Mrs. Dearborn handed the pages back to her niece. "The remainder of the missive is meant only for you, my dear."

Betsy exhaled the tight breath she'd been holding. "Thank you for . . . sharing your letter with us, Miss Olsen."

Mrs. Dearborn gathered up her things. "When shall we come again, Mrs. Ross? Anne leaves for New York in a fortnight."

Betsy rose to accompany the ladies back through the house. In the corridor, she caught a glimpse of Sarah hovering in the shadows. The women departed after agreeing upon a date in which Miss Olsen could return for her final fitting and Betsy hurried back to the parlor, expecting to find Sarah weeping uncontrollably. Instead, she found her sister pacing back and forth before the hearth.

"We must get word to William at once! I am certain he does not know that seventeen thousand German soldiers are headed this way. It is our duty to alert the men, Betsy." Her eyes were wild. "If Miss Olson can travel to New York City, then, why cannot I?"

"Sarah, I own that the news about the German soldiers is distressing, but I hardly think it advisable that you rush off to New York to warn the Patriot army that the Germans are coming."

"You and I could both go! George could go with us. Father might even agree to come along. And we shall take food!" she added fervently.

"Do sit down, Sarah. Oh, my, after all that, Mrs. Dearborn hardly touched her tea."

"Give it to me!" Sarah cried. She snatched up the cup and flung the contents through the opened window. "There. If it were not one of your precious china teacups, I'd toss it out as well. How you can be civil to that horrid woman, Betsy, I do not know."

"Do sit down, Sarah, you seem quite overset."

"That seventeen thousand German soldiers are on their way to kill my husband does indeed overset me! I can neither sit still, nor can I be silent."

"Very well, then. I shall endeavor to get word to . . . to Joseph," Betsy offered, wondering if she should not, instead, get word to François. Surely this was precisely the sort of information he would want to pass along to the Secret Committee of Correspondence.

Sarah turned a wide-eyed look on her sister. "Perhaps Joseph would agree to come along. You must ask him."

"Well, I-I . . . perhaps, there is another way, Sarah."

"What do you mean *another* way?"

"Perhaps there is another way to warn the rebel army that the Germans are coming."

* * * * *

It took the rest of that day and into the evening before Betsy managed to calm her sister and she did so only by promising to appeal to Joseph for help. But, bright and early the next morning, before Betsy had determined how to reach Joseph when she hadn't the least notion where he was at the moment, Sarah appeared on her doorstep with another plan in mind.

"You must read this!" Sarah instructed, hurrying after Betsy back downstairs where she'd been eating her breakfast. The minute Betsy sat down, Sarah thrust a folded up newspaper beneath her nose.

"What is it?" Betsy glanced at the paper whilst chewing up the oatmeal in her mouth.

"On my way home last evening, I stopped at the newsstand and purchased copies of every single Philadelphia and New York newspaper I could find. I sat up long into the night pouring through the news pages, and only this morning discovered this in the *New York Post*. I am persuaded it is the very solution to our problem."

Squinting at the tiny print, Betsy read aloud: " *'IF the YOUTH who left LEXINGTON with the rebel army above one year ago can remember that he ever had a Mother, be informed he will soon be deprived of that blessing except he immediately writes particulars, or personally appears before her.'* "

"Not that," Sarah cried. *"There!"* A finger tapped lower down in the column of print. *" 'YANKEE DODDLE to REDCOATS – SURRENDER or DIE!'* "

Still not taking her sister's meaning, Betsy gazed up at her agitated sister.

"We must place an advertisement in the *Post!*" Sarah exclaimed. "William said in his letter that he read the *New York Post*. We can tell him, and every other Patriot soldier, that the German soldiers are coming!"

"Oh-h-h." Betsy fully understood her sister's urgency in wanting to warn her husband of this fresh and imminent danger. If she had known of the peril John faced on that horrible day last January, she would have done everything in her power to warn him.

"I haven't a clue how to go about placing an advertisement in the newspaper," Sarah added. "Do you suppose the *New York Post* has an agent here?"

"Perhaps Dr. Franklin could help," Betsy suggested. "He publishes a newspaper."

Sarah's countenance brightened. "We must go to him at once, Betsy. Do make haste!"

Entering Dr. Franklin's noisy newspaper shop that morning the girls spotted him removing printed pages from the rack of one of the clacking presses. Before the ladies told him the nature of their visit, Franklin took the precaution of ushering them into his private office and closing the door. Betsy was grateful when the kindly gentleman exhibited no signs of bemusement when Sarah outlined what Betsy realized must seem an unconventional solution to their problem.

"To place an advertisement in the newspaper is, indeed, a unique method of distributing information of this sort," Franklin remarked, "but I suppose it is as good a way as any."

"Then you will help us?" Sarah asked anxiously.

"Indeed, I will help you, Mrs. Donaldson." Franklin nodded. "But I beg your leave to allow me to decide how best to handle the matter."

"But, my husband and the entire rebel army are unaware that seventeen thousand German soldiers mean to raise arms against them. Does this mean that we are also now at war with Germany?"

"On the contrary, Mrs. Donaldson. We have no grievance with Germany; nor they with us. The British have merely hired Hessian soldiers to assist them in their fight."

Betsy had said little since they arrived. As Sarah frantically laid out her plan, it had occurred to Betsy that given Franklin's knowledge of covert activity, he no doubt knew exactly how, and to whom, to pass along this important information. She touched her sister's elbow. "We really should allow Dr. Franklin to resume his work, Sarah."

"But . . . you will . . . when shall I expect to read the advertisement in the *Post,* sir? Quite soon, I hope. The men must be warned at once, sir; at once!"

Franklin smiled. "Would it put your mind at ease, Mrs. Donaldson, if I told you that General Washington himself will be made privy to this information before the day is out?"

"Oh, yes, sir! I am vastly relieved, sir. I confess I did not sleep a wink last night."

Franklin looked past Sarah to Betsy. "Take your sister home, Mrs. Ross, and see that she gets a nap. I daresay some warm milk is in order." He ushered them to the door. "I am grateful to you ladies for your diligence. I am certain General Washington will be quite pleased, as well."

"I am persuaded we did the right thing, Betsy," Sarah declared as the two walked back down High Street that hot summer morning.

"Indeed, we did," Betsy agreed, thinking that because they'd told Dr. Franklin, there was now no need for her to get word to François, which, she had to admit, was in itself rather a relief.

CHAPTER 13

When the shadows lengthened that afternoon, Betsy, weary of stitching on Miss Olsen's ball gown, decided to stretch her limbs by walking down to the wharf to see if Joseph's ship was still in the harbor. Because he had not yet returned to collect his mending, Betsy was growing a trifle worried. The cool breeze off the water made the walk all the more pleasant. A few horse-drawn wagons lumbered along the cobbles and from somewhere Betsy heard the call of peddlers reluctant to give up whilst they still had something left on their carts to sell.

"Fresh wegtables, ratish, vaterkress, lettis, und peas!"

Her lips pursed. Yesterday she might have smiled at the farmer's quaint German accent. Today it sent shivers up her spine. She hoped Sarah had managed to put aside her worries over the German soldiers and rest a spell this afternoon.

"Good day, Miz Ross!" A woman sweeping her doorstep hailed Betsy. "I saw ye steppin' out th' other night. Looked pretty as a picture, ye did!"

"Thank you, Mrs. Burton." Betsy paused.

"Quite a fine carriage yer young man come for ye in. Too fine for the likes o' me!" With a laugh, the woman returned to her sweeping.

Betsy smiled at her youngsters, a flaxen-haired boy and girl, playing nearby. A pang of regret stabbed her. She and John had dreamt of having children one day. Now, she wondered if she would ever marry again and be blessed with little ones of her own.

Pushing down painful memories of the promising life she'd once had with John, she crossed Front Street and approached the wharf. Despite the late hour, the quay still teemed with activity. As on the night she and Toby were here, dozens of multi-sailed ships fought for space in the harbor. Ranged in close to one another, she wondered what kept the sails and rigging from becoming entangled. The snapping of sails, the thud of wood against wood, and the ever-present pounding of waves against the pier assaulted her ears while the pungent stench of horse dung, fish, and brine made her want to pinch her nostrils together.

She kept to the far side of the wharf as she watched burly sailors heft chests and kegs from the dock onto waiting wagons. Whinnying horses stamped their hooves as seamen hurled heavy containers over their backs. Lifting her gaze above the din and confusion, Betsy scanned the waterfront for . . . what? Now that she was here, she hadn't a clue how to differentiate one ship from another. Joseph's bark would likely not have a banner stretched across the mast proclaiming it the *"Swallow"*. Thinking perhaps the name of the ship was inscribed somewhere along the bow, she moved from her place of refuge across the cobbled thoroughfare to the pier. And instantly halted.

Ten yards ahead she spotted Joseph speaking with . . . *François!* Her stomach muscles tightened. *What could they be discussing?* Ducking her head, she hurried away and in minutes found herself back on Front Street. Perhaps she'd stop at Joseph's aunt's home instead. If need be, she could even deliver Joseph's mended clothing and the flag there. In minutes, she reached the widow Ashburn's lovely home shaded by tall oak trees.

An elderly housekeeper confirmed that Mrs. Ashburn was indeed at home and directed Betsy into a drawing room facing the shady side of the house. Glancing about, Betsy recalled the many times she'd been here with

Joseph back when he was courting her. Virtually nothing had changed. The same pictures graced the walls, the same sofas and chairs sat about the chamber; the same cushions placed at intervals upon them.

When Mrs. Ashburn, a wiry woman of some sixty years with graying hair entered the room leaning upon a cane, Betsy was pleased to see that, minus the cane, she, too, looked exactly the same as she had half a decade earlier.

Mrs. Ashburn expressed delight that Betsy had called and after they warmly embraced, both took seats on a sofa overlooking the portico. In a casual manner, Betsy asked after Joseph and Mrs. Ashburn said she hadn't seen her nephew in several days and didn't know whether or not he was even in the city. Betsy was still vastly annoyed over spotting Joseph speaking with François. *What were the men talking about? What was Joseph keeping from her?*

"How fares your husband, dear?"

Upon hearing the unexpected question, a rush of moisture sprang to Betsy's eyes. "M-my husband passed away in January, Mrs. Ashburn."

"I am so sorry, my dear. I had not heard. Winter was especially deadly this year. I assume it was the influenza."

"No." Betsy shook her head. "John died of injuries he received in a warehouse explosion. Perhaps you did not hear." *But Joseph knew of it.*

Mrs. Ashburn's brow furrowed. "Might you be referring to the explosion that occurred the night of that dreadful blizzard?"

Betsy's head jerked up. "Yes. John's friend said the warehouse simply burst into flames. John had been on guard duty that day and Tom Hull was coming to take his turn."

"I do recall hearing of it." Mrs. Ashburn nodded thoughtfully. "What did the authorities make of it?"

"Nothing," Betsy replied sharply. "So far as I know, it was declared an accident. No one ever came to ask John what happened that night."

"Hmmm."

Betsy's eyes remained glued to the older woman's face. *Did she know something about the explosion? Had Joseph not told Betsy everything* he *knew about it?*

"I recall Pete, my man-of-all-work, mentioning something peculiar about that night. Pete insisted on returning home that evening rather than staying the night here. Said his grandson was ill. At any rate, the next morning, Pete said that on his way home, the snow was blowing so hard he stopped in at Mr. Rockaway's Pub for a quick nip. Pete said a young fellow in the tavern seemed quite agitated, kept peering out the window, couldn't seem to sit still. Pete said that when a lull came in the snowfall, he rose to leave, as did the young man. But once outdoors, the fellow seemed confused, asked Pete which way to Dock Street, said the blizzard had him turned around. Pete noticed the fellow was carrying a package, which he said he needed to deliver that night. When the Watch came along, Pete said the pair of them walked off together. He assumed the Watch had offered to show the fellow the way to Dock Street."

Betsy's nerves tensed. "Might I please speak with Pete, Mrs. Ashburn?"

The woman's gray head shook. "Pete succumbed to influenza a few days later. Poor soul. His illness came on so quickly and he went so suddenly. I warned him not to go out that night."

"What of his grandson? Perhaps he might recall what his grandfather said about the man with the package. His height, the color of his hair, anything."

"Pete's grandson marched off to war within a week of his

grandfather's passing. Haven't heard a word from the boy since. I am so sorry, dear."

"I never believed the explosion was an accident." Betsy's breath grew ragged. "I am certain that fire was set a-purpose."

"What of the night watchman? Pete said the two of them walked off together. Perhaps the Watch could tell you . . . "

"His frozen body was found floating in the river the next morning."

"Oh, my, goodness," Mrs. Ashburn gasped. "To be sure, it does sound quite suspicious. Pete may have actually spoken with the man responsible for the explosion."

"And, ultimately John's death," Betsy exclaimed. "I never believed the warehouse could simply burst into flames on its own. Pete said the man was carrying a package?"

Of a sudden, the bell on the front door jangled and before the summons was answered, both women heard the door open and then close. In seconds, Joseph strode into the room, a cheery grin on his face. "My two favorite women in the same place."

A mix of emotions churned within Betsy. "Hello, Joseph."

"Where have you been keeping yourself, young man?" his aunt wanted to know, although a smile softened her wrinkled countenance.

"I just came from your shop, Betsy. Went to retrieve my uniforms and flag. I expect you have 'em ready by now, eh?"

"Yes." She choked back the questions burning in her mind.

Mrs. Ashburn's smile traveled from her nephew to Betsy. "It's good to see the pair of you together again."

The threesome fell to discussing other things and before long Mrs. Ashburn summoned the housekeeper to inform her there would be three for dinner that night.

Soon after the meal, Joseph and Betsy took their leave, but not before Betsy promised Mrs. Ashburn she would call again soon.

"Seeing you lifted my aunt's spirits considerably," Joseph remarked as the two of them advanced to the flagway. "Makes me glad I was out of pocket. Aunt Ashburn has missed you."

"I will indeed call again. I feel as if I no longer have a mother and I am quite fond of your aunt."

Lamps on the street corners and a silvery slice of moon cast shadows on the cobbled street. When Joseph asked Betsy how she fared, she coolly told him about her lucrative new commission from the Loyalist ladies. She also told him what his aunt had just said regarding the warehouse explosion.

"I had no idea Aunt Ashburn knew anything of it," Joseph marveled. "But, then, I never asked. So, I take it you've not seen the Frenchman."

Unable to contain her upset a second longer, Betsy exploded. "No, I have not. But *you* have! I saw you talking to François earlier, Joseph. What were you talking about?"

He exhaled. "I wasn't going to say anything."

"I thought I could trust you, Joseph. What were you and François . . .?"

"I didn't want to upset you."

"Well, as you can clearly see, that you are keeping something from me *does* upset me."

He held up both hands as if to forestall further assaults. "Very well, then. My first mate, MacGregor said the Frenchie had approached him wanting to know where we were headed. The Frenchie said he'd give us a fair price for any weapons we managed to confiscate from the British."

"François asked about *weapons?* Why? What did you say? Surely you did not strike a bargain with . . . "

"Hell, no! I told him . . . well, I'd rather not repeat what I told him, but I don't believe he'll be approaching another member of my crew again." Joseph took her arm and they continued to walk, although in silence.

Betsy longed to believe him. "Will you be bringing back weapons?" she asked gently.

"That's my plan. Word is two British barks are en route from England loaded with supplies for the army. I intend to take 'em on"

"But there are *two* ships!" Betsy cried.

"There'll be two of us." Joseph grinned. "A friend of mine has also fitted out his ship. Between us, the Brits don't stand a chance."

"Oh, Joseph, do be careful." Betsy suddenly realized those were the last words she'd spoken to John before he left home that fateful day.

Upon reaching her doorstep, Betsy unlocked the door and Joseph followed her inside. She did not want to believe he was lying to her. She lit a candle and upon reaching the parlor, set it down and went straightaway to fetch the scarlet coats and flag. She'd known Joseph more than half her life and he'd always been truthful with her. If she had not fallen in love with John Ross and married him, she'd likely be wed to Joseph now. She had no reason not to trust him.

"I found a bit of gold braid in my cupboard and added it to one of the coats." She held it up for him to see. "From a distance, it might appear the wearer has attained quite an impressive rank."

Joseph laughed. "Looking out for my welfare, eh, lass?"

Betsy smiled and when Joseph reached to catch her about the waist and pull her close, she hesitated only slightly. She *so* wanted to trust him.

Gazing warmly down into her shuttered eyes, Joseph dipped his head and without a word, settled his lips upon hers. The kiss was gentle. Although Betsy fought the warm feelings stirring within her, at length, she relaxed and twined both arms up around his neck. For a long moment, they stood thusly together while nearby the shadows cast by the candlelight danced upon the painted yellow wall.

"Promise me you'll be careful, too, Betsy. I've no right to say it, but I wish you'd leave off seeing the Frenchman altogether. I don't want him, or any other man save me, coming around."

Betsy laid her head upon the seaman's strong chest. "If my association with François continues it will simply be to learn whatever I can that will expose John's killer."

"I wish you could let that go. Nothing you learn now will bring John, or Toby, back."

She gazed into his worried hazel eyes. "What I learned from your aunt today makes me more determined than ever to uncover the truth. The warehouse explosion was not an accident, Joseph. Someone set that fire a-purpose. The same someone who killed my husband."

Exhaling a resigned breath, Joseph drew away, and instead, took her hand. Together, they walked through the darkened house to the door. Lamplight filtering through the shop window illuminated his rugged features as he bent again to kiss her cheek. "When I return, love, perhaps I can help you find the answers you seek."

"Promise me you *will* return, Joseph." She patted the bundle he carried, the flag wrapped around the scarlet coats so as to make them less visible. "And that's an order, Captain."

"Hey, matey, from the looks of my uniform, I far outrank you."

They both laughed. As he skipped down the steps, Betsy stood in the doorway to watch him saunter off down the street. She did trust Joseph and she did not regret allowing him to kiss her tonight. In her heart, she also did not believe John would fault her for the small stirrings of warmth she was beginning to feel for another man.

Much, much later that night, lingering fears at the back of Betsy's mind worked their way to the surface; fears about how very *quickly* Joseph had appeared at her door the night the intruder held a knife to her throat. And that it was *he* who'd pointed out the secret compartment in the little box. Odd in itself was that Joseph had suddenly appeared at her door at all, after so many years away.

No, she chided herself. She was being silly. If Joseph had wanted the box or what was inside it, she would have willingly given it to him the first time he came to see her. He wouldn't have had to break into her home or threaten her. It was François she must be wary of, not Joseph. If she were to learn anything about spying, or subterfuge, or sabotage, it would come from François.

However, as she was drifting off to sleep, another question rose to the surface of her mind.

Why did François now suddenly wish to purchase weapons?

CHAPTER 14

A few days later, Sarah came to thank Betsy again for taking her to see Dr. Franklin. When Betsy said she was certain he had delivered the message to General Washington, Sarah remarked that she would not rest easy until she heard from William and knew for certain that he was still alive. Seating herself in Betsy's parlor, where Betsy was busy sewing, Sarah said conversationally, "I happened to see François at the market yesterday. He is such a charming young man, and so very kind."

Although it was a struggle not to protest, Betsy said nothing and continued to sew as Sarah went on.

"He was helping his little mother negotiate the cost of her goods. The poor woman's English is woefully lacking. I told him you were making a ball gown for Miss Olsen and that it was every bit as lovely as the gown you made for yourself."

Betsy glanced up. "Did you mention to him anything about the contents of Miss Olsen's letter?"

"I told him I was here when the young lady and her aunt came for a fitting and that they shared a letter with us, yes; although I mentioned nothing that was said. Rachel was with me. I did not wish to spoil the day by becoming . . . overset. I must say our little sister was quite taken with François. She thought him very handsome."

"You introduced Rachel to François?"

"The gentleman and I were conversing. It would have been rude not to make them known to one another. Is there some reason why I should not have?"

"No, I . . . suppose not. How is Rachel faring? She must be quite the young lady now." A trace of sadness crept into Betsy's tone. She missed her younger siblings, Hannah, Rachel and George.

"Indeed, she is. As I mentioned before, she favors you, the same chestnut hair, only she wears hers loose and flowing down her back. Her eyes are the same brilliant blue as yours and her skin every bit as lustrous. Although not yet sixteen, she appears a good deal older. Her figure is . . . well, Rachel is quite developed for her age. And I daresay, a bit too flirtatious for her own good."

"Oh, dear," Betsy murmured. Given her tender years, Rachel could easily be taken in by François's flowery phrases. "Considering how I disappointed our parents, I expect they will endeavor to keep a tighter rein on Rachel."

"Indeed," Sarah agreed with a laugh.

A half hour or so later, Sarah said she must pop off.

"Sarah." Betsy followed her sister into the corridor.

"Yes, dear, what is it?"

Betsy hesitated. She wanted to say that it would be unwise for Rachel to see François again, but perhaps if her parents kept a tight rein on their youngest daughter, the warning would be for naught. "Please tell Rachel that I miss her terribly and that I would love to see her again."

"Rachel misses you, as well, Betsy." Sarah kissed her sister's flushed cheek.

"According to our agreement, *madame,* you should have got word to me that a pair of Loyalist ladies had called upon you," François Dubeau angrily declared.

Betsy and the Frenchman were alone in her parlor; Betsy on the sofa, François glaring down upon her from a superior position before the hearth. That a storm was brewing behind his dark eyes had not escaped her notice.

"I had every intention of telling you last evening at the Fighting Quaker meeting," Betsy said defensively, "but you were not there."

"I have left off attending those radical gatherings and I daresay, you should, as well."

"I have no intention of leaving off . . ."

"I *forbid* you to attend another meeting of that rebel group!"

Betsy's eyes widened. "You *forbid* me?" Anger knotted her stomach.

After a few tense seconds, François cleared his throat and began afresh. "Forgive, me, *madame.* What I meant to say is that to forward your ruse as being sympathetic to the Loyalist cause, it would behoove you to leave off associating with known Patriots. To gain the trust of those we wish to learn from is paramount."

"I see." The smallest whit of Betsy's anger dissolved. "You could have said as much rather than ordering me about as if I were a child."

François took a seat on a wing chair adjacent to the sofa. "Your sister, Mrs. Donaldson, mentioned that she was here the day the Loyalist woman read from a letter she had received from a British officer in New York." When Betsy did not reply at once, he prompted, "Well? Was there anything of import in the letter?"

Betsy's lips thinned. Given his surly attitude, she had half a mind to reply: *'No, nothing at all.'* But, given his surly attitude, she expected that to not dangle some tantalizing morsel of intelligence before him would serve only to ramp up his ire. The two of them were in her home alone. After dark. With Joseph away, and therefore no hope of him coming to her rescue, should she require rescuing, she felt somewhat vulnerable. In a tight voice, she said, "The writer spoke mainly of the British officer's fine accommodations and that . . ." her voice trailed off.

"And, that . . . *what?*"

"That a goodly number of Patriot soldiers were deserting. The writer said the rebels were eager to trade information for food." She rushed on. "Which was quite distressing to Sarah. You see, her husband—"

"What more did the letter say?" A hard gaze pinned her.

Betsy paused. Apparently her reluctance to reveal more merely told him there *was* more, and that for some reason she was choosing to withhold it.

"Did Miss Olsen's letter say anything regarding troop movements, or additional British warships arriving in New York harbor?" He leaned forward, an expectant look on his admittedly handsome face.

Growing more uncomfortable by the second, Betsy had no idea how François would react when he learned that she'd given the information to Dr. Franklin instead of him. Squirming, she said, "Now that I think on it, there was a brief mention of . . . additional troops arriving."

"Was a number mentioned?"

Betsy sprang to her feet. "Must you persist in badgering me?"

He, too, stood, which meant he was again towering over her. "I am not badgering you, *madame*. Instead of working with me as you agreed, you seem bent upon withholding whatever information you overheard." Scowling, he grasped her arm.

Her blue eyes snapped fire. "Unhand me this instant!"

Although his broad chest heaved, he did loosen his grip. "By all that is right, *madame*, I could insist that you hand over a portion of whatever you earn for making that vulgar scarlet gown." A scornful gaze darted toward the fluff of red silk draped over a chair. "Were it not for me, you would not have received the commission."

"I find your attitude intolerable, sir. You appear to find Loyalists *and* rebels beneath you."

"Colonists *are* beneath me." His upper lip curled. "Provincials, the lot of you."

"And yet you claim to be one of us."

He ignored her. "I came prepared tonight to give you a gold guinea merely for telling me what you learned from the Loyalist woman's *lettre!* Instead, you renege on our agreement. Why? Because *you* believe you are better than I? *Pah!"*

Betsy rubbed the red place on her arm where he had grasped her. "I am not reneging. As it turns out, I have already passed along what I learned from Miss Olsen's letter."

His brows snapped together. "How dare you make an agreement behind my back with another sp . . . with another man."

"I told Dr. Franklin."

"And who gave you permission to do that?"

"*Permission?*" She blinked. "I do not need *your* permission to do anything, sir. I am free to do whatever I please." She knew she was making the Frenchman angry but tonight he was vexing her beyond measure.

"Did Dr. Franklin compensate you?"

"I did not *sell* the information to him. I freely volunteered it."

"*Quelle stupide!* I am fast losing patience with you, *madame!*" He moved toward the door. "I no longer care to know what you learned from the *sotte mademoiselle*. No doubt, it was nothing of import."

Although incensed by the disagreeable Frenchman, Betsy did not want him to leave. In all likelihood, she would never have another opportunity to learn anything regarding Philadelphia's spy underworld. With effort, she swallowed her pride. "Forgive me, François. I-I should have come straight to you. My sister was quite overset after hearing the distressing news and to placate her, I suggested we consult with Dr. Franklin."

"Why did you not tell me you were *ami* . . . a friend of Dr. Franklin?"

"Dr. Franklin attends the same church where John and I worshipped."

He strode back to the chair he had vacated. "So, you are aware that Franklin is a spymaster, that he runs agents, *oui?*"

Because Betsy did not think it wise to further anger him, she replied, "I am aware the brilliant Dr. Franklin has many areas of expertise."

"*Bien sûr.*"

Of a sudden, Betsy realized that when angered, François reverted to his native language. Tonight he had used more French phrases than she had ever before heard from him.

He held up a hand. "*Pas de problème.* Since you have already turned over this bit of information, there is no need now to write a report and send it through . . . *proper* channels. However, *madame,*" he pinned her with an icy glare. "Do you, or do you not, wish to continue our association?"

"I do wish to help the Patriot Cause, François. Truly I do."

He flicked a bit of lint from the velvet cuff of his coat. "It is no matter to me. Given your . . . unique profession, I merely thought that you would *souvnet* . . . that is, be in a position to overhear sensitive matters being . . . *discuter.*"

Although he seemed to be making a concerted effort to control his anger, from his continued use of French, Betsy surmised his efforts on that head were failing miserably. He was as irritated with her now as ever. Apparently he had hoped she would be able to supply him with a great deal of information and did not wish to dismiss her any more than she wished to break all ties with him.

In a calm tone, she said, "François, if you will tell me exactly what I must do when I have information to pass along, I give my word that in future I will do precisely as you say. How exactly am I to get word to you, sir?"

From his coat pocket, he withdrew a scrap of paper. "*C'est* . . . this is my direction. When you have a report, *madame,* send a message to my home and I will come for it. You are a woman and I have no wish to put you in harm's way, therefore I will not ask you to venture beyond your *domicile.*"

"I appreciate your concern for my safety."

Rising, he strode toward the door. "If I am out of the city, you will deliver your report to another committee member. *Au revoir, madame.*"

Betsy followed him through the darkened house and after bidding him good night, closed the door and secured the bolt. A part of her hoped that no other person of the Loyalist persuasion ever again visited her shop so that she would never again be obliged to entertain the annoying Frenchman. The one measure of relief she felt came from his remark that he did not wish to put her in harm's way. Whether or not that sentiment was true remained to be seen.

CHAPTER 15

Early the following week, Mrs. Dearborn and Miss Olsen arrived for the latter's final fitting. When the gown fit perfectly as it was, the ladies insisted upon leaving with it. As Mrs. Dearborn made no mention of discharging the vast sum she owed Betsy for making the gown, Betsy was reluctant to let it go. Watching the shiny black Dearborn coach rumble away, the scarlet confection clutched in the older woman's arms, she wondered how she'd go about collecting such an immense sum of money? John had always taken care of that side of their business.

The next morning, when Mrs. Dearborn's carriage again drew up to the curb, Betsy was relieved when upon stepping into the foyer, the woman promptly handed her a pouch jingling with coins. Miss Olsen, she gaily announced, was already on her way to New York City and by week's end would dance the night away in a whirl of scarlet finery.

"Make no mistake, my niece will return to Philadelphia with a ring on her finger!" she declared with high satisfaction.

Smiling, Betsy was also pleased when Mrs. Dearborn suddenly remembered she had brought along some mending and sent her footman to fetch it. Although the woman told her there was no hurry to complete the task, once she departed, Betsy turned to it at once, as she had no other work to do. The following afternoon, the simple project complete, she decided to walk to Mrs. Dearborn's home to deliver the garment and perhaps collect the small sum due for it, as well.

While awaiting Mrs. Dearborn to join her in the spacious withdrawing room to which she'd been shown, Betsy became aware of the deep rumble of men's voices coming from an adjacent chamber. Cocking an ear, she distinctly overheard one of the men declare that British Admiral Lord Richard Howe, General William Howe's brother, would soon be arriving in New York harbor accompanied by upwards of one hundred warships and thousands more reinforcement troops. Realizing the significance of what she had inadvertently overheard, Betsy's cheeks grew hot and her pulse began to pound.

"Good afternoon, my dear!" A rustle of silk accompanied Mrs. Dearborn's shrill voice into the chamber where Betsy sat perched upon a straight-backed chair, her blue eyes round. "There was absolutely no need for you to come all this way on my account, dear! Oh, my, Mrs. Ross, you look quite flushed. Are you feeling unwell?"

"N-no, ma'am, I-I feel quite well, thank you."

"You do not look at all well to me."

After insisting that Betsy remove to a chair situated beneath an opened window, she rang for a housemaid and when the black girl appeared, instructed her to fling open additional windows and bring sustenance at once. In no time the Negro servant returned bearing a pitcher of lemon water and a plate of small sugar cakes.

"I daresay you simply overexerted yourself walking such a distance, my dear. I am persuaded you will feel better in no time. However, I will not hear of you returning home on foot. I expect my husband has concluded his business; I shall have him escort you home. I would come as well, but I am expected elsewhere this afternoon."

Mrs. Dearborn exited the room and moments later Betsy heard *her* voice coming from the adjacent chamber. Her eyes rolled skyward. To endure a ride across Philadelphia in the company of a Loyalist gentleman was the last thing she wished to do.

As it turned out, there were two gentlemen, Mr. Dearborn, a portly gentleman of some fifty years and a younger man named Mr. Tuttle, who, throughout the short journey, more than once cast an appraising eye at the pretty young lady seated across from him, her hands folded primly in her lap, her gaze fixed on a point somewhere beyond his left shoulder. As neither of the gentlemen addressed Betsy throughout the duration of the drive, she remained silent. But grew increasingly overwrought as her companions spent the entire sojourn continuing to discuss the exact numbers and anticipated arrival of fresh British troops as if she were not sitting right there taking in every word!

The men even launched into a description of the British attack the previous month on Charleston, South Carolina, remarking on how the rebels had apparently been engaged for some time preparing their "welcome" for the British. Betsy knew very well that the Charleston rebel's *welcome* had not been of a friendly nature and the outcome was so *un*friendly that the attack on Charleston had been deemed a rousing Patriot victory. What she did *not* know, until this minute, was that plans were afoot for General Clinton's defeated soldiers to also be shipped north to join General Howe in New York City. *Dear Lord, what military secrets would the men reveal next?*

That her heart was drumming so loudly in her ears by the time the open-air carriage wheeled up before her shop nearly prevented Betsy from expressing her gratitude to Mr. Dearborn for seeing her safely home. His polite response was: "I hope we did not bore you to pieces with our talk of war, Mrs. Ross."

A nervous squeak escaped Betsy before she scampered into her shop and a few seconds later, her pulse quickened again when another rap sounded at the door and the intrepid Mr. Dearborn stepped inside.

"Forgive me, Mrs. Ross. It quite slipped my mind that my wife instructed me to give you this." He dropped a few coins into Betsy's trembling palm. "Good day, ma'am."

A shaky smile wavered across Betsy's flushed face. "T-thank you, sir."

Closing the door to her shop, Betsy stood at the window and watched until the Dearborn carriage wheeled off down Mulberry Street. Then she spun around. *Pencil and paper!* She had to write down every single word she had just overheard. This would comprise her first report to the Secret Committee of Correspondence and it must be perfect!

In no time, Betsy had completed her report and as François instructed, dispatched a note to him via messenger. However, Betsy was puzzled when by eventide the Frenchman had not appeared at her door. *Had he decided to terminate their association, after all?* An image of the gold guinea he'd mentioned the other evening popped to mind, although the coin now had wings and was fluttering beyond her grasp.

Mid-morning of the following day, François's sister Minette arrived.

"My brother," the little blonde's expression was guileless, "he go to New York to attend *soiree* he say much important. He wish me to give you theeze." The missive Minette handed Betsy was impressively sealed with a dollop of red wax.

"I see," Betsy murmured. Uncertain what this new turn meant, she gazed at the sealed note and without ripping into it, slipped it into her apron pocket. "Will you join me in the parlor?"

"*Oui*." The pretty girl smiled with pleasure.

Her mind awhirl, Betsy led the way through the house. Perhaps François had truly cast her off and was using this benign method of telling her. After all, he'd said nothing of his plans to travel when last he saw her. She also wondered if the *soiree* he had journeyed to New York to attend could possibly be the same ball Miss Olsen would be attending? François said he came to this country with numerous letters of introduction in his pocket, the majority to homes of Loyalists. Was he now in New York consorting with the enemy?

Suddenly aware that the sweltering summer sun spilling through the opened window was making the small parlor feel especially close, Betsy withdrew the sealed note from her pocket, and began to fan herself with it.

"Would you care for a glass of lemon water, Minette?"

"*Oui*. Lemon water would be quite nice. *Merci*."

"I shall fetch it at once." Betsy sprang to her feet.

Below stairs in the kitchen, she wasted no time ripping into the note.

'In my absence, madame, deliver reports to: M'sieur Paul Trumbell. 47 Vandemere Lane.'

Betsy's brow furrowed. She'd expected more than a mere name and direction; an explanation, perhaps, regarding his whereabouts. Stuffing the page back into her pocket, she hastily prepared the light refreshment and carried it on a tray up the steep stairs to the parlor. Considering the anger François had displayed a few nights ago when she had not done as he asked, she must now do precisely as he said. Moreover, since the intelligence she'd overheard yesterday at the Dearborn home was of a timely nature, perhaps she should deliver her report straightaway.

Above stairs, Betsy fairly gulped down her lemonade, then mumbled an excuse to Minette about an urgent need to deliver something, and in less than a quarter hour, was on her way to Vandemere Lane. Why, she demanded of herself again, had François *suddenly* traveled to New York City? And if his decision to go had *not* come about suddenly, why had he said nothing of his plans to her the other evening? Was this, perhaps, a test to determine if she would follow his instructions without question? She recalled him saying he would not place her in harm's way therefore it did not occur to her now that she might be heading straight into danger.

Upon reaching Vandemere Lane, a winding thoroughfare, which she could not help noticing was quite near Dock Street, the location of the fateful warehouse explosion, she easily found number forty-seven and without hesitation, rapped upon the jamb of the opened doorway. Bright sunlight at her back all but obscured the interior of the cramped enclosure.

When Betsy finally caught sight of the barrel-chested man striding through the narrow building, she sucked in her breath . . . not because she recognized him, but because she'd never before beheld such a giant of a man! His neck was thick, his chest and forearms bulky; his legs the size of tree trunks. She also noticed that as he drew near enough to distinguish her features, he seemed to flinch. *What could there possibly be about her to fear?*

"M-Mr. Paul Trumbell?" Betsy pushed down her rising anxiety.

"Who's askin'?" came the brusque reply.

Her stomach muscles tightened. This area of Philadelphia, rife with dilapidated houses and abandoned buildings, was not a neighborhood she would normally frequent. Now standing toe-to-toe with one of its inhabitants, she elected not to reveal her identity and instead coolly replied, "M'sieur Dubeau asked that I deliver this to you, sir."

When the man stretched forth a hand, his fingers resembling sausages, Betsy noted that the first and middle fingers of his right hand were stained with splotches of something dark; ink, perhaps? A furtive glance past him into the interior of the building, now shaded by his large frame, revealed an assortment of pen and ink drawings tacked to the wall; drawings, which looked a good deal like maps. Paul Trumbell was a cartographer. Who, she also noted, wore a very large knife strapped to his belt.

The very second she spotted the sheathed weapon, she nodded *adieu* and without uttering a parting word, whirled around and hastened back up the street the way she'd come. Never again, not *ever*, would she agree to meet with Paul Trumbell, or allow the huge man into her home. The over-sized creature was far too unsettling and she wished never to see him again.

As she lay abed that night mulling over the events of the past two days, overhearing the men talking at the Dearborn home, carefully composing her report and delivering it, she wondered if the course she had set for herself was, indeed, wise or prudent? The more she thought about Paul Trumbell, the more it gnawed at her that she might have encountered the man before. The fellow she'd glimpsed in the alleyway when Toby was killed was quite large. She hadn't been close enough to ascertain just *how* large, but there was no question that he carried a knife. But why would Paul Trumbell kill Toby? Unless, as Dr. Franklin suggested, Toby had been acting as a courier for *both* sides and had been found out. Also, the intruder who barged into her home had wielded a knife. And he seemed quite large and was certainly muscled. Was it possible that upon seeing her today, Paul Trumbell had recognized *her?* He had definitely flinched when he saw her standing in his doorway. The little box hidden in her kindling bucket contained a map, crudely drawn, yes; but nonetheless a map. She knew of no rule that said an artist could not also be a spy . . . or a killer.

Suddenly, she sat straight up in bed. François had said Secret Committee member's identities were never revealed! Yet, François knew her name and he was obviously well enough acquainted with Paul Trumbell to know his.

Her pulse quickened.

What did it mean? Had Toby been working for Paul Trumbell and for some reason, the giant had killed the boy? Why? Could that mean there was also a connection between François and Toby? Had she stumbled upon a pair of British spies and did not even know it? If François was a British spy, as she was beginning to suspect, why was he so insistent upon her spying upon the British if he were already one of them? And why did he wish to purchase weapons stolen from the British? Not a bit of it made sense. As things now stood, she had way too many questions, and *no* answers.

CHAPTER 16

August 1776

At the next Fighting Quaker meeting, members were brought up-to-date on the state of the war in New York. Rebel commanders were still wondering when and from where the British would strike next. General Washington was begging Congress to supply him with additional troops and much-needed provisions. More and more rebel soldiers were giving up the fight and either heading home, or switching sides in the hope of enjoying more hospitable conditions. That evening fliers were circulated amongst the members indicating where a man could enlist . . . various pubs facing the waterfront, or inns and taverns along King's Highway. Of special interest was that cash bonuses and free farmland were now being offered to new enlistees who served out a full term.

The August night was hot, and on the way home, Betsy, Minette and Emma, who had earlier untied the long sleeves from their gray gowns in an effort to stay cool, talked about what they had learned at the meeting. Betsy asked Minette if François had yet returned from New York and what, if any, news of the war had he ferreted out whilst there?

"François no yet return from *heez* jour-nay," Minette replied.

"Why did your brother go to New York and with whom does he stay?" Emma asked.

Betsy was glad Emma asked the questions as it saved her the trouble of attempting to learn the truth from Minette without appearing to pry.

"François stay with *bon ami* from *Anglais* school."

Because she could not resist, Betsy did inquire if her brother's English friend was a Loyalist?

Sighing, Minette nodded. "I sometime wonder how my brother stay friends with those loyal to *Anglais* king."

"If François knew about the offer for free land," Emma said, "he might be persuaded to join the rebel army. I intend to tell my cousin Thadius about it. He has not yet enlisted but I daresay this generous offer might be sufficient to persuade him."

"I wish we could think of a way to help our troops," Betsy said. "With winter coming on, the men will need warm mittens, and mufflers, and warm woolen stockings."

"Perhaps we might make mittens and stockings and send them to the soldiers," Emma suggested. "We could begin knitting now before winter sets in. Mother would help."

Betsy leapt on the idea. "Perhaps we could go door-to-door and ask ladies to donate cast-off clothing, and yarn. The three of us, and any other Patriot woman who'd like to help, could gather at my shop to knit."

"How shall we get the clothing to the men?" Emma asked.

"Perhaps François know where to deliver things," Minette supplied.

"Having so recently been in New York," Betsy remarked, "François should know exactly where our Patriot troops are quartered." *And, if he did not know* . . .

Before parting ways that evening, the girls decided to begin knocking on doors the very next day. However, as Betsy was nibbling bread and jam the following morning, it occurred to her that for *her* to openly solicit donations for the rebels would clearly disavow her claim as being sympathetic to Loyalists. Therefore when Emma and Minette appeared on her doorstep, she said she thought it best if she remained at the shop so as to be on hand if ladies should arrive to deliver yarn, or clothing. When Betsy's friends left, she began laying out supplies in preparation for an afternoon of sewing with the women.

Before Minette and Emma returned, Sarah appeared, excitedly waving a letter she had just received from William.

"He knows!" she cried. "William says the troops know that German soldiers are en route to New York!"

Betsy's eyes widened. *Perhaps this spy business had merit, after all.*

"I am convinced is it due entirely to *our* efforts to get word to General Washington! Just think of it, Betsy, it is almost as if we've become *bona fide* spies!"

Betsy smiled tightly. Though she longed to share with Sarah her efforts in that area, she dared not. "What more does William say?"

"I shall read his letter to you." Before Sarah took a seat, she asked, "What are you preparing to work on now?"

"Emma and Minette and I have decided to knit mufflers and stockings for the troops," Betsy continued to rummage through storage bins in search of colored yarn. "Would you like to help?"

"Of course, I shall help. But, first, I will tell you what William wrote." Sarah's eyes scanned the page. "He says that although the uncertainty is vastly unsettling, every day that the British do not attack gives the rebels another day to strengthen their fortifications. He says every morning when the men awaken they brace themselves for an attack which thus far has not come. His Excellency, General Washington believes there is '*something exceedingly mysterious in the conduct of the enemy.*' William says the troop's desperate need for bullets is so great the men have begun to dig lead from church windows in order to recast it as bullets."

"Oh, my." Betsy looked up. "Apparently desperate times indeed call for desperate measures."

"He says that in lieu of ammunition, the men are filling barrels with dirt and arranging them in rows so if the British attempt to climb over their fortifications, they can roll the barrels down upon them." A worried frown marred Sarah's features. "What a dreadful way in which to protect oneself. I do so wish we might make *bullets* to send to the men along with warm stockings."

"If Joseph is successful in capturing the British ships he means to plunder, perhaps he and his crew will abscond with the enemies own ammunition and distribute it amongst our troops."

"Oh, Betsy, do you think he will succeed?"

At that moment, Emma and Minette stepped into the shop exclaiming over their success in canvassing the neighborhood. Minette crossed the room to dump the contents of her apron onto Betsy's worktable. "I receive much yarn for stockings. And such pretty colors, *oui?*"

"More than a dozen ladies agreed to help," exclaimed Emma. "Some are coming now."

A whirlwind of activity ensued. Sarah stayed on to help as the women arrived carrying yarn and knitting needles. Although the ladies chatted and laughed as they knitted, they were all aware of the serious nature of their mission. When Sarah relayed the contents of the letter she'd received, other women chimed in with tales of appalling conditions their menfolk were enduring. One remarked that a staggering number of men had succumbed to malaria; that even Commander Nathanael Greene had contracted the dreaded disease. Still, before sundown, more than a dozen pairs of red, green, yellow and blue woolen stockings had begun to take shape.

"I do hope the bright colors will not give away our army's position to the British," remarked one woman with a laugh.

"I daresay the warmth the stockings will provide will offset any harm the bright colors might cause," Betsy said. She thanked the ladies for their help and was gratified when many declared they'd come again tomorrow.

Although Betsy was uncertain if further efforts on her part to spy on the Loyalists would prove useful to the rebel troops, she was certain that to supply even a few of the rebel soldiers with much-needed warm stockings would protect more than a few toes from frostbite come winter.

Quite weary that night from her exertions, Betsy had only just climbed the stairs to bed when an insistent rapping at her front door set her pulse pounding.

Holding a sputtering candle aloft Betsy retraced her steps back through the darkened house to the front door. *Who could be calling at this hour?* So far as she knew, both Joseph and François were away and Sarah never went out alone at night.

Rap-rap-rap!

Whoever it was had no intention of leaving without rousing her.

"Betsy, it's me. Joseph. Open the door."

Her eyes wide, Betsy set down the candle and anxiously unlatched the front door. "What is it, Joseph? Are you hurt?"

"No." He rushed inside, bringing with him a sweep of humid night air. "I cannot stay long but I had to see you before I set sail again."

He latched the door himself, and snatching up the candlestick, rushed through the house. The flickering flame threw shadows on the painted walls as Betsy, enjoying the fresh outdoorsy scent that trailed after the ruddy seaman, hurried to keep up with his long strides. It surprised her when instead of entering the parlor, Joseph headed for the rear door. He handed the candlestick to her before lifting the heavy bar that lay across the door.

"Where are you . . .?"

"I leave on the morrow but before I go, I wanted to bring a few things to you . . ." The rest of his words were lost as he charged out the back door and seconds later, returned lugging a bulky parcel. He set it down in the middle of the parlor, a perplexed Betsy holding the candle aloft.

Joseph hurried back outdoors and returned with an even larger crate, which he set alongside the first. "Turned out the British ships we plundered were carrying a good deal more than guns and ammunition. Light another candle, love."

Betsy did so while, across the room, Joseph ripped into one of the crates. The room now fairly glowing with light, Betsy was astonished as Joseph drew out one lovely gown after another, a dozen or more pairs of frilled sleeves, half a dozen stomachers, lacy chemises and scores of petticoats. Also in the box were dozens of pairs of silk stockings, soft slippers, kid gloves, and even a ruffled parasol!

Nearing the bottom of the first crate, Joseph gazed up at her. "Thought ye might like to leave off wearing your gray frocks for a spell, lass."

Her eyes alight Betsy fell to her knees. "I've never seen so much finery in all my life!" She reached to stroke a blue silk gown.

"The color of that one matches your eyes," he said. "Here, try the slippers. Softest kid I've ever felt. I'll wager there will be some mighty disappointed officer's wives in New York City."

"Oh, Joseph, perhaps I shouldn't . . ."

"Rubbish! You've heard tales of British soldiers looting Patriot's homes and taking whatever they like. You've as much right to this as they."

Betsy tried on the slippers and reaching for the parasol, began to dance around the room. "I feel like a princess in these slippers. They're as soft as a cloud!"

He sat back on his heels. "You'll look like a princess wearing these frocks." He dug to the bottom of the box. "Never seen so many unmentionables all in one place."

Betsy parked both hands on her hips. "I would think it unlikely you have *ever* seen unmentionables!"

Joseph roared with laughter. "Try on this bonnet, love."

Betsy carefully settled the frothy confection adorned with lace and ribbons atop her chestnut curls. "I shall wear it to church on Sunday."

Joseph gazed up with admiration. "If I were here, sweeting, I'd accompany you. Got myself several new pairs of breeches, and coats with velvet cuffs. Linen shirts, too. And shoes with silver buckles."

Betsy held up a pretty stripped gown. "Oh, Joseph, do I dare wear such lovely things? What will people say?"

"Hang what folks say. Your Uncle Abel imports finery from all over the world; they'll assume he's supplying you with new frocks."

"What's in the other box?" Betsy asked.

"More of the same." Joseph laughed.

Betsy's eyes widened. "I don't know what to say."

He rose to his feet and caught her about the waist. "Say you'll think of me every time you wear one of these fancy gowns." He gazed down into her glittering blue eyes. "Just promise me you'll not wear one of them if you step out with the Frenchman again. By the by, I've learned something about him that will interest you."

"I've no intention of *ever* stepping out with François again!"

"Good." He drew her closer. "I think about you every night before I drift off to sleep, Betsy." His warm breath fanned her tousled curls as he lowered his head for a kiss.

"I think about you too, Joseph." She snuggled against his muscled chest. "I prayed you would return home unharmed and God has granted my request. I am so thankful."

"Unfortunately, I am not here to stay."

She frowned. "Must you sail away so soon, Joseph? Why?"

"I've prisoners aboard the *Swallow* and dozens of crates of muskets and ammunition. We're off to New York. I only put in here to see you.

Brits had drifted so far off course, turned out we were closer to Philadelphia than New York. My friend's bark sailed on ahead. I'll catch up to him tomorrow."

"How can you be safe with British soldiers aboard your ship?"

"Not soldiers. Limeys. I may hire one or two. The rest I'll turn over to the rebels when I drop anchor there."

"But how will you know where to go? They say New York harbor looks as if all England is afloat."

"I know coves and inlets the British know nothing of. I've sent word ahead to a rebel commander to be on the lookout for us."

"But those waters are sure to be dangerous," Betsy protested.

"Even if we blow off-course, two more ships entering New York harbor flyin' the Union Jack will scarcely be noticed, let alone remarked upon." He drew her hand to his lips. "By the by, the red coats you adorned with all that gold braid did the trick. We boarded those Tory ships and plundered 'em without firing a single shot. Easiest thing I've ever done."

Betsy joined in his satisfied laughter. "I'm glad I could help."

"I figured you deserved a share of the spoils." He bent to kiss her again, then straightened. "I must go now, lass. Bar the door behind me."

"Thank you for all the lovely gifts, Joseph, and promise me you'll be careful."

He dashed out and Betsy heard him cluck the horse pulling the cart into motion and it clatter off down the street. She assumed the equipage belonged to his aunt and that he'd gone to see her before he hurried here.

Back in the parlor, Betsy fell to her knees and spent another half-hour drawing costly items from the crates. Uncovering half a dozen woolen cloaks, she decided at once to share her bounty with her sisters, and Emma and Minette. At the bottom of the box she found enough black tea to also distribute amongst her friends and Sarah, as well as, sugar, spices and coffee. Gazing with wonder at all the treasures, she hoped that in addition to the weapons Joseph was taking to New York, there was also a supply of warm men's clothing, and foodstuffs for the troops.

Eventually, Betsy climbed the stairs to her bedchamber. Joseph was indeed trustworthy and she had nothing to fear from him. Before drifting off to sleep, however, she realized he had neglected to tell her what he had learned about François.

CHAPTER 17

Several afternoons that week Sarah, Minette, Emma, and a half dozen other ladies came to Betsy's shop to knit. The pile of woolen stockings, mufflers and mittens grew. Betsy stored them, and the used clothing the ladies had donated, in the pantry off the parlor. Exactly how to go about delivering the much-needed supplies perplexed all the ladies.

One day as the women prepared to depart, Betsy asked Sarah to linger a while longer. Once alone, she told Sarah of Joseph's late night visit and showed her much of what he'd brought, now stashed in cupboards in her bedchamber and the sitting room. The tea, sugar and spices, of course, were in the kitchen. Spreading out the handsome new woolen cloaks on her bed, they each chose their favorite color and Sarah left carrying three, one for herself and one each for Rachel and Hannah, Betsy's two other sisters still living at the Griscom home.

"We shan't be cold come winter this year," Sarah exclaimed. "Do convey our sincerest gratitude to Joseph."

Betsy was pleased she could do something nice for her sisters.

Later that week, Mrs. Dearborn and Miss Olsen appeared at Betsy's shop door, both women atwitter over the resounding success of Miss Olsen's campaign in New York City.

"My niece is now affianced to Captain Charles Lancaster!" Mrs. Dearborn gaily announced. "Anne now needs a wedding gown and *trousseau*."

"Have you white silk on hand, Mrs. Ross?" Miss Olsen inquired, her cheeks flushed with happiness.

"Indeed, I do have white silk, although I fear there may not be enough to fashion the entire gown, unless . . ." Betsy's voice trailed off as she headed across the room to where a dozen ells of fine fabric leant against the wall.

"Unless, what?" Mrs. Dearborn demanded.

Moving aside several bolts, Betsy drew out one that appeared to have yards and yards of white silk wound around it. "There appears plenty here for a gown, although we may have to make the flounces from a contrasting fabric . . . patterned brocade perhaps, or white lace, over a slimmer skirt and the stomacher of brocade with white ribbons."

"Oh, how lovely!" Miss Olsen exclaimed.

"Might you show us a sketch of that design, dear?"

"Certainly." Reaching for a lead pencil, Betsy set down her idea. To ascertain how much time she'd have to sew the gown, she inquired of Miss Olsen when she and Captain Lancaster planned to be wed?

The young woman turned to her aunt. "I have forgot, did Charles say the attack on the rebels would take place at the end of *this* month . . . or next?"

Betsy's head jerked up.

"I believe your young man said the invasion was planned for the end of *this* month," Mrs. Dearborn replied, her distracted gaze fixed on Betsy's sketch.

Although her heart nearly leapt from her chest, Betsy caught herself before an all-out gasp escaped her. *The British planned to attack at the end of this month? August?* Again, she'd been made privy to an important military secret; something His Excellency, General George Washington and the entire Continental Army were on pins and needles to know!

"At any rate," Miss Olsen turned to Betsy, "we shall wait until the rebel soldiers have vacated the city so no bothersome old battle will interfere with our wedding."

"We've at least a fortnight or more before Anne will need the gown. Will you have sufficient time, dear?"

Still reeling over what she'd just learned, Betsy nodded tightly.

As soon as the women quitted her shop, she hastened to write a report . . . only . . . she didn't know what to do with it. Minette had made no mention of François having returned to Philadelphia. It was possible he had also learned the exact date of the British attack from his Loyalist friends in New York. However, because Betsy hadn't spoken with him, she couldn't be certain. And because she refused to return to Paul Trumbell's dwelling, she saw nothing for it but to head straight to Dr. Franklin.

Tacking a hastily scribbled note to her shop door saying that an urgent matter had called her away that afternoon and the ladies would have to meet elsewhere to sew, she quickly made her way up High Street to Dr. Franklin's print shop.

Once there, she breathlessly inquired of a clerk if she might speak with the proprietor. Before the young man could form a reply, Dr. Franklin flung open the door to his private office.

"How nice to see you again, Mrs. Ross. Do come in. I was just having a bite to eat; you are welcome to join me."

"Forgive me, sir, I do not mean to intrude."

"Nonsense, what might I do for you today?"

Once Franklin had secured his office door, Betsy explained her reason for calling. Behind his spectacles, the older man's eyes widened.

"This is excellent news, indeed, Mrs. Ross. I shall dispatch a rider straightaway." Casting a furtive glance through the pane of glass fronting his office, he reached for a fresh copy of the newspaper and handed it to her. "Take this with you and do not return to your home right away."

Alarm shot through Betsy. "Is something wrong, sir?"

Franklin escorted her to the door. "These are dangerous times, my dear. You have made more than one call upon me of late. It would not do to arouse anyone's suspicions regarding the nature of our . . . association. Call upon a friend before you return home, or perhaps stop at the market. I shouldn't wish any harm to befall you."

"Thank you, sir." Gazing anxiously up at him, a whit of Betsy's anxiety dissolved when Dr. Franklin winked at her. A shaky smile on her face, Betsy quitted the print shop and leisurely strolled back down High Street.

A bit later, when she did reach home carrying a parcel of fresh butter and a wheel of day-old bread she'd just purchased from the baker, another wave of anxiety washed over her when she glanced over one shoulder and spotted François headed her way. That he had not yet seen her gave her a few moments to compose herself. Laying aside her packages and the newspaper, she hastily tore off the note tacked to the door and wasted additional time fumbling for the key and slowly inserting it into the lock.

"*Bonjour, madame.* I see you have been to market."

Betsy looked up. "Indeed, I have, sir. And I see you have returned from your travels." She smiled as if she were pleased to see him.

François scooped up her packages and tucking them beneath his arm, followed her into the shop. Betsy did not particularly want him to come below stairs with her, so she left him in the parlor while she hastened to the kitchen before rejoining him above stairs.

"I came to give you this." François reached into his pocket and withdrew a few folded-up paper bills.

"Continentals?" Betsy's tone was flat. "I clearly recall you saying that Secret Correspondence members were paid in coin."

"As you know, coin is scarce these days. For the nonce, this will have to do."

Betsy's lips tightened as she took the worthless paper money and dropped it onto a nearby table. "Perhaps I shall find a hungry merchant who will accept these as payment for a . . . carrot, or a potato."

"Once more, you disappoint me, *madame,*" he scoffed. "We are all of us working for the good of the country. If you were truly loyal to the Patriot Cause, you would perform the small part you play for nothing."

"And do you perform the small part you play for nothing?" When his lips pursed, she pressed, "What, if anything, did you learn of import from your Loyalist friends in New York City?"

Giving a tug to the points of his plum-colored waistcoat, he replied, "*Ma petite* journey was merely for pleasure."

That he was reverting to the use of French sounded an alarm bell in Betsy's head. No doubt her impertinence had angered him. She smiled with satisfaction. Because the day was warm and the room especially close, she crossed it to fling open a window. "I suppose Minette mentioned that we are knitting stockings for the rebel troops. Might we count upon your help in delivering the warm clothing? We thought that since you have so recently been in New York City you would know the whereabouts of our army."

With a snort, François muttered, "Come winter, I expect the entire rebel army will have been driven into the sea."

Because a gust of wind had caused the panes of glass in the window to rattle, Betsy did not hear his response. "Excuse me, sir, what did you say?"

"I said I . . . expect I should be going and when the time comes, we shall see."

"Ah."

"I take it, *madame,* that *you* have heard nothing of import and therefore have nothing further to report."

"No; nothing at all." Betsy followed him through the shop. "But, if you are absent from the city in future, sir, do not ask me to deliver a report to Mr. Trumbell."

He flicked a gaze her way. "And why ever not?"

"I do not like the man."

"Committee members are not required to *like* one another, Mrs. Ross."

"How fortunate for you, sir. Good day."

Closing the door on the disagreeable Frenchman, Betsy turned her attention to other things. She had a wedding gown to make and only a few short weeks in which to complete the complicated task.

A few days later, Sarah called to tell Betsy that their sisters, Rachel and Hannah, were delighted with their new cloaks.

"Rachel chose the wine-colored one, similar to the burgundy-colored one you chose. I declare were you and Rachel standing side-by-side, one would be hard pressed to tell the difference between you. You are *so* alike!"

Not looking up from her sewing, Betsy smiled, albeit sadly. She longed to see her sisters again. "So that left the brown plaid for Hannah."

"She adores it, as I do the green." Sarah laughed. "I confess I am almost looking forward to winter so I can wear my new cloak. Mother was pleased by your generosity."

"I hope you did not tell her where the cloaks came from."

"I said you received them in a shipment and rather than attempt to sell them, decided to make each of us a gift."

Betsy grinned. "There is a particle of truth in that." She glanced up. "Could I persuade you to help me with these flounces, Sarah?"

"Indeed. I see you have cut the strips, shall I commence to gather them?"

"Yes, please. I've cut the fabric on a bias, which means the flounces will fall in a more pleasing fashion from stomacher to hem."

Sarah threaded a needle. "I am certain this gown will be every bit as lovely as the previous ones you've made."

"I am most grateful to have received another lucrative project. One's money seems to disappear so quickly these days."

"The Lord is taking splendid care of thee, Betsy."

"Indeed, He is. Have you heard from William?"

Sarah shook her head.

"Will you be writing to him soon?"

"I write to my husband every night and send my letters to him every Monday morning. By then, I own, the packet has become quite bulky."

Betsy wanted to reveal to Sarah, without unduly oversetting her, what she had learned of the impending British attack. She schooled her tone to remain calm. "When Miss Olsen was last here, she mentioned her fiancé saying that the British mean to launch their surprise attack upon the rebels at the end of this month."

"Oh!" Sarah leapt to her feet, the flounce in her lap falling to the floor. "I must alert William! Did you tell Dr. Franklin? If not, we must . . ."

"Indeed, Sarah; I relayed the news to Dr. Franklin mere minutes after I learned of it. I am certain the details are already in General Washington's hands, and the troops have been alerted. However," she aimed a stern look at her sister, "I must insist that you *not* mention this to anyone, Sarah. I assume you are still meeting with the ladies to knit."

Sarah nodded. "We gather at Mrs. Burton's home now. I shall do as you ask, but . . . why must I remain silent about something so very important to all of us?"

"Dr. Franklin advised it," Betsy fabricated. "If the British learn their secret is being bandied about, they are likely to alter their plan." Truth was, Betsy did not want word that she had failed to report such important information to François to filter back to him through Minette.

"Then, of course, I shall say nothing. By the by, there is something I have been meaning to tell you."

"What have you to tell me, Sarah?" Betsy murmured absently.

"Something that concerns . . . Rachel. She has met a young man with whom she is quite enamored and . . . he seems also to fancy her."

Betsy's needle continued to whip in and out of the white silk. "Rachel is very young to have fallen in love."

"No younger than when John Ross was courting you," Sarah countered.

"What does our mother say? Does she find Rachel's young man agreeable?" When Sarah did not reply at once, Betsy looked up; her blue eyes a question.

"Mother does not know of the *tendré*."

Betsy smiled. "So, you have been assisting the couple to meet up just as you helped John and me those many years ago."

"Rachel and her young man seem very well suited. He is a good bit older than she, but he is quite solicitous of her and most respectful."

"Given his age, surely you do not allow her to see him alone."

"Rachel has been alone with him," Sarah admitted. "She enjoys dancing as much as you did at that age."

"I did not attend a public dance with John until I was . . . at least seventeen."

"I believe the first time you sneaked out of our parent's home to attend a dance with John, you had just turned sixteen."

"Rachel is but fifteen," Betsy said. "I would like to meet her young man."

Sarah said nothing.

Betsy glanced up. "Sarah, I said I would like to meet Rachel's young man. Perhaps *I* might chaperone them. Perhaps when Joseph returns, he and I might accompany them to a dance. I am certain if our mother knew of the plan, she would approve."

Sarah remained silent.

"Sarah, I would like to meet Rachel's young man," Betsy said more firmly. Her eyes searched her sister's shuttered gaze.

"You have already met him."

Betsy's face became a question. "Well, then . . . who is he?"

"Promise me you will not be angry."

"I promise nothing of the sort. Tell me at once with whom our sister fancies herself in love."

"Rachel's young man is . . . François."

"Ouch!" Betsy's astonishment was so great she accidentally pricked her finger with the needle. Thrusting the injured finger into her mouth, she just as quickly removed it. *"François!"*

"Now that you are with Joseph," Sarah rushed on, "I did not think you would mind Rachel seeing François. He sent her a note from New York and even brought her back a gift; a lovely bottle of French *parfum*. Rachel adores it. She is quite smitten with him."

"Why have neither you nor François spoken of this to me? I saw him only a few days ago and he said nothing."

"I expect his reluctance to tell you stems from the fact that . . . well, François has mentioned that the pair of you often . . . quarrel."

White-hot anger bubbled up inside Betsy. Feeling inordinately warm, she set down her sewing, untied the sleeves from her frock and flung them aside. "We quarrel because François is insufferable!"

"Do calm yourself, Betsy. The *tendré* is likely to be fleeting. As you pointed out, Rachel is only fifteen."

Betsy's nostrils flared. "And, as you pointed out, she is smitten with him. Yet you allow her to see him *un*-chaperoned. He is *French, Sarah.* Which means he has no scruples. I've a mind to alert our mother myself. I have no doubt that she and Father would bring this . . . this flirtation to an end straightaway."

Having finished the flounce she was gathering, Sarah rose to lay it on the table and fetch another length of fabric. "I am persuaded it will come to nothing, Betsy."

"And I am persuaded of only one thing," Betsy exclaimed. "François Dubeau is not a man to be trusted!"

"Perhaps you still harbor feelings for him, Betsy."

"I harbor nothing of the sort! I am overset because I do not wish to see Rachel ill-done by, as she most assuredly will be by that scoundrel!"

"François has been all that is charming towards both Rachel and myself. As the elder and therefore, wiser, of us, I can assure you he is most trustworthy."

"Elder or no, clearly you are unaware of the unspeakable things a man such as François could do to an innocent girl like Rachel. And if you refuse to do nothing to deter him, then I have no choice but to take matters into my own hands."

"That will make Rachel quite unhappy."

"Better unhappy than ruined."

"You are being unfair, Betsy. François is not the sort of man who would . . . "

"*Any* man is the sort of man who would ruin a silly, simpering miss who fancies herself top over tail in love with him."

"Rachel is not a silly, simpering miss!"

"She is if she trusts François Dubeau. I will not be deterred from this, Sarah, so you may as well leave off trying to dissuade me. I will not sit idly by and let that reprobate take advantage of our Rachel; I will not."

Sarah exhaled. "Very well, Betsy. Say what you must to him, but promise me, you will give him ample opportunity in which to defend himself. François Dubeau is a wonderful man."

Betsy's lips tightened. Clearly, there was no point in discussing the matter further. Sarah appeared as smitten by the Frenchman as poor, lovesick Rachel. Make no mistake; she would indeed confront the man. This ill-considered romance must be brought to an end straightaway and that's all there was for it.

CHAPTER 18

Before Betsy could decide how best to approach François in regard to not seeing Rachel, a note arrived from Mrs. Dearborn inviting her to a reception to announce Miss Olsen's engagement. Betsy wasn't certain whether or not gentlemen attended engagement parties, but it was possible François would also be present and if so, she intended to take full advantage of the opportunity to confront him.

The afternoon of the party, she received another note from Mrs. Dearborn saying a carriage would collect her that night. Betsy thought the woman's offer was very kind and said as much to Sarah when she came to help her dress. Although still officially in mourning, Betsy had decided to wear one of the beautiful frocks Joseph had brought her; this one made of a stunning gray silk, which, when she moved, shimmered to violet. She had not yet been brave enough to wear a single one of the pretty new gowns, nor had she shown them to Sarah.

"What a lovely gown," Sarah exclaimed upon entering Betsy's bedchamber and spotting the violet silk upon the bed. Darker violet bows marched down the stiff stomacher and a frill of violet lace hung from the elbow-length sleeves. Sarah fingered the rich fabric. "It is simply breathtaking. When did you make it?"

"It was amongst the things Joseph brought," Betsy replied, tying the strings of her petticoat around her waist. "Might you help lace me up, please?"

"How fortunate that you had such a beautiful gown on hand."

"Indeed," Betsy murmured, aware of the tension crackling in the air between herself and Sarah, whom she had not seen since the afternoon they quarreled.

Once dressed and her coiffure perfect, Betsy said, "I have not given up my resolve to speak with François about Rachel. If he is present, I intend to broach the topic with him tonight."

"François will not be there," Sarah replied coolly. "He and Rachel will be at my home. I am preparing dinner for the three of us. You may rest assured that tonight they will be properly chaperoned."

"I see."

Betsy thanked Sarah for her help and once the Dearborn chaise drew up, both girls walked to the flagway. After a liveried footman assisted Betsy into the coach, she waved goodbye to her sister. She felt quite grand being driven to yet another *soiree* at another fine mansion on Society Hill. She wished Joseph were there to accompany her, or at least see her wearing the lovely frock.

At the party, certain now that she would not come face-to-face with François, Betsy mingled easily with the society matrons and ladies with whom she was already acquainted. All were wearing their finest silks and satins, as were the few gentlemen present in the Dearborn drawing room. Betsy soon ascertained that earlier in the evening, a special dinner had been served for a select group of Miss Olsen's closest friends. The guests now arriving had been invited only to attend the grand reception afterward.

"You always look so stylish, my dear," remarked a woman Betsy had met at the Shippen's dinner party. "Wherever do you procure such stylish gowns these days?"

Before Betsy could reply, another lady said, "I'll wager she made it herself." She addressed Betsy. "I understand you are making Miss Olsen's wedding gown."

"Indeed, I feel honored to have been chosen to do so."

"Mrs. Ross also made the stunning scarlet ball gown Miss Olsen wore in New York City when Captain Lancaster proposed to her," said another. "Everyone remarked upon its beauty."

"Thank you, ma'am," Betsy murmured.

"You are very talented, Mrs. Ross. I daresay ladies in New York are quite jealous of us here in Philadelphia."

Before Betsy could respond, Mrs. Dearborn stepped up. "A bit of a crisis has arisen, my dear. I was hoping you could assist."

"Certainly," Betsy replied.

"Please, excuse us." Mrs. Dearborn drew Betsy away.

Thinking that perhaps Miss Olsen had torn a ruffle, or a bow at an elbow needed retying, Betsy accompanied Mrs. Dearborn up a winding staircase.

"You do carry needle and thread, do you not?"

"Yes, ma'am. And also my thimble."

"Splendid. Not a single one of my maids is the least bit clever with needle and thread."

Having gained the second floor of the house, Betsy quite enjoyed the impromptu tour. Admiring the silk-clad walls upon which hung portraits of Dearborn ancestors, quick glances into opened chambers revealed polished cherry-wood tallboys, gilded commodes, and assorted costly artifacts.

"I had half expected to see your young man here this evening," Mrs. Dearborn said. "I am certain I had an invitation sent 'round."

"My . . . young man?"

"M'sieur Dubeau. You recall I greeted you the day I spotted the pair of you strolling in North East Square. I thought to myself then, I hope she is not taking time away from sewing Anne's wedding gown in order to promenade with her young man." Mrs. Dearborn's tone was a trifle accusing.

Betsy grimaced. Apparently the woman had spotted François and Rachel together on the square. "Miss Olsen's gown is coming along nicely," Betsy assured her. "You may bring her in on Monday for a fitting."

"Splendid. Here we are."

Mrs. Dearborn sailed into a chamber, which to Betsy's surprise was overflowing with gentlemen, which clearly explained the lack of same below stairs. As nearly every man was smoking pipes or fat cigars, smoke hung like puffy clouds above their heads. At least a dozen gentlemen were ranged about a pair of billiard tables and several more were leaning over a desk at the bottom of the room. That the walls of the chamber were lined with books told Betsy this was Mr. Dearborn's study.

Heading through the throng of gentlemen towards those gathered around the desk, Mrs. Dearborn addressed her husband. Betsy recognized him as the man who had escorted her home the day she walked here. "Mrs. Ross has agreed to repair Captain Lancaster's coat."

When Mr. Dearborn stepped aside, Betsy's breath caught in her throat. Three of the gentlemen on the opposite side of the desk were wearing buff breeches and scarlet coats adorned with gold braid. Lethal-looking scabbards hung at their sides. Gripped with fear by her first sight of British army officers, Betsy edged a small step backward.

"Do come here, Charles," Mrs. Dearborn motioned to one of the soldiers. "We made special arrangements for Captain Lancaster and a few of his friends to come to Philadelphia tonight as a special surprise for Anne," the woman explained to Betsy. "Unfortunately, whilst traveling,

Captain Lancaster rent the sleeve of his coat. I hoped you could mend it before he joins us downstairs."

Betsy nodded mutely as the handsome young captain removed his scarlet coat. She worked to calm her rapid pulse as the British officer walked from behind the desk and stood near enough to her that she could feel the warmth from his breath fanning her cheek as he pointed out the small tear on the sleeve of his jacket. Her fingers trembled as she took the coat, it still warm from the heat of the young man's body.

"Gentlemen, do step away from the desk and allow Mrs. Ross to be seated while she sews," Mrs. Dearborn instructed.

As the officers parted, Betsy was startled by the touch of Captain Lancaster's fingers on her elbow as he guided her around the desk to the empty leather chair sitting behind it.

"When Mrs. Ross is finished with your coat, Charles, you and your friends will please join us below stairs. The drawing room is quite thin of gentlemen and I daresay, the ladies are growing restless for want of masculine attention."

Although her remark elicited a few chuckles, Mr. Dearborn and his companions all turned back to whatever they'd been studying on the desktop.

Although Betsy's head was bent over her work, she was keenly aware that once again she was in a prime position to overhear whatever it was the gentlemen were discussing. From her position behind the backs of two British officers, she caught a glimpse of what was so raptly claiming their attention. A map. *Of what?* However hard she strained to see, she could make out nothing. Nor was she was able to distinguish much of anything the men were saying. The deep timbre of their voices blended with the crack of billiard balls and the shuffle of feet upon the wooden floor.

Still, she caught phrases like "General Clinton believes . . ." and "Here are the five roads leading to . . ." and "Long Island shall be the first . . . ." In minutes, she clearly heard one gentleman say, " . . . will be child's play to drive the rebels from Manhattan."

Her heart thumped. *The men were discussing plans for the surprise attack on the rebels!* If only she could get a good look at the map. But . . . *how?*

Nearly completed with the repair, she heard Mr. Dearborn's voice. "You say a full two thirds of Howe's troops mean to launch the surprise attack . . . *here?*" Betsy assumed the older man was at that instant pointing to a specific spot on the map. Tilting her head, she attempted to peek through the crook of a red-coated elbow, but . . . to no avail.

Just then the billiards game broke up. Betsy heard raised voices and laughter as the men racked their cue sticks and quitted the room.

For a few seconds, all was silent until Mr. Dearborn said, "I shall just mark this spot on the map for Anne. Like most women, she understands little to nothing of the war, but she does like to know where you and your regiment are, Lancaster. Right here, you say?"

"I shall mark the precise spot for you, sir. And, before I return to New York on the morrow, I shall tell Anne exactly where I shall be."

"Nearly done with the repair, Mrs. Ross?" Betsy jumped when Mr. Dearborn addressed her.

"Indeed, sir; I was just tying off the thread." After biting it in two, she shook out the garment and rising, handed it to Mr. Dearborn. "Here you are, sir."

Holding up the scarlet coat, he pulled out the sleeve. "Why, I cannot even see where it was rent. Splendid work, Mrs. Ross! Here you are, Lancaster, good as new."

The older man helped the captain shrug into his redcoat while Betsy busied herself replacing the needle and thread inside her reticule in such a way that she would not prick her finger the next time she dipped into it.

"And here you are, Mrs. Ross." Mr. Dearborn withdrew a couple of gold coins from his pocket.

"Oh, no, sir." Pasting a smile on her face, Betsy glanced at Captain Lancaster, who was still examining the sleeve of his coat. "It was a privilege to assist one of our . . . brave young men."

"You are too kind, Mrs. Ross." Inclining his head, Dearborn returned the coins to his pocket. "Come along then, we shall all escort you below stairs."

At that moment, Betsy's gaze dropped to the floor. "I . . . seem to have misplaced my thimble, sir." She gazed about here and there. "It must have slipped from my finger as I . . . ."

"Gentleman," Dearborn announced solemnly, "the lady has lost her thimble."

Betsy laughed. "I am certain I shall find it in no time, sir. Do make haste to escort Captain Lancaster below stairs. I shouldn't wish to cause another moments delay in keeping him from dear Miss Olsen."

"Very well, then." Dearborn's tone conveyed his relief over being released from the obligation of diving beneath the desk in search of something as trivial as a thimble. "If you fail to find it straightaway, Mrs. Ross, do not hesitate to ring for a maid to assist you. Come along, gentleman."

"I shall only be a moment, sir." Already Betsy had fallen to her knees and was groping about on the wooden floor beneath the desk, hoping the floorboards were free of dust and would not soil her lovely silk gown.

The moment she heard the gentlemen's voices receding down the corridor, she sprang upright and with wide eyes attempted to memorize every single word the officers had scrawled upon the map.

She took it all in: the exact position of General Howe's ships in the harbor, the location of the commanding officer's headquarters and more importantly, the X where Captain Lancaster had said two thirds of General Howe's army would launch a surprise attack upon the rebels: a thin squiggly line that clearly said *Jamaica Pass Road.*

Her heart beating like a drum in her ears, Betsy scooped up her reticule and breathlessly scampered from the room. If she weren't the last person to exit the chamber, and therefore the very one upon whom suspicion would fall, she would have folded up the map, stuffed it into her reticule and quitted the house straightaway. As it was, she must be content with having seen what she had seen and knowing the *exact* location of the proposed British attack upon the rebel troops in New York City. How she would be able to smile her way through the remainder of the evening with this important information burning like a hot coal in her mind she hadn't a clue.

CHAPTER 19

"I have never been afraid of the force of the enemy. They, like the Frenchman, look one way and row the other." . . . *General Heath to General Washington, August 1776.*

The next morning, Betsy was unprepared to receive a caller before she'd had time to dress or pour her first cup of coffee. Pulling open the door, she found François Dubeau standing on the doorstep. It galled her when upon rushing inside he did not wait for her to *offer* him a cup of coffee, but instead ordered her, as if she were a serving wench, to fetch him one.

Her lips pressed together, Betsy headed to the kitchen for the kettle and while climbing back upstairs, attempted to gather her wits in order to confront her early-morning caller about terminating his courtship of her younger sister Rachel. But before she had a chance to say a word, he confronted her on a topic of his choosing.

"I was informed you spent last evening with the Dearborns, *madame*. If you tell me you heard nothing of import, I shall refuse to believe you. British officers were present, were they not?"

Betsy's brows drew together. *Had did he know that? Mrs. Dearborn had said the presence of the British officers was a surprise.* "I have not had sufficient time in which to set down what I overheard last evening, sir. It is quite early and as you can see, I have only just arisen." She pulled her wrapper closer about her body, beneath which she wore only her nightshift.

"You may forgo writing a report and relay the information to me. The British attack is slated for the end of this month and today is the twenty-fifth. The attack could come as early as today, or tomorrow."

Aware that timing was critical, Betsy had already decided *not* to supply François with this particular information, as she wasn't entirely certain he would pass it along. For all she knew, he was working *for* the British. He'd just confirmed that he already knew *when* the attack was to take place. Perhaps he already knew what she had learned: precisely *where* the attack was to take place, although why he was pretending otherwise made no sense. Still, she had decided to call upon Dr. Franklin this morning. In his hands the message would surely end up where it ought. However, with the disagreeable Frenchman now scowling down upon her, she had to say something. Perhaps she'd tell both men what she knew. "I learned that the

British intend to launch their surprise attack upon the rebels from the Jamaica Pass Road."

"Rubbish!"

Stunned by his reaction, Betsy grew defensive. "I saw the map. The men were gathered around Mr. Dearborn's desk studying it. Captain Lancaster drew an X upon that very spot. The Jamaica Pass Road," she repeated.

François paced. "Perhaps, *madame,* you do not know how to correctly read a map. A far more likely spot for ambush would be the Gowanus Road to the west, or perhaps the Bedford Road to the east."

So . . . he did *not* know from where the British meant to attack. She feigned exasperation. "Dear me, perhaps I did misread the map. They are quite complicated, and I own, by the time I got a glimpse of it, I had consumed one or two, perhaps three, goblets of wine. As you know, I rarely imbibe. It is quite possible . . ." She tapped her chin for effect. "Now that I think on it, I recall seeing *two* X's on the map. I confess I am not certain where the X lay."

"Which X?"

"Either of them."

François snorted. "As a spy, *madame,* you have proven worthless." He regarded her with contempt. "As are most women."

A finely arched brow lifted. "I take it your opinion of women applies also to Rachel?"

"I have no idea of whom you speak."

"I am referring to my sister, you boor! The one you dined with only last evening."

He waved a hand. "An *enfant.* The *demoiselle* merely amuses me."

That he had reverted to peppering his speech with French words did not escape Betsy's notice. "I have told you what I overheard last evening, sir. It is your choice whether or not to believe me." She smiled archly. "Rest assured I shall pass along your high opinion of my sister to her." She rose to collect his nearly full cup of coffee. "Good day, sir."

Saying nothing, the Frenchman stalked from the house. Betsy hurriedly dressed and made her way up High Street where she relayed the news regarding the Jamaica Pass Road to Dr. Franklin.

"The Jamaica Pass Road, you say?"

"Yes, sir, I saw the X drawn upon the map. I heard the men say the plan was forwarded by General Clinton, whom I understand is familiar with the terrain as I recall reading in the newspaper that he grew up in that area."

"True." Franklin nodded, his tone considering. "Unfortunately, I have it on good authority that for whatever reason, our troops are not guarding that particular road."

"Which may explain why it is the very one the British have chosen to use," Betsy pointed out.

Again, Franklin nodded. "I will dispatch the intelligence at once. You have become an excellent spy, Mrs. Ross."

"Thank you, sir, I confess it was . . . purely accidental."

"Nonetheless, I insist upon paying you the same as I do my other informants." He withdrew a gold coin from a box in a desk drawer and pressed it into her palm. "I pray this information will not arrive too late to be of use to General Washington. Be mindful as you go about your business, Mrs. Ross. You must not unwittingly place yourself in danger."

"Thank you, sir. I will make every effort to remain alert."

* * * * *

The following morning Betsy walked to the market and found the entire square abuzz with excitement. Asking questions, she learned the British had launched a surprise attack upon the rebels in New York City in the wee hours of *this very morning*. Stunned, she endeavored to learn more but as no one possessed any details regarding the attack, other than the fighting was still going on, she had to wait out the long hours of the day until the evening newspapers appeared on the stand.

The news correspondent said that in the early morning hours of the *previous* day, His Excellency, General George Washington, uncertain when and from where the British would attack, had through his telescope, calmly watched General Howe's men go about their daily parade. Yesterday afternoon, Washington had drafted a note to the Continental Congress here in Philadelphia saying that from *'the general appearance of things, the enemy planned to make their attack upon Long Island from the water.'* Instead, in an unexpected move this morning, a two-mile long column of ten thousand redcoats had launched a surprise attack upon the Patriot army . . . *from the Jamaica Pass Road!*

Betsy gasped.

As the newspaper account gave no further details such as the number of casualties on either side, apparently the omission meant that nothing more was known.

Betsy's thoughts whirled as she laid aside the newspaper and turned back to her sewing. She could work a few more hours this evening by candlelight. What, she wondered, had happened to Dr. Franklin's dispatch? She had had serious doubts that François would pass along the intelligence, but why had Dr. Franklin's missive not gotten through, or had it, perhaps, arrived too late? Perhaps the courier had been waylaid, or even overtaken, and killed. She shuddered, recalling an image of poor Toby bleeding to death in the alleyway. A sad sigh escaped her. Dr. Franklin may think she had become a creditable spy, but truth was, she'd made precious little progress in either of *her* investigations. She was no closer to uncovering John's killer than she was Toby's.

The hours of the following day ticked by slowly. Betsy expected any moment to receive a frantic visit from Sarah, wringing her hands over William's safety. Because Betsy knew firsthand how it felt to lose a beloved husband, she fully understood her sister's fragile state of mind. Also aware that her new Loyalist lady friends were subject to the selfsame heartache, it was now difficult to view them as the enemy. Mrs. Dearborn had been as concerned for Betsy's health that day when she had walked to her home as Betsy was now for Sarah . . . and Anne Olsen, whose beloved Captain Lancaster was also fighting this war.

She worried also for Joseph. He'd had plenty of time now to complete his mission in New York and sail back down the coast to Philadelphia. She prayed the British had not captured his ship and killed him, or any one of his men.

As the afternoon dragged on, Betsy sat alone in her parlor sewing on Miss Olsen's wedding gown, pausing every time she glanced up at the clock to pray for the safety of the Patriot troops, and for Joseph and his men. The city seemed ominously quiet today; only a few carriages clattered by on the cobbles. The entire city was on prickles, wondering when the fighting in New York City would end, and would the British claim victory, or would the rebels manage to hold their own? At times, Betsy raised her head from her work and found herself straining to hear sounds of gunfire, or the boom of a cannon, as if the battle were taking place right here. But all was silent. Not even the birds in the treetops dared chirp. The city appeared to be holding its collective breath. Near sundown, a sharp rap at her door startled her.

Tossing aside her work, Betsy sprang to her feet and spotting Joseph on the threshold, she cried, "You are safe!" Tears of joy welled in her eyes as she flung herself into his arms.

"I've only just arrived." Joseph lifted her off the floor, her feet dangling as he carried her back inside the house. When he set her down, they hurried into the parlor. "The wharf is abuzz with tales of the fighting and from what I've been able to make out, our boys did not fare well."

"Oh, Joseph." Betsy's face fell. "I read where the British attacked during the wee hours of yesterday morning. I've heard nothing since. What are they saying now?"

"Evidently a high wind worked against the British fleet, which explains why all the fighting took place on land. Cornwallis attacked from the northeast, Hessians bore down from the Flatlands, and Highlanders swooped in from the west."

"Oh-h," Betsy moaned. "So many soldiers shooting at our little army."

"Word is there were upwards of twenty-two thousand Lobster-backs attacking us from three sides. The rebels were vastly outnumbered. Even with the guns and ammunition I delivered our boys simply could not reload fast enough."

"Does this mean our army is . . . gone? Is the war over and we have lost?" Moisture pooled in Betsy's eyes. "Will the British now march into Philadelphia and hang us all as traitors?" Tears trickled down her cheeks.

Joseph gathered a weeping Betsy into his arms. "Mustn't give up so easily, love. We've still breath in our bodies. Depend on it; we'll find a way out."

Over the next hour, Joseph told Betsy how he'd managed to skirt past the British fleet in New York harbor and how, under the cover of darkness and a soupy fog, he had handed over the British soldiers' own guns and ammunition to the waiting rebel troops.

"Rebels weren't particularly happy to accept a dozen prisoners, but they took 'em."

"With our army's food so scarce, I can understand their reluctance to share what little they have with British sailors."

"Feeding prisoners is part and parcel of war."

"I expect it is." Betsy glanced toward a window and noted it was now quite dark. "I know Sarah is worried to pieces over William. I don't know how she'd cope if she learned he'd been taken prisoner. Perhaps I should go and console her. I thought she might come 'round today. I fear she's still vexed with me for not wanting Rachel to see François."

"Ah. So, the Frenchie is courting your sister now, eh?"

Betsy nodded. "Yesterday, he grilled me regarding what I'd learned at Miss Olsen's engagement party. Oh." Her expression brightened. "I wore one of the pretty frocks you brought me, Joseph. All the ladies thought it quite lovely."

"I'll wager you were the most beautiful woman there." He leaned to kiss her cheek.

"When I told François what I had learned, he scoffed. But it turned out to be true. The British *did* attack from the Jamaica Pass Road. François said I was useless as a spy. Oh," Betsy paused as another thought struck, "you never told me what you had learned about him."

"Ah, yes. Seems the Frenchie has been in the business of selling secrets for quite some time. When he lived in England, he spied on them for the French; then during the year he was in New York, he joined the Sons of Liberty there and carried Patriot secrets back to the Brit . . ."

"Are you saying François lived in New York *before* he came here?"

Joseph nodded. "Fellow I know named Jeffrey Sills joined the Sons of Liberty up in Massachusetts. Dubeau was also a member, but when they discovered he was the mole who gave away the location of their munitions stockpile, he disappeared. Jeffery and I were at a pub on the waterfront one night when, in strolled your Frenchman. After he left, Jeff spilled what he knew about him. Apparently Dubeau hasn't a loyal bone in his body, although his first leanings are to his own country, France; the British next, and . . . well, he appears to be as rude and arrogant towards us colonials as any other Frog I've had the misfortune to meet. Most think they're superior to anyone not fortunate enough to have been born French."

Betsy's head shook. "François led me to believe he had only just arrived here straight from England. Minette never said otherwise. But, then, I suppose she hasn't a clue what her brother has been up to. I trust Minette completely. I *never* trusted François. I've suspected all along that he was working for the British."

"He is a known spy, Betsy. If I were your father, I'd forbid your sister Rachel from seeing the turncoat." His brow furrowed. "Isn't Rachel still a little girl?"

"She's fifteen and according to Sarah, quite grown up." Betsy cast another anxious gaze toward the window. The sooner she alerted Sarah to the truth about François, the better. "I really should go see Sarah."

"It's late, pet. Can't it wait until tomorrow?"

"Sarah's distraught and now that I know the truth about François, I must tell her. He has already caused a riff to spring up between us. I do so wish to mend it."

"Very well." Joseph took her hand. "I know when you've set your mind to something there's no deterring you. I should show my face to Aunt Ashburn. I expect she's also worried about me."

Betsy crossed the room to fetch her shawl. "It will soon be time to wear my new cloak." Smiling, she wrapped the shawl about her shoulders as Joseph closed the window and latched it.

"Is the rear door barred?"

Betsy nodded and on the way through the house, she told Joseph she'd given new cloaks to each of her sisters and meant also to give Minette and Emma each one.

"Quite generous of you, love." They stepped outdoors and Betsy locked the door. "Shall I pop in again tomorrow evening?"

Betsy smiled. "I hoped you would."

"How about if I walk with you now to Sarah's? I worry about you being out alone at night."

"It's only a short distance. Tell your aunt I said hello and I shall call soon."

"Now that I'm home, I expect she'll insist we join her for dinner one night, or perhaps several." He bent to kiss her cheek. "Good night, love."

Once Betsy reached Sarah's house, she found her sister's pale blue eyes red-rimmed from hours spent weeping.

"Oh, Sarah." Betsy hugged her sister. "For all we know, William is snug in his tent tonight."

Sarah's voice shook. "For all I know, my husband is lying wounded or . . . dead. They say our entire army was decimated."

"We don't know that for certain. We must wait to see what the morning newspapers say."

Due to her sister's overwrought state, Betsy decided against upsetting her further by revealing what she'd learned about François. Instead, she extracted a promise from Sarah to come to her shop the following day and sit with her while she sewed. In Sarah's kitchen, Betsy heated up the kettle of mutton and potatoes hanging on the spit and after both girls had eaten, she warmed milk for Sarah and insisted she retire for the night. After seeing her sister settled in bed, Betsy quietly took her leave.

Outdoors, the night sky was black as pitch, the city streets ominously silent. Although she felt some trepidation over being abroad at such a late hour, Betsy pulled her shawl tighter about her shoulders and bravely set out. She'd gone only a short distance when strong fingers grasped her elbow and a deep voice said, "Continue walking. Do not turn around."

Betsy instinctively turned toward the tall man who was propelling her forward. "Uncle Abel! You gave me a fright!"

"To walk the streets alone at night is foolhardy, girl. You're being followed."

Betsy's eyes widened. "C-can you see who is following me?"

"A large man wearing a cap pulled low over his brow. I happened to be approaching from the opposite direction and saw him fall into step behind you when you left Sarah's home. I circled around to catch up to you. I've been to see your parents."

"How are they faring? How is Rachel?"

"Everyone is well. I had hoped to put their minds at ease regarding the war."

"Do you have fresh news about what is happening in New York?"

"Our troops were chased deeper into Brook Land Heights. Fortunately, that area is heavily fortified. To dislodge our troops will prove difficult. For now, they say all is quiet."

"That's a relief. Sarah and I both feared our entire army had been decimated."

"Our entire army was not under siege."

"How do you know this, Uncle Abel?" Betsy aimed an anxious gaze up at the elderly Quaker. His black felt hat was also pulled low over his brow.

"I pay informants to keep me abreast of what is happening along the seaboard." He flung a look over one shoulder. "I believe your stalker has fled."

Betsy exhaled a relieved breath. "I am so grateful you were on hand, Uncle Abel."

In minutes, they reached Betsy's doorstep.

"I'll see you in and make certain your windows and doors are secure."

Inside, Betsy lit a candle and held it aloft while her uncle inspected window latches and the rear door. "Everything appears tight. Do you have any idea who might have been following you?"

"No." Betsy shook her head.

"I understand you've been seen with a Frenchman, a man named Dubeau."

"I-well, it . . . it might have been . . ."

"Word is a Frenchman here runs agents. They say he plays both sides. Come to think on it, a double spy could have been responsible for young Toby's death. Toby approached me once."

"Approached you? About what?"

"Asked if I needed help. I knew what he meant."

"But, why would Toby ask you about . . . spying?"

"I just told you I pay informants. It's important I know which waters are safe and which are not. I'm perceived to be Loyalist, but I make no distinction from whom I purchase goods."

"Are you . . . also a spymaster?"

"No; not to the degree Franklin is, or the Frenchman, whose true identity remains unknown. There are scores of Frenchmen in Philadelphia. Perhaps the double agent is Dubeau, perhaps not." Long strides carried him to the door. "The man is said to be ruthless. Extremely cunning and extremely dangerous." At the door, he paused. "Do not go out alone at night again, girl."

Betsy thanked her uncle for rescuing her and locked the door behind him. Heading back through the darkened house, she realized she'd learned more about François tonight than she had in the six months she'd known him. And, not a bit of it good.

The question now was . . . would she be able to convince Sarah of the truth about the man?

And would the truth make any difference to Rachel?

Furthermore, who was stalking Betsy? And, *why?*

CHAPTER 20

Betsy was pleased when Sarah arrived the following day. She put her to stitching bows onto the stomacher of Miss Olsen's wedding gown, hoping that by keeping her mind occupied, she might cease worrying over her husband's safety for a spell. Due to Sarah's fretful state, Betsy again opted not to mention anything about François, nor did she tell her sister about the alarming event of the previous night as she'd walked home alone.

That evening, when Joseph arrived, she surprised him by having supper already on the table. "You cooked a meal for me?" He seemed delighted that she had gone to such lengths on his behalf.

After the two had eaten their fill of bubble and squeak, a dish made from cabbage and sausages that John had especially enjoyed, Betsy prevailed upon Joseph to accompany her to a Fighting Quaker meeting.

"Perhaps we'll learn more about what is afoot in New York. If the news is good, we could call on Sarah and tell her." After a pause, she said, "Only we must let her believe *you* brought the news to me. Sarah doesn't know I'm a Fighting Quaker member. I've purposely not told her of my involvement."

When the Fighting Quaker members, all anxious for news from New York, were told that rebel casualties resulting from the attack on Long Island were estimated to be upwards of one thousand men, alarmed cries arose from every corner of the crowded hall. Apparent now was that General Howe's long-range plan was not only to take control of the Hudson River, but advance up it and seize Albany, thereby cutting off New England from the lower colonies. Because the British had spent the summer months enlarging their naval power and bringing over additional troops, the British army was now so strong they could easily overtake the far fewer rebel troops encamped there. Patriot strategists predicted that unless the Continental Army surrendered Brook Land Heights that Howe would launch an all-out attack upon the Patriots and very likely slaughter what remained of the rebel forces in a single deadly campaign.

"Oh, dear," Betsy lamented as she and Joseph left the meeting, "the news from New York is so grim I fear telling Sarah would only further upset her."

"The news is quite grim," Joseph agreed.

"Perhaps for the remainder of the evening you and I should just sit on the sofa and talk."

After a pause, Joseph said soberly, "Perhaps when you least expect it, I shall steal a kiss."

Despite her downcast state, Betsy giggled.

Joseph's lips twitched. "If the British have beaten us and hanging is to be our fate, I daresay we should seize the moment and make hay whilst the sun, or . . ." he glanced up, "the moon shines."

Betsy sighed. "I expect you are right."

At home, Betsy and Joseph snuggled close on the sofa and Joseph made good on his threat to steal a kiss. Later Betsy told him what had happened the previous night as she walked home from Sarah's house and how Uncle Abel had come to her rescue. Joseph was far more alarmed than Betsy expected.

"Who could have been following you?" he demanded and when she didn't answer at once, he growled, "Think, love. Could it have been the Frenchman? Have you unduly angered him?"

"François and I did not part on good terms, to be sure, but I do not believe it was he who was following me. Why would he when he feels free to simply barge in here and demand that I fetch him a cup of tea? Uncle Abel said it was a *large* man. François is not so very large. Tall, yes; but not overlarge." She worried her lower lip as she thought back. "It was quite dark last night. I never caught so much as a glimpse of the man. Uncle Abel merely said that a large man with his cap pulled low was following me. The only large man I know is . . . Paul Trumbell."

"Who is Paul Trumbell?" Joseph demanded. "Another one of your suitors?"

"No!" Betsy cried. "Paul Trumbell is most assuredly not one of my suitors. *You* are my only suitor."

"Well, that is reassuring." He relaxed a mite. "So, who is this Trumbell character and why would he wish you ill?"

Betsy told Joseph about the report she'd written about General Clinton's troops being sent north from Charleston and how François had instructed she deliver the report to a man named Paul Trumbell. She also told him how she was certain she'd seen a flicker of recognition on Trumbell's face when he caught sight of her. "I've since wondered if perhaps *he* was the man who broke into my house and held a knife to my throat. I've even wondered if perhaps it was not he who killed Toby. I cannot be certain as I did not get a good enough look at the man who stabbed Toby to ever recognize him again. But Trumbell doesn't know that. It's possible he *thinks* I recognized him from the alleyway and now he fears that because I know his identity, I'll alert the authorities. Perhaps he means to rid himself of me first."

"Why would Trumbell kill Toby?"

Betsy shook her head. "I don't know. Dr. Franklin said Toby was working for the British. We now know François is working for the enemy. François is acquainted with Trumbell." She paused. "I've not yet sorted out the puzzle but there is obviously a connection between François and Trumbell. Still, I haven't a clue why Toby was killed." Her head shook. "It's all so confusing."

"Perhaps I should pay a call upon Paul Trumbell."

"Oh, Joseph, promise me you'll not confront him. We know nothing for certain and besides, he is a giant of a man, quite the largest man I have ever seen. Not that I believe you cannot defend yourself, but I daresay Paul Trumbell could easily overtake several men at once."

"Then, I'll take along a few friends to assist me should I require . . . assisting." Rising, he said, "I refuse to let anyone threaten you, Betsy. Now that I've found you again, I will not let some ruffian take you away from me."

"He wears a knife at his belt, Joseph."

"And I carry a pistol in my pocket. Where does he live?"

"It's late, Joseph."

"It's never too late to pay a call upon a killer."

Betsy spent the long hours of the following day worrying and wondering what had happened last night when Joseph paid his late night call upon Paul Trumbell. She realized she had come to care deeply for Joseph and depended more and more upon him to look out for her. Were Paul Trumbell to plunge his knife into Joseph's belly, as she suspected he had done to Toby, she'd *insist* the authorities investigate that crime!

Throughout the long day, her worried thoughts fixed also on Sarah, who did not come to the shop that day. Mid-way through the long afternoon, Betsy did receive a call from Mrs. Dearborn and Miss Olsen, both eager to learn how the latter's wedding gown was coming along.

Although her heart wasn't in it, Betsy graciously greeted her guests, offered them tea and pretended to be cheerful as the two bragged about the British army's rousing victory in New York City.

"It's just as I thought," Mrs. Dearborn gleefully declared, "the rebels will soon be chased out of New York altogether and Anne and her young man can enjoy their wedding festivities without any interference from a silly old war!"

"But Charles says he's been assigned to look after that rebel general they captured," Miss Olsen fretted.

Betsy's ears perked up. "W-what general would that be?"

Mrs. Dearborn glanced at Betsy. "Excuse me, what did you say, dear?"

"The general Miss Olsen just mentioned; the one the British captured. I wondered what was his name?"

"Oh, I do not recall the man's name, Sullivan, Mulligan, what does it matter? When all's said and done, they shall all be captured. Have you given any thought, dear, to what sort of traveling costume would be suitable for Anne? She and her new husband will be leaving on a wedding trip immediately following the ceremony and . . ."

"Actually I *have* given the matter some thought," Betsy said crisply, suddenly feeling irritable over having to listen to the Loyalist women gloat over the British army's victory. She snatched up a piece of paper and quickly sketched one of the very costumes Joseph had confiscated from the British ship he had plundered. The gown fit her a tad bit too snugly but it would fit Miss Olsen's trim figure to perfection. To sell it to the girl would save Betsy the trouble of having to smile her way through several more visits from the enemy. She passed the sketch to Mrs. Dearborn.

And was relieved when a split second later, the older woman exclaimed, "Why, with a bonnet and gloves to match, this would be a stunning traveling costume!"

"It is quite lovely, Mrs. Ross. What color would you suggest?"

Betsy head's tilted to one side. The frock was made of ivory linen trimmed with brown braid. "I can see this design made up in ivory linen trimmed with brown braid."

"Absolutely perfect!" enthused Mrs. Dearborn. "How fortunate we are to have found you, Mrs. Ross. I daresay you are as talented as any Paris *modiste*. But will you have sufficient time to complete both costumes, the wedding gown *and* the traveling suit?"

"I've hired a helper," Betsy fabricated, "who I shall put to work at once on the traveling suit." *And my helper will receive all the credit for having made it.*

"When do you expect to have both costumes completed? I assure you when Anne receives word from her Captain that it is safe to travel; we shall depart for New York straightaway."

Betsy rose to her feet, the action signaling to her clients that the interview was over. "Both gowns will be ready in less than a fortnight, madam. I shall get word to you the minute I snip the final thread."

Mrs. Dearborn beckoned to her niece. "Come along, Anne. We must not keep Mrs. Ross from her work."

Betsy sighed with relief as she watched the Dearborn carriage wheel away from the curb. In a few days time, the wedding gown would be finished and very soon after that, she'd declare the traveling costume also complete. With luck, she'd never be obliged to see the Dearborn women again. Returning to her parlor, she settled down to sew.

Sometime later, roused by another rap at the door, she hoped this time it would be Joseph. "Tell me at once how you fared last night with Paul Trumbell," she blurted out the minute she saw that it was indeed he.

In the parlor, Joseph slid onto the sofa and began to relate the details of his late night adventure with the giant. "I chose three of my largest men to accompany me and as we approached Trumbell's building, which, by the by, is in quite a rough and tumble area of Philadelphia, Betsy. I don't ever want you to venture there again. Anyhow, the four of us pretended to be deep in our cups, raising a ruckus and whatnot. When I spotted Trumbell's door standing ajar and candlelight flickering from within, I knew he was there. Sure enough, it wasn't long before he appeared, an angry scowl on his face and that long knife attached to his belt. He is one giant of a man."

"Did you notice the ink stains on his fingers?"

Joseph's brow furrowed. "Well, I . . . wasn't exactly looking at his fingers. Why? Should I have been?"

"I believe he's a cartographer."

"I believe he's a forger!" Joseph dug some wadded up pieces of paper from his breeches pocket. "While my men distracted him, I crept into the rear of the house and found these. Does this look familiar?" He handed a crumpled page to Betsy. "I recall you telling me your report mentioned General Clinton."

"This is my very report! Apparently it was never passed along."

"Not the way you wrote it. Now, take a look at this."

Betsy read the second page aloud. "No worries from General Clinton. Troops are garrisoned north of Charleston awaiting orders from Howe." Betsy gasped. "I don't understand. This tells the rebels they have *nothing* to fear from Clinton."

"Exactly." Joseph produced several more messages and half-finished copies in which the meaning was reversed. "Apparently Trumbell attempts to closely replicate the original writer's handwriting, but in the doing, he turns the words around so that when the report reaches its destination, the original message has been reversed."

"This is despicable! If General Washington receives conflicting intelligence from his spies, how does he determine what to act upon?"

"It's no wonder the British took our troops by surprise on Long Island."

"My last message to General Washington warned that the enemy planned to attack from the Jamaica Pass Road. Fortunately I also handed the intelligence off to Dr. Franklin, but it obviously arrived too late to be of any use. Or perhaps Washington received a false report from François and acted upon it instead. What are we to do now, Joseph?"

"I know what I'd like *you* to do. I'd like you to give up this spy business altogether, but since I know you won't, I'd suggest that when you write a report, you twist the words around so that when Trumbell re-twists them, perhaps the meaning will appear as you originally intended."

Betsy began to pace. "That seems far too complicated. I'm certain that whatever information I deliver to Dr. Franklin will reach its intended destination unaltered. I mean what are we going to do about François's perfidy? He and Paul Trumbell are profiting from passing along false information."

"What a minute, love. You're not suggesting that you and I attempt to take down both the giant *and* a notorious spy, one whom even your uncle declares is cunning and dangerous?"

Betsy parked both hands on her hips. "Well, someone has to do it. Even if Paul Trumbell did not kill Toby, he and François must be stopped. They are British spies!" She thrust up her chin. "If you will not help me, Joseph, then I have no choice but to go it alone."

Joseph's eyes rolled skyward. "Very well, love. How do you propose we bring down a pair of ruthless British spies?"

CHAPTER 21

"I'll think of something," Betsy said.

The following evening, Joseph collected Betsy early, telling her his aunt had requested they join her for dinner that night. As they walked to her home, Joseph relayed the news he'd heard on the wharf that day regarding conditions in New York.

"The Battle of Long Island was a slaughter," Joseph began. "Two of our generals were either captured, or killed. General Stirling and . . .”

“General Sullivan.”

“How did you know that?”

“I heard it from the Loyalist women yesterday. Miss Olsen said her fiancé was ordered to guard the general they’d captured. Do go on, please, Joseph.”

“Apparently General Washington reached the Heights just after the fighting commenced and from an elevated position above the battlefield, he watched the battle unfold before him through his telescope. One soldier heard him mutter, ‘*Good God! What brave fellows I must lose today!*’ ”

“Oh, dear,” Betsy murmured. “We must not tell Sarah such disturbing news.”

“Apparently, Washington actually saw the British army advancing from all three sides but was unable to get word to any of his commanding officers. It’s said the Hessians soldiers chased our troops through the trees and plunged bayonets through their chests even as the men paused to reload their muskets.”

“Oh-h,” Betsy moaned. Such distressing details of battle always sickened her.

“Four or five hours into the battle, a few commanders gave their troops leave to run for their lives. Our boys tried again and again to cut through British lines to reach safety but in the end, only ten men succeeded. A good many were shot down as they tried to slog through a muddy creek. Over fifteen hundred rebel troops were killed.” Joseph paused to draw breath. “The rest were taken prisoner. As things now stand, what’s left of our army is bottled up behind their own fortifications; trapped by British forces with no way to climb out. Our men may be putting on brave faces, Betsy, but bravado and empty muskets will not win this war.”

"All the same, you and I must put on a brave face for your Aunt Ashburn. I do not wish to unduly alarm her either."

"At this juncture, not a one of us is *unduly* alarmed."

Early the following morning, Betsy walked to the High Street market. Browsing through the stalls, an empty basket slung over one arm, she deliberated over what to purchase with the few coins left in her pocket. Of a sudden, her concentration was shattered when a messenger clattered up on horseback, swung down from the saddle and began to shout that during the night General Washington and the entire Continental Army had escaped from beneath the very noses of the British! Amidst gasps of disbelief and a volley of questions, Philadelphians learned that in an astonishing move during a torrential rain storm last night the entire rebel army was ferried across the Hudson River and every last soldier was even now safely ashore in Manhattan. Left behind on Long Island, the breathless rider exclaimed, were only a few old cannon too deeply sunk in the mud to pull out.

Following the messenger's proclamation cheers erupted in the marketplace and instead of frowning, everyone was smiling. Merchants especially welcomed the good news for suddenly folks began buying up all they could carry for special celebratory dinners. Betsy could hardly wait to finish her shopping and rush to Sarah's side to tell her the good news.

"They are *safe?* All our men are safe!" Sarah cried.

"Well," Betsy modified, "those that were not killed in the fighting, or . . . taken prisoner."

"Oh." Sarah's face fell. "Then it is too soon to rejoice. I must not get my hopes up lest they be dashed to the ground when I learn that William was struck down on the battlefield, or taken prisoner. Oh, Betsy, how shall I bear it?"

"God will give thee strength to bear every trial, Sarah; just as He did me. Would you like to come and stay with me? Your presence helped me through my time of trouble. Perhaps now I can help you."

Sarah considered, but in the end, declared she mustn't risk being away from home if William should return to Philadelphia wounded and need her there to care for him. Besides, she had . . . other considerations. "Rachel, for one," she said. "Oh, Betsy, I know you do not wish it, but our Rachel is quite in love with her Frenchman."

Betsy's lips thinned. She had hoped the matter would not arise today. But, now that it had, she had no choice but to reveal the truth to Sarah about François. "I'm so sorry for Rachel," she began, her mind casting about for how to proceed. She had never divulged to Sarah that she'd actually been spying on the Loyalist women, plus Sarah knew nothing about the Secret Committees of Correspondence.

"Sarah, please trust me when I say that Rachel must never see François again. That is all I can divulge at the moment. I truly do have Rachel's best interests at heart." Betsy shifted in her chair at Sarah's kitchen table, both girls' hands wrapped around warm cups of black tea.

"I do not understand your opposition to Rachel's courtship, Betsy. I would expect you'd be happy our sister has found love."

"Our sister has *not* found love, Sarah. To find love with François is not possible."

"You are being unkind."

"Sarah, there is a great deal that neither you nor Rachel know about François." After a pause, she blurted out, "Joseph has uncovered undeniable proof that François is a spy!"

"That is absurd!" Sarah scoffed. "I do not believe it! François is all that is kind and charitable; he is . . ."

"Loyal to the British!" Betsy exclaimed. "François is selling secrets to our army that in the end will harm every last one of us, perhaps even result in William's death."

Sarah blanched. "I . . . I cannot believe it."

"Nonetheless, it is true. Even Uncle Abel warned me against François."

"What has Uncle Abel to say to this?"

"Apparently word is circulating that *I* am seeing François. Uncle Abel told me what he knows of the Frenchman in an effort to warn *me* against him. I am now trying to do the same for Rachel. And you." She did not mention that her uncle was uncertain whether or not François was the double spy, but it didn't matter. Betsy was certain that he was.

Sarah's chin trembled. "You must own that your claims seem quite outrageous . . ."

"I am speaking the truth," Betsy insisted. "Surely you can see that Rachel must not be allowed to see François again." She waited, praying she had said enough. She did not wish to cause further pain by revealing what François *truly* through of Rachel, that she merely amused him; that he was trifling with her and that when not with her, he could barely dredge up a memory of who she was!

"W-what exactly did Uncle Abel say?"

"That François is a ruthless double spy, who is extremely cunning and dangerous."

Sarah exhaled a weary sigh. "Oh, Betsy. It is all too much to take in. I am far too worried over William to think of anything else. Rachel is planning to see François this very evening. I fear I shan't be able to persuade her otherwise."

"Would you like me to try?" Betsy knew she was treading on thin ice. If Rachel found *her* here when she arrived at Sarah's home this evening, the girl might bolt. So far as Betsy knew, Rachel still believed, as did their parents, that Betsy must be shunned. On the other hand, Rachel was clearly proving that she, too, had a rebellious streak and was unafraid of opposing their parent's strict Quaker beliefs. "What time do you expect Rachel to arrive this evening?"

"She is typically here just after sundown."

"Then, I shall arrive a bit before. Between us, we shall surely be able to convince Rachel of the truth."

By half-past seven of the clock that evening, neither Rachel nor François had arrived at Sarah's home for the proposed outing. Sarah told Betsy and Joseph, who had insisted upon accompanying Betsy, that either Rachel had changed her mind, or that the lovers had made alternate plans and failed to alert her.

"One other time," Sarah said, "Rachel quite by accident ran into François on his way here to collect her and I knew nothing of it until much later. Perhaps that was the case tonight."

"Did Rachel have plans to stay the night with you?" Betsy asked.

"She typically does when she steps out with François. I assume she meant to tonight."

"So," Betsy calculated, "if our parents are not expecting her to return home this evening, there is no point in asking them where she might be."

"Unless her plans changed, our parents believe she is here with me."

A worried gaze slid to Joseph. "What do you think we should do?" Betsy asked him.

He shrugged. "Thus far, the Frenchman hasn't harmed your sister; perhaps he'll not harm her tonight." He addressed Sarah. "Do you know what their plans were for this evening? Were they to attend a public dance?"

Betsy answered the question. "Due to the war, entertainments of every sort are now in abeyance. All public dances have been suspended."

"I don't know what their plans were," Sarah replied. "They often merely walk to North East Square, or they walk as far as South East Square. They sit on a bench and talk; then he escorts her back here."

"What time do they usually return from their walk?" Joseph asked.

"The time varies. It is nearly eight of the clock now. Sometimes he brings her back by nine, sometimes as late as ten. I am certain she is safe, Betsy. Despite your ill feelings toward him, François has been all that is good and kind toward Rachel. I am certain he will not harm her."

"Very well," Betsy replied. "For the nonce, I suppose I've no choice but to leave matters as they are." She rose, as did Joseph. "But I've not given up my resolve to alert Rachel to the man's true character. Given what I've told you, Sarah, I would expect you'd be eager to break all ties with him also. His loyalty clearly lies with the British. That makes him our enemy."

Sarah flinched. "It is difficult to think of him that way."

Irritated, Betsy bit back a saucy retort. "Let us be off, Joseph."

When they were alone, she exploded. "At times it is all I can do not to shake Sarah from her complacency! François's duplicity could have already played a part in killing Sarah's husband and yet, she seems unwilling to distance herself from him. I cannot fathom it, I cannot."

"I take it you've not abandoned your resolve to expose his crime."

"Indeed, I have not!" Betsy's blue eyes snapped fire. "I have every intention of confronting him the very next time I see him. Perhaps I shall have him arrested. And hung," she added.

"Promise me you will say nothing to him unless I am there to protect you. He is a dangerous man, love, and once he realizes you're aware of his duplicity, there's no saying what he will do."

Betsy squared her shoulders. "Perhaps we should pay a call upon him together then. Would tomorrow evening suit?"

"Tomorrow evening it is," Joseph agreed.

CHAPTER 22

Early the following morning an insistent rapping at the door roused Betsy from a deep slumber. Throwing a wrapper on over her nightshift, she hastened downstairs to see who could be calling at such an early hour. Through the shop window, she noted the sun was only beginning to burn off the morning mist. It was far too early for anyone but street vendors to be out and about. Pulling open the door a crack, she was surprised to find a distraught Sarah on the doorstep. Wearing a stricken look on her face, the older girl rushed inside.

"Rachel is gone!"

Blinking sleep from her eyes, Betsy repeated in a raspy voice, "Gone . . . where?"

"Vanished! We haven't a clue where she is! When she did not appear at my home last evening, I retired at the usual hour, thinking she had indeed changed her plans. But not above half an hour ago, our parents were rapping at my door, demanding to know if Rachel was with me. She had, indeed, changed her plans last night, telling our parents she would *not* be staying the night with me, so when they discovered her not at home this morning, they naturally grew alarmed. Now, none of us knows where she is! I came at once to alert you."

Betsy shook her head to clear it. "Has our father summoned the authorities?"

"I do not know. A moment ago, they were rushing off to call on Rachel's girl friends to inquire if they know of her whereabouts." Sarah choked back a sob. "Oh, Betsy, I should have listened to you. François has done something dreadful to our sister and it is all my fault!"

"I take it you've not told our parents about Rachel seeing François."

Sarah shook her head. "I didn't have the heart to tell them. Father is persuaded that since she was not with me, they'll find her with one of her friends. I knew I must alert you at once, Betsy. What are we to do?"

"Well, since you are dressed, Sarah, you should go to François's home and demand that he tell you what he has done with Rachel."

Sarah brushed away the tears in her eyes. "I-I have already been there."

Betsy's brows drew together. "What did he say?"

"Oh, Betsy, it is just as you feared."

"*What*, Sarah? What did he say?"

"François is also gone."

Betsy's stomach lurched. "They've run away together." She drew a sobbing Sarah into her arms.

Once in the parlor, Betsy bade her sister sit on the sofa while she padded downstairs to the kitchen to put on the kettle. *What must they do now?* Given that no one knew precisely how long the couple had been gone, it would be impossible to determine how far they'd got, let alone *where* they were headed.

As Betsy scurried around the kitchen placing cups and saucers on a tray, cutting slices of bread and reaching into the cupboard for a pot of jam, she wracked her brain in an effort to determine how best to proceed with so very little to go on.

Above stairs she and Sarah wordlessly sipped tea and munched on bread and jam. Finally Betsy said, "I should dress and go for Joseph. You may remain here or return home. I'll ask Joseph to dispatch a party of men to go in search of them, although with no idea which direction they headed, it will be difficult to determine where they might have gone." Gathering up the soiled dishes, she said, "It is your decision whether or not to apprise our parents of the situation. If Rachel has indeed run off to become François's wife, there is nothing that you, nor I, nor anyone, can do to alter what might have . . . already occurred. Sooner or later, our parents will learn that Rachel is not alone."

Sarah choked back a sob. "But, they will also know that *I* assisted Rachel in deceiving them."

"Indeed, they will Sarah. But you are not the only one at fault. Eventually they will know the part we both played in this."

"You did nothing wrong."

"I'm as much to blame as you. It was I who brought François Dubeau into our lives." When a fresh sob escaped her sister, Betsy added, "I realize you meant no harm by helping them. I'm still grateful for what you did for John and me. If it weren't for you, I'd have never seen John at all beyond the hours we spent at Mr. Webster's upholstery shop. It's just that, none of us had any reason to mistrust John's intentions. Unfortunately that is not the case with François."

"I should have listened to you at the outset."

"At the outset, I did not know what I've since learned about the Frenchman."

Sarah opted to return to her own home while Betsy walked to Joseph's Aunt Ashburn's home in an effort to get word to him. After learning of the problem, the widow Ashburn sent her man-of-all-work to the quay with instructions to board Joseph's ship and tell him an emergency had arisen and for him to come ashore at once.

"I assume you are aware that Joseph is planning to set sail again soon," Aunt Ashburn told Betsy.

"No," Betsy murmured. "He has said nothing to me. I had no idea he was planning to leave again so soon."

Mrs. Ashburn sorrowfully shook her head. "Like it or not, my dear, a man of the sea feels at home only on the water." She reached to squeeze Betsy's fingertips; the two seated side by side in her cool drawing room. "That he has remained so long in port is due entirely to you. My nephew is very fond of you, my dear."

Betsy exhaled a shaky breath. "I am quite fond of him."

"Well, we mustn't fret. Joseph will most assuredly set aside his plans now and help you find your sister. You would do well to return home so as to be on hand when he arrives. Come to see me again, won't you, dear?"

Betsy nodded. "Thank you, Aunt Ashburn. I suppose if Joseph is bent on leaving us, we must comfort one another." She reached to embrace the older woman before she departed.

Betsy had been home only a short while when another rap sounded at the door. Thinking it was surely Joseph, she raced through the shop to fling open the door, but blanched when she saw that it was not he on the doorstep. Betsy glared at the tall Frenchman, finely turned out this morning in smooth calfskin breeches and a forest-green cut-away coat. "What have you done with Rachel?" she demanded.

François brushed past Betsy into the shop. "I have done nothing with your sister, or *to* her, for all that."

"Rachel had plans to be with you last night!" Betsy rushed to catch up to him as he strode toward the parlor. "I demand to know what you have done with my sister! Rachel did not come home last night!"

"Have you tea made, *madame?*" François took up his customary stance before the hearth, one long leg crossed over the other at the ankle, an elbow propped on the mantlepiece. "Pray, fetch me a cup. I've a matter of great import to take up with you."

"What you have done with my sister?" Flinging herself at the infuriating man, Betsy began to pummel his chest with both balled up fists.

To fend her off, the Frenchman merely shoved her aside with an arm. "My tea, *madame.*"

Betsy staggered a step backward. "How dare you order me about like a serving wench! Either you tell me what you have done with Rachel, or I shall summon the authorities and have you arrested!"

He snorted. "And what crime would you charge me with?"

"Kidnapping! Spying!"

"Do calm yourself, *madame.* The truth is, when your sister failed to show up for our tryst last evening, I sought pleasure . . . elsewhere."

"You are despicable." Her nostrils flared.

"So, you have poisoned your sister against me, which explains why she did not show up last evening." He tweaked his cravat. "My tea?"

"I do not serve tea to *British spies,*" Betsy ground out.

Her rage merely amused him. "So, you have discovered the truth . . ."

"And you do not deny it?"

"Deny what? You and I, *madame,* we are cut from the same cloth. I am no more ashamed of what I do than . . . apparently you are."

"I am doing nothing so reprehensible as you, sir! I agreed simply to report to you whatever I overheard from the Loyalist women. But you, *you* and Paul Trumbell, you twist every morsel of information so that it . . ."

"I have merely found a way to turn a tidy profit." He ambled to a window and bent to peer out. "My family, we are poor *émigrés. Mon père* is frail; she does not so well speak the language. You cannot expect me to send Minette into the street to earn a living as a . . . well, to earn a living. Selling secrets to whomever is willing to pay for them allows me to put food on our table and clothes on my back!"

"And very fine clothes they are, too!" Betsy sputtered. "If you think to gain by demanding a ransom for the return of Rachel, you are sadly mistaken, for my parents have no wealth."

"Rachel. Rachel. I told you I merely find the *ingénue trés amusant.* Of her disappearance, I know nothing."

He was angry. If the storm brewing behind his dark eyes was insufficient to alert her, that he had resorted to the use of French clearly did. "What do you want from me, François?"

He coughed. Then coughed again. "*Madame,* I am parched. If not tea, then I beg you . . . some water, please."

Huffing, Betsy exited the room and returned in seconds carrying a mug of tepid water. She had lost all patience with the insufferable Frenchman and while below stairs had reached a decision. "I have decided to summon the authorities and have you arrested as a British spy," she announced coolly. "It is my sincerest hope that you hang for your crimes."

He did not respond; instead he drank the water and set the empty mug on a nearby table. Betsy found his arrogance intolerable. Folding her arms beneath her bosom, she watched as he withdrew an elegant lace-edged handkerchief and delicately wiped the droplet of moisture that lingered still upon his lips. Refolding the handkerchief, he arranged it just so into the breast pocket of his green velvet coat, then turned a sullen gaze upon her.

"Before you accuse *me* of spying, *ma chérie,* be aware that I can easily obtain proof that it is *you* who is the British spy; not I."

"If you are referring to the reports which Paul Trumbell copied, *forging* my handwriting so it would appear that *I* had written them, after he twists the messages around . . ."

"So." His lips twitched. "You have uncovered our clever little ploy." A dark brow cocked. "Obviously there is *twice* the money to be had selling the same secret to two different agents, although, as you pointed out, one does have to do a bit of . . . altering. If you turn me over to the authorities, *madame,* rest assured I shall return the favor. As to which of us is guilty will, of course, depend upon the political leanings of the authority. A Patriot constable will not take kindly to one who spies upon the rebels in order to aid the British; whereas a Loyalist magistrate will frown upon one who divulges British secrets to the rebels. As things now stand, *ma petite,* spying for the British will likely be . . . rewarded. The noose around your pretty neck will, no doubt, be very tight."

Betsy seethed inside. Although she was loath to admit it, his reasoning did have merit. Most of the high-ranking authorities in Philadelphia today were Loyalists. A few even served on the Continental Congress. To accuse François of spying would, indeed, be to also point a finger at herself. Dr. Franklin would vouch for her veracity, of course, but to ask him to do so would place him in jeopardy. Not even to save herself from the hangman's noose would she expose Dr. Franklin. He was doing far too much to aid the Patriot Cause. For now, François had the upper hand.

"Very well. I shall say nothing against you."

He inclined his head a notch. "As I said, *ma petite,* you and I, we are *très* alike. I recall it was the lure of monetary gain that prompted you to agree to become a spy. It is for the same reason that I continue in my chosen profession." An elegantly clad shoulder lifted and fell. "To say truth, I care not who wins this silly war. Win or lose is no matter to me. When the fighting is over, I shall return to France, or perhaps England, and do as any sensible man would do, find a wealthy heiress to take to wife, or perhaps a widow possessed of a large fortune. For the nonce, I must rely solely upon my wit. Fortunately, I am possessed with a great deal of it."

Betsy's chest rose and fell but rather than further inflame the despicable creature, she swallowed the saucy retort that very nearly leapt from her lips. "You have yet to tell me why you are here, François. What do you want from me now?"

"Ah. Yes." He brightened. "My purpose in calling upon you this morning, Mrs. Ross, concerns a profitable venture I conceived of only last evening. Word is circulating that the South Sea trader, ahem, the . . . *privateer,* with whom you consort, recently met with success in plundering a vast quantity of British guns and ammunition. I wish to know where the pirate has stashed the weapons. You will ask him and tell me where I might find them."

"What interest have you in weaponry?"

"I intend to sell them to the Continental army, of course. Everyone knows the poor rebels are always in want of muskets."

Betsy didn't flinch. "The guns have already been delivered to the rebel army. Joseph and his men took them to New York only a few days before the battle began."

He chuckled. "And still the wretches lost."

"There are no more guns to be had, François, therefore," she lifted her chin, "I see no reason for you to linger."

"You are lying." His gaze turned menacing as he took a step towards her. The scowl on his face was so alarming that Betsy edged a step backwards. "It is common knowledge," he spat out, "that militiamen in every colony up and down the seaboard have stockpiled guns and ammunition in abandoned barns or warehouses."

The mention of weapons in warehouses caused Betsy's heart to leap to her throat. "W-what do you know of that?"

"More than you think I do, *madame*. I know that your husband guarded such a stash." His gaze narrowed. "What you do *not* know is that I was in Philadelphia that day. I trudged through that miserable blizzard, frozen to my bones as I searched for . . ."

"You killed my husband!" Betsy gasped. Tears sprang to her eyes as her chin began to quiver. "W-Why? Why did you do it?"

"For money, of course," he replied. "I collected quite a handsome sum for that bit of sabotage. Although now that I think on it, I could have made a great deal more if I had figured a way to confiscate the weapons and sell them for profit. Ah, well . . ."

Quaking with outrage, Betsy sank to her knees as sorrow and grief overtook her. "I *will* have you arrested. I *will!* You will hang for killing John. You will *hang!*"

François's tone hardened. "I have friends in Manhattan who will testify that I never left New York during the entire month of January. My family will testify that I did not arrive in Philadelphia until late spring. The night you and I met at the Fighting Quaker meeting, I had only just arrived, presumably straight from England. Official documents I carry attest to that fact. To accuse me of murdering your husband will only make you look like the hysterical female you are."

Betsy managed to choke back her sobs and at length, lifted her head. "You are a vile creature. What have you done with my sister?"

"Pah!" He grasped her wrist and roughly dragged her to her feet. "I know nothing of the whereabouts of your silly sister. But, I can promise you this, *madame,* unless you tell me where your pirate friend has stashed the weaponry he stole, you will never see *either* of your sisters alive again!"

He flung her from him as if she were a whimpering lapdog, then he stormed back through the house. Betsy heard the front door slam shut behind him. Sinking to the floor, she gave in to the gut wrenching sobs that overtook her.

François was the man at the wharf that night, the man Pete saw, the one who grew confused by the blizzard and asked the way to Dock Street. The package he carried must have contained some sort of solution that ignited the fire, causing the explosion that ultimately claimed John's life. And, unless she now wished to sacrifice the lives of both Sarah and Rachel she had no choice but to do as the monster said. Otherwise, the assassin who murdered her husband would also kill her sisters.

CHAPTER 23

Not until much, much later that day did Joseph appear at Betsy's door and the news he brought was not good.

"My men and I fanned out today to comb the city and well beyond it. We asked at every inn and tavern on both sides of the river if a young couple had stopped in late last night or early this morning. I, myself, questioned every ferryman north and south of here to inquire if any of them had ferried a couple bent on marrying across the Delaware River."

Her soul still aching over what she had learned from François that morning, Betsy said softly, "François has not left Philadelphia."

Joseph's brows snapped together. "You have seen him?"

Betsy nodded as they both sat on the sofa in the parlor. "He was here."

"What happened, love?" Joseph's expression grew concerned. "What did the blackguard say to you?"

Hot tears burned Betsy's eyes as both hands covered her face. "Oh-h, Joseph." Her shoulders shook as the ache in her heart throbbed afresh with each breath she drew.

Slipping an arm about her, Joseph pulled her to him. "Is it Rachel, love? Did they find her?"

Wrenching sobs consumed Betsy. She had not wanted to cry; she had not wanted to tell Joseph what she had learned today. She had intended to keep her grief private. But all day, despite her growing fears for Rachel, thoughts of John filled her mind. How much she missed him, how dearly she still loved him, how much she would *always* love him.

"Oh, Joseph." The horrible truth inside her fought for release. Yet, she bit it back. She dared not tell him. If Joseph learned the whole truth, she could not count upon him to remain silent. To confront François would place *both* her sisters, and him, in danger. She could not risk that. Swallowing her tears, she drew on what little strength remained within her. "I-I . . . fear something dreadful has happened to Rachel."

"Clearly, you have worried yourself sick, love." His tone was soothing. "We'll find her. We'll keep looking until we do." He gazed into her tear-filled eyes. "I vow I will find your sister, and bring her home safely."

Sniffing back tears, Betsy nodded. "Might we go and see Sarah now? I want to assure her that you and your men are determined to find Rachel." And she wished to assure herself that Sarah was still safe.

Although the September night air had grown chilly, Betsy's new burgundy-colored cloak was still a bit too warm to wear this early in the season; all the same, she draped it around her shoulders before they set out. On the way to Sarah's home, she haltingly told Joseph more of what François had said that morning, admitting that he and Paul Trumbell were both double spies, and what it was that he now wanted from both her and Joseph.

"He wants to know where you and your men have stored the guns and ammunition you took from the British. He said that unless I tell him, I will never see *either* of my sisters alive again."

"The thieving traitor," Joseph spat out. "I assume you told him we have already given the weaponry to the rebels."

"He didn't believe me. He believes you have hidden the guns. If I don't tell him where to find them, he swore he would kill both Rachel *and* Sarah."

"So, now you want to warn Sarah to be on her guard against him."

"Oh, Joseph," Betsy blurted out. "Sarah knows nothing of my spying on the Loyalist women or that I've assisted François in his perfidy. I am so distraught, I can no longer think straight. I don't know what is safe to say to anyone anymore."

He slipped an arm around her shoulders. "Don't fret, love. We shall simply assure ourselves that Sarah is safe and tell her she mustn't allow the Frenchman into her home ever again."

"And that she also must not go out alone at night," Betsy added anxiously, recalling the unknown man who had followed her. "Sarah rarely ventures out after dark, so perhaps I've nothing to fear on that score."

"Until we find Rachel and bring her home safely," Joseph said, "we shall also keep a close watch on Sarah."

Although Sarah was beside herself with worry over Rachel, she expressed gratitude to Joseph for his commitment to finding their beloved sister. She told them her parents had learned from Rachel's friends that Rachel had, indeed, slipped from the house late last night to go a friend's home in order to borrow a lacy shawl. "I expect she wished to wear it the next time she saw François," Sarah said. "Rachel's girlfriend said she left her home about nine of the clock last evening."

"So, unless Rachel met with François quite late," Joseph put in, "she did not, in fact, see him at all last night."

"Evidently not." Sarah murmured. "Which begs the question, when *did* she meet up with him? Much, much later last night, or perhaps very early this morning? And if it were this morning, then why was he not . . .?"

Betsy could stand it no longer. "Rachel is not with François."

Sarah's head whirled around. "How do you know?"

"I saw him today. I confronted him about Rachel. They have not run away to be married but that is not to say he knows nothing of her whereabouts."

"O-oh!" Sarah wailed. "What if he has . . . but *why* would he harm Rachel? Why does he not let her go?"

Both remorse and guilt gripped Betsy. Not a bit of this wretched business was Sarah's, or Rachel's, fault. It was all due to *her* obsession to uncover the truth about what had happened to John. She would never have agreed to François's spying venture if she hadn't believed it would lead to the answers *she* sought. Instead, things were now much, *much* worse than they had been before. Not even Joseph knew the whole truth. "Please, don't worry, Sarah. Joseph has promised to find Rachel. He'll not give up until she is safely home." She darted an anxious gaze at Joseph, who nodded and said . . .

"I promise on my life to find your sister, Sarah. In the meantime, if François should appear at your door for any reason, do not invite the scoundrel in. The man is not to be trusted. You must also promise not to go out any more than necessary, and most especially not at night. I am persuaded the Frenchman is not above attempting also to snatch you."

Betsy was glad to hear Joseph's strong words and that Sarah appeared to heed his warning. When Joseph rose to go, Betsy reached for her cape. "Promise me, Sarah, you'll not speak to François, or allow him into your home ever again."

"I promise." Sarah walked with her guests to the door. "I will never again speak with the Frenchman." Gazing at Betsy, a sad smile softened her strained features. "Wearing that burgundy-colored cape and with your hair flowing loose down your back, you look exactly like Rachel. You are both so beautiful." Tears filled her eyes. "Our parents are mystified over Rachel's disappearance. Our father elicited the help of every man in Friends Church to search for her but all their efforts were for naught."

Betsy pushed down the fearful thoughts swirling in her mind. "We must take comfort in knowing that Rachel did not marry the . . . *him*." She had almost said 'reprobate' but since she now believed the blame for everything rested squarely upon her shoulders, she thought it best to cease pointing fingers. *She* was the guilty party, she and no other.

Far, far into that night, an alarming thought caused Betsy to sit straight up in bed. *What if François was telling the truth?* What if he had no knowledge of Rachel's whereabouts? He appeared to have been taken by surprise when Betsy told him of her disappearance. *What if he were telling the truth?* Never once had she detected the slightest hint that he was deriving pleasure over the girl's disappearance. Rather it seemed he could not care less. Given the man's cunning nature, perhaps when he saw how distraught Betsy was, he'd merely leapt upon the circumstance as a means of coercing *her* to do his bidding . . . to tell him the location of the guns and ammunition Joseph had plundered from the British ships. That Rachel was *already* missing strengthened his position, and to threaten that the same misfortune would befall Sarah provided François an even stronger hold over her.

Betsy pondered the reckoning for several minutes, then wondered if someone *else* could have snatched Rachel, and if so, who?

Sarah had remarked tonight on how very like Rachel Betsy looked in her new cloak, her hair hanging loose down her back in the identical manner that Rachel wore her hair. It was equally as cold last night as it was tonight. Rachel would have very likely donned her new cloak when she set out from their parent's home to walk to a friend's house in the dead of night. Rachel's new cloak was similar in color to Betsy's. In the dark, Rachel would have looked very like Betsy.

Someone had been stalking Betsy.

Someone who thought she could identify *him* as Toby Grimes's killer.

Suddenly Betsy knew that François had *not* spirited Rachel away.

Paul Trumbell had.

CHAPTER 24

The following day, Betsy could hardly wait to tell Joseph what she was certain now was the truth, although *which* particular criminal had kidnapped Rachel did not change the awful fact that her sister was still missing. Because Betsy knew that Joseph and his men would again spend all day searching for Rachel, she did not expect to see him until later that evening. As the long hours of the day dragged on, she found it more difficult than usual to fix her thoughts on the task before her, completing Miss Olsen's wedding gown.

At length, the garment was finished and Betsy wasted no time sending a message to Mrs. Dearborn telling her so. Within the hour, both women arrived at Betsy's shop to collect the wedding dress and traveling suit. Miss Olsen was elated when she tried on the pretty traveling suit and found it fit her like a glove.

"You are a marvel, Mrs. Ross!" the girl's aunt declared. "I cannot think how you managed to complete both costumes in such a short stretch of time."

"My new helper did the bulk of the work on the traveling suit," Betsy replied softly.

"Well, both garments are exquisite and I, for one, could not be more pleased!"

"I am pleased, as well, Mrs. Ross," Miss Olsen said shyly.

The two women rose to take their leave, the action causing a stab of alarm to course through Betsy as once again Mrs. Dearborn had made no mention of discharging the large sum she owed for not one, but *two* garments. Deciding not to put herself through the additional stress of waiting and wondering if and when she'd be paid, Betsy advanced to her desk. Snatching up a piece of paper, she jotted down a few figures. "Here you are, Mrs. Dearborn. I have set down the charges due for both gowns."

"Oh, yes, dear." Mrs. Dearborn turned around. "I quite forgot."

Betsy presented her calculation to the woman and was relieved when she promptly handed over the entire sum.

"We are off for New York on the morrow," Mrs. Dearborn announced gaily. "We have only been awaiting word from you that Anne's gowns were ready before we set out."

"I wish you much happiness in your married life, Miss Olsen," Betsy said. "May you have a pleasant and safe journey to New York City."

"La!" Mrs. Dearborn laughed. "Now that the war is over, I have no doubt we shall be quite safe indeed."

The war was over? Betsy had heard nothing regarding the war in the past few days, not since her sister disappeared. "What is the latest news on that head, ma'am? I have been so busy sewing I confess I have not kept up."

"Well, let me see." Mrs. Dearborn paused. "Last night over dinner I recall Mr. Dearborn remarking that the rebel general who was taken prisoner following last month's battle has been granted safe passage in order to come to Philadelphia to appeal to the Congress for a peaceful resolution to the conflict."

"Oh!" Betsy's eyes widened. "That is quite good news, indeed."

"Anne and I are certain now that what little remains of the poor defeated rebel troops will be gone from the city by the time we arrive." She pulled a face. "I daresay I shouldn't wish to encounter a single one of the wretches. From all accounts, the rebel soldiers are not a pretty sight. Ill-clothed and every last one filthy dirty." She laughed. "It is said one can actually *smell* the rebels from as far as five miles away."

Betsy swallowed a curt reply. "Do come to see me when you return from New York, Mrs. Dearborn."

"Indeed, I shall. You may count upon it, my dear!"

Closing the door behind the Loyalist ladies, Betsy thrust Mrs. Dearborn's offensive remarks from mind, her thoughts fastened instead upon what the woman had said regarding the conflict heading for a swift and peaceful conclusion. If that were true, then neither the rebel troops *nor* the British would have a further need for guns; therefore François would have no one to sell them to, which meant he could not continue to blackmail her into doing his bidding. A modicum of relief washed over her. Until a second later when she realized that Paul Trumbell kidnapping her sister had nothing whatever to do with the war. Trumbell had snatched Rachel for his own reasons. Once again, terror overtook her.

It was after sundown that evening when Joseph finally appeared at Betsy's door, his crestfallen features perfectly reflecting her dejected state.

"No luck today either," Joseph remarked as he followed Betsy into the parlor. "Did you hear anything from Sarah today?"

"I have not see Sarah today." Both sat down upon the sofa. "But, I did hear a bit of good news about the war." Betsy quickly told him what Mrs. Dearborn had said and how she believed it greatly lessened the stronghold François had upon her. "If the war is indeed coming to a peaceful conclusion, he will no longer need to sell weapons and will have no reason to threaten me with harm to either Sarah or Rachel."

Joseph's response was skeptical. "I find it difficult to believe that our rebel troops will give up so easily, Betsy. Not unless we're assured that a good many of our demands will be met . . . sanctions against foreign imports lifted, and various taxes removed. "No." He shook his head. "I do not believe the war will end so quickly or easily, not by a long chalk."

The optimism in Betsy's blue eyes faded. "What shall we do now?"

"Oh." A sudden thought struck Joseph. Reaching into a pocket, he withdrew a scrap of cloth. "I realize you have not seen your sister in a spell, but is it possible she might have been wearing a garment made from this when she disappeared?"

Betsy examined the tattered piece of cloth. Brushing the dust from it, she held it near the candlelight. "The cloth is woolen and although dusty, is not old. It appears to be the same sort of cloth our new cloaks are made from. And it's the right color." Excitement rose within her. "Sarah said Rachel chose the wine-colored cloak, which is similar to the burgundy one I chose. Where did you find this?" she breathlessly asked.

"Along the edge of the Germantown highway fronting an overgrown field. Was quite early this morning, just after we set out. I confess I forgot about it until now."

"It's the only clue anyone has turned up. Might we go there? Now? *Please?*"

"It's late, love, and a storm is brewing. It'll be too dark to see anything along the road, and certainly nothing beyond it."

"Joseph, we must go! Rachel could be lying in that field injured or . . . or worse! We must find her!"

"Very well." He rose to his feet. "It's chilly tonight, Betsy; get your cloak and we'll head out."

Betsy hurried to fetch her cloak. "Perhaps we should take your cart. If we find Rachel injured and unable to walk . . ."

"We'll take Aunt Ashburn's cart." He ushered her ahead of him to the shop door.

"We *must* find her, Joseph; we must!"

On the way to Aunt Ashburn's home, Betsy told Joseph of her conviction that it was *not* François who had spirited Rachel away but was instead Paul Trumbell. And why.

"That does make sense," he agreed. "I haven't seen Rachel since she was a little girl, but Sarah seems to think the pair of you bear a striking resemblance to one another."

"Enough that in the dead of night Trumbell could easily mistake Rachel for me."

At the Ashburn home, Joseph alerted his aunt that he and Betsy were taking the horse and cart in order to scour the Germantown highway in search of Rachel Griscom.

"I didn't want you to hear a noise and think thieves were making off with Priscilla and the cart," he added before he and Betsy headed for the shed behind the house.

Carrying an oil lamp, Betsy waited while Joseph went inside and came back out leading the sleepy horse behind him. It soon became apparent the animal was not taking kindly to having its sleep disturbed or being hitched to the cart at night.

"Whoa there, boy. Settle down," Joseph coaxed, slipping on the harness and tugging the straps taunt. "He generally doesn't go anywhere at night."

"I thought you said the horse's name was Priscilla," Betsy murmured, hugging her cloak tighter about her as she waited.

"It is."

"Priscilla seems an odd name for a male horse."

"Well, given that he's no longer . . . *entirely* male, it seemed appropriate."

Betsy grinned, forgetting for a scant second the serious nature of their errand.

Once she and Joseph climbed aboard the somewhat rickety cart, they set off, the sleepy-eyed horse clip-clopping over the cobblestones through town. Even before they left the city, Betsy pulled up the hood of her cloak as cold wind whipped about her ears. The night air, pungent with the smell of impending rain, felt quite chilly. As they reached the Germantown road, Joseph flicked the reins in an effort to hurry the horse along. But it balked when of a sudden two riders on horseback galloped past them, their mount's hooves flinging pebbles and debris up behind them, causing Betsy to close her eyes and duck her head.

"Damn," Joseph grumbled. "C'mon, boy, giddya' up!"

Presently he said, "I believe it was right about here that I spotted the cloth." He slowed the horse. "Snagged on a twig, or bit of brush."

"Might we head off the road into that field, or . . . would it be too treacherous for . . . Priscilla?"

Joseph chuckled. "It does sound silly when you say his name." He glanced about. "What do you say we tie him up over there, and you and I tramp farther into that field? My mate and I searched both sides of the road this morning and a good way into these woods. Perhaps you and I could go beyond those trees." A hand indicated the dense thicket up ahead.

Betsy nodded as Joseph headed the horse and cart across the field and into a small clearing surrounded by a copse of birch trees. After securing the reins around a tree trunk, he helped Betsy to the ground. Guided by the haze of moonlight flickering through the gathering storm clouds, they picked their way through the thick overgrowth.

At length, Betsy pointed at something up ahead. "Look, just there, I am certain I see something flickering."

"It's a light." Joseph took the lead and before long they spotted what appeared to be several weathered outbuildings. As they drew nearer, it became plain that one of the structures was little more than a primitive lean-to and the larger one, although dilapidated, could have once sheltered cows or horses.

"Do you see that?" Betsy asked in a low tone. "The light looks to be coming from *inside* the barn."

At that moment, they both heard the sound of a horse neigh.

"I heard a horse . . ." Betsy strained to better see through the sheen of mist that had begun to fall. She cocked her head. "I'm certain I can hear voices on the wind."

"Sh-h-h," Joseph hissed. He ducked behind a tree, pulling Betsy with him.

"Perhaps it's the men on horseback," she whispered.

"Could be."

Keeping to the shadows cast by the tall trees, they crept closer.

"It sounds as if they are arguing," Betsy said softly. She tugged at Joseph's coat sleeve. "I heard one of them say *'muskets',*" she whispered.

"Either we've come upon a meeting between a pair of spies, or . . ."

"Or, *what?*"

From their aspect, neither could clearly make out anything, but soon, they both spotted a lone horse and rider emerge from the opposite side of the barn and begin to pick its way through the high grass toward the opposite end of the thicket that Betsy and Joseph had just come through.

"One of them is leaving," Betsy said softly.

"Which means if there were only two to start with, I like the odds now a good deal better."

"Are you carrying your pistol?"

Joseph patted his pocket. "I only hope there aren't more men inside."

In seconds they heard the sound of the horse reaching the dusty road and its hooves break into a gallop. The noise must have also reached Priscilla's ears, for he let out a whinny. The disturbance brought the second man into view.

"Who goes there?" he shouted into the darkness.

Both Betsy and Joseph ducked; their heads and shoulders hidden by the tall grass they'd just tramped through.

Joseph risked a peek upward, then motioned for Betsy to follow him. Both walked bent over, making their way through the high weeds in a circular path and eventually coming up behind the barn. One by one they ran across the clearing to the backside of the building. Betsy, unable to curb her eagerness to find out what, or *who,* was inside, inched along the perimeter in search of a space between the weathered boards wide enough to peek through.

Apparently her movements were not as noiseless as she intended, for again, a male voice shouted, *"Who goes there?"*

Betsy had now reached the opposite side of the building and standing on tiptoe in order to see inside, she gasped. *"Rachel!"*

In one corner of the abandoned building, she saw her younger sister tied to a beam, her hands bound behind her, a wadded up piece of cloth stuffed into her mouth. White-hot anger surged through Betsy. Giving no thought to her own safety, she ran back around the perimeter of the building in search of the entryway, but the split-second she gained the backside of the barn she stopped short when she spotted a very large man emerging from the opposite corner. Paul Trumbell.

Where was Joseph?

Her heart hammering in her ears, Betsy noiselessly stood with her body flattened against the rough wooden planks of the barn. Suddenly, the thud of something, or someone, hitting the ground startled her. She held her breath as the unmistakable grunts and curses of a scuffle reached her ears.

In size, she knew Joseph was no match for the giant. An anxious gaze scanned the ground in search of a rock, or stray length of timber, that she might swing at the massive man. Her hopes were dashed when she saw nothing, and realized again that she had no choice but to remain where she was and pray that Joseph's efforts to subdue the giant would prove successful.

Seconds later, when the ear-splitting sound of a shot rang out on the cold night air, Betsy's heart plummeted to her feet. Gulping past the fear spiraling through her, she again groped along the splintery planks of the building in order to peek around the corner. Once there, all she could see was the shadowy figure of a lone man, the one holding the smoking pistol, as he stood gazing down upon the other. A gust of wind whipping through the treetops allowed a flicker of moonlight to illuminate the killer's face.

"Joseph!" Betsy screamed, running from behind the barn toward the man holding the gun.

His eyes did not leave his prey. "Stay back, Betsy."

She halted in mid-step. "Rachel is tied up inside the barn!"

Pocketing his pistol, Joseph turned away from the body lying on the ground. "Let's get her and be gone before this fellow's friend returns. I don't relish killing two men tonight."

"Is that one . . . dead?"

"Either that or he suddenly fell into a very sound sleep."

In seconds, the two of them reached a wide-eyed Rachel. Sobs of joy over finding her sister alive nearly prevented Betsy from being able to render assistance in untying her sister but she did manage to remove the gag from the frightened girl's mouth.

"B-Betsy?"

"Yes, sweetie, it's me." Betsy hugged her sister, who despite her disheveled state did, indeed, sufficiently resemble her that at first glance it appeared she was gazing into a mirror.

Tears filled the younger girl's eyes as behind her Joseph worked to unloosen the ropes that bound her wrists and ankles. "I heard a shot. You did not kill François, did you?"

"François was here?"

"Yes, moments ago. He and the other man stood outside talking. Please tell me you did not kill François!"

"No . . . not François."

"We need to get out of here *now*," Joseph insisted, flinging the last of the ropes aside.

"My cloak!" Rachel pointed to the soiled garment lying in a heap on a pile of dusty straw.

Joseph snatched it up and all but dragged the two women along with him out of the building and far away from it.

For most of the drive back to town, the threesome scarcely spoke.

Turning onto Sassafras Street and heading down the cobbled thoroughfare toward Betsy's childhood home, she twisted around to address Rachel, huddled in the back of the cart. Betsy hadn't said much to her sister thus far because she didn't quite know what to say. It was apparent Rachel still harbored warm feelings toward François as evidenced by her fear that he might have been the one who was shot.

"Rachel," she began, "You must promise me you will never see François again. He is not the kind, thoughtful man you believe him to be, sweetie, he is . . ."

"He saved my life!" Rachel cried. "The other man, the one who snatched me, he meant to kill me but François would have none of it! I am alive now because of François and none other!"

Betsy refrained from pointing out that Joseph deserved a good deal of the credit for saving her life. After all François had left her tied up inside the barn and it was Joseph who rushed in to untie her. Instead she said, "François Dubeau is a notorious spy, Rachel, a ruthless killer, who works for the British." Everything in Betsy wanted to scream, *He killed John!* but she resisted. "The reason he spared your life is because he is using *you* to threaten *me,* and in order to do that, he was obliged to keep you alive. François wishes me to procure information for him, which I do not wish to provide. He said if I did not meet his demands, he would kill both you *and* Sarah."

Rachel's frightened blue eyes filled with tears. "I don't believe you." She trembled. "I-I love him!"

"It's the truth, Rachel. You must *not* see François again. He will find a way to snatch you again, and the next time, he will *not* spare your life." That Rachel appeared now to be listening somewhat gratified Betsy. "Joseph, tell her what you learned about François."

Joseph repeated what had been told him, vehemently adding that François Dubeau was indeed a dangerous man and not to be trusted. "Rachel, your sister has your best interests at heart. It is unfortunate, but the truth of the matter is, the Frenchman has only been trifling with you."

When fresh sobs overtook Rachel, Betsy attempted to comfort her. "You've had a frightful scare, Rachel, but I beg you to heed what Captain Ashburn says. François is a dangerous man and he will not . . ."

The talk continued on in that vein until Joseph halted the cart in front of the Griscom home on Second Street. Giving her sister a final hug, Betsy and Joseph watched the girl, whose tangled hair and torn clothing bespoke the frightening experience she'd just endured, scamper up the walk and rap at the door. In the darkness, tears filled Betsy's eyes when she saw her father fling open the door and heard her parent's cries of joy as they embraced their lost daughter, then, lovingly draw her into the house. Despite her longing to join in her family's elation over Rachel's safe return, Betsy merely murmured, "Please take me home now, Joseph."

Before Betsy went up to bed that night, she asked one last favor of her seafaring friend. "I think it best that you return to the barn and . . ."

"Bury Trumbell," Joseph supplied. "I quite agree. When François returns tomorrow and finds Rachel gone, his first thought will be that Trumbell disobeyed orders and went ahead with his plan to kill her, which will undoubtedly anger him."

"He'll then set out to extract revenge upon Trumbell," Betsy added. "Perhaps by then, we'll know more about what is happening with the war, whether or not the conflict is truly over." A weary sigh escaped her. "I am so sorry to have drawn you into this, Joseph."

He wrapped his arms about her as they stood in the foyer of her shop. "Your problems are now my problems, Betsy. Whatever troubles you, troubles me. I care deeply for you, lass. I want nothing more than to be with you now and forevermore." He lowered his head to press his lips to hers.

Twining her arms up around his neck, Betsy returned the kiss. "I care for you as well, Joseph, but . . ."

He smiled, albeit sadly. "At this juncture, I'll not press you for anything more, Betsy. Just know there isn't anything in this world that I wouldn't do for you."

Betsy buried her head in his shoulder. The feel of his strong arms wrapped around her and the fresh outdoorsy scent that always accompanied him, comforted her beyond measure. She gazed up at him. Moonlight filtering through the shop window cast shadows across his ruggedly handsome face. Suddenly, a feeling she had not experienced in a long, long time washed over her. She did care for this man. She'd felt drawn to him as a girl, but the pull she felt now was a thousand times stronger. "I care deeply for you, as well, Joseph."

He hugged her to him again, then, reluctantly extricated himself from her arms. "I still have work to do before this night ends."

"Be watchful, Joseph, please. We've no assurance that François will not return to the barn to check on Rachel tonight."

Joseph chuckled. "If he does, he'll not find me alone. I plan to take reinforcements this time."

Betsy smiled. "And I plan to prepare a nice dinner for you tomorrow night."

He gave her another peck on the cheek. "Then I'll make certain I am still alive to eat it."

CHAPTER 25

The storm raged all night and only began to let up the following morning. Upon awakening, Betsy wondered if Joseph and his men had become drenched whilst digging Paul Trumbell's grave, or had they managed to complete the task before the hard rain began to fall? After dressing, she wrapped her cloak about herself and hurried out to the newsstand for a copy of the *Pennsylvania Packet*. Soon after returning home, Sarah rapped at her door.

Shaking raindrops from her cloak, she followed Betsy into the parlor where a warm fire crackled in the hearth. "I'm so very grateful to you and Joseph for finding Rachel. Our parents are also deeply indebted to you."

"I'm grateful that Joseph persevered," Betsy said. "Would you like some tea, Sarah? I've just poured myself a cup."

"Indeed, I would. Thank you." Sarah settled herself onto a wing chair whilst Betsy fetched the teapot. "I confess I still feel quite distressed to have had no word from William."

Betsy handed her sister a cup of the steaming brew. "I was just reading in the morning paper that General Sullivan, who you recall was captured by the British last month on Long Island, arrived in Philadelphia a few days ago to meet with the Continental Congress. The committee that our statesmen appointed is now in New York meeting with General Howe to negotiate the terms of the peace treaty. I believe the war is nearly over, Sarah," she declared.

"Oh." Sarah brightened. "Surely that means William will be returning home soon. That is if . . ." her smile faltered, "if . . . he is still alive."

"Do not lose faith, Sarah. We found Rachel alive. I am certain William is, as well."

"I pray you are right, Sister."

The girls fell to discussing other news and eventually the conversation returned to Rachel.

"She said she never did know why she was kidnapped," Sarah remarked. "She said that the large man, whose name she never learned, was surly and uncommunicative, that the morning after he tied her up in the barn, François came and assured her that he would not allow the man to harm her. She said that every day someone, either the man who took her or another one, brought her food and untied one hand so she might feed herself."

"Given all that Rachel endured, it's understandable she is still confused and frightened by the experience."

"What do you and Joseph make of it? Rachel said you told her François wanted to keep her alive because he was threatening you for some reason."

Betsy set down her teacup. She had feared Sarah would probe for answers to questions she still did not wish to answer. Without revealing any of the particulars regarding François's threat, Betsy confirmed only that he was indeed threatening her and that it was vastly important that neither Sarah nor Rachel ever see him again. "François must not be presented with the opportunity to harm either you or Rachel," Betsy concluded firmly.

"Our parents have declared that Rachel will never, *ever* be allowed to leave the house alone again and most certainly not after dark. She is forbidden to walk to my home, or to any of her girlfriend's homes. Our parents mean to keep a close watch on their youngest daughter now."

"I am glad to hear it."

"Rachel has proven far more rebellious than you or I ever were. Oh, did I tell you?" Sarah smiled. "Hannah is soon to marry. Which means our father now has only one more daughter to marry off."

"I knew Hannah had a beau but I did not know their romance had progressed so far." Betsy smiled. "I do hope her marriage will not fuel Rachel's dream of marrying François."

Sarah sighed. "I fear she does still fancy herself in love with him."

Betsy squirmed. Quite clearly, not all danger from François Dubeau was behind them.

That evening, Betsy grew anxious awaiting Joseph's arrival. She'd spent several hours that afternoon preparing a delicious meal of pastry pies filled with shredded mutton, potatoes, carrots, and leeks, and had seasoned the mixture with the tasty spices Joseph brought her. She had also considered preparing a pot of green peas, but after reading an account in the morning paper that a plot to kill General Washington had been uncovered when two chickens fell over dead after eating green peas that Washington had merely pushed around on his plate, she decided against it.

Still the delicious aroma of what she had prepared wafted up from the kitchen as she drew two fine china plates from the cupboard and arranged everything just so on the table in the parlor. She regretted having no flowers to brighten the table and instead settled on a painted blue and white figurine depicting a couple dancing the minuet. She and John had received the whimsical statuette as a gift when they married.

When Joseph finally arrived, Betsy greeted him with a barrage of questions concerning his previous night's adventure.

Shrugging out of his heavy woolen coat, Joseph said, "We decided it would take far too long to dig a hole large enough to bury Trumbell, so . . . we merely dragged him into the barn and set fire to it."

"Oh, my." Betsy grimaced.

"Blaze shot right to the sky. We watched until the roof caved in, then we fled. I didn't worry about the fire spreading to the woods, since by then rain had already begun to douse the flames."

"So." Betsy sighed. "It's done." She paused. "We've committed a crime, Joseph," she murmured with sad finality.

He drew her into his arms. "It couldn't be helped, love. We've no way of knowing whether or not Rachel would have survived her captor."

"I'm loath to admit it, but I daresay it was due to François's intervention that we found Rachel alive. Trumbell would have killed her straightaway, thinking he was doing away with me. As I've said before, I'm certain Trumbell killed Toby. Although, I haven't proof and I don't know why he did."

"Something to do with spying, no doubt."

Betsy rested her head on Joseph's shoulder. "I've worried about you all day, Joseph."

He kissed the top of her head. "Well, it smells as if you managed to put aside your worry long enough to prepare a delicious dinner."

Betsy smiled as the two took seats at the table and settled down to enjoy the tasty meal. It felt as if she'd prepared a special dinner for her husband, who'd returned home to her at the end of a long day. She'd even put on one of the lovely dresses Joseph had brought her and noticed that he was more finely turned out tonight than usual in an ivory damask shirt, dark blue knee breeches, ivory hose and buckled shoes instead of the rugged boots he typically wore.

"You look lovely in that pretty frock," Joseph said later when she came up from the kitchen bearing a tray laden with spiced apple tarts and cups of steaming hot coffee.

"Thank you, sir. You look quite handsome yourself tonight."

"I've not had much of an opportunity to wear my new finery," Joseph said with a self-conscious grin.

Later, after he'd nudged the fire to a blaze and they were settled side-by-side on the sofa, Betsy snuggled closer to him.

"Sarah conveyed my parent's gratitude to us for rescuing Rachel."

"I'm glad you insisted we go out there last night. If my men and I had trekked further into the woods yesterday morning, we might have found her a good deal sooner."

"But Trumbell might not have been on the premises then," Betsy pointed out. "And now he is safely gone from our lives." After a pause, she said, "You mustn't feel guilty for what you did, Joseph. When one takes into account Paul Trumbell's many transgressions, Toby's vile murder, crimes committed against the Patriots, kidnapping Rachel and breaking into my home . . . *twice*, I daresay he deserved . . ."

"Justice for the giant was, indeed, a long time coming," Joseph agreed. "To be honest, I don't feel the least bit guilty about taking his life. By the time I jumped him, he had already pulled his knife. I was merely defending myself."

"You were defending all three of us. He would have killed you and me; then felt compelled to slay Rachel to ensure she'd not speak of our deaths to anyone."

Joseph heaved a sigh. "Unfortunately, Trumbell is not the first man I've killed. In my line of work, I rather expect he'll not be the last."

Thinking further on the troubling experience, both fell silent. Presently Betsy said, "I wonder what François thought when he discovered the barn burned to the ground. Did he think Rachel had also burned to death?"

"Perhaps he thought Trumbell set the fire in blatant disregard of his orders."

"François's threat is all that hangs over our heads now."

"Which may come to nothing," Joseph said. "Newspapers today were full of stories regarding the meeting of our delegates with the British generals in New York."

Betsy looked up. "Do you think it means the war is truly over?"

Joseph's head shook. "I still cannot fathom our troops giving up so easily."

Betsy stared into the fire. "But wouldn't it be wonderful if the war could end with no further bloodshed?"

"In all likelihood, love, I just don't see that happening."

A few evenings later, in the hope of learning the truth about the current state of the war, Betsy attended a Fighting Quaker meeting and was astonished by what she heard from the group's leader that night.

CHAPTER 26

"We think (at least I do) that we cannot stay in New York and yet we do not know how to go, so we may be properly said to be between hawk and buzzard." . . . General Joseph Reed in a letter to his wife, September 1776.

Reported at the Fighting Quaker meeting was that following the disaster on Long Island last month, dissention was now rife between the rebel troops and their Patriot commanders, including General Washington, whose leadership was being openly questioned not only amongst his own men, but amongst his fellow officers. In a letter Washington wrote to Congress, whom he blamed for the haphazard manner in which war matters were being handled, Washington himself had disdainfully referred to his troops as *'contemptible, untrained, and unfit to bear arms.'* It was said that General Washington was now in a quandary as to what to do in the event the British drove his troops from the relatively safe foothold the army now had in Manhattan. Did the Philadelphia Congressmen want the city left standing to be used as winter quarters by the enemy, or should the rebels burn it to the ground behind them if, and when, they left?

A Fighting Quaker member stood and lashed out at many colonial newspapers, the bulk of which were Loyalist owned, whom the fellow maintained had of a purpose lulled Patriot citizens into the false hope of a peaceful conclusion to the war by playing up the peace talks whilst, even as the negotiations in New York City were underway, British troops were advancing up Long Island towards Kip's Bay, presumably preparing again to attack. Following this disclosure, every Fighting Quake member cried out with both alarm and outrage.

More informed Fighting Quaker members all agreed that without Long Island, New York would be lost. And, as everyone knew, the British now occupied Long Island. With Washington's troops thinly scattered from one end of York Island to the other meant that any single Patriot regiment could provide only feeble protection to whichever rebel fortification the British chose next to attack.

"With our men scattered thither and yon," one member declared, "not a single outpost holds sufficient men to fight off the far larger, and stronger, British army. Furthermore, at this juncture, insufficient time remains in which to reconsolidate our troops into one unit should the need arise."

"Washington's regiment," chimed in a young man sitting near Betsy, "is garrisoned at Harlem Heights while Henry Knox's men are trapped in the downtown area with no way out should the middle section of Manhattan Island be hit next."

At that disclosure, a shudder shot through Betsy. *Henry Knox was Sarah's husband William's commanding officer.* This was the first time in months she'd heard any mention of the location of Commander Knox's troops.

The final question put to the group that night was: should Washington remain to fight what could very well become the final and bloodiest battle of the war, or should he once again attempt to withdraw his troops as best he could given their dissimilar locations? More importantly could the rebels escape for the second time in less than a month, or would the British army launch yet another surprise attack upon the rebel troops and this time, quite likely destroy the entire Continental Army?

Everyone agreed that the outlook for the Patriots had never looked quite so grim.

Betsy came away from the meeting with her heart in her throat. The war was definitely not over. On the way home that night, she and her friends, Minette and Emma, all agreed that they had indeed been led to believe that the war was headed for a swift and peaceful conclusion when all along quite the opposite was true.

As the girls were nearing Betsy's shop, Minette announced that a few mornings ago, her brother had departed again for New York City. The unexpectedness of that disclosure caused Betsy's head to jerk up.

"François has gone to New York . . . again?"

"Oui."

"But . . . *why?* Forgive me," she faltered. "I-I do not mean to pry. It's just that, as we learned tonight, the situation in New York is quite volatile."

"That is why he go," Minette replied. "François learn that General Washington be in great need for . . ." she lowered her voice, "brave men to spy on the British for heem. He promise to pay his new spies *très bon.*"

"Oh," Betsy nodded.

To line his pockets with gold would indeed be sufficient reason to lure François to New York despite the threat of further fighting. However, with Rachel now free of the Frenchman, his sudden departure might also mean that, for the nonce, he had abandoned his quest to ferret out the location of the guns Joseph had plundered from the enemy and to resell the weapons to the rebels for a profit. Far simpler would be the task of altering a few ill-come-by messages and presenting them to General Washington as *bona fide* intelligence.

Crawling into bed that night, Betsy's apprehension heightened as she thought further on François traveling to New York for the express purpose of spying for General Washington when, in truth, his loyalty lay with the British. Now, more than ever, the great rebel general needed reliable intelligence he could act upon with confidence. The more she thought on it, the more she became convinced that General Washington should be warned against the Frenchman. François Dubeau was a *double* spy and the disloyal wretch posed an enormous threat to the Patriot Cause.

But whom could she tell?

Because Dr. Franklin was one of the delegates appointed to meet with the British generals in New York to negotiate the peace settlement, he was presently away from Philadelphia.

Still, she felt duty-bound to tell someone. She had to protect the Continental Army and every Patriot in America from a ruthless double spy bent on destruction. François Dubeau *had* to be stopped!

CHAPTER 27

"I only regret that I have but one life to lose for my country." . . . Nathan Hale, before being hung by the British for spying, September 22, 1776.

Before Betsy could fix upon a manner in which to expose François Dubeau for the double spy he was, the headline splashed across the front page of the *Pennsylvania Packet* the following morning brought her to her knees.

"British Take Manhattan Island!"

Her heart thudded in her ears as she read the terrifying words printed in bold letters on the page: *"So terrible and incessant a roar of guns few in the army have ever heard before! With more than eighty cannon pounding point-blank at the rebel troops, the barrage continued well above an hour. From his command post on the crest of Harlem Heights five miles to the north, His Excellency General George Washington heard the roar of the cannon and saw the smoke rising in the distance. Washington flung himself onto his mount and galloped at a race to the south. Reining up near a cornfield about a mile inland from Kip's Bay, he observed disorder all about him, men running for their lives in all directions, leaving behind muskets, cartridge boxes, canteens and knapsacks. Drawing his own sword, Washington began to shout orders, but all was chaos. Amidst the smoke and flying sod and sand, the rebel soldiers had little opportunity to fire back. Men were cut down and buried where they fell. What is left of the Patriot army is now on the run. Late last evening as many as nine thousand additional redcoats swarmed onto Manhattan Island."*

Betsy's heart lodged in her throat as she attempted to digest the horrible news.

In another notice, Patriot General Nathanael Greene was quoted as saying the rebel army's *'cowardly flight in the face of the enemy was shameful, scandalous, and disgraceful. It was a miserable, disorderly retreat.'* The final sentence in the long column of gray print caused Betsy's heart to stand still. "*General Henry Knox and the bulk of his regiment are still unaccounted for.*"

Stunned, Betsy flung aside the newspaper. To convince Sarah that her husband was still safe would likely now be an impossible task. This latest British attack had taken things from bad to worse. The world she and her family and friends had known all their lives was being ripped from beneath them. To Betsy it felt as if her very breath was being squeezed from her lungs. The British would now surely take Philadelphia and every Patriot amongst them hung as a traitor to the crown. What chance did any of them have for escape? Where could one run that the British would not follow with bayonets pointed at their backs, or muskets aimed at their hearts?

Any moment, Betsy expected an overset Sarah to rap at her door. When her sister failed to come, Betsy saw nothing for it but to rush to her side. Either Sarah had not yet heard the awful news, or she'd heard it and was far too distraught to walk the few short blocks to Betsy's home to seek solace.

"Uncle Abel told me," Sarah muttered in a tight voice after she answered Betsy's knock at the door and Betsy explained her reason for coming. "He didn't want me to be alone when I read the account of the battle and the . . . horrible aftermath."

"I'm so sorry, Sarah." Betsy gathered her weeping sister into her arms. Leading her to the kitchen, the older girl dropped onto a chair while Betsy put on the teakettle, then, joined her sister at the table.

"Joseph often hears a good bit of news on the wharf," Betsy offered. "Perhaps later today I'll learn more regarding this latest battle from him."

"I'll never see my husband alive again." Sarah's head dropped to her arms folded before her on the table. "William is already dead."

"Sarah, please; you mustn't give up hope. We feared that Rachel was dead, and yet she came home to us safe. God will look after William and also bring him home. Please, do not let your faith waver."

In an attempt to console her grieving sister, Betsy remained with Sarah all day and even agreed to stay the night.

The following morning when Betsy returned home, she found a note from Joseph slid beneath the door. In it, he said he and his men were setting sail for an undisclosed port and that he'd come to see her the minute he returned to Philadelphia. Once again, Betsy's heart sank. She had craved Joseph's reassurance, had desperately needed his strength. Instead, just as Sarah was awaiting her husband to come home, she must now also wait, and worry, for Joseph's safe return.

Betsy *did* have an inkling where Joseph was off to. He'd told her the last time they were together that he'd learned of a stash of British muskets, cannon and gunpowder secreted in a fort a hundred miles or so south of

Philadelphia and that the fort was not only well hidden, it was virtually
unguarded. Quite possibly it was unguarded, Betsy thought, because every
single British soldier on the continent had been deployed to slaughter the
rebel troops on Manhattan Island.

Scanning the newspapers later that day, Betsy read in miscellaneous
war news, or as she termed it, *belated* war news, that Congress had issued
a resolution against the burning of New York City, reasoning that when it
was retaken by the Patriots, it would be of more use to them if the city
were left standing. Of course, whether or not to burn New York City was
now a moot point as the Patriots had already been driven from it. The
Pennsylvania Packet also reported that the peace talks with General Howe
had indeed taken place on September 11 on Staten Island, but that when
the delegates from the Continental Congress learned that whatever terms
they agreed upon would also have to be sanctioned by the king in London,
the committee dispersed with no definitive agreement reached. Yet one
more bit of war news being reported a day after the fair, Betsy muttered
irritably. Quite obvious now was that peace for the Patriots, and
independence for all Americans, would be a long time coming. If it came at
all.

A fortnight later, with Joseph still away, Betsy decided one morning before
going to the market to pay a call on the widow Ashburn. Perhaps she had
received word from her nephew and would know if Joseph had completed
his mission, and whether or not he and his men were safe.

"Joseph rarely writes to me when he's away," the older woman told
Betsy. The two were seated in Aunt Ashburn's cool parlor. No fire blazed
in the hearth even though the late September days were quite cool. "He
stays far too busy on board ship to write and, of course, to get a missive to

anyone from hundreds of miles out to sea is nigh on impossible. I confess that when my boy set out this time, I did not have a good feeling about the voyage. There is far too much unrest in the world today. The stories one reads in the newspapers are quite distressing."

"Indeed." Betsy nodded. "I read only this morning that above five hundred buildings in New York City did burn to the ground a few days ago. British General Howe is blaming the blaze on those of our troops who were unable to escape the city following the last awful battle. Perhaps it means my sister Sarah's husband, William, who we *think* was trapped in Manhattan, is not dead after all. At least, that bit of news provided us with a glimmer of hope."

"We are living in terrible times." Aunt Ashburn sighed. "I pray daily that my Joseph will return home unharmed." Morning light filtering through the cloudy windowpanes of the Ashburn parlor illuminated the wrinkles crisscrossing the older woman's face. Her furrowed brow revealed the deep concern she felt for her beloved nephew.

"I suppose when Joseph leaves the city not even he has any notion when he might return," Betsy murmured sadly. She drew her shawl closer about her shoulders in a futile attempt to ward off the chilly air eddying about the room.

Aunt Ashburn nodded. "Since Joseph never knows what he'll encounter on the high seas, to predict his return is nigh on impossible. Even without the threat of war or hostile ships lurking about, any number of unforeseen things can happen at sea. Anything from a mild storm to a deadly hurricane could befall him. And with the sea now full of British ships . . ." her voice trailed off. When moisture pooled in the gray-haired woman's eyes, she withdrew a damp handkerchief to dab at them.

"Joseph will come home safely to us." Betsy reached to squeeze the older woman's cool fingertips. "He's an accomplished seaman and quite a clever fellow, you know."

Aunt Ashburn smiled wanly. "My Joseph is a clever boy, isn't he?"

Betsy attempted to push down her own worries for Joseph's safety. "I am on my way to market, Aunt Ashburn. Are you in need of anything?"

"I could ask the same of you, my dear. Only a few days ago my housekeeper was lamenting the fact that food and provisions have become quite scarce of late. About all one can be certain of finding at market these days is spoiled meat and stale bread."

"Oh, my." Betsy grimaced. "I did notice last week there seemed to be a marked shortage of fresh meat and virtually no vegetables at all."

Aunt Ashburn struggled to her feet. "Come, dear, I will share what I have on hand with you."

"Oh, no, I couldn't," Betsy protested.

"I insist. With only me and my housekeeper hereabouts, there are times when our food spoils long before we have a chance to prepare it, let alone eat it."

Because Aunt Ashburn would not take no for an answer, Betsy returned home from her visit carrying a sack of flour under one arm. A wedge of mutton and several quarts of fruit and vegetables, which the older woman's housekeeper had preserved for winter, were tucked in her basket.

The next time Sarah came to see Betsy, she, too, remarked on how there now seemed less and less foodstuffs available at the market. "And the price for what is there has become quite dear."

"I had expected the money I earned from sewing Miss Oslen's wedding gown to see me through winter," Betsy said. "But after paying this month's rent, I wonder that I shall have enough left to see me through another month, let alone another quarter."

"I do not believe William would have gone off to join the fighting if he had foreseen the difficulties those of us left behind would face."

Although she hadn't yet heard from William, or his commanding officer, Betsy noted her sister was putting on a brave face and carrying on as if William would come marching home any day now. Betsy wasn't certain what had caused the marked change in Sarah's outlook, but she put it down to her steadfast faith in God. Betsy appealed to the good Lord every day to bring both William and Joseph safely home.

One day in early October, Betsy read in the newspaper the sad account of an eager young schoolmaster from New Jersey named Nathan Hale who had bravely volunteered to spy for General Washington. Unfortunately, in only a few days time, the young man had been apprehended by the British and promptly hanged for his crime. Although she felt quite sorry for the patriotic fellow, clearly Nathan Hale was not as devious, or as cunning, a spy as François Dubeau. Otherwise she might be reading an account of his demise.

Setting aside the newspaper, Betsy realized she'd become so caught up in following the distressing war news, and Sarah's plight, and her own fear for Joseph, that she'd taken no further steps to curb François's deadly mission in New York. The only good she could see in his departure was that with François gone from Philadelphia and Paul Trumbell dead, she no longer had a pressing need to worry over Rachel's safety. Plus she had accomplished what she'd originally set out to do, uncover who was responsible for the explosion that took John's life and learn the identity of Toby Grimes's killer . . . although she still had no concrete evidence that

Paul Trumbell *had* actually killed Toby, or why the boy had been slain. Still, to halt François Dubeau before his dastardly deeds further damaged the Patriot Cause was of paramount importance. And it had also fallen to her to accomplish that feat.

CHAPTER 28

"The air and hills smoked and echoed terribly. The fences and walls were knocked down and torn to pieces; men's legs, arms, and bodies mingled with cannon and grapeshot all around us." . . . a Pennsylvania soldier following the Battle of White Plains, New York. October 1776.

Because Betsy knew the peace talks in New York had come to nothing, she expected that by now Dr. Franklin had returned to Philadelphia, so the only thing she could think to do toward exposing François Dubeau's duplicity, and perhaps getting word to General Washington that a double spy had traveled to New York for the express purpose of joining his intelligence gatherers, was alert Dr. Franklin.

Upon entering the noisy newspaper office that October afternoon, she was surprised when the young clerk promptly told her, "Dr. Franklin has left the country, Mrs. Ross."

"Left the country? But, I expected he would have returned from New York by now." Betsy was fairly yelling in order to be heard above the noisy clack of the presses churning out the evening newspaper in the cluttered print shop.

"No, ma'am." The clerk leaned toward her over the counter, his tone dropping to barely above a whisper, which meant Betsy had to strain in order to hear him and only by reading his lips did she make out what he was attempting to convey. "Dr. Franklin departed last week for France."

"France!" Betsy blurted out in a normal tone, then cast a surreptitious glance over one shoulder. "Dear me; I had no idea he was planning to embark on such a lengthy voyage." And certainly not *now,* she thought. The notion of an overseas journey at this time of year was . . . well, not wise.

The clerk smiled sagely. "Dr. Franklin purposely kept the news of his journey and his destination under wraps. Philadelphia is a-swarm with British spies these days," he informed her.

Betsy's brow furrowed. Were British spies scouting out Philadelphia in preparation to overtake the city, she wondered.

"Is there anything else I can do for you today, ma'am?"

"No . . . thank you, sir, that will be all." Distracted by the chilling thoughts swirling in her mind, Betsy turned to go.

"Would ye like a fresh copy of the evening news, ma'am?"

Betsy nodded absently and accepted the still damp copy of the newspaper the clerk handed her. Thanking the fellow, she tucked the paper under one arm and quitted the noisy print shop to return home.

Why would Dr. Franklin choose to make an arduous voyage overseas *now?* Everyone knew that with winter close upon them, now was the worst possible time of year in which to make a crossing. And why did he go to France? Did his destination have anything to do with the war? Could he possibly mean to appeal to the French government for French troops to aid in the colonies fight for independence, just as the British had solicited, and were receiving, help from German mercenaries?

Heading home, Betsy continued to mull the matter over. Were France to agree to aid the colonies, especially if they supplied money, as well as soldiers, might mean the rebels still had a fighting chance. She could think of no other plausible reason why the busy statesman would suddenly wake up one day and decide to embark upon a sea voyage to France. Plus, she reasoned, Dr. Franklin had departed in secrecy in order to conceal not only his *plan,* but also his *destination* from the prying eyes of British spies, who, according to his clerk, were a-swarm in the city.

Before Betsy reached home that day, she took a whit of pleasure from realizing that all on her own, she had unraveled a well-kept state secret. On the other hand, she had accomplished nothing in regard to warning General Washington against the duplicitous Frenchman. Perhaps she could write a letter, but who could she trust to deliver it? And would anyone here even know where Washington was? There were other newspapers in the city, but she suspected they were Loyalist owned, so to reach General Washington through another newspaperman did not seem a viable option. She longed to discuss her dilemma with Joseph, but he was adrift somewhere upon the high seas. Once again, she was left with no choice but to wait . . . and wonder.

At the next Fighting Quaker meeting, news of the war proved as dismal and bleak as the daily reports Betsy read of it in the newspaper.

In quite a dejected tone, the group leader told the members that in mid-October four thousand British soldiers had outflanked the rebels below their own fortifications at Harlem Heights. Upon spotting a sea of redcoats advancing towards them, the far-outnumbered rebel troops had simply abandoned their posts and retreated northward toward White Plains, New York.

Just yesterday, on October 28, British General Howe had dispatched a combined force of thirteen thousand redcoats and Hessian troops up the northern road towards White Plains. Suddenly, it was said, one column of marching redcoats turned sharply to the right and headed straight towards Chatterton's Hill, where only a small company of Patriot militia stood guard. Although General Washington quickly ordered additional troops to scramble atop the higher hill, it was too few too late. The attack on the rebels was vicious and deadly. Washington at once pulled his troops even further north to North Castle, leaving General Greene behind to hold Fort Washington with a regiment of only three thousand men.

"The small bit of good news at this juncture," the group leader said, "is that at North Castle, our troops will be able to take on fresh supplies and provisions. I understand a good many New Englanders up that way are sympathetic to the Patriot Cause." The remark met with only feeble applause.

At this juncture, both the rebel troops and Fighting Quakers were all left wondering where the British would strike next? Would the entire rebel army be wiped out before the bitter hostilities ceased? As things now stood, the Patriot troops had lost not only Long Island, but the whole of Manhattan, and now White Plains, New York.

Walking home from the meeting that night, Betsy, Minette and Emma glumly discussed the dismal state of their world.

"Only a few short months ago, we were all in high spirits," Emma lamented. "We were so elated as we watched our boys gaily march off to war on Independence Day. Since then, we've not had one word of good news."

"I have received only one letter from Caleb since I wish heem *'Au revoir'* in August," Minette said.

"I've heard nothing from Joseph," Betsy added, "and he isn't anywhere near the fighting."

"Has Sarah heard from William?" asked Emma.

Betsy shook her head.

"Well." Emma sighed. "We've a goodly supply of mufflers and mittens ready to deliver to the rebel army. I wonder where our troops will winter? And will we be able to get the warm clothing to them?"

Betsy and Minette turned palms upward.

Betsy silently wondered when the much-needed French reinforcements would arrive?

One afternoon in early November, Joseph surprised Betsy by appearing at her door. Because she had begun to lose all hope for his safe return, she fell into his arms, tears of joy swimming in her eyes. "Praise God, you are safe!"

"I only just arrived, love, and came straight to see you." He hugged her small body to his much larger one.

Because it was an especially warm fall day, they decided to walk to Aunt Ashburn's to tell her Joseph was home. Betsy purposely did not ask if his mission had been successful. She knew he'd divulge the details of his journey, good or bad, of his own accord. Instead, they spoke of the war.

"It appears now the British have changed their entire plan of attack," Joseph said. "Word on the wharf is that a sen'night ago, after taking White Plains, the entire British army suddenly did an about face and headed off in a southwesterly direction toward the Hudson River and King's Bridge.

Appears now they intend to penetrate the Jerseys and then . . . unfortunately, head on down to Pennsylvania."

"Oh, Joseph. What will we do if the British march into Philadelphia?" Betsy thought again of the French troops that she fervently hoped Dr. Franklin would be successful in acquisitioning and that the French soldiers would arrive in time to save them from the British.

"We fight. Even now, my men are organizing a reserve unit of soldiers willing to shoot any man wearing a red coat. I daresay I'm careful not to wear mine ashore." He grinned. "We plan to arm the new militia with the very muskets and gunpowder we just stole from the British."

"Your mission was successful then?" Betsy asked breathlessly.

"In a manner of speaking. Despite the Union Jack I hoisted and the British uniforms we donned, we still met with a good bit of resistance when we attempted to seize the enemy weapons." He shrugged. "In the end, the two paltry British guards gave in and helped us heft the heavy crates onto the deck and store 'em in the hold. They even shook hands with us and wished us well before we hove anchor and sailed away."

"But why did it take you so long to return to Philadelphia?" Betsy wanted to know.

"Gale winds and a torrential rainfall befell us about fifty miles south of here. Took on so much water, I feared we'd sink." He grinned down at her as they crossed busy Market Street. "All the time my men and I were sloshing through knee-deep water, I kept thinking about how much I wanted to see your pretty face again. And, here I am."

"I'm so glad, Joseph. Your aunt has been frightfully worried about you, as have I."

"I've missed you, too, Betsy."

At her home that evening, Betsy hastily prepared supper for the two of them and whilst they ate what remained of the boiled mutton she'd prepared the day before, she brought Joseph up to date on what was happening here at home.

"Mostly we've all just kept our heads down scouring the newspapers for news of the war. Poor Sarah still hasn't received word from William. I can't help but fear for him."

"And what of François?" Joseph asked, reaching for the last wedge of day old bread lying on the platter. "Is the blackguard still pestering you?"

"Minette hasn't mentioned her brother since he left for New York, ostensibly to volunteer his services to General Washington to spy on the British. I tried to get word to His Excellency through Dr. Franklin but learned that *he* had suddenly departed for France. *I* think . . ." Betsy told Joseph her theory regarding Dr. Franklin's secret mission.

"Well, if that's the case, we've cause to rejoice," Joseph replied. "On the down side, if French reinforcements do come, it will be spring or early summer before they arrive."

Betsy's face fell. "Why so long?"

Joseph shrugged. "As a rule, armies generally don't fight during the winter months. They'll likely pitch tents or throw together some sort of shelter and lay low waiting out the harsh weather, then, resume fighting in the spring."

"Oh-h." Betsy sighed. "And now we must also wait out the long winter. I fear we have a very long way to go before this dreadful war is over."

Joseph pushed up from the table. "What do you say we wait some of it out on the sofa?" His tone turned playful. "I've been thinkin' about kissin' those sweet lips of yours for a mighty long time, love."

Rising from the table, Betsy smiled up into his hazel eyes as he led her to the sofa where they settled down before a warm fire, and for the next hour, nary a thought of war, or fighting, entered either of their heads.

CHAPTER 29

"The movements and designs of the enemy are not yet understood." . . .
General George Washington in a letter to John Hancock, November 1776.

In the coming weeks as Betsy awaited further news of the war, she and Joseph attended Sabbath services together several Sunday mornings at Christ Church. On one especially sparkling Sunday afternoon following a mid-day meal with Aunt Ashburn, Betsy and Joseph strolled up Walnut Street to South East Square. Walking arm-in-arm through the park, the sun felt warm on their backs despite the crisp autumn breeze. Betsy reveled in the peaceful sounds of birds chirping as they darted here and there amongst the colorful red and yellow leaves.

"Autumn is a lovely time of year, almost as lovely as springtime," she remarked. "If it weren't for constant threats of war hanging over our heads; I would truly enjoy autumn this year."

"We've also the threat of snow coming and . . ."

Suddenly, Betsy ceased listening to Joseph, for a scant three yards up ahead she caught sight of another couple strolling on the red brick path. Her blue eyes snapped fire.

"Look! Rachel and *François!*" She pointed at the pair. "I cannot believe the audacity of that man!"

Jerking from Joseph's grasp, Betsy quickly closed the gap between the two couples. "How dare you!" she cried, coming up alongside the elegantly attired Frenchman and her beautiful younger sister.

"Betsy!" the startled girl cried.

"Do our parents know where you are this afternoon?"

Rachel lifted her chin. "Pray, leave us be!"

"Yes, Betsy," taunted the Frenchman. "Leave us be."

Upon reaching them, Joseph took her arm. "Come along, sweetheart."

Betsy jerked free of his grasp. "Do our parents know . . .?"

"Betsy, please." Again, Joseph took her arm. "Beg pardon, sir," he addressed the taller gentleman. "Good afternoon, Miss Griscom." He politely touched his cap.

"It was a pleasure to see *you* again, Captain Ashburn."

François inclined his head a notch.

As the accosted couple resumed their stroll, Betsy continued to glare at them. "I am so angry I cannot speak!"

"Yet you managed to convey your feelings quite well to your sister and her beau."

"Her *beau!*" Betsy cried. "If you recall, only a few short weeks ago, her *beau* was bent upon killing her!"

"Well, apparently she has forgiven him," Joseph muttered.

"Oh!" Whirling around, Betsy headed back the way they'd come. "I refuse to watch the two of them together! I refuse!"

As Betsy lay abed that night, various scenarios played out in her mind; each a method of doing away with François Dubeau. Because she had brought the man into their lives, it was clearly up to her to protect, even prevent, her far more innocent, and apparently, *lovestruck,* younger sister from falling prey to the scoundrel's trap. She simply could not let the reprobate harm her sister. But beyond snatching Rachel and holding her prisoner *here,* how could she stop the pair from seeing one another? She simply *had* to find a way to beat François Dubeau at his own game.

That François called at her shop the following afternoon came as no surprise to Betsy.

"What do you want?" Not inviting the elegantly dressed gentleman into her shop, Betsy regarded him with a fiery gaze, her arms folded beneath her bosom.

"Is that any manner in which to greet a friend?"

"You are the last person in the world I would call a friend. What do you want?"

A shadow of annoyance crossed the Frenchman's handsome face as he nonetheless brushed past Betsy into the foyer.

She continued to stand near the opened doorway. "Unless you state your business at once, sir, I shall summon the authorities."

He whirled to face her, his black eyes mere slits in his face. "And tell them what? That you and your pirate friend *murdered* M'sieur Paul Trumbell?"

Betsy's gaze did not waver. "It will be your word against mine."

"Your sister Rachel was also there. I assume she witnessed the crime."

"As *you* well know, Rachel was tied up in the barn; consequently, she saw nothing. Nor did I for all that. I was hiding on the opposite side of the building. I heard a shot and when I peeked around the corner, it was far too dark to see a thing. I have no idea who fired the shot. For all I know it could have been *you*. Rachel mentioned you also being there that night."

"If it weren't for *my* intervention, Trumbell would have killed your sister the night he nabbed her. Trumbell is the impetuous one . . . as evidenced by the reckless manner in which he stabbed your young helper."

Betsy gasped. "Paul Trumbell *did* kill Toby! I knew it."

François shrugged. "The boy had it coming. One does not take money and then fail to discharge an assignment."

"W-what had Toby promised to do that he did not . . . "

François smirked. "You are so innocent, *ma chérie*. Your young friend bragged that *he* could poison the great General Washington the next time the statesman visited your shop."

"Oh!" Betsy did recall asking Toby to carry the heavy tea tray up the steep stairs to the parlor the day the delegation called to ask her to sew a flag. Her heart sank. "Toby was just a boy."

"Who lied. Unfortunately, by the time he told Trumbell he could not complete the task, he had already spent the money we had given him. Apparently that angered Trumbell, and without considering the consequences, he recklessly felled the boy on the spot."

"Toby's father was away fighting. He had been left alone to care for his family."

"Which is none of my concern," François countered. "As I said, Trumbell is, rather *was,* the impetuous one. I would have persuaded the boy to complete the task. To drop a bit of poison into a teacup is not difficult. *Pas de problème.* In a few hours," he grinned wickedly, "the victim falls ill, then keels over dead."

Betsy felt sick to her stomach. "You are a ruthless, evil man," she said through gritted teeth. "And mark my words, one way or another, I shall bring you down."

"Oh, I am so very frightened of you, *ma petite*." Casting a gaze around the workroom of her shop, he advanced to a table and scooped up a pair of sharp pointed shears. "It is you who should be frightened of me. You know far too many of my secrets." Eyeing her coldly, he did not elaborate. Then.

Betsy saw something in his gaze she had never seen before. Cold, hard, hatred. Though shivers of fear crept up her spine, white-hot anger kept her from retreating onto the flagway in order to escape the madman. She watched as he separated the blades of the shears and began to pick at his fingernails with one pointed tip.

"*Très* sharp," he said, a lethal gaze pinning her. "Although I am not the impetuous one, had I a mind to, I could easily . . . ensure your silence this very moment." He half-smiled. "A dreadful shame, the pretty *mam'selle* fell upon her own shears and . . . bled to death."

Betsy did not flinch. It was three of the clock in the afternoon and above half a dozen people were parading along the walkway. Because she was visible to all of them, she felt reasonably safe. "You are wasting my time, François. I insist you leave at once."

"Have you tea made, *chérie*?"

"I am not your *chérie* and I do not offer tea to traitors."

"Ah. A pity." He tossed the scissors aside. "I had thought we might adjourn to the parlor. There is something of a . . . private nature I wish to discuss with you."

Betsy did not budge.

"Very well, then. We shall speak here. First, I wished to apprise you of *my* success with His Excellency, General Washington. My new employer has proven quite generous. He rewarded my efforts on behalf of the . . . Patriots quite handsomely."

Betsy's lips firmed. "I can imagine how meticulously you performed your duties."

"Indeed, I did." His tone was mocking. "Before quitting New York, His Excellency entrusted me with a packet of documents with instructions to deliver them immediately upon my arrival here in Philadelphia."

Betsy's eyes narrowed. If the wretch pulled the packet from his pocket and declared he had no intention of delivering it, she would snatch up the scissors and plunge them into *his* silk clad chest. Then as he lay bleeding upon the floor, she would deliver the missive herself. "Where are the documents now?"

He rubbed his chin. "I seem to have . . . misplaced them." He turned both palms up. "Quite careless of me, I own. Perhaps I left them on a table at an inn where I paused to sup, or . . . perhaps I accidentally gave them to a friend."

One of Betsy's finely arched brows lifted.

"As you know, several of my friends are British officers."

"*Get out!*" Betsy lunged at the tall man. *"Get out!"*

Amusement etched on his face, François grabbed her wrists causing her to struggle to free herself from his grasp. "I quite like a spirited woman."

"Unhand me! I never want to see your murderous face again! *Get out!*" Unmindful of the ruckus she was causing, Betsy's screams grew louder. *"Get out! Now!"*

"You all right, Miz Ross?" came a male voice from the doorway of the shop. "I heard screamin'."

At once, François released her.

Her bosom heaving with rage, Betsy turned to the uniformed man. "This gentleman was just leaving."

The Watch stepped past Betsy into the shop. "Miz Ross would like you to leave now, sir."

His jaws grinding together, François stepped past Betsy and the older man. Before exiting, he cast a final look of loathing at her. "This is not over . . . *salope.*"

Her nostrils aflare, Betsy said nothing. She had never before been called a bitch. François Dubeau was a vile man. *Step into her parlor, indeed! She was no one's fool.* Still, she could not help wondering if he had, indeed, come here today intent upon killing her? Fortunately, the Watch had intervened before he had a chance to do so.

It was quite some time before Betsy's anger subsided and when it did, her thoughts turned to Toby. Poor, sweet lad. She had always assumed his father was a Patriot, now she wasn't certain. Quite possibly the boy did not understand why the war was being fought. He had obviously become drawn into spying as a way of earning much-needed money for his mother and siblings. Obviously when he'd reported to Trumbell, or François, that General Washington had called at her shop and that she served the great man tea, *they* had leapt upon the idea of . . . oh, why was she further upsetting herself by ruminating on what *might* have happened? Still she kept returning to it. Perhaps after thinking about what he'd been told to do, poison the rebel leader, Toby's conscience had prevented him from carrying out the deadly assignment. Her heart ached for the boy whose death had been in vain, since as it turned out, General Washington never again visited her shop.

Although Betsy now knew the truth about Toby's death, and she also knew who killed John, unfortunately, learning the truth did not mean all her troubles were over.

"It was dreadful, Joseph," Betsy became agitated all over again when she relayed the vexing details of the Frenchman's visit to Joseph later that evening. "He was deliberately taunting me, telling me how Toby was slain because he refused to put poison in General Washington's tea, and how *he* had betrayed Washington by handing over the general's private correspondence to a British officer."

"I agree the Frenchman's actions are despicable, Betsy, and young Toby's death was most unfortunate, but you mustn't continue to overset yourself. You attempted to warn General Washington against François. I own it's regrettable that you were unable to do so, but it appears nothing more can be done. Let us pray no real harm resulted from his latest prank."

"*Prank?* This was not a prank, Joseph! You said yourself that François is a cunning and dangerous spy. He does not engage in pranks! He is a killer." Her eyes squeezed shut as she bit her lower lip to keep from revealing that François had threatened to kill her this afternoon. She did not want Joseph, who was also a trifle impetuous, to rush out and put a bullet through the man's heart. It was too risky. The action would make Joseph a target for retaliation; or worse, he would be caught and hanged for the crime. She could not let that happen. Instead, she had no choice but to conceive her own plan to trap the man, and she would not tell Joseph anything of it.

She had also intended never to tell Joseph about the part François played in John's death, however, later this afternoon as she thought over her confrontation with the contemptible man it had occurred to her that if François discovered that Joseph's ship was now anchored in the harbor chock full of muskets and gunpowder, there was no saying what he might do. He had single-handedly caused one deadly explosion. Her refusal to supply François with the information he sought regarding the weaponry meant it was possible he could wreak the same havoc again. An explosion aboard the *Swallow* would not only kill Joseph, it could wipe out his entire crew who also lived aboard the ship. Moreover, a blaze on one ship in the harbor could easily destroy half a dozen other ships also anchored nearby.

"I . . . have not told you everything François has done," Betsy began softly.

Joseph exhaled. "Something told me there was more, sweetheart. You are far too overset. Tell me what is plaguing you now."

Betsy told Joseph all that François had said the day he denied involvement in Rachel's kidnapping; that it was *he* who caused the Dock Street explosion that eventually claimed John's life. "I refuse to watch you die in the same dreadful manner John did. Or, any one of your crew.

"François is a heartless killer, Joseph, and he must be stopped."

Convinced of the impending danger now, Joseph leaned forward. "Tell me what you want me to do, Betsy."

"For now, I merely l want you to sail the *Swallow* some distance away from Philadelphia and store the weapons and ammunition you took from the British in an . . . undisclosed location. Swear your men to secrecy. François appears to be quite masterful at uncovering the truth. He must not discover where you store the cargo."

The following night Joseph told Betsy his aunt had a friend with a little-used rock barn behind his stone farmhouse at a place called McKonkey's Ferry.

"Even if François does learn I've stored the weaponry there, to burn down a building made of stone will not prove a simple task," he assured Betsy.

* * * * *

A sen'night later, both Betsy and Joseph attended a Fighting Quaker meeting and were as stunned as everyone by the war news now filtering down to them from New York.

On Friday, November 15, British General Howe had sent one of his officers, under cover of a white flag, to deliver a message to the rebel commander at Fort Washington. The message was terse. *"Surrender at once or face annihilation."*

The following day, Saturday, November 16, four Patriot generals, George Washington, Israel Putnam, Nathaneal Greene, and Hugh Mercer, convened to discuss what should be done regarding the British officer's threat. During the interval the generals were deliberating, the enemy suddenly descended upon the rebels. The initial assault was an unrelenting pounding of cannon aimed at Fort Washington's outer walls. Seconds later, four thousand Hessian troops headed down from the north while British General Cornwallis's entire regiment, plus a battalion of Highlanders, simultaneously struck from the east. Before the rebel troops had a chance to fend off the unexpected assault, another force of three thousand redcoats came marching up the hill from the south. In a matter of minutes, above eight thousand British troops, more than *four* times the number of rebel soldiers that had been assigned to defend Fort Washington, had committed to slaughtering every last rebel inside the fort.

One soldier reportedly said, "When I saw a cannon ball blow off parts of two men's heads, I ran for the fort."

Following the ferocious battle, the remaining Patriots who were left standing were marched from the fort between two lines of Hessian soldiers and ordered to lay down their arms. The defeat of Fort Washington, agreed all the Fighting Quaker members, was yet one more disastrous loss for the rebel army's now quite battle-weary soldiers.

As Betsy and Joseph walked home that evening, she murmured, "I shudder to think what is in store for us now. A fortnight ago we thought the British were headed straight for Philadelphia. Now it looks as if the war might end before it comes to that."

"When and where the enemy will attack next cannot be predicted. I honestly don't believe either side knows how to end this conflict. I suppose the fighting will continue until there's not a man left standing. And then, we'll still be obliged to deal with the king. Looking back, it seems foolish that we set out to take on the whole world."

"We chose to fight because our Cause is just!" Betsy cried. "We are an independent nation and we should be allowed to conduct our lives as we see fit."

A lop-sided grin softened Joseph's features. "I do not wish to fight with you, Betsy. No doubt I'd lose. I quite agree with the Patriot Cause, but anyone with half an eye can see that we have far fewer men and resources than the entire British Empire. At any rate, with winter fast approaching, the fighting will no doubt cease for a spell. At least until spring."

"And then what?" Betsy muttered glumly.

"We must take this one day at a time, love." He brought her gloved hand, clasped warmly in his, to his lips. "Have you spoken with Sarah recently? I'm certain you told her about seeing François and Rachel in the park. What does she say about your sister's rekindled romance?"

Betsy sighed. "She says Rachel is convinced that the larger man, the one who snatched her, would have killed her if François had not intervened. Rachel is persuaded that if you and I had not appeared in the barn that night, François would have returned and set her free."

Joseph grimaced. "And what of your parents? Are they aware that Rachel has resumed her courtship with the Frenchman?"

"Sarah said they still refuse to allow her to go out alone after dark, which, does reassure me; but what is to prevent our younger brother George from escorting Rachel to Sarah's home of an evening and then François coming later to collect her?" Betsy's head shook sadly, causing the hood of her cloak to slide down her back. In the lamplight her rich chestnut hair gleamed like burnished copper. "I daresay Rachel is as headstrong as I was when I was her age. I was just as determined then to see John as Rachel is now to see François. And Sarah was equally as eager and charitable to help John and me as she is now to help Rachel."

"Have you considered that perhaps François truly cares for Rachel?"

"François is incapable of caring for anyone but himself," she snapped.

"Rachel is a very pretty girl. The two of you do look enough alike to be twins."

"François is a killer and by his own admission, he is merely trifling with my sister," Betsy replied. But, what did it matter, she asked herself. Some way . . . somehow . . . the lover's ill-fated romance would come to an end. In the meantime, she must also be vigilant for her own safety. François's threat that he wished to see her dead felt like the blade of a guillotine poised to come crashing down upon her head. And she had no way of knowing when the blade would fall.

CHAPTER 30

"I feel mad, vexed, sick and sorry. This is a most terrible event. Its' consequences are justly to be dreaded." . . . *General Nathanael Greene in an anguished letter to fellow commander Henry Knox following the fall of Fort Washington.*

A few days later, Betsy read in the *Pennsylvania Packet* that General Charles Lee was so furious over the loss of Fort Washington that he tore out some of his hair. The war correspondent said that not only had the British taken above one thousand rebel soldiers prisoner after the Battle at White Plains, but following the surrender of Fort Washington more than twice that number were marched into the enemy camp as prisoners. The loss of nearly four thousand men from an army already devastated by sickness and desertion was a bitter blow to the morale of both the rebel troops and their commanders. At Fort Washington, the British made off with vast quantities of arms, tools, tents, blankets and over one hundred cannon. It was a devastating loss. The *Packet* declared the Continental army was now crying for any man fit enough to hoist a musket to his shoulder and fire it.

Reading further Betsy's heart sank when the newspaper reported that British commanders were astonished to discover how many of the captured rebel soldiers were boys not yet fifteen years of age, all *'indifferently clothed, filthy, and without shoes'*. Betsy prayed her younger brother George, who she remembered as being quite high-spirited, did not take it into his head to march off to war. Thinking it was bad enough that his Uncle William suffered from want of warm clothing and food reminded

Betsy that the closet off her parlor was still crammed full of clean shirts, breeches, and scores of pairs of cast-off shoes. Unfortunately, neither she nor the ladies who had helped gather the clothing had any notion how to get the much-needed supplies to the rebel troops.

The following day, newspaper headlines screamed of yet another devastating loss to the already dwindling rebel forces. Under cover of darkness, the reporter said, on a cold rainy night General Howe had dispatched four thousand British and Hessian troops across the Hudson River. The enemy battalion had to make its way up a steep, almost perpendicular, footpath before they could attack the last rebel holdout, Fort Lee. The perilous climb provided General Washington sufficient time to rush from his command post to the fort and shout orders for the men to abandon the garrison at once. Unfortunately, all their supplies had been left behind—guns, tools, hundreds of tents, even their breakfast which had just been put on the fire to cook. When the British arrived, they found the fort deserted, except for a dozen soldiers who'd gotten into the rum supply the night before and were falling down drunk. Those soldiers were the only ones taken prisoner that day.

Betsy shook her head, wondering if perhaps a far more trustworthy spy than François Dubeau had been responsible for warning General Washington of the impending attack upon Fort Lee? In an ironic twist, she offered up a quick prayer of thanksgiving that François was now in Philadelphia, meaning he was safely out of reach of General Washington and unable to wreak further havoc for the rebel troops with his twisted intelligence.

The alarming outcome of the Fort Lee loss was that General Washington and his retreating troops were now presently fleeing from the

British, both armies plunging deeper into New Jersey, ostensibly headed straight toward Philadelphia.

Her heart in her throat, Betsy laid aside the pages of the *Packet*. Clearly evident now was that despite winter weather setting in, British General Howe meant to chase the rebel soldiers . . . here.

"Uncle Abel says the British will soon overtake Philadelphia," Sarah glumly announced the following afternoon as she entered Betsy's shop, her warm woolen cloak flapping about her legs as a gust of icy cold air accompanied her indoors.

"Come warm yourself by the fire, Sarah."

Once the girls had drawn up chairs as close to the blaze as was prudent, given their long skirts, Sarah said, "If our troops do reach Philadelphia, at least I might be able to discover if William is still alive."

Betsy nodded. All the dreadful war news she'd read in the newspaper the past several days had so lowered her spirits that to summon even weak words of hope for her sister was more than she could manage. "I pray George will not join the fighting."

"Our brother still clings to the Quaker point of view. He will not fight, and our parents would never allow it."

"You would not help him, would you, Sarah? Even if he wanted above all things to go?"

"No!" Sarah looked askance. "I would not wish the worry and fear I've suffered these past months over my husband's safety upon anyone, least of all our mother."

"I am exceedingly glad to hear you say that." Betsy considered whether or not to tell Sarah she had uncovered the truth about Toby's death, but decided against it. She also did not reveal to Sarah anything that had happened the afternoon the Watch escorted François from her shop. Or that she had seen François with his mother and Minette yesterday morning at market. Although Betsy had longed to greet her girlfriend, who looked fetching in the blue woolen cloak Betsy had given her, she thought it fortunate that the threesome had not spotted her. She had already filled her basket and was ready to depart when they began to browse amongst the stalls. Still, the unexpected glimpse of François had caused her stomach to roil with fear and her breath to grow short. Now, she said, "I cannot help but continue to worry for Rachel's safety. So long as she continues to see François . . ."

"Betsy, do leave off complaining about Rachel and François. I am aware that you detest the man, but I'm sick to death of hearing you speak disparagingly of him. Perhaps *he* will join the fighting . . ."

"For *which* side?" Betsy demanded. "Forgive me, I will honor your wishes and cease to speak ill of him. But, I refuse to cease *thinking* ill of him."

"I am far too concerned for the safety of my own husband to fret over Rachel and her romantical intrigue."

"Fine." Betsy rose and taking up the poker, prodded the charred logs in the hearth until one fell apart and rewarded her with a shower of sparks.

"Perhaps I should be going," Sarah said suddenly. Snatching up her cloak, she flung it about her shoulders.

"Please do not leave in a huff, Sarah." Betsy followed her sister, her chin held aloft as she quitted the room. "It's bad enough that our world is at war, I cannot bear it when you and I are at odds."

In the dimly lit corridor, Sarah softened. "It is not my wish to bicker with thee either, Sister."

"Then we must cease quarreling altogether." Betsy drew Sarah into her arms and for a long moment, the frightened sisters clung to one another.

When they parted, Betsy noted moisture glistening on Sarah's lashes. Weeks and months of worrying over whether or not her husband was dead or alive was indeed taking a toll on her. Although Betsy could not bring William safely home, she could continue her quest to eliminate one troublesome faction that continued to threaten the Griscom family. François Dubeau. Precisely how she would accomplish *her* goal, however, before he accomplished *his* continued to elude her.

CHAPTER 31

"These are the times that try men's souls. The summer soldier and sunshine patriot will, in this crisis, shrink from the service of his country; but he that stands it now, deserves the love and thanks of man and woman. Tyranny, like hell is not easily conquered." . . . *Thomas Paine, 1776.*

December, 1776

The next morning, clutching her shawl about her shoulders, Betsy sat with her back to the kitchen fire before the small table she'd dragged closer to the hearth. To pass the morning below stairs meant she could conserve firewood by not building up the fire in the parlor until much later in the day. Because her supply of logs seemed to be rapidly diminishing of late, she'd begun to suspect that during the night, one, or more, of her neighbors were helping themselves to her woodpile. But since she hadn't been able to catch the culprit in the act of carrying off the costly logs, she could not point fingers.

After finishing her breakfast, Betsy opened the *Pennsylvania Packet* and was stunned by the bold headline splashed across the front page.

"BRITISH PUSHING TOWARD PHILADELPHIA!"

Her heart plummeted to her feet.

"Dear God, the British are here!"

The newspaper further reported that the enlistments of two thousand Patriot troops from the New Jersey and Maryland militias had expired in early December and that those regiments, and others, had without so much as a backward glance calmly walked away from the war.

Betsy's head dropped to her chest as she worked to push down her tears, her fear and her anguish.

Reading further; Nathanael Greene was said to have written in a letter to John Hancock here in Philadelphia: *'Two brigades left us at Brunswick. The enemy is within two hours march and fast advancing upon us, with some redcoats in sight. I ordered the bridge over the Raritan River at Brunswick destroyed. But truth be told, my remaining forces are totally inadequate to halt the enemy when they do reach us.'*

Betsy could feel her heart thudding in her ears.

Greene added that despite burning the bridge behind him, he and his men watched with dismay as the British merely forded the river on foot. A bitter skirmish ensued, with British and Patriot cannon firing upon one another. *'By time we left Brunswick, we had not three thousand men left, a very pitiful army upon which to trust the liberties of America.'*

Although Betsy hadn't the heart to read further, she felt compelled to do so.

Cornwallis's redcoats now occupied Brunswick, said General Greene, and Hessian soldiers had declared everything within Patriot's homes was booty. New Jersey Loyalists were every bit as villainous as the Hessians, Greene added, freely leading the German soldiers to the homes of their Patriot neighbors and watching whilst the men stripped the poor women and children of everything they had to eat or wear, then the enemy soldiers savagely ravished the mothers and daughters whilst compelling the horrified fathers and sons to witness their brutality.

Upon reading that, Betsy lurched to her feet, stumbled up the stairs to the ground floor and unbarring the back door, fell sick to her stomach mere inches beyond the doorstep.

When Joseph called later that evening, he found Betsy curled into a ball upon the sofa in the parlor, the fire in the hearth a bed of white ash.

"What is it, love? Have you taken ill?"

"I am sick to death of this dreadful war." Tears gathering in her eyes, Betsy choked out, "T-The British will be here at-t a-any moment and all our lives will be over."

Sliding onto the sofa, Joseph gathered a weeping Betsy into his arms. "The war is not yet over, love." He held her close and when, at last, she grew calm, he rose, ostensibly to build up the fire. But not finding a spare stick of wood anywhere indoors, he exited the rear door only to return a few minutes later.

"You've no firewood, love."

"My wood seems to be burning itself up."

"Meaning?" His brow furrowed as he advanced into the room.

"The logs appear to be walking away."

Joseph huffed. "Wood thieves are striking with greater frequency all over the city. Well, I cannot leave you here all night without warmth." He snatched up his coat. "I shall return straightaway."

Within an hour Betsy heard Joseph's rap at the back door. She opened it and watched him cart several armloads of wood into the house, depositing as much as possible near the hearth in the parlor and carrying twice that much below stairs and stacking it on either side of the kitchen hearth. "There." He brushed the dust from his hands. "I've stacked no wood outdoors, so at least you can rest assured that what I brought tonight will not disappear before daybreak."

As he and Betsy returned to the parlor, his tone brightened. "The good news is that just now a crier on the wharf was shouting that General Washington and the entire Continental army are at this moment crossing the Delaware River from New Jersey."

Betsy eyes widened. "General Washington is *here?* In Philadelphia?"

"Coming ashore just north of here. Bonfires are blazing all along the coast lighting the way for our troops. Apparently our army means to dig in and winter here."

"Oh, that is good news, indeed. But . . . have we sufficient men and arms to fight off the British when they follow our troops?"

"Our new volunteer militia, over one thousand men that I and my crew helped to recruit and arm, plan to join forces with Washington's army at first light tomorrow. Only moments ago the crier said that General Washington declared that to defend Philadelphia from the British is his first priority."

"Oh-h." For the first time in days, the flicker of a smile lit Betsy's flushed face. Twinning her arms around Joseph's neck, she clung to him.

"I am so glad you came tonight, Joseph. I was feeling so forlorn. Thank you for the firewood. I don't know what I would have done come morning."

He drew back and gazed down into her glittering blue eyes. "So, you admit you cannot get along without me, eh?"

Her smile turned sheepish. "I desperately need your help, Joseph."

"So, there it is," he said with high satisfaction.

Before leaving, Joseph told Betsy he meant to load up his aunt's cart with the supplies he'd confiscated from the unguarded British fort. "I've tents, knapsacks, and blankets aplenty. Even now, my men are collecting whatever tools we can scrape together from farmers hereabouts. Our army will need picks, axes, shovels and hammers to build winter huts and chop wood. My men and I will deliver the supplies tomorrow."

"But . . . how will you know where to find the troops?"

He blinked. "In all likelihood the smell will lead us straight to 'em."

Betsy grinned. "I've heard our men have become quite filthy."

"If the Delaware weren't so icy cold, I expect Washington would order his men to bathe in the river before they come ashore."

The remark elicited something akin to a chuckle from Betsy. "I wonder if our entire army has reached Pennsylvania?"

"Crier said all but General Lee."

"Lee and his men have not yet arrived?"

"Apparently his *men* are on their way. Crier said General Lee was captured and taken prisoner this morning at Trenton."

"Oh, how dreadful."

"Said he was captured wearing only his dressing gown and slippers. Seems he was breakfasting at a tavern near Trenton when half a dozen British officers burst in and surprised him. Lee didn't even have time to reach for his pistol, which he probably hadn't carried down to breakfast with him anyhow."

"God help us, where will it end?" Betsy sighed. "I expect more to the point is *how* will it end?"

"In victory!" Joseph enthused. "Victory for the Patriots! Victory for the Rebels, and for all of us Americans. And don't forget that, love." He drew her close for a good night kiss, and some minutes later, rose to take his leave. "I've a full day ahead of me tomorrow."

"You'll come again tomorrow night?" Betsy asked anxiously.

"Not even the British could keep me away."

Minutes after he'd gone, Betsy realized she should have asked him if he would take the men's clothing, warm mufflers, mittens, and socks the ladies had knitted to the troops.

Sarah came by early the following morning, alarmed that British forces had now drawn so near the city, but equally as relieved as Betsy that General Washington's troops were also nearby.

"Perhaps William is amongst the soldiers," she said breathlessly as Betsy snatched up an empty basket and the two set out for market that cold winter day.

Outdoors, the bustle and confusion on the city streets puzzled Betsy. "What is going on?" she exclaimed. "I've not been out of doors in several days."

"It's the same everywhere," Sarah said. "Now that everyone knows the British are coming, they are fleeing the city. Neighbors on either side of me last night were burying their valuables in the backyard by candlelight."

As Betsy and Sarah advanced up the avenue, Betsy's wide-eyed gaze darted to the right and left. Neighborhood merchants were boarding up shop windows. Other frightened folk were spilling from their homes carrying furniture and armloads of clothing. At the curb, men hastened to tie their family's belongings onto the beds of wagons and carts. The cobblestone street bustled with horses laden with goods and possessions as frightened citizens vacated the city.

"It's an exodus," Betsy murmured. "Where are they fleeing *to?*"

"My neighbors to the west have friends in Virginia. The Fullers across the way are headed for the Carolinas."

"Our parents will not leave Philadelphia, will they?"

Sarah shook her head. "I expect Father will simply drape his Union flag from an upstairs window and hope for the best."

Betsy's lips thinned. Of course, he would. The Griscoms and most all other Quakers up and down the seaboard were perceived to be Loyalist. She wondered if when the British troops arrived, would Joseph hoist his Union flag atop the *Swallow's* mast in an attempt to save his ship, and quite possibly his life?

Joseph apprised her of his plans that afternoon when he unexpectedly arrived at her shop.

"I've just learned that General Washington has ordered every ship and vessel of a size within sixty miles north and south of here be destroyed."

"Destroyed?" Betsy's eyes widened with alarm. "But, why?"

"To prevent the British from crossing the Delaware in pursuit of the rebels."

"Oh, Joseph, that's dreadful. What are you going to do?"

"Leave."

"*Now?*"

"Not right this minute. The *Swallow's* hemmed in. But as soon as the ships that are blocking her leave port, I'll be right behind them. I've no choice, love. I'll not hang around here and watch my ship burn."

"Have we time to take a load of supplies to the army before you go?"

Joseph looked quizzical. "What do you wish to take to the men?" He cast a gaze around her shop and noting the colorful silks and satins, fancy tassels and trim, said, "I doubt the men will take time to hang up frilly curtains in their huts."

Betsy was halfway to the rear of the house. "I've a closet full of . . ."

In less than a quarter hour, Joseph had piled the men's clothing, mufflers, and mittens onto the bed of his cart and was about to pull away from the curb when Betsy ran back out onto the street. "I'm going with you!" Pulling her cloak snugly about her, she scrambled up on the platform beside Joseph. "We must collect Sarah. She's beside herself wondering if William is encamped here with the troops."

Without a word, Joseph slapped the reins over Pricilla's back. Sarah was overjoyed when Betsy and Joseph wheeled up before her home that blustery December afternoon. But three quarters of an hour later, when the cart bounced into the woods to the west of King's Highway beyond Philadelphia, both women were shocked by the gruesome sights that greeted them there. To the right and left amongst the tall trees, all was chaos and confusion. They saw a few soldiers hacking up small trees they'd felled; others sat huddled around feeble fires, apparently too weak to move. Several makeshift tents had been pitched, the flaps and loose ends snapping in the brisk breeze. Hugging tattered blankets about their rail-thin shoulders, clearly not a single man was properly clothed for a winter's day spent out of doors. Some of the men, Betsy noted, wore both shirts *and* breeches; others wore only one or the other. Most all of the men were without shoes. Instead of proper footwear, the men had wrapped filthy rags about their legs and feet. In place of hats or caps, they'd wound strips of cloth around their heads. Most every man looked frighteningly emaciated. Both Betsy and Sarah lamented that they'd not brought along food.

"I see no need to go any further, Joseph. Stop right here," Betsy said.

The three set about distributing the contents of the cart. In moments, skeletal-thin arms reaching for the woolen mufflers, mittens and socks surrounded them. Before the women's eyes, men who wore no clothing at all beneath the ragged blankets they clutched, turned around and letting the blanket drop to the ground, pulled on clean breeches and shirts, then sat down to tug on stockings and shoes. Turning back to face the women, most men had tears in their eyes and could manage only a nod of thanks, others murmured a heartfelt, "Thank you, ma'am."

Sarah began to ask each and every man if he knew the whereabouts of a soldier named William Donaldson.

"He's with Henry Knox's regiment, sir. Do you know him? Have you seen him?"

Betsy also began to ask. "Might you be acquainted with a soldier named William Donaldson, sir?"

"Donaldson? No, ma'am."

"Sorry, ma'am. Might I have another pair of them nice wooly stockings, please, ma'am? My buddy there, he . . ."

"Of course; here you are, sir. We're very happy you're here. Our prayers are with you." Betsy fought to keep tears at bay. She'd had no idea how pitifully wretched the Patriot army had become, or how sparse and shameful were the conditions under which they lived. How these poor courageous, ill-fed men could summon the courage and energy to fight yet one more battle was far and away beyond her comprehension.

"We *must* bring food!" Sarah exclaimed. She turned to Joseph. "Might we go back to the city now, please, and bring back food? *Please?*"

"Sarah?" came a frail-sounding male voice from behind them. "Sarah, is that you?"

Sarah spun around and spotting a tall, thin man clutching a filthy scrap of blanket about his bare shoulders, she blinked, and then cried, "William? *William!*" Dropping the items of clothing in her hands, she burst into tears and flung herself into the arms of the gaunt man, his own tears of joy weaving white trails in the filth darkening his face.

Watching the touching scene unfold before her, fresh moisture gathered in Betsy's eyes. Sobs of joy caught in her throat as she turned toward Joseph, who was also blinking away tears.

"Praise God, William is alive," she said.

"Indeed. Praise the Lord," Joseph murmured.

Sarah sobbed all the way back to the city. "He refused to come home with me," she repeated over and over. "Why would he not come home with me, Betsy? *Why?*"

"William is a not a deserter, Sarah. He's a soldier. His place is with his men."

"He could return to camp tomorrow." She sniffed. "He had no clothes. He looks as if he's eaten nothing in weeks, perhaps months."

"All the men want for food." Betsy hugged her distraught sister. "We shall return tomorrow, with food."

"Betsy," Joseph said soberly. "I'll not be here tomorrow."

"Aunt Ashburn will lend us the cart, won't she? And Priscilla?"

Joseph nodded. "I am certain she will."

* * * * *

Joseph helped Betsy from the cart that afternoon and despite the cold December air swirling about them, he kissed her goodbye as they stood on the walkway before her shop door.

"My plan is to sail at least a hundred miles downriver, leave the *Swallow* in the care of a skeletal crew; then the rest of my men and I will either walk back, or perhaps ride, if we can manage to get a couple of horses on board before we shove off."

Gazing up into his serious hazel eyes, a brisk wind sent the hood of Betsy's cloak tumbling down her back. "Do be careful, Joseph."

"If all goes according to plan, I'll be back before Christmas. Otherwise . . . try not to fret. I don't expect there'll be any fighting whilst I'm away. With the holidays close upon us, both armies will be hugging their campfires. Depend on it, love, there'll be no fighting for quite a spell."

Betsy nodded, hoping against hope that Joseph was right. As he hurried back to the cart at the curb, she scampered after him. "Joseph!"

He paused. "What is it, love?"

"Don't forget to ask Aunt Ashburn if Sarah and I might borrow the cart and Priscilla tomorrow so we can take food to the men."

Grinning, he scooped her again into his arms. "Here I thought you'd come running after me for one last kiss."

Betsy smiled. "That, too." Their lips met and when Joseph drew away this time, Betsy realized it was on the tip of her tongue to say "I love you . . ." Only she was glad she hadn't, for the name that would have followed was not Joseph . . . it was John.

As Betsy stood watching Joseph's cart lumber away, all the worries she had tried to push to the back of her mind came rushing again to the fore.

As they had re-entered the city just now, she'd caught a glimpse of her sister Rachel walking with François down High Street. He was looking straight ahead; Rachel, an arm twined through his, was gazing adoringly up at him as if hanging onto his every word. The sight had caused Betsy's heart to lurch to her throat . . . and also made her think of John, and who had been responsible for his death.

There was no saying what skullduggery the loathsome Frenchman was planning now. To know that he could be lurking anywhere, ready to strike at her was, at the very least, disconcerting. But what could she do? With Joseph leaving the city she could no longer count on him to protect her, or come to her rescue. Her only choice was to redouble her efforts to remain vigilant and pray that François did not make good on his threat to kill her, or preface his attack by hurting, or killing, either of her sisters.

CHAPTER 32

"Our only hope now is upon the speedy enlistment of a new army. If that fails, I think the game is pretty near up." . . . General George Washington, December 1776.

As those Philadelphians who steadfastly refused to leave the city became increasingly aware of the deplorable conditions of the rebel army camped nearby, they willingly tightened their belts in order to share their own scarce provisions with the troops. Not a day passed that at least a dozen wagons and carts, loaded with clothing, blankets, and food, rumbled up

King's Highway in order to deliver the much-needed goods and supplies to the starving men.

In the next few weeks, Sarah's spirits visibly rose as she and Betsy made above half a dozen trips back and forth to the army camp. The girls took meat pies, vegetables and baked goods for William and as many of his men as their meager offerings could feed. On two occasions, Betsy's younger brother George accompanied them, he being especially fond of his Uncle William and happy to see him again. Betsy was pleased for the opportunity to see George again for she'd not seen her little brother since he was a boy. George Griscom was now a strapping young man of nearly seventeen, far taller than Betsy and quite good-looking.

One day as Betsy and Sarah returned to town, Sarah fretted that they could not take enough food to feed every single soldier.

"It's the vast number of ill men I feel sorry for," Betsy replied as she carefully wheeled the cart onto the dirt road leading back to the city. Once they'd gained the dusty highway she slapped the reins over Priscilla's back. "If so many of our fellow Philadelphians hadn't fled the city, I'm certain even more would be eager to help the troops. It's fallen to so few of us to care for them. And with our own supplies dwindling, I fear we may all soon want for food and medicine."

"Nonetheless," Sarah replied, "we cannot let a single man starve. We must press on, even if we've nothing left on our own tables to eat."

"You heart is far more generous than mine, Sarah."

"That is untrue, Betsy. It has not escaped my notice that you are spending far more time than usual in your kitchen preparing stews and meat pies to take to the troops."

"It gives me something to do. I've no sewing to occupy me these days. And with Joseph still away . . ." her voice trailed off. With Joseph still away, she did, indeed, spend a great deal of time in her underground kitchen, but she made sure that whilst cooking every single door and window in her home was securely latched against unwanted intruders.

"I do so wish William's commanding officer would grant him leave to spend Christmas with me." Sarah's tone sounded wistful.

"Perhaps he will. Joseph declared it unlikely there would be any fighting until spring."

Sarah's eyes cut round. "You have not heard?" she asked softly.

Another wagon was fast approaching; the pair of horses galloping clean down the center of the highway. Betsy pulled on the reins to slow Priscilla's progress. "Heard what?"

Sarah chewed on her lower lip. "I expect I shouldn't say anything. William insisted I tell no one."

"Tell no one *what?*" Betsy demanded. "If William has said something to you of the army's plans, I insist you tell me at once, Sarah. What is it? What is General Washington planning?"

Sarah inhaled a ragged breath. "William said that . . . General Washington is planning to launch a surprise attack upon the Hessian troops in Trenton. Perhaps before Christmas."

"But Christmas is next week!" Betsy gasped. "To do so at this juncture would spoil everyone's holiday."

"William says that more than half the army's enlistments will expire the first day of the New Year," Sarah explained. "If Washington does not launch an attack now, he'll have very little army left come next year."

"Oh, I-I did not know that." Betsy knew there had been a strong push of late to enlist more men, but until now she hadn't fully understood the reason for the urgency. Given that there would be no actual fighting until spring she had wondered why they wished to take on more soldiers now, considering the shortage of supplies. Suddenly it occurred to her that if Sarah knew of the army's secret plan, perhaps . . . *others* knew of it as well. "Sarah, have you spoken of this to anyone?"

"I've said nothing to anyone. William swore me to secrecy."

"It is imperative that you abide by his wishes, Sarah. William's life and the lives of all our soldiers depend upon it. Promise me you will say nothing to Rachel."

"I have not seen Rachel . . . alone, in weeks. Not since I learned that William is alive. Since then, my husband has occupied my thoughts to the exclusion of all else. I have not spoken with Rachel," she said again.

From her sister's agitated tone, Betsy could tell that Sarah was growing irritated, quite likely because she suspected that Betsy was about to once again proclaim that François Dubeau was a British spy and if Sarah told Rachel of the rebel army's plan, that . . . . She fell silent, desperately hoping that Sarah had indeed said nothing to Rachel and that no one had said anything regarding General Washington's secret plan . . . to François.

Much, much later that evening, Betsy began to wonder *how* the Patriot army planned to cross the Delaware River if every ship and boat in the vicinity had been destroyed? So far as she knew, other than a few small ferryboats, there was nothing left for miles around still afloat. The few ferryboats that had been spared were capable of carrying only two or three passengers at a time, consequently it would take hundreds, perhaps thousands, of trips across the river before every single rebel soldier could be carried to the opposite shore; and vice versa were the enemy to somehow seize these small boats in order to attempt a reverse crossing. Moreover, as slow as the little rowboats traveled, to cross the river in one of them would prove a suicide mission for it would be child's play for the waiting army to pick off each and every man before he had time to climb

out of the shallow boat and dive for cover. But, she assumed General
Washington knew what he was about and had a viable plan in mind.

Considering this new development, however, meant that she had no
choice but to set her own secret plan into motion now. She had conceived
the idea soon after Joseph left the city and had been quietly considering all
aspects of it since.

CHAPTER 33

*"Expense must not be spared in procuring intelligence in regard to the
enemy's strength, situation, and movements. Without this we wander in a
wilderness of uncertainties."* . . . *General Washington, December 1776.*

At a recent Fighting Quaker meeting, a plea had been read from General
Washington begging private citizens to help with covert activity. Of
course, the announcement had caused Betsy's stomach to churn as she had
no reason to believe that François was not still in General Washington's
employ. Which meant with Hessian troops occupying Trenton just across
the Delaware River, intelligence and false intelligence must be flying with
lightning speed back and forth across the river, the duplicitous Frenchman
profiting hand over fist.

Several Sundays ago at services, an acquaintance had mentioned to
Betsy that John's sister Joanna Ross Holland was wintering in Trenton
whilst her husband was away fighting with the Continental army. Both
Betsy and her friend had expressed concern for Joanna's safety, hoping

that with Hessian soldiers now occupying the township that Joanna and the kinswomen with whom she was staying were not being forced to share lodgings with the enemy. Although Betsy often thought of her former sister-in-law and longed to see her, she had not spoken with Joanna since John's funeral nearly a twelvemonth ago.

That Joanna was now in Trenton gave Betsy a valid reason to venture across the Delaware River and into the village. On the down side, the location of the ferry landing on this side of the river was a goodly distance from Philadelphia and it was an equal distance from Trenton on the opposite shore, meaning she might not be able to comfortably walk the entire way there and back in one day. Consequently she'd be obliged to stay the night in Trenton and pray that she'd be gone from the village before the fighting began, depending, of course, upon *when* the surprise attack commenced. One other disturbing matter, one that vastly troubled Betsy, was the possibility of stumbling upon Hessian soldiers either on her way to Trenton or on the way back. Recalling the newspaper account of the atrocities committed by Hessian soldiers upon women caused her more than once to thrust all thoughts of the risky undertaking from mind.

But, she kept returning to it.

She may never be afforded another such golden opportunity again. And she would never forgive herself if she did not take full advantage of it now. If Joseph were here, he would, of course, attempt to talk her out of the notion, or insist upon accompanying her. Even if she told him nothing of her plan, he would no doubt sense her preoccupation as she contemplated it and when he finally wrenched the truth from her, *then* he would talk her out of it.

In the end, Betsy knew she had to move forward. To succeed would mean she had done all in her power to avenge John's death *and* prevent

François Dubeau from feeding additional false information to General Washington and further damaging the Patriot Cause. If Washington meant to launch a surprise attack upon Trenton, Betsy meant *before* the attack to provide the great leader with factual information that would help, and not hinder, the rebel troop's all-important maneuver.

As Betsy and Sarah set out for the rebel camp the following day, Betsy casually mentioned to her sister that she was thinking of going to Trenton on the morrow to see Joanna.

"You cannot be serious!" Sarah exclaimed. "Hessian troops are occupying Trenton!" She lowered her voice. "It is where General Washington means to launch his surprise attack."

"All the more reason for me to go *now*," Betsy replied. "The village may soon be destroyed and once it is, I may never have another opportunity to see Joanna. She will return to her home in Baltimore and in all likelihood, I shall never . . ."

"So, you mean to *warn* her?"

"No, that is not what I . . . "

"You told *me* to keep silent and now *you* mean to warn . . ."

"I have no intention of giving away our army's plans, Sarah. And neither must you. I do need your help, however. I need both you *and* George to come along tomorrow . . ."

"You want George to escort you to Trenton?"

"No."

"Actually now that I think on it, that is quite a good idea, Betsy. I would feel much better about this foolish notion of yours if George were along. He could . . ."

"No, Sarah. For George to escort me would be far too dangerous. The Hessian soldiers might mistake him for the enemy and cut him down. I refuse to risk our brother's life!"

"But you will risk your own. And for no good purpose that I can see," Sarah persisted.

Betsy's lips pursed. She had not anticipated having to quell Sarah's many objections. "Sarah, I intend doing this whether or not you think it is a good idea. I need George to come along tomorrow merely to drive the cart since I did not think you could manage it alone."

Sarah's gaze turned quizzical. "You need George to drive the cart *where?*"

As they were at that moment nearing the bend in the road where one could clearly see the Trenton ferry fronting the Delaware River, Betsy pointed across a desolate field. "There."

Sarah's long gaze followed.

"I will ride this far with you and George, then I shall take the ferry from that point across the Delaware to Trenton. You and George may then resume your trek into the woods to the Patriot camp as usual."

"Are we to wait here for you to return at the end of the day?"

Betsy shook her head. "I intend to stay the night with Joanna and return the following day."

"I cannot like it, Betsy."

"Nonetheless, my plan is fixed. You must do your part and see that George is waiting with you when I arrive to collect you tomorrow morning. Early. It is imperative that I leave as early as possible so that if, for some reason, I am obliged to return tomorrow evening, I shall reach Philadelphia by nightfall."

"Night falls quite early these days, Betsy." Sarah's lips thinned. "Though I am loath to admit it, you will indeed be better off staying the night with Joanna. That does not change the fact that you will be walking straight into the enemy's arms. You recall reading the newspaper accounts about what Hessian soldiers do to women; and . . . without George along to protect you, you will be vulnerable and . . . *un*protected! I do not like this plan of yours, Betsy, I do not like it one bit."

Betsy did not particularly like Sarah reminding her about the Hessian soldiers forcing themselves upon women, but once again, she pushed that nagging fear aside. And the following morning, anticipating the highly-charged day before her, she drew the cart to a halt before Sarah's home quite early indeed; and was vastly relieved to see both her sister and brother emerge from the house carrying an armload of food that she expected Sarah and their mother had spent the previous evening preparing.

Also to her great relief that morning, the winter weather was cooperating beautifully. It was a brisk cold December day and the sky was clear with not the least hint of foul weather on the horizon. Betsy had packed her basket with a dozen freshly baked corn cakes, carefully wrapped in oilcloth, and on top laid a package done up in tissue paper containing a fringed silk shawl she'd made for Joanna as a Christmas gift.

As planned, once the party of three arrived at the bend in the road adjacent to the river, Betsy had no trouble finding an eager ferryman to accept the few cents she paid him to row her across the Delaware to the New Jersey side. She waved goodbye to Sarah and George, who sat worriedly watching from the cart, before climbing into the small boat.

Seated alone in the ferryboat in front of the oarsman, Betsy prayed she was not embarking on a fool's errand; that she was not walking straight into a tangled snare from which she might never escape. Perhaps she should have asked George to come along. But no, to have done so would pose too great a threat to his life. The only course open to her was the one she had chosen. *"Dear Lord,"* she prayed, *"please be with me and see me safely home tomorrow evening."*

Reaching the opposite shore, the ferryman told her the trek into Trenton from that point was not quite as far as it was into Philadelphia on the Pennsylvania side. Nonetheless, as she set out alone, Betsy was unable to push down the anxiety rising within her as she headed straight toward the enemy-occupied village. Anticipating the cold weather and the long walk back home that night, or the following afternoon, she had donned heavy woolen stockings and a woolen petticoat beneath her Hodden gray gown, it covered by her new burgundy woolen cloak. She also wore a scarf wrapped about her neck and knitted gloves. To outward appearances, she looked as warm as toast; inside, fear chilled her to her bones.

A short way up River Road, she passed a couple of farmers, one leading a few sheep somewhere; another pulling a donkey with heavy loads of firewood strapped to its flanks. Eventually the trees on either side of the path thickened and she found herself alone. Minutes later, she spotted a pair of provost guards leaning against a tree, the distracted men conversing with one another. Stark terror knotted her insides as she paused to inhale deep breaths of courage. Slowly setting her feet in motion again, she could not help noticing the soldiers' handsome blue uniforms trimmed with scarlet braid. On their heads were close-fitting brass helmets with feathery red plumes. Their appearance alone, so unlike the poor unkempt rebel troops, bespoke their . . . foreignness. Betsy slowed her step, her long gaze casting about for a way to skirt around the Hessian guards, who had not yet seen her. Suddenly one soldier glanced up, then in an instant, both men sprang to attention and leveled their muskets straight at her.

290   Marilyn Clay

"Halt!" the men shouted in unison.

Panic shot through Betsy. She was alone on a deserted stretch of road with two enemy soldiers who, if they chose, could rape and then kill her with no one the wiser. She hardly dared breathe as the men approached her, their dark gazes menacing.

"State your business!"

"I-I am on my way to Trenton, sir. I am . . ." She squared her shoulders. "Expected." She prayed the German soldiers understood English.

The men exchanged a few unintelligible words; then using the sharp bayonets that extended from the end of their muskets, they motioned her forward.

Betsy drew shallow breaths as the Hessian soldiers marched her at bayonet point ahead of them straight into the township of Trenton. Despite the fear knotting her stomach, her alert gaze took in every aspect of her surroundings. Here and there along the road clusters of grenadiers stood guard, all smartly turned out in dark blue uniforms and wearing the same odd-shaped brass helmets on their heads. A few yards up Front Street, the armed soldiers ushered her onto King Street. The small party continued a bit beyond Second.

Betsy noted that nearly every house they passed had a Union flag fluttering from an upstairs window or draped over the banister, the corners flapping in the brisk breeze. She had heard that virtually the entire town had suddenly professed undying loyalty to the crown and from the look of it that did appear to be the case. Of a sudden the soldiers, in whose custody she now considered herself to be, again shouted, *"Halt!"*

They'd stopped before a two-storey house with a wide porch and a waist-high railing. Standing sentry here were another half dozen Hessian soldiers, each carrying muskets with sharp bayonets protruding from the ends. Swords sheathed in scabbards hung from their belts. Betsy noticed these men all had mustaches that looked to have been stiffened with boot blacking and their hair was pulled into queues that hung down their backs from beneath their helmets. All the men looked inordinately clean, a stark contrast to the filthy rebel soldiers. To her immense relief, not a one appeared to pay her any heed.

Without being told, Betsy assumed she had been brought to their commanding officer's headquarters. *Was she now about to come face-to-face with the much-feared German commander, Colonel Rall?*

In moments, she was ushered inside the house and to a large room in the center of it where a tall, gray-haired man of some fifty years, his dark blue uniform decorated with considerably more stripes and insignia than his subordinates, sat behind a cluttered desk. The man glanced up, but said nothing as his assistant addressed her.

"Welcher name?"

"Mrs. Ross, sir."

"State your business, madam."

Before Betsy had a chance to reply, she was startled when another soldier snatched the basket from her arm and began to rifle through it. *Would the men gobble up the corn cakes?* She grimaced when she saw the soldier strip off the tissue paper covering Joanna's Christmas gift. Flinging it aside, he roughly shook out the folds of the silk shawl.

"Wofür ist das?"

"Please sir, it is a gift for my sister-in-law. I do not wish to deliver it soiled."

"Voss ist das?" demanded Colonel Rall, his narrowed gaze also eyeing the red silk.

Did the colonel not speak English?

"I am bringing a Christmas gift to my sister-in-law," Betsy said again. To her surprise, Colonel Rall reached to snatch the shawl from his assistant and handed it back to Betsy.

"A handsome gift, *fräulein.*"

A smile of relief wavered across her face. "Thank you, sir." *So, he spoke a bit of English and thankfully, she understood a bit of German.*

Rall eyed her up and down. "You are Quaker woman, *yah?*"

"Yes, sir." Betsy nodded. She hoped her telltale garb would also attest to her political persuasion.

"Loyalist?"

Betsy winced before thrusting up her chin and replying in quite a steady tone, "Indeed, sir. As is my sister-in-law."

"You have family in Trenton?" asked the assistant whose English seemed tolerably good.

"Yes." Betsy replied and before being asked also provided Joanna's direction, explaining that her sister-in-law was visiting here. She also revealed the names of the persons with whom Joanna was staying. Then, her heart in her throat, she breathlessly awaited the Hessian commander's response. *Would the colonel let her proceed, or would he order her to quit the village at once without granting her permission to see Joanna?*

Her anxiety mounted as Colonel Rall turned to address his assistant . . . in German. He spoke a few foreign words also to the Hessian soldiers who had escorted her into the village.

"Die Frau ist nett, und sie ist hübsch."

The soldiers all nodded as Rall's assistant declared, "Proceed."

With no further comment from Colonel Rall, the soldiers motioned her from the house and once outdoors, silently led her deeper into the village.

Were they taking her to where her sister-in-law was staying, or . . . elsewhere, Betsy wondered.

Eventually the soldiers paused before a tidy home with a Union flag fluttering from a window. When both soldiers nodded toward Betsy, she scampered up the steps and rapped at the door.

"Betsy!" Joanna Holland cried with surprise when she flung open the door and spotted her former sister-in-law standing on the stoop.

"I've come for a visit, Joanna." Betsy smiled at the older girl, whose dark hair and eyes provided an aching reminder of her beloved John.

"How did you know I was in Trenton?" Joanna ushered Betsy inside. "Did you come alone? How did you get past the pickets?"

Betsy blinked away the moisture that had sprung to her eyes. "I've brought you a Christmas gift, Joanna." She pulled the unwrapped shawl from her basket.

"Why, thank you; it's lovely, Sister; but you took such a risk coming!"

Overhearing the commotion in the foyer, Joanna's elderly cousins appeared from the rear of the house. Joanna presented Betsy to the pair.

"The pickets let her through," Joanna marveled.

Betsy nodded. "Colonel Rall asked if . . ."

"You spoke with Colonel Rall?" Joanna's eyes widened.

"Indeed. He asked why I had come and I told him I was bringing a gift to my sister-in-law whose husband is away fighting . . ."

"Oh, Betsy, you didn't!" Joanna gasped, a hand flying to her breast.

"They will surely come for us now!" cried one cousin. She wrung her hands together while a stricken look appeared on the face of the other.

Betsy gazed from the elderly women to Joanna. "I didn't tell Colonel Rall *which* side your husband is fighting for, Joanna."

"Oh, praise the Lord, Betsy. You gave us a dreadful fright."

"I see you have a Union flag fluttering out front."

"It's the only way to insure staying alive here," Joanna said softly as if fearing the Hessian grenadiers who'd escorted Betsy to the house might still be loitering outside. Listening.

"How far did you travel, dear?" asked one of the cousins.

"Just across the river. I live in Philadelphia. I would like to stay the night if it's no trouble."

"You must stay longer," Joanna insisted. "Christmas is but three days away. You mustn't be alone on Christmas Day, Sister."

Betsy smiled. Joanna was aware that her immediate family, save Sarah, no longer included her in special gatherings. "Thank you, but I should return home before . . . bad weather sets in."

"We have been lucky thus far," one cousin said and the other nodded. "Although I fear our luck will not last much longer. Winters here can be quite brutal indeed."

The four women then ambled toward the parlor and passed an enjoyable afternoon talking quietly over cups of warm, but somewhat watery, apple cider.

That night, Joanna led Betsy into her bedchamber. "Do come and sit with me by the fire. It will be hours before it's quiet enough for anyone to sleep." She drew a chair up before the hearth for Betsy.

"It does seem a bit noisy out," Betsy murmured. Whilst the women had been eating their evening meal, there seemed to be some sort of disturbance coming from the street. Betsy hoped it was not General Washington and his troops launching their surprise attack.

"The Hessian soldiers drink and carouse till all hours." Joanna's eyes rolled skyward. "They like to play cards. Villagers who live near Trenton

Tavern say the noise coming from there continues long into the night. With Christmas fast upon us, I expect the celebrations will become *very* loud, indeed. Yet," she added, "despite the late hours the soldiers keep, Colonel Rall insists they parade bright and early every morning. We happened to witness the spectacle one day. Some of the men were still so drunk from the previous night's revelries they could scarcely stand upright. I am certain you noticed the Hessians are quite finely fitted out."

"Indeed, they are a decided contrast to our poorly clad troops." Betsy held her hands, palms out, before the fire. "My sister Sarah's husband William is encamped near Philadelphia. We see him often." She sighed. "It breaks my heart that our troops are suffering so, but there is simply not enough food or supplies to go around. Do you . . . know where Thomas is?" As her sister-in-law had not once mentioned her husband's whereabouts, Betsy hoped nothing dreadful had happened to him.

Joanna paused before softly replying. "Thomas is serving under General Greene, although, at the moment, I cannot say for certain *where* his regiment is encamped. Apparently some of our troops are still on the move." She smiled serenely. "I am confident the Lord will keep him safe." She seemed to dismiss her own concerns. "Tell me how you are faring, Sister. These past months cannot have been easy for you."

Betsy gazed into the fire. "It is difficult to believe that this time last year, John and I were cozy together in our little house on Mulberry Street; grateful that we'd made a go of our upholstery business and looking forward to another happy year together. Then . . ." Tears welled in her eyes. "Oh, Joanna, I shall miss John as long as I live." Somehow she felt closer to her beloved John now that she was here with his sister. "With the Lord's help," she concluded bravely, "I am bearing up."

Joanna reached to squeeze Betsy's fingertips. "You are as pretty as ever, Sister. I am certain you will marry again. John would not want you to be alone. He loved you dearly, and he would want you to be happy."

Betsy smiled. "I-I have been seeing Joseph Ashburn. He is also away now, but I-I expect him to return to Philadelphia soon, perhaps in a . . . matter of days."

"Ah." A smile played at Joanna lips. "So Captain Ashburn is the reason you wish to return home so quickly. Well, I am glad you will not be alone on Christmas Day. No one should be alone on Christmas, Sister. Least of all you."

After the women had enjoyed a leisurely breakfast the following morning, Betsy announced she must head back.

"Which way will you go, dear?" asked one of the cousins.

"If I am allowed to, I shall return the way I came; ferry across the river below Trenton, then when I reach the other side, simply walk back to Philadelphia."

"Ah." The gray-haired woman nodded. "I have it on good authority that another, much *larger* company of British soldiers is positioned below Assunpink Creek."

"Oh." Betsy's ears perked up. This was the very sort of information that would prove useful to General Washington. Truth was, she had every intention of calling upon the rebel commander before she returned to Philadelphia.

At the door, Betsy and Joanna embraced.

"Thank you for the lovely shawl," Joanna said. "I will think of you every time I wear it." She brushed a stray tear from her eye. "Do promise me you'll be careful. You took such a risk coming," she said.

"It was lovely to see you, Joanna. Perhaps after the war we shall—"

"Indeed, we *shall* see one another again after the war. I love you with all my heart, Betsy Ross."

"I love you, too, Joanna."

Betsy was not surprised when upon leaving her sister-in-law's home, she was halted only a few feet down King Street. Once again, the menacing-looking grenadier escorted her straight to Colonel Rall's headquarters, but this time the door to the inner chamber where she'd been interviewed the previous day was tightly shut. From within Betsy could hear the deep rumble of men's voices. Concentrating upon the sounds, she realized that one voice coming from within the chamber sounded suspiciously familiar.

The one speaking French.

CHAPTER 34

It had not occurred to Betsy that she would actually come face-to-face with François Dubeau *in* Trenton, but as it now appeared that that might actually be the case, she determined to stay alert and perhaps turn the unexpected encounter to good advantage. Although she strained to hear what was being said inside Colonel Rall's office, she could make out nothing. Of a sudden, she was astonished when the unmistakable jolt of laughter . . . and not just a mild titter, but hearty guffaws . . . rang from the inner chamber. Suddenly, the group of smiling men burst forth from the office and poured into the room where Betsy sat. Amongst them was the tall, elegantly clad Frenchman.

"Mrs. Ross," Dubeau sputtered, obviously taken aback over finding her sitting there.

That the Frenchman was acquainted with Betsy seemed also to come as a surprise to Colonel Rall.

"You are acquainted *avec* Quaker woman? *Yah?*"

François said nothing but Betsy noted the muscles of his jaws grinding together. The glare he directed her way would have felled a man had it been an arrow.

Colonel Rall turned to address Betsy, now standing. "Your visit with relative concluded, *yah?*"

"Yes, sir. I request your permission now to be on my way, sir."

"M'sieur Dubeau," Colonel Rall turned to a tight-lipped François. "You will please to escort the *fräulein* home. She is returning also to Philadelphia, *yah?*" The commanding officer looked to Betsy for confirmation.

"Indeed, sir."

"You will escort the *fräulein* home," Colonel Rall instructed firmly.

Betsy cringed when she noted the gleam that suddenly appeared in the Frenchman's black eyes. "*Certainment.*"

Although the travel arrangements were not to her liking, apparently she was to have no say in the matter.

Setting out for the ferry, two Hessian grenadiers walked ahead of Betsy and François while another pair followed close behind. Neither Betsy nor François spoke. After traversing the entire length of River Road in silence, their escorts halted at the far end of it with the ferry landing in plain sight.

As Betsy and François walked the last quarter mile to the waterfront alone, she turned to boldly address her companion. "I could not help overhearing laughter coming from within Colonel Rall's office. What did you and the Hessian soldiers find so amusing?"

He shrugged. "Nothing."

"Must you lie about everything, François? I distinctly heard laughter coming from Colonel Rall's chamber. The men were still laughing when they emerged."

His lips twitched. "It amused them when I said the Patriot army was a rag-tag bunch of illiterate farmers from whom they had nothing to fear."

"Oh." After giving his reply only a bit of thought, Betsy realized that to paint the rebels as ill-bred and ignorant could very well be to their advantage. If the Hessians believed they had nothing to fear from the Patriot army, they'd be more apt to let down their guard, consequently when the surprise attack came, both the suddenness and the force of it could wreak even greater havoc. Unless, of course, they had been forewarned and knew the attack was coming. Had François alerted them?

"What brought *you* to Trenton, *madame?*"

"I came to deliver a Christmas gift to my sister-in-law . . . that is, my *former* sister-in-law," Betsy replied, alluding to the fact that her husband John was no longer with them.

He grasped her meaning. *"Madame,* when I set fire to the munitions warehouse, I did not know the man guarding it was your husband. If you recall, at that juncture, we were not yet acquainted. I was merely carrying out an assignment," he added defensively.

Betsy worked to remain calm. It would be exceedingly foolhardy of her to anger the Frenchman. The journey ahead of them was of sufficient duration that should he wish to, he could easily find a way to slay her with no one the wiser. Sarah, and her sister-in-law . . . should she ever learn of Betsy's demise . . . would simply believe some disaster had befallen her on her way home. Biting back an angry retort, she said quietly, "I understand."

"So, in addition to visiting your sister-in-law, were you also . . . spying?"

"I have given up spying." Betsy's lips pursed. "However, I take it *you* have not abandoned your duplicitous career."

A snort of contempt told her that for him to abandon such a profitable venture was unlikely indeed. "Before returning to Philadelphia, I intend to pay a call upon General Washington," François said, "and tell him . . . something."

"So, you do not intend to escort me home as Colonel Rall instructed?"

His shoulders lifted and fell. "You may wait, if you like, while I . . . conduct my business with the general."

"So, you *have* learned something of use to General Washington?" she pressed.

He snorted. "I did not say that. I have not yet decided what I shall tell the general."

"I take it you know *where* in the woods the general has set up headquarters." Betsy slid a sidelong look at him. She had no notion where General Washington's headquarters were located, meaning she'd have no choice but to search out the great man on her own once she reached the opposite side of the river, which would make her return trip to Philadelphia take considerably longer than it otherwise should.

"Of course, I know where his headquarters are. The man is my employer."

"So . . . exactly what of import *did* you learn from Colonel Rall today?"

He directed a contemptuous look her way. "You do not expect me to share information with you, do you?"

Betsy's lips pressed together. To persist in this vein would be pointless, since whatever the man said would, no doubt, be devoid of truth. Had she been alone with him on this lonely stretch of road after dark, she would be saying nothing. But, as it was broad daylight and the ferry landing lay only a few steps ahead of them, she said, "As it happens, I intend to pay a call upon General Washington myself this afternoon."

"And, what pray, have *you* to reveal to the Virginia farmer?"

"Nothing of import. I merely mean to wish him and Lady Washington a pleasant holiday. With the fighting in abeyance until spring, I expect he will welcome a respite from his duties."

Upon reaching the riverbank, François very ungallantly stood aside and allowed Betsy to pay the fellow standing near the ferryboat for their return trip across the river. She hoped she was not being foolhardy embarking upon the crossing in François's company. Perhaps the fact that a ferryman would also be along would prevent the odious creature from attempting anything sinister. She considered waiting on shore for another boat, but noting the bank of ominous-looking storm clouds that had rolled in made her abandon that notion. To wait for another ferry would mean she'd run the risk of the tiny boat capsizing due to a strong wind or a heavy downpour. Either way danger was eminent.

Casting an anxious look at François as they both climbed into the small boat, Betsy experienced additional trepidation when of a sudden, another ferryman, a small, wiry sort of fellow who looked as if he might not have sufficient strength in him to wield the oars, let alone row the entire way across the mile-wide river, also climbed in and scooped up the oars. Praying the weather did not take a nasty turn before they gained the opposite shore, she perched rigidly on the center bench, tightly grasping the edge of the vessel at her side with a gloved hand.

Unfortunately, they had scarcely reached the middle of the wide expanse of water when great gusts of wind kicked up. Alarm shot through Betsy when she noted white foam forming on the crests of the churning waves. She tightened her grip as the fierce wind pitched the tiny boat to and fro.

The choppy black water reminded her of the night, just above three years ago, when she and John had crossed the Delaware River in order to be married. With John at her side, she had felt perfectly safe. Today, with François seated next to her, she felt anything but. Especially when, of a sudden, he leaned down to whisper into her ear. "How easy it would be to shove a young lady overboard. I wonder how quickly her head would disappear beneath the waves?"

With her free hand, Betsy tugged her cloak tighter about her shoulders. "Were you to do away with me in that fashion, sir, you would also be obliged to toss the ferryman into the river, otherwise he would report your crime and . . . "

"You are privy to far too many of my secrets, Mrs. Ross. Surely you realize that I have no choice but to kill you."

Betsy's breath caught in her throat. She cast a wild gaze about for some object, *anything*, with which she might defend herself should he decide to act upon his threat. But, she saw nothing lying about, not a length of rope, or a spare oar. She flung a furtive glance over one shoulder toward the ferryman.

François laughed; an evil, mocking sound. "To look to the captain of our little vessel will do you no good, *mam'selle*. To toss such a frail fellow overboard will be less trouble than to push you over the edge. He would not be expecting it."

Betsy's heart thrummed in her ears. Given the tumultuous weather, were François merely to stand up in the tiny rowboat would be sufficient to tip it over, and send her, and perhaps the old man, as well, tumbling into the icy waves.

François again leaned towards her. "I take it you do not swim, *ma petite?*"

Betsy edged away from him, but as the craft was so very narrow, she was already pressed quite close to the side. "Do leave off badgering me, François." Her tone sounded far more calm than she felt. "If the boat were to tip over, you would surely drown along with the rest of us."

Suddenly, reaching past her to grasp the edge of the boat on her side, his other hand clasping the opposite rail, he said, "Shall we see what happens when I . . ."

"You there!" shouted the ferryman. "Yer frightenin' the lady!"

Over the sounds of the rushing wind and the splashing waves, Betsy expected the elderly man hadn't heard a word François had said, but fortunately, his actions had been duly noted. She was vastly relieved when François let go of her side of the boat. With a gloved hand, she continued to cling to it.

Despite the old man's interference, however, François was not ready to abandon his ominous threats. In seconds, he said, "I expect it would be more expedient simply to . . . shoot you."

Betsy turned a horrified gaze on him and when she saw him pat a bulky object in his coat pocket, her breath again deserted her.

"I never walk into an army camp without a loaded pistol." He grinned wickedly. "Most especially when it is the . . . *enemy* camp."

Betsy fought to still her pounding pulse. *Dear Lord, please help her survive the river crossing, and reach home safely.*

Apparently the Lord heard her prayer for mere minutes before they reached shore, François abandoned his evil threats. After dragging the boat onto dry land, the ferryman gallantly handed Betsy out. She fervently thanked both him and God for seeing her safely ashore.

François had stepped from the boat and gained the road well ahead of Betsy, his hands thrust deep into his pockets, his dark head bent against the stiff wind. Betsy held onto the hood of her cloak as she hastened to catch up to him, although not *too* close.

On this side of the river, the sky was darker and in the distance thunder rumbled. Betsy hoped that François did, indeed, know the way to General Washington's headquarters and that he was not planning to lead her further into the woods where he could easily put a bullet through her heart and walk away unobserved.

Following at what she hoped was a safe distance; he walked only a short way up the road before veering off to the right. Surrounded by dense woods, Betsy purposely straggled behind, stepping over fallen tree limbs and carefully picking her way through thick brush and debris, all the while keeping a sharp eye on the Frenchman. When an armed sentry came into view and she saw François approach the man, an enormous breath of relief escaped her. When François motioned back toward her, she suspected he meant to gain the general's ear before she did, perhaps in an attempt to discredit her before she had the opportunity to address the great man herself.

However, the sentry waited until Betsy caught up to them, then he led both of them even deeper into the woods until at last they came upon a clearing where a vast number of tattered white tents stood. Eventually, the soldier, a rifle slung over one shoulder, turned toward Betsy.

"Your name, miss?"

"Please tell General Washington that Betsy Ross wishes to speak with him, sir."

As the guard stooped to enter one of the tents, François aimed a lethal glare at her. "Washington is a busy man, *madame*. You are wasting everyone's time."

In a few moments, the sentry reappeared. "The general will see you now."

Both François and Betsy took a step forward, but to her surprise and no doubt, François's, the guard laid his musket across the Frenchman's broad chest.

"The lady first, sir."

Betsy had spoken with His Excellency General George Washington and his pretty little wife, Lady Washington, upon many occasions at Christ Church where they all worshipped. In addition, the general had been amongst the delegation of statesmen who had called at her shop last spring requesting she make a banner to represent the thirteen colonies. Today, however, surrounded by three of his advisors, all impeccably turned out in buff and blue coats, calfskin breeches and polished black boots, General Washington, standing over six feet tall, seemed far more regal and imposing than she remembered. Waves of uncertainty commenced to erode her confidence.

"T-thank you for seeing me, sir." A shaky smile flickered across Betsy's flushed face.

"Mrs. Ross." Although the general did not smile, his tone was cordial.

"Sir, I-I have just come from Trenton and wished to impart to you some of what I learned there before I return home."

General Washington's expression revealed only mild curiosity. "Please be seated, madam." He indicated a flimsy, slat-backed chair that had previously been occupied by one of his advisors, for when Betsy sat down she noted the seat still felt warm. As it was especially cold both outdoors and inside the tent, she was grateful for the slightest bit of heat.

"Thank you, sir." Her wide-eyed gaze took in the clutter of papers and crudely drawn diagrams spread upon the makeshift table where the general and his advisors had gathered. Two other officers, to whom she was not introduced, moved toward another corner of the tent and now stood a bit apart from her and the general, the men rubbing their hands together in a futile effort to stave off the chill. A third officer moved to stand before the tent flap, perhaps to guard it from intruders, or merely to keep it from flying open due to the stiff wind rustling through the treetops.

"What did you wish to see me about, Mrs. Ross?"

"I have a great deal to tell you, sir, but first I-I wonder if you are acquainted with a man, a *Frenchman,* by the name of François Dubeau? He claims to be in your employ as an . . . intelligence gatherer. Some weeks ago M'sieur Dubeau traveled from Philadelphia to New York for the express purpose of seeking a position with you as an informant."

Washington's white-wigged head shook. "I am unacquainted with any gentleman by that name, madam. To protect my informants from possible detection, true names are never used."

"Oh." Betsy suddenly felt like a child telling tales out of school. "Well, sir, some months ago, M'sieur Dubeau approached *me* with the notion of . . . of spying on those customers who come to my upholstery shop, those who profess loyalty to the crown, that is. I agreed to do as M'sieur Dubeau asked but I later learned that the information I passed along to him was altered and when passed along, presumably to you, sir, the message became quite the opposite of what I originally intended."

Washington leaned forward. "Are you saying, Mrs. Ross, that this M'sieur Dubeau is a . . . *double* spy? That the man is, in fact, working *for* the British?"

Betsy nodded eagerly. "Yes, sir, that is exactly what I am saying, sir."

She told him about the message her friend Captain Ashburn had recovered along with a copy of the altered one, which clearly proved that her original message had been reversed. Watching the general closely, it pleased Betsy to note that the great man appeared now to be listening quite intently.

"Sir, I attempted to get word to you in New York that the British planned to attack from the Jamaica Pass Road, but when I told M'sieur Dubeau what I had learned he scoffed at the notion. I was certain that it was correct, sir, for I clearly saw the map with an X marking the spot. The next morning, I hastened to tell Dr. Franklin but apparently the information arrived too late to be of any use to you. I'm dreadfully sorry, sir. Dr. Franklin has passed along more than one message which I have directed to you, sir."

"I see." Washington drew breath. "Precisely *where* did you see this map of the proposed enemy campaign in New York City, Mrs. Ross?"

Betsy told him about sewing Miss Olsen's wedding finery and that she'd been invited to attend the young lady's engagement party where British officers were present and how she came to be in the same room with the officers. "I pretended to lose my thimble and was left alone in the room to search for it and therefore was able to get quite a good look at the map, sir."

Following that disclosure she was certain she saw the hint of a smile play about the great man's lips. "A unique ploy, to be sure, Mrs. Ross."

"Thank you, sir." Betsy nodded. "On more than one occasion in the past months, sir, M'sieur Dubeau has openly confessed to me that he is a double spy. He said that you had recently entrusted him to carry a packet of important documents from New York to Philadelphia and that he had deliberately placed the packet in the hands of a British officer." At that disclosure she was certain she heard the collective intake of breath from the other officers inside the tent. "M'sieur Dubeau grew up in England, sir, and he continues to correspond with a number of British officers who are in this country fighting against us. Only minutes ago, as we were crossing the Delaware River from Trenton, M'sieur Dubeau indicated that he has no intention of abandoning his career as a double spy."

Washington frowned. "Am I to understand that you and this . . . M'sieur Dubeau traveled to Trenton . . . together?"

"Oh, no, sir." Betsy shook her head. "I went to Trenton to see my sister-in-law, Joanna Holland, my . . . my *late* husband's sister. Perhaps you remember Mrs. Holland from Christ Church. She and her husband, who is now serving in the *rebel* army, often sat in the same pew with John and me. Anyhow, whilst I was visiting with Joanna, she and her cousins told me quite a number of things that I thought might be of interest to you."

At this juncture, Betsy knew she had the general's full attention as well as that of the other officers in the tent. She felt them draw a bit closer as she continued in a low tone, telling the general the exact location of Colonel Rall's headquarters, the number of Hessian soldiers that both she and her sister-in-law had observed in the village and that the soldiers very often stayed up long into the night drinking and playing cards at Trenton Tavern and that they were often still drunk the following morning. "Often too drunk to stand for inspection," she said, adding, "it is expected that with Christmas drawing near the late night revelries will escalate to an intolerable degree."

She went on to tell him the exact number of armed sentries she'd encountered on the River Road and did her best to describe the weapons the Hessian soldiers carried. "The men's uniforms are very clean, but I couldn't help noticing, sir, their muskets did not appear . . . immaculate. I saw mud caked on them. The men often stand leaning upon their rifles, which appears to not be a good idea to me, sir, as that might push dirt or debris up the nozzle or . . . whatever you call the part of the musket that protrudes. All the soldier's rifles had bayonets on the ends. I am quite certain of that."

"Well done, Mrs. Ross." The general sat back. "The intelligence you have gathered is quite useful, indeed. Is there . . . anything further?"

"Umm. Yes, sir, I was told that quite a large company of British soldiers are encamped below Assunpink Creek."

"Ah." The general glanced at his men, then looked back toward Betsy as if expecting her to divulge even more.

"Before I left Trenton this morning, sir, I was taken again to Colonel Rall's headquarters but upon arriving, I was obliged to wait as he was entertaining visitors. I couldn't make out what the men within his chamber were saying, but I did hear laughter, sir. *Laughter!*"

"Laughter?"

She nodded. "Very loud laughter. The men were still laughing when they emerged, sir, and M'sieur Dubeau was amongst them. Since both he and I were headed for Philadelphia, Colonel Rall insisted that M'sieur Dubeau escort me home."

"That was . . . thoughtful of him," the general murmured.

"M'sieur Dubeau is waiting outside, sir. I do not know what he means to tell you today as only moments ago, he said he had not yet decided. But . . . some weeks back, François, his given name is François, at any rate, he confessed to me that," her chin quivered, "that he alone was responsible for the explosion at the munitions warehouse in Philadelphia nearly a twelvemonth ago, where my late husband John Ross was standing guard. If you recall, sir, my husband perished from his wounds."

"I do recall that unfortunate accident, Mrs. Ross. Please accept my sincere condolences for your loss, madam."

"Thank you, sir." Claps of thunder so loud that voices could not be heard above the clamor afforded Betsy a much-needed moment in which to regain herself. Thinking that she would surely be obliged to walk the entire way back to Philadelphia in a torrent of cold rain, she rose to depart. "That is all I have to say, sir. I will leave it to you to determine which of us, M'sieur Dubeau or myself, is being truthful."

The general walked behind her as she edged towards the soldier standing guard at the entrance to the tent. "Oh, one other thing, sir. M'sieur Dubeau is waiting outside and . . . he is carrying a pistol, which he said is loaded."

She heard the collective gasp of alarm from all the uniformed men inside the tent.

"I see." Standing quite near her, General Washington again asked, "Is there anything else you wish to tell me, Mrs. Ross?"

"Oh, yes. I nearly forgot, sir." Betsy smiled up at the dignified man. "Did you find the muskets and gunpowder? Upstream at McKonkey's

Ferry, in the stone barn behind the rock farmhouse? We thought a stone building would be more difficult to burn down."

"We?"

Betsy's anxious features softened. "My friend Joseph Ashburn is a privateer, sir. Those particular muskets formerly belonged to the British. On Captain Ashburn's most recent voyage, he absconded with them. In order to protect them from M'sieur Dubeau, who intended to steal them and sell them to you, I persuaded Joseph to stash them in a safe place for *our* army's use."

"Ah." The appearance of a genuine smile on the general's lips vastly pleased Betsy. "We did indeed find the weapons. Please extend my gratitude to Captain Ashburn. Thank you for coming to see me today, madam." General Washington inclined his head before turning to one of his subordinates. "Harris, please see to an escort for Mrs. Ross. The lady is returning to Philadelphia and it would not do for her to travel alone."

One of the officers snapped to attention. "Certainly, sir. Anything else, sir?"

Washington cocked a brow. "Disarm M'sieur Dubeau before you show him in."

"You may depend upon it, sir."

Some minutes later, seated on one of two horses clip-clopping toward Philadelphia, Betsy had no idea what the outcome of her interview with General Washington would be. All she knew for certain was that she suddenly felt quite lightheaded over having been awarded the opportunity to speak with the great general and to finally unburden all that had weighed so heavily upon her mind these past weeks. Her relief was so great, in fact, that she could not halt the sob that rose in her throat or the rush of hot tears

that began to trickle down her cheeks. Aware of the several sidelong
glances the uniformed officer who rode beside her cast her way, she had no
idea what the young man thought the trouble might be, but as he did not
inquire as to the nature of her distress, Betsy did not venture to explain.

Less than a mile down the roadway, the dark clouds overhead
unleashed the icy rain swelling them; therefore, whether or not Betsy was
crying, or rain was dampening her cheeks became a moot point. Despite
the downpour, Betsy felt safe and comfortable cantering alongside an
armed soldier of the Continental Army, her long-awaited and much
anticipated mission now behind her. Although she could not help
wondering if General Washington had seen fit to arrest François on the
spot, she hoped at the very least, he would refuse to believe a single word
the Frenchman said; for whatever François conjured up, Betsy knew it
would be nowhere near the truth.

CHAPTER 35

*"Christmas Day at night, one hour before day, is the time fixed for our
attempt on Trenton. For Heaven's sake, keep this to yourself, as the
discovery of it may prove fatal to us."* . . . *General George Washington,
December 23, 1776, in a dispatch to General Reed in Philadelphia.*

The following day being the eve of Christmas, it did not surprise Betsy
when Sarah rapped at her door quite early.

"I simply had to know if you are safe," Sarah said. "I am so glad you
are home."

"Do come in out of the cold, Sarah."

Betsy closed the door behind her sister and the girls hurried into the parlor where Betsy had been seated before a crackling fire sipping rather weak tea. Although the beverage was more steaming hot water than tea, she offered her sister a cup, thinking that to hold the heated mug in her hands would warm them. It was frightfully cold that day; the howling wind blowing so hard it caused all the windowpanes in the house to rattle. Ice crystals had formed on every pane of glass and it was not yet ten of the clock in the morning.

"I am certain it will snow before the day is out," Betsy said, settling herself on the sofa beside Sarah.

"I am grateful the worst of the foul weather held off until you returned," Sarah said. "Is Joanna well? Is her husband safe? Does she know where his regiment is?"

Smiling, Betsy relayed news of her sister-in-law and her trip, without mentioning a word of what had transpired after she returned to the Pennsylvania side of the river yesterday afternoon.

"I rode nearly the whole way home yesterday in freezing rain."

"You *rode?*"

Pausing, Betsy quickly fabricated a small falsehood. "Soon after it began to sprinkle, I was fortunate enough to come upon another traveler also headed this way and gladly accepted the offer of a ride in the bed of his wagon. I arrived home drenched to the bone."

"Oh, my. I hope you did not take a chill. How do you feel today?"

"Quite well, thank you." Betsy took a sip of tea. "I sat by the fire all last evening to dry my hair. My clothes are still draped over chairs in the kitchen drying. Did you and George go to the rebel camp yesterday?"

Sarah nodded. "Uncle Abel took us in his cart. Mother and a number of other Quaker women had prepared a good many dishes for the men to enjoy over the next several days, it being Christmas." She looked down, her blue eyes troubled. "I am so thankful to have been able to see William again. But, he said that since the weather is turning nasty it would be best if we did not come again for a while." Her chin trembled. "I hope that does not mean . . ." Her tone grew anxious. "I-I suppose if the army means to launch an attack upon Trenton *before* Christmas, it will have to be . . . today, or . . . tonight."

Betsy's brow furrowed. "Surely the rebels would not attack *tomorrow*, on Christmas Day."

"I pray they will not attack at all!"

Betsy reached to pat her sister's hand. "The Lord has kept William safe thus far."

Sarah sniffed back worried tears. "Surely neither army will fight in such foul weather."

Betsy recalled the maps she had seen spread out on the makeshift desk inside General Washington's tent. Had she interrupted the officers discussing strategy for their proposed attack? Given that all boats of a size in the vicinity had been destroyed she still could not fathom *how* General Washington meant to transport the troops across the Delaware River especially if a blinding snowstorm ensued, an event that now seemed imminent. In all likelihood, ice floes were already forming on the river. *Did the troops make their crossing last night? Perhaps they were even now on their way to Trenton. Or, were they already there and fighting?* When a shudder rippled through her, she offered up a silent prayer for a quick end to the battle, and for William *and* Joanna's safety.

She and Sarah talked a bit longer and when the gunmetal gray sky grew even grayer, Sarah decided it best to return home before snow, or sleet, began to fall. "Has Joseph returned home?" she asked Betsy as they walked back through the house.

"I don't know. I have not spoken with Aunt Ashburn since I went for the cart the day I left for Trenton. I am certain he'll come to see me the minute he returns to town."

"I do hope it will be soon. I feel dreadful that you're alone today, Betsy, on Christmas Eve. I can hardly bear to think of you alone tomorrow, on Christmas Day."

"I shall be fine. Promise me you'll set aside your worries and enjoy a pleasant day with our family."

Sarah embraced her sister. "It isn't right that Mother and Father continue to shun thee, Betsy."

"Don't fret, Sarah. I expect Joseph will come home today, and if not, then surely tomorrow."

But, Joseph did not come. By late afternoon on Christmas Day, Betsy had all but given up hope that she'd see him that day. Fluffy white snow now blanketed the entire city and this morning, the snow had turned to ice. Wind gusts whipped mounds of snow into whirling funnels. Were Betsy to open her front door today, piles of snow would cascade into the foyer. The winter storm had become an all-out blizzard, reminding Betsy of that horrible day nearly a twelvemonth ago when John set out to take his turn at guard duty.

As dusk fell on that holy day, Betsy stood alone gazing from the front window, her eyes blanched as she strained to peer through the ice crystals on the windowpane for Joseph. Staring out over the wintry landscape she imagined his shadowy form taking shape out of the foggy whiteness. She remembered that bleak winter afternoon last January when she had stood at this very window, anxiously watching John's huddled form disappear into the thick falling snow. Unbidden tears sprang to her eyes and although she tried, she could not dislodge those heart-wrenching memories from mind.

Turning from the window, she hurried back through the gloomy darkness into the parlor. Grasping the poker that stood propped against the hearth, Betsy attempted to shove around what remained of the few smoldering logs in the fire until she had created a nest of sorts, then, she carefully dropped a fresh log onto the glowing embers. Watching sparks leap upward, her thoughts turned to the hundreds of young men encamped not far from here in the frozen woods. To imagine those skeletal, vacant-eyed men finding warmth on a day such as this was not possible. Even if the men sat crowded together inside their tents in a futile attempt to escape the howling wind and the snow and ice and stay warm by huddling close to one another, she knew they would not succeed. She prayed the troops were not on the march today; every last man hungry and poorly clad as they tramped through knee-high snow on their way to, or from, the ferry on the New Jersey shore.

She also wondered if François had returned to Philadelphia, or had General Washington detained him? Reaching for a warm woolen shawl, Betsy wrapped it about her shoulders and curled her legs up beneath her body on the sofa. Of a sudden, it occurred to her that other than the howling wind and now the hiss of ice hitting the windowpanes, she'd heard virtually no sounds at all today. Not even a dog barking. Truth was, she had also not laid eyes upon a single soul since yesterday morning when Sarah came to see her. So far as she knew the houses on both sides of her stood empty, the occupants having packed up and departed some weeks ago, taking what they could with them and hiding the rest in cellars or holes they managed to dig in the ground before it froze so hard no tool could penetrate the earth. With so few citizens remaining in Philadelphia the city had become a virtual ghost town. The world seemed so silent today that if she did not know better, she'd think she was the only person alive in it.

Why did being alone on Christmas Day feel so *lonely?*

It was not that she missed having gifts to open or exclaim over. Even as a child, Griscom family members had not exchanged gifts at Christmastide. Their strict Quaker upbringing did not hold with that. Thinking back on her childhood, she did recall that upon a few Christmases her mother had presented the girls with new white caps, sans frills, of course, for Quakers did not hold with that either. A sigh escaped her as she stared into the flickering flames. No, what she truly missed on this lonesome Christmas Day was . . . family. Laughter. Good things to eat, sugary treats for the little ones and a sumptuous dinner of hot meat and vegetable compotes and afterward, perhaps mincemeat pie, or sweet pumpkin bread.

Until the time Betsy was six, she'd had a good many little brothers and sisters, and of course, older sisters. Now, except for Rachel and George, all the younger ones had perished, most before reaching the age of three. When she was a little girl, Betsy used to pretend her mother's new babies were dolls. Now, she wondered how her mother had held up each year bringing yet another new babe into the world; then, in a few short years forced to watch her precious little ones sicken and die. Now that Betsy knew how it felt to lose someone she loved, she did not want to ever feel such heartache again. To love another person was often painful in itself; but to *lose* the one you loved, and for no good purpose, was unbearable.

Fresh tears sprang to her eyes. This time she did not attempt to halt them, but gave in to the gnawing self-pity that threatened to strangle her. At length, becoming aware of cold air eddying about the room, she slipped onto the floor and held her palms up before the fire in an effort to warm them.

Would this wretched day never end?

The hours were not merely dragging by; they were *crawling*.

It felt as if everyone else in the world were surrounded by loved ones and . . . she had no one. When tears of self-pity again pooled in Betsy's eyes, this time she angrily brushed them aside.

Where was Joseph?

She pulled herself to her feet and hurried back through the house to peer from the front window yet again. Had he returned to Philadelphia and just not come to see her today, or . . . had the blizzard detained him somewhere along the road?

Dear Lord, please, do not let Joseph freeze to death in his haste to return home. And, please God, do not let our troops freeze to death in the woods.

Thank goodness, she and her sister, and others in the city had managed to get *some* warm clothing to *some* of the men encamped amongst the tall trees. Unfortunately, the women hadn't been able to clothe all of them. Or feed all of them. Hundreds of the men still had little to nothing to eat, and most still had no shoes.

How in God's name would our brave soldiers summon the strength to march barefoot over frozen ground or manage to fight once they reached Trenton . . . if they reached Trenton?

She rubbed a spot on the frosty windowpane and attempted to peer through it. Because no agitated crier had galloped through the streets of

Philadelphia calling out the news of a rebel attack upon Trenton, Betsy assumed the surprise attack had not yet taken place. *Dear Lord, please do not let the men attempt to fight in this weather!* Anyone with half an eye could see that it was far too cold out-of-doors today for man or beast. The general and his advisors may have *wished* above all things to attack Trenton before Christmas, they may have gathered around their maps and charts and meticulously *planned* their attack, but as the day wore on and the weather grew more treacherous, Betsy became more and more convinced that no surprise attack upon anyone would take place today. For General Washington to even consider crossing the Delaware River on a night such as this was unthinkable.

CHAPTER 36

Early the following morning, a rap at the door drew Betsy from the parlor. Pushing open the door as far as the mountain of snow pressed against it would allow, she peered around the edge and spotted a bundled-up Sarah attempting to brush snow from the landing with her hands.

"Sarah, it is far too cold for you to be out-of-doors!" Betsy peeked around the doorjamb.

"I've brought food." A thick woolen scarf wrapped nearly to her ears muffled Sarah's reply.

Betsy spotted a cloth-covered platter resting on the icy flagway.

"Do stop shoveling snow with your hands. Your gloves will be soaked clean through. I shall get the broom."

Some minutes later, after the two had managed to brush aside
sufficient snow from the threshold to enter the house, both girls were
seated in the parlor, warming themselves before a crackling fire. Sarah's
wet cloak, muffler and gloves were spread out on the hearth to dry. She'd
put the pewter platter containing generous portions of the Christmas dinner
the Griscom family had enjoyed the previous day on the table in the corner.

"Was everyone there for dinner?" Betsy asked, eager for news of her
siblings and other family members who might have been present at the
Griscom home.

"A good many, yes. Rachel and George, of course, and Deborah and
Everard. Susannah and Ephraim, and Hannah and Grif, plus a good many
little ones. Did I tell you Hannah and Grif have taken a house next door to
Susannah?"

"How nice for them. Is everyone well?"

Sarah nodded. "All are fine, although Deborah was sniffling and
Everard talked incessantly about how gloomy his textile cleaning business
has become these days. Otherwise everyone was in good spirits. There was
an abundance of lighthearted chatter and laughter."

"It sounds as if you all had a merry time," Betsy murmured wistfully.
"I recall how jolly Christmases used to be when we were children and all
of us were home together."

"Yes," Sarah agreed. "We were quite happy then." After a pause, she
said, "Uncle Abel paid us a call last evening."

"Oh? I take it he is well. And his sons?"

"All well." Sarah nodded.

"Did he bring news of the war?" Betsy lowered her voice as though
fearful that someone might be listening. "Has the attack on Trenton taken

place? Uncle Abel's informants generally keep him abreast of what is afoot."

"He said nothing of it."

"Well, apparently General Washington saw the folly of attempting to cross the Delaware River during a blizzard and . . . "

"All the men agreed that neither army will engage in battle before spring," Sarah interjected. "Both Father and Uncle Abel said we have nothing to fear on that score."

"That is quite good news. I am glad to hear it."

"However . . ." Sarah said, "as I was helping Mother and Hannah in the kitchen, I . . . overheard the men discussing . . . other war news."

"Oh? Do tell me what was said."

Sarah's gaze grew shuttered. "Uncle Abel said that . . . two men in the rebel camp had been hanged."

Betsy drew back. "But, why? Of what crimes could *our* men have been found guilty of?"

Sarah's tone was so low Betsy had to strain to hear. "It was determined that they were . . . spies."

"Oh-h." Betsy sucked in her breath. "Did . . . Uncle Abel mention either man's . . . name?"

"No." Sarah pinned her sister with a stern look. "It occurred to me that perhaps you might know the name of at least . . . one of the men."

"Why, no, I do not," Betsy replied breezily. "I've heard nothing of it. Of course, I've not spoken to a soul since you were here the other day." A nervous little laugh escaped her.

One of Sarah's pale brows lifted. "Uncle Abel said that . . . one of the spies was a Frenchman, that he was a ruthless man who had no scruples about killing anyone who blocked his path."

Betsy's heart drummed in her ears. *So, at last, François had been hanged for his many crimes.* The thought froze in her mind.

"Are you certain you know nothing of this, Betsy? Uncle Abel said that a woman had brought the Frenchman to General Washington's attention." Sarah's tone became gentle. "Perhaps you have not told me *everything* about your sojourn to Trenton, Betsy."

"Does Rachel know?"

Because Betsy could see no benefit in telling Sarah the sordid details, she continued to deny any knowledge of the Frenchman's hanging, and in minutes deftly steered the conversation to other matters, namely, the tribulations both girls had endured the past year and those over which they had, with God's help, managed to triumph.

"I am persuaded the New Year of 1777 will be brighter," Betsy said, unable to conceal the lilt in her tone. To be rid of someone bent upon killing her meant that the New Year would, indeed, be brighter for her. "I have every confidence the war will end soon, perhaps *very* soon, and William will come marching home, safe and well, and all in a piece."

Sarah managed a shaky smile. "I do hope you are right, Betsy. I cannot help but worry for him; and for all our fighting men." At length, Sarah cast a long gaze toward one of the frosty windows in the parlor. "I see it has begun again to snow. I expect I should return home before the snow turns to sleet, again." She knelt to retrieve her still-damp cloak, scarf and gloves. "Promise you will get word to me when Joseph returns home and most especially if he brings fresh news of the war."

"I will, Sarah." Betsy embraced her sister. "Thank you for coming today; your presence has cheered me." A self-conscious laugh escaped her. "I confess my holiday has been . . . somewhat lonely."

"And yet," Sarah cast a sidelong look at her, "you seem to have borne it well."

"I am certain I will see Joseph today."

As the long hours dragged by, Betsy's certainty about seeing Joseph that day began to wane. However, just before dusk a rap at the door sent her spirits soaring. This time she did find Joseph on the doorstep stamping clumps of brown snow from the soles of his sturdy boots.

"You are home at last!"

Smiling broadly, the burly seaman, his blond hair ruffled from the wind, scooped a beaming Betsy into his arms and twirled her around. "I've missed ye', love."

"I am so glad you are home, Joseph; do, come in. I've just put my supper on the table. There's plenty for both of us."

Arm-in-arm they hurried through the house to the parlor where Joseph shrugged out of his snow-sodden coat and drawing up a chair, draped the wet garment over the back of it. Across the room, Betsy set another plate and fork on the table.

"Sarah brought samplings of our family's Christmas dinner to me this morning. The roast venison and vegetables smell delicious. Are you hungry?"

"I haven't had a decent meal in days."

As they ate, Betsy listened raptly as Joseph relayed news of his travels. "Turns out I'm not the only privateer who was bent on saving his ship. Three more vessels sailed downriver with me. We all dropped anchor near one another."

"And then you all walked back to Philadelphia?"

"I walked for a ways, then I bought a sway-backed nag off a fellow I met at an inn. Turned out that nag sure didn't like tramping through snow." He laughed. "I daresay I'd have made faster progress on foot. But no one would buy her off me so I had no choice but to keep plodding along on her back."

"Did you stop to see Aunt Ashburn before you came here?" Betsy handed him the platter of flatbread she had baked that afternoon.

"Briefly." After taking a piece of bread, he set the platter down. "I wanted her to know I was safe, plus I had . . . other news to impart."

"What other news, Joseph?" Betsy's eyes widened. "Has something dreadful happened?" *Had the attack taken place after all?* She had not yet told Joseph anything about her trip to Trenton . . . or of François's death.

A broad grin split his face. "On the contrary, this news is good."

Of a sudden, whoops and shouts coming from outdoors startled them.

"What could that be?" Betsy cried.

Scrapping back their chairs, they both ran through the house and out onto the snow-covered flagway.

"Washington has taken Trenton!" shouted a man, waving his arms as he attempted to run down the ice-encrusted street.

"Trenton has fallen!" another man called from nearby Third Street.

Men, women and children began to spill from houses further up and down the street, each taking up the jubilant call.

"The rebels have taken Trenton!"

"The war is over!"

A look of wonder on her face, Betsy gazed up at Joseph. "Is it true? The war is over? And we have won?"

Joseph shook his blond head. "Let us go back inside, love, before you catch a chill."

Seated once again at the table in the parlor, Joseph's demeanor sobered. "It is true that General Washington and the rebel army did cross the Delaware River in the dead of night . . ."

"When?"

"Last night."

"But, *how?*" Betsy exclaimed. "Washington had no boats and surely the river was frozen solid!"

"Apparently the army managed to secret away a sufficient number of Durham boats, you know the sort, deep-bottomed, generally used only for freight, but sturdy enough to haul dozens of men and apparently, even cannon and horses. At any rate, under cover of darkness, General Washington and his entire army of twenty-four hundred men did make it across the Delaware River and . . ."

"And launched a surprise attack upon Trenton," Betsy breathlessly completed the sentence.

Joseph's brow furrowed. "You knew of the army's plan?"

"Yes." Betsy nodded. "Do go on."

Joseph shook his head. "You amaze me, lass. Evidently the attack went well. Colonel Rall was killed . . ."

"Oh-h-h. He seemed such a nice man."

"You were acquainted with Colonel Rall?" Joseph sputtered.

"Do go on, please," Betsy urged.

"Well, the way I heard it our army captured above nine hundred Hessian soldiers and we lost only two men. They said a couple of our boys were wounded during the battle, but judging from the look of the troops I saw just a bit ago, I daresay half a dozen more won't last the night. Some are so weak and exhausted they can barely stand, let alone walk. Although I must say, all our boys were wearing good sturdy boots."

"But where did they get . . .?"

"Hessians were barefoot." Joseph chuckled. "And the German soldiers also wore no coats. Our boys were wearin' 'em, turned inside out, of course."

Betsy laughed.

"Seems our boys also got away with I don't-know-how-many cannon, drums, weapons and who-knows-what-else."

"You heard all of this just now on the wharf?" Betsy marveled. "Before you arrived here?"

"Actually I learned of it an hour or so ago. Ran into some of the army re-crossing the Delaware a few miles downstream; mainly our boys bringing prisoners across. I believe some of 'em must have helped themselves to the enemy's rum. A couple were falling down drunk; but laughin' and shoutin' at the top of their lungs over their victory." His eyes twinkled. "Anyhow, despite my nag draggin' her feet, I arrived here a good bit ahead of the men. Aunt Ashburn was pleased to hear the news. Two of her housekeeper's sons are garrisoned here."

Betsy handed Joseph the platter containing the last scrap of bread and pushed aside her own empty plate. "Did the soldiers say exactly when our army attacked?"

"Sometime this morning."

"And it has taken all day for word to reach us?"

"Well, after the smoke cleared and the Hessians surrendered, our troops had to round up the prisoners, seize their weapons and strip 'em, then put on their new boots and coats, rest a spell, perhaps eat a bite while General Washington and the rest of his staff conferred. Then once they decided what to do, the entire company had to reassemble and begin the long trek back. Plus the river is still full of ice floes. I expect that slowed the army's progress both going and coming across the river."

"Of a certainty," Betsy murmured.

"The bad news is . . ."

Betsy sucked in her breath. "There is also bad news?"

He nodded. "A bit ago, I heard that Cornwallis is already headed south bringing eight thousand fresh British soldiers this way."

"Oh-h-h." Betsy's shoulders sagged. "That means there will be *more* fighting across the river. How on earth will our little army push back eight thousand soldiers? And if we lose the *next* battle," she fretted, "the British will surely take Philadelphia."

Joseph reached to pat her hand. "Don't take on so, love. I'm home now. I'll protect you."

Both the tenderness in his voice and the heartfelt expression on his face lifted Betsy's spirits. "You don't plan to leave again soon, then?"

His gaze warm, Joseph shook his blond head. "Perhaps not until spring. And perhaps not even then if . . . well, perhaps, not even then."

Betsy let out the breath she'd been holding. These past weeks had been filled with one peril after another. "I am so glad you are home now, Joseph."

His tone was gentle. "As am I, Betsy." He pushed back his chair. "Let us go sit by the fire."

Betsy smiled. "I'd like that."

Joseph placed another log onto the fire and after prodding it till it burst into flames, he settled himself next to Betsy on the sofa. "Now, I want to know how, and when, you met Colonel Rall."

Betsy inhaled an uneven breath. Now was as good a time as any to relay her news. "Whilst you were away," she began, "I . . . took a little trip.

I had learned that John's sister Joanna was visiting nearby, so I took a ferry across the Delaware River and went to see her . . . in Trenton."

His brows snapped together. "You were in Trenton? *When?*" he demanded. "Trenton has been overrun with Hessians since . . . well, since a good long while."

"As you can see, Joseph, I am quite safe. Joanna and I had a nice visit. And on the way back, I . . . had an escort. Although, he . . . did not return the entire way with me back to Philadelphia."

"He?"

After a pause, she said, "François."

"François escorted you to Trenton?"

"I did not say that. I encountered François . . . *in* Trenton."

Joseph turned to face her. "You are not making a great deal of sense, Betsy."

She looked down. A part of her had not yet absorbed the finality of François's death, or . . . the part she played in it. But, swallowing her reticence, she pressed on and in minutes, had relayed the entire story to Joseph, leaving out nothing.

Wagging his head, he muttered, "So, the frog is dead. Good riddance to him, I say."

"Oh, Joseph." Betsy reached for her shawl and draped it around her shoulders. "I cannot help but feel somewhat guilty. François's death is due entirely to me."

"Absolutely untrue," Joseph declared firmly. "The man's despicable actions led to his death. Washington would not hang a man based on the testimony of a single person, and certainly not that of a woman. If your Uncle Abel knew of Dubeau's crimes, then it's a certainty Washington knew of them as well."

"But he said he was not acquainted with him, that he did not know the names of any of his spies."

"That may be, but I'll wager he knew *of* him. Or one of his subordinates did. You merely sought justice and brought the lout to it. Despite the danger you placed yourself in, Betsy, you performed a great service for our country."

A relieved smile replaced the anxiety on Betsy's pretty face. "I did, didn't I?" She wound an arm through Joseph's and snuggled closer.

"Most assuredly."

"Still," Betsy murmured, "François must have had . . . *some* good qualities. Minette will surely miss her brother. As will Rachel."

"Your sister is well rid of the ruffian."

They both fell silent, each lost in their own thoughts as they gazed into the red and orange flames of the fire. The hiss from the burning logs blended with the soft patter of snowflakes against the windowpanes. For the first time in weeks, Betsy began to feel relaxed and warm. Joseph's presence was, indeed, reassuring. She rested her head against his shoulder.

Both his fresh outdoorsy scent and his nearness comforted her. Over the past year, she had come to rely more and more upon this strong, self-assured man. Now, with John's death fully avenged, perhaps it was time to look to the future. John wanted her to be happy. Both his sister and Sarah had reminded her of that. Both had assured her that John did not want, or expect, her to go on alone. With her year long trial now behind her, she was free at last to focus on the future. She smiled when Joseph's arm dropped from the back of the sofa to settle around her shoulders.

"You have accomplished all you set out to do, Betsy. You have been very brave."

She turned to gaze up into his warm hazel eyes. "I have, haven't I?" The slight tremor in her voice betrayed the emotion building within her. "John's death has truly been avenged," she said softly. "And Toby's."

Joseph drew her closer to him. "So," he gazed down into her glittering blue eyes. "I assume François's death will mark the end of your spying career. Spying is far too dangerous for a woman."

Betsy hedged. "But you must admit it can be quite thrilling. Except for the night you and I rescued Rachel, I don't believe I was ever in any real danger."

Joseph scowled. "You just said the Frenchman nearly pushed you from the ferryboat!"

"True . . ." She paused to consider. Were François not already dead, she supposed he would still be intent upon killing her, but she chose not to think about that now. "I cannot tell you how . . . *useful* I felt relaying important information about the Hessians to General Washington. He, and his advisors, actually *listened* to me, Joseph. They hung onto my every word. It was all quite thrilling."

"Betsy." The one word spoke volumes.

"Spying is no more dangerous than what you do," she protested. "You flirt with danger every day that you spend bobbing about on the high seas."

"I'm a man. To flirt with danger is my lot in life. I won't always be around to get you out of whatever scrape you get yourself into."

Taking no small umbrage at that, Betsy sat up straighter. "I have managed to get myself out of a good many scrapes on my own, sir."

"Nonetheless, you are a woman, and by all that is right you should have a man by your side and a couple of little ones playing at your feet."

A smile softened Betsy's lips. "What exactly are you suggesting, Captain Ashburn?"

"Firstly, I'm asking for your word that you will abandon this dastardly spy business." When she did not answer, he pressed, "Do I have it?"

Betsy coyly replied, "I cannot say for certain if I shall give up spying, or not. As you pointed out, the war is not yet over. We do not know what will happen next. Until the war is truly over and done with, I expect General Washington will continue to need reliable intelligence. Anything is possible."

"Very well, then, if anything is possible; is it possible?" Of a sudden, his voice grew raspy. "That you would consider . . . becoming my wife?"

Betsy's smile widened. At length, her blue eyes began to twinkle and she said, "For the nonce, sir, the best I can do is give you my word that I will think seriously upon . . . both matters."

"Come here you little minx." He drew her into his arms and settled his hungry lips upon hers.

Betsy snuggled closer to her swarthy seaman. To be sure she would give Joseph Ashburn's proposal of marriage a great deal of thought. She would be foolish not to. But because she was not yet ready to give up her own hard-fought freedom, she could not say for certain if she was ready yet to abandon spying. She may be a mere woman, but she had General Washington's ear. The great man now trusted her . . . as did many of Philadelphia's Loyalists now. Indeed, she concluded sagely, at this juncture, anything *was* possible.

* * * * *

On the following day Philadelphia newspapers joyfully reported news of the Patriot victory at the Battle of Trenton on December 26, 1776. Said General George Washington: *"This is a glorious day for our country. Our thanks must be to God, and these brave, young Americans who fought for our independence."*

AUTHOR'S HISTORICAL NOTES

Apart from the delegation of statesmen who reportedly visited Betsy Ross at her upholstery shop in the spring of 1776 to ask her to sew a banner to represent the unification of the thirteen colonies, history tells us virtually nothing of Betsy Ross's life between the death of her first husband John Ross in January 1776 and her subsequent marriage to privateer Joseph Ashburn in June 1777. It is during this gap in Betsy's life that I chose to set *The Accidental Spy*. In my fictional story Betsy Ross is drawn into Philadelphia's dangerous underworld of Revolutionary war spies and double agents. She interacts with many real historical figures: among them her siblings—Sarah, Rachel and George. Historians differ as to how many siblings Betsy actually had, possibly because so many died as children, and whether Betsy was the seventh or eighth child born to Rebecca and Samuel Griscom. I also found discrepancies regarding the birth dates of some of her siblings, including George and Rachel, so in my fictional tale, it is possible that their ages may be off by as much as a year.

After Betsy eloped to marry John Ross in 1773, the Quaker community and Betsy's parents did "shun" her for marrying outside the Quaker faith but history is unclear if they continued to shun her following John's death. For the purposes of my fictional story, I chose to have Betsy continue to live at the home on Mulberry Street, where she may or may not have lived with John Ross while they were married and to have her parents continue to shun her, since throughout the remainder of her life, Betsy never returned to the Quaker fold. After being given several opportunities to seek forgiveness for marrying outside her faith, Betsy failed on numerous occasions to appear before the Quaker Women's Committee, who eventually issued a formal statement declaring that they could "no longer esteem her a Member in Fellowship with us." Thereafter Betsy Ross was known as a Free Quaker. History substantiates that Betsy did join a group called Fighting Quakers and that many members were, like her, known as Free Quakers.

Whether or not the house at 239 Arch Street (in 1776 also known as Mulberry Street) in Philadelphia, now a museum and memorial to Betsy Ross is, in fact, the actual house where Betsy lived in 1776 and conducted her upholstery business is also in dispute. According to Marla Miller, author of a scholarly work titled *Betsy Ross and the Making of America,* no official records exist citing precisely *where* Betsy Ross lived from 1775 to 1780, which encompasses the time period in which I set *Accidental Spy.* The layout and number of rooms in Betsy's home, in my story, may or may not be correct. We have no way of knowing today exactly how many rooms were in the house or how they may have been arranged in 1776.

History does not substantiate that Sarah's husband William Donaldson ever served with the rebel army, but that he was instead a shipbuilder. In 1776, Sarah and William were already the parents of a little girl named Margaret. As did Betsy when she married John, Sarah had also eloped with William but following a "satisfactory report" from the Friends committee who handled her case, she was readmitted as a member in good standing to the Quaker community, known as the Society of Friends. I discovered that not all Quakers used "thee" and "thy" in their everyday speech; for some these were affectionate terms used only toward family members. Also many Quakers did not celebrate Christmas, as they viewed every day as holy, therefore one day was no different from another. History tells us that some Quaker families exchanged gifts at Christmas while others did not.

Despite the exceptions cited above, I made every effort to remain true to substantiated historical fact in my story both in regard to Betsy's life and to the events of the Revolutionary war in 1776. History confirms that after the British swarmed into New York, George Washington *did* become desperate for reliable intelligence and *did* issue a plea for civilians to act as informants, i.e. spies. An especially interesting and entertaining book on this subject, *George Washington, Spymaster* by Thomas B. Allen cites an incident where Washington discovered that one of his own bodyguards, Thomas Hickey, was a British spy and at a hastily convened trial (court martial) over which Washington presided, he found Hickey guilty of "mutiny, sedition, and treachery" and ordered him hanged on the spot as *"a warning to every soldier in the army."*

During the war years, it was common for Patriot-owned newspapers to *not* report negative news about General Washington, or his battle loses. However, as a way for my characters (and readers) to stay abreast of the war, I chose to let them read about *all* war battles, whether victorious or not, in their local newspapers.

Early in the Revolutionary war the Continental Congress did grant privateers permission to capture, board, and plunder British ships without fear of penalty or punishment. Also true is that after Washington and his Continental army reached Pennsylvania in early December 1776, he at once issued an order for all ships of a size within a specified distance from Philadelphia be destroyed in order to prevent the British from crossing the Delaware River in pursuit of the rebels.

The second Continental Congress did meet in Philadelphia in 1775-76 and Congressman John Nixon did read aloud the newly penned document called *The Declaration of Independence* from the steps of the State House on Chestnut Street. The original document used the word *un*alienable as opposed to *in*alienable which we use today. However in 1776, the public reading of the declaration and parade were actually held on July 8, as opposed to July 4, the day later designated, and which we now commemorate, as Independence Day.

In my research, I came across many references to the Secret Committees of Correspondence. The first Secret Committee of Correspondence group was organized in Massachusetts by Sam Adams as a way of quickly spreading war information throughout the colonies. It was similar enough to the Sons of Liberty that the two groups were often mistaken for one another. Apart from the historical references I make in my story in regard to the Revolutionary war, *Betsy Ross: Accidental Spy* is to be regarded as a purely fictional tale. No historical records anywhere suggest that Betsy Ross ever engaged in covert spy activity. At the time of her death, Elizabeth Ross Ashburn Claypoole was an ordinary Philadelphia citizen whose death notice in the *Pennsylvanian* listed only her name, age, and date of death—the afternoon of January 30, 1836. She was 84. No one knew then that Betsy Ross was destined to become an American icon.

Fascinating Facts About Early Philadelphia . . . Did you know?

The first public fire truck in Philadelphia was purchased in 1719; and America's first medical school opened in Philadelphia in 1765. In July 1775, Benjamin Franklin established the first American Post Office in Philadelphia and was named the first Postmaster General.

During the Revolutionary war, a British soldier wore the same uniform winter and summer. It was made of heavy wool with a stiff leather collar (so he'd stand up straight) and his white knee breeches were so tight that they had to be put on wet. When they dried, they became even tighter. His supply pack weighted over 135 pounds and had to be worn on his back even into battle. British soldiers were required to wear their hair in a tight ponytail with a curl over each ear, the curls held in place by a smelly mixture of powder and grease, which caused flies to swarm around the soldier's face. The brass helmets had no brim and were of no use in the sun. It was thought that the more uncomfortable a soldier was, the madder he would be and the more aggressively he would fight the hated rebels.

As punishment for treason against the British, when a rebel traitor was caught, he was hanged until nearly dead; then the soldiers cut him down, cut out his intestines and set them on fire as the half-dead traitor watched. Then the poor wretch was beheaded; his body cut into four pieces and put on a spike for all to see.

Patriots, or rebels, referred to the enemy as Loyalists or Tories, an Irish word meaning bandit or thief. Patriots declared that a "Tory was a thing whose head is in England, whose body is in America, and whose neck needs stretching." Sadly, Patriots were also known to beat their hated Loyalist brothers (the enemy) then tar and feather him.

Some say the origins of the *tune* to the song we know today as *Yankee Doodle Dandy* dates back to fifteenth-century Holland where it was sung, with different words, of course, at harvest time. In the sixteenth century, the British changed the lyrics to be derisive towards Oliver Cromwell. New lyrics penned by the British during the American Revolutionary war poked fun at the colonists who the British saw as poorly educated farmers who wore ill-fitting clothes and had no class. However, Rebels quickly took up the tune, wrote their own lyrics and marched off to battle singing: *"Yankee Doodle is the tune Americans delight in. It suits for feasts, it suits for fun. And just as well for fighting."*

In 1777 when the British occupied Philadelphia, General Cornwallis needed to determine the number of vacant houses that were available to quarter his men. A door-to-door, house-to-house count was conducted and when completed, revealed there were 5,470 houses in the entire city, 587 of them unoccupied, with 287 being stores. The total population was determined to be 21,767 citizens, exclusive of the British soldiers. This count became the first census taken in America.

In 1783 at the close of the Revolutionary War, Washington presented an award to three soldiers whom he felt had acted with outstanding courage. The award consisted of a badge made of purple cloth. Washington called it the *Badge of Military Merit*. The honor was virtually forgotten until 1932, when upon the 200th anniversary of George Washington's birth, the badge reemerged as the "Purple Heart" and was awarded to soldiers who had been wounded in action.

During the revolutionary war period, the towering mounds that women created with their hair could reach as high as three feet. After decorating the mound with ribbons, flowers or artificial birds, women coated their hair, or wigs, with animal fat mixed with cinnamon and cloves, then the whole thing was dusted with flour to make it white—white hair being a sign of wisdom. At fancy-dress balls, the air often looked like it was snowing due to the profusion of flour, or powder, blowing off everyone's heads, men included, as they danced. Usually a special room was set aside where the ladies could go to have their hair re-powdered, giving rise to the phrase "I'm going to the powder room."

As men and women lost their teeth due to age, or decay, they often placed cork balls, called *plumpers,* into their cheeks to keep them from looking caved-in.

The red rouge that women used on their cheeks and lips was made from crushed cochineal bugs, which were red. The substance was also used to dye the red coats worn by British soldiers.

Women's dancing slippers were often made from silk, which generally did not last beyond one night of dancing at a ball. A *really* wealthy woman's dancing shoes were made from dog skin; therefore in those days the expression "putting on the dog" came to mean one was preparing for a lively evening of dancing.

A popular and best-selling book of the 1700s was a book on how to dance, which showed the steps for 918 different dances!

During this period, forty newspapers were published in the thirteen colonies, six of them owned, run and edited by women.

In colonial days, a person convicted of a crime had the inside top of his or her thumb of his right hand branded with a hot iron—*T* for thief, *M* for murderer and so on. A person caught and convicted a second time was sentenced to the gallows. The present day custom in a court of law of a person being asked to "raise your right hand" dates back to colonial times when as soon as a person was brought before a judge, he asked them to raise their right hand so he could look at their thumb to determine if they had ever before been convicted of a crime.

There were a good many slaves in Philadelphia during the revolution. When a slave was asked how long he/she worked each day, the answer would likely be "from can to can't" meaning from when I "can" see daylight to when I "can't" i.e. from sunrise to sunset.

We've all heard of the famous revolutionary woman named Molly Pitcher, right? What we may not know is that her real name was Mary Ludwig Hays. On a sweltering June day in 1778 it was so hot that soldiers on the battlefield began passing out from the heat. Mary, whose nickname was, indeed, Molly; grabbed an old pitcher and began running between the battlefield and a nearby stream to bring water to the men. However, that day the thirsty men merely called out: "Molly! Pitcher!" Thereafter the name stuck. In truth, there were hundreds of "Molly Pitchers" during the revolutionary war and these brave women's efforts to bring the soldiers water no doubt saved many a young man's life. God bless our American Patriots everywhere and God bless America, the greatest country in the world!

MARILYN CLAY is the best-selling author of over two dozen books, among them nineteen novels, three books for children and numerous non-fiction titles. A professional commercial artist for many years, Marilyn designed the Romance Writers of America's RITA Award and was presented with the first silver statuette at RWA's National Conference in San Francisco when the award was unveiled. A former University Editor for the University of Texas at Dallas, for sixteen years Marilyn published *The Regency Plume*, an international newsletter focused on the Regency period in English history, the time in which her seven Regency romance novels are set.

Following visits to Colonial Williamsburg and Philadelphia, she began to write about the American colonies. *Deceptions: A Jamestown Novel,* and *Secrets And Lies*, both books originally released in hardback, are set in 1620s Colonial Jamestown. Both are now available online as Ebooks.

Marilyn Clay's newest historical suspense series features Miss Juliette Abbott as the clever young sleuth who sorts out crime in the Regency era. *Murder At Morland Manor, Murder In Mayfair, Murder In Margate, Murder At Medley Park, Murder In Middlewych, Murder In Maidstone* and *Murder At Montford Hall* are all available in print and ebook formats. *Murder On Marsh Lane* will be out soon. All of Marilyn Clay's non-fiction titles have been named to Amazon's Top 100 Best-Selling E-books lists in their respective categories. For more information on Marilyn Clay's novels and artwork, please visit the author's website at Marilyn Clay Author.

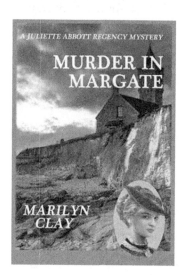

All seven of Marilyn Clay's Juliette Abbott Regency Mysteries are available in print and Ebook formats from Amazon and other online retailers. New titles in the series will follow soon. For more information, contact the author, Marilyn Clay, at marilynclay@yahoo.com

Made in the USA
Middletown, DE
03 January 2024

47177667R00189